321684AB1 Prior, Philip Hugh. Born 31 May 2232, New York General Hospital. First son of Prior, Lyle Martin, and Prior, Ava Leonard. Wgt. at birth 5 lb. 3 oz. . . . EXAMINED AT N.Y. EUTH CLINIC 10 JUNE/EUTHANASIA RECOMMENDED

Walton glanced at his watch: the time was 1026. He had set up the schedule himself: the gas chamber delivered Happy sleep each day at 1100 and 1500. He had about half an hour to save Philip Prior . . . and to jeopardize the Equalizor system that protected Earth's survival, his position—even, probably his life.

FROM
MASTER OF LIFE AND DEATH

"Silverberg's success in maintaining complete clarity and strong narrative drive while manipulating unnumbered plots and complex concepts is a technical triumph, and results in a lively and enjoyable book."

Fantasy and Science Fiction

CONQUERORS FROM THE DARKNESS

—————— AND ——————

MASTER OF LIFE AND DEATH

ROBERT SILVERBERG

SF

ace books

A Division of Charter Communications Inc.
A GROSSET & DUNLAP COMPANY
360 Park Avenue South
New York, New York 10010

CONQUERORS FROM THE DARKNESS

Copyright © 1965 by Robert Silverberg

MASTER OF LIFE AND DEATH

Copyright © 1957 by A.A. Wyn, Inc.

An Ace Book

First Ace printing: July 1979

2 4 6 8 0 9 7 5 3 1

Manufactured in the United States of America

Conquerors from
the Darkness

Contents

Introduction

THERE WAS A TIME, way back when, when I wrote a lot of action-and-adventure science-fiction. It was never my own prime preference as reading matter; I like to think of myself as a cool and cerebral man, and the things I enjoy most to read tend to be cool and cerebral books, and after 1966 or so the fiction I wrote was generally cool and cerebral fiction, even when I was writing of violent or passionate events. I have long admired the sword & sorcery work of Fritz Leiber and L. Sprague de Camp and a few other masters of that genre, and I recall even finding some pleasure in the bloody epics of Robert E. Howard, but the stuff is not a natural part of my diet and never has been.

Nevertheless, I wrote a lot of it before I was thirty, and mainly before I was twenty-five. This was a matter of economic necessity rather than personal preference. In those days the going rate for stories in the science fiction magazines was two or three cents a word, or even less, sometimes a good deal less. For books, most writers could hope to earn no more than $2000 or so, and often half that. Which meant that a writer who turned out 3000 words of fiction a day, five days a week, and sold every word of it, could count on earning an annual income of $15,000 or thereabouts—before taxes. That doesn't sound too awful, considering the value of the dollar back in the 1950's, but it isn't too great either; and if a writer fell ill for a few weeks, or took a vacation, or hit a dry spell, or wrote two or three stinkers in a row, that cut a deep gash in his income.

I will not plead poverty. I was actually writing *more* than 3000 words of fiction a day, sometimes two or three times that much, and I was selling every word, and even though I was being paid at a minimal word-rate I was earning a very nice living, probably as good as that of anyone in the field at the time. But in order to sustain such high-volume production, I had to exploit every market that was available to me, for I knew that if I tried to write nothing but the kind of science fiction that appealed personally to me as a reader I'd lose 70% or more of my income. Hence the action-and-adventure stuff.

There was a magazine for a while, circa 1956–58, called *Science Fiction Adventures*, edited by Larry T. Shaw. Larry had grown up in the bad old days when science fiction magazines had names like *Planet Stories* and *Thrilling Won-*

der Stories, and the stories were full of bug-eyed monsters and heroes with ray-guns. Though himself a sophisticated and intelligent reader, he felt considerable nostalgia for the junk s-f of his boyhood, and was sure that a market existed for it among readers. So he edited a sophisticated and intelligent magazine called *Infinity* to express his adult tastes, and he edited rip-snorting old *Science Fiction Adventures* to indulge his sentimental taste for the wilder, gaudier action fiction. I wrote for both magazines. I gave *Infinity* the most elegant stories I had in me, and for *Science Fiction Adventures* I closed my eyes, took a deep breath, and brought forth in a completely unselfconscious way all sorts of ferocious epics of vengeance, conspiracy, perdition, and blaster-play. In fact I must have written half the stories in the magazine. I was its star author.

Some of my *Science Fiction Adventures* stories were silly beyond easy description, and some were pretty decent pulp adventure, and a few actually were quite good science fiction, making allowances for the conventions of the form. I didn't feel especially depraved or corrupt writing them; I had certainly enjoyed reading stories of that type when I was thirteen or fourteen, and I saw no harm in earning a chunk of my living supplying the reading needs of a later crop of adolescents, particularly when they represented so big a segment of the science-fiction public. (If I could have earned my entire living writing complex novels like *The World Inside* or *Tower of Glass* or *Shadrach in the Furnace* back then, I probably would have felt a lot happier about everything. But I couldn't.)

The third issue of *Science Fiction Adventures*—April,

1957—had a wonderfully garish Emshwiller cover, bright orange background, lovely brunette in fur bikini showing terror at stage center, hideous gray shaggy Thing with Big Teeth menacing her from three corners of the painting. Just above her head bold black letters proclaim the presence in the issue of a story called "Spawn of the Deadly Sea," by Robert Silverberg.

"Spawn of the Deadly Sea" was a typical *Planet Stories* title—they were big on words like "spawn," "vassal," "juggernaut"—and the story, rich in color, violence, brooding mists, feudal morality, and resonant names, was precisely the sort of thing *Planet Stories* had published in the 1940's and very early 1950's. I loved writing it. Editor Shaw loved publishing it. The readers loved it too. ("It was, to say the least, terrific," declared one in a letter published a couple of issues later.) Triumph! Not only had I given people all sorts of adrenal satisfaction, but I had earned myself $225 in the fine fat dollars of November, 1956, when I was newly married and scrambling to pay for the furniture and the high-fidelity set. (In looking up how much I was paid for the story, I discovered that "Spawn of the Deadly Sea" was actually editor Shaw's title. What I called it was "Sea-Lords of Forgotten Terra," which also was a typical *Planet Stories* title, though not quite as zippy.)

We jump forward quite a few years—to June, 1964. I am no longer a struggling beginner pounding out penny-a-word pulp to meet the bills. Now I am a well-established pro who writes for the hardcover publishers, for the likes of Macmillan and Putnam and Holt, Rinehart & Winston, and my economic problems now center not around paying for the furniture but in keeping up the mortgage payments on the imposing mansion I have bought in the northern reaches of New York City. (Writers have a mysterious fondness for buying big fancy houses. Talk to Sir Walter Scott about it. Talk to Mark Twain.) For Holt's excellent editor Ann Durell I did a science-fiction novel called *Time of the Great Freeze*, which got good reviews and was a significant commercial success, and then a biography of the Assyriologist Austen Henry Layard, one of my heroes. For the next book she wanted more science fiction. And so I trotted out good old "Spawn of the Deadly Sea" and proposed its expansion into a novel, and she agreed, and in June of 1964 I did the job.

The original story provided the framework, but there are new characters, new incidents, and a general redevelopment of the material. I also undertook a considerable depulpifying of the prose. Compare, for example, the first paragraph of "Spawn"—

> The Sea-Lord ship was but a blurred dot on the horizon, a tiny squib of color against the endless roiling green of the mighty sea. It would be a long time before the men of the sea would draw into the harbor of Vythain—yet the people of the floating city were already congealed with terror.

—with the opening lines of the novel that I originally called *Water World,* and then *The Star Beasts,* and which Ann Durell dubbed *Conquerors from the Darkness*—

> The ship of the Sea-Lords was little more than a blurred dot on the horizon now, a tiny, bob-

bing squib of color against the endless roiling green of the mighty sea. It would be a few hours yet before the men of the sea drew into the harbor of Vythain and came ashore. Even now, though, the people of the floating city were beginning to shiver with terror at the knowledge that the swaggering, arrogant Sea-Lords would soon be among them.

Many small changes there. Some of them were done for the purpose of padding—or expansion, if you like: the addition of an extra adjective here and there. One, in the second sentence, repairs a syntactical blunder. But also the pulp overstatement of "congealed with terror" gives way to the milder "shiver with terror," and the deliberately archaic "but a blurred dot" in the first sentence becomes "little more than a blurred dot" in the book. So it goes, sentence by sentence, the hyped-up conventions of the pulp epic disappearing.

But I think the fun remains. It's a good romantic adventure on the high seas, not exactly what people think of when they think of Silverberg novels, but one should try to unsettle one's public's preconceptions now and then. The red blood of heroes flows freely, and so does the golden-green ichor of monsters. They don't write 'em that way any more. At least, I don't. Too bad, maybe.

—Robert Silverberg
Oakland, California
February, 1978

The Coming of the
Sea-Lords

THE SHIP OF THE SEA-LORDS was little more than a blurred dot on the horizon now, a tiny, bobbing squib of color against the endless roiling green of the mighty sea. It would be a few hours yet before the men of the sea drew into the harbor of Vythain and came ashore. Even now, though, the people of the floating city were beginning to shiver with terror at the knowledge that the swaggering, arrogant Sea-Lords would soon be among them.

A harsh whisper had gone running through the city a little past midday: "The Sea-Lords come! Their ship has been sighted!" And everyone in Vythain turned to his neighbor to ask, "Is it true? Do they come?"

It was true. Old Lackresh, the graybeard who was manning the spy tower, had been the first to sight the black sails, and he had flashed the signal. Flags of gold and green had risen to the staffs atop the lookout post, relaying the word to those below: The Sea-Lords come!

In the busy streets of the city, life froze suddenly. Commerce came to a halt. The purchasing of fish and the scraping of scales ceased at once. The menders of sails folded their work, put away their awls and thread. In classrooms, teachers with taut faces cut short their words in midsentence. The writing of books and the making of songs were interrupted. Everything stopped. This was no time for normal daily activities. The Sea-Lords were coming, making their way across the panthalassa, the great sea that covered the whole world. They were heading for the city of Vythain to collect their annual tribute.

The hundred thousand people of Vythain awaited the coming of the Sea-Lords with fear, for there was no predicting the mood of the men of the sea, and they might do great harm if they felt destructive. All Vythain cowered, all but one of its inhabitants. One alone waited eagerly for the coming of the Sea-Lords.

That one stood now on the concrete pier that jutted from the flank of the city. He took his post down where the oily slick of the sea licked angrily against the base of the floating city, and stared outward at the vast expanse of water with open, unashamed curiosity.

For Dovirr Stargan, this was a long-awaited day.

Dovirr was eighteen years old. He had grown to manhood tall and broad and powerful, with the strength of a young shark. His dark hair curled wildly almost to his shoulders, and was held in place by a thin band of silver. His light tunic was of blue linen, too flimsy to shield him well against the brisk breeze coming from the sea. Burly arms, bare to mid-bicep, jutted from his sleeves. His eyes, midnight black and set wide in his face, were trained outward, fixed on the still-tiny ship that was approaching Vythain.

Dovirr was waiting—waiting for the coming of the Sea-Lords. Looking out across the heaving bulk of the sea, he scowled impatiently as the Sea-Lord vessel slowly made its way toward the city.

Hurry, he urged it silently. Hurry and get here, Sea-Lords! I'm waiting for you!

From somewhere high above came the shrill sounds of trumpet blasts, three of them, splitting the sudden silence of the city. Dovirr glanced up. Councilman Morgrun, the leader of the city, had appeared. He stood on the parapet atop the wide, sweeping flat face of the Councilhouse, lifting one hand to draw all eyes toward him.

The Councilman was delivering the usual warning. "Citizens!" he cried, and loudspeakers echoed his words all around the city. "Citizens, the Sea-Lords approach! Remain in your houses! Make no attempt at resistance while the tribute is being delivered! The Sea-Lords will not harm us if we do not give them cause."

Down by the pier, Dovirr spat angrily. Coward! he thought, as Councilman Morgrun's words bounced from the red-painted walls of the waterfront warehouses. Coward and city of cowards! Morgrun was still speaking, his words rolling out over the amplifiers that had been left behind by the Dhuchay'y, the Star Beasts, those long-forgotten, long-departed conquerors of abandoned Earth.

"The piers are to be cleared as well!" Morgrun ordered, and the amplifiers roared out the old man's high-pitched voice. The words rebounded and became jumbled: "The piers the piers the piers."

Dovirr smiled. He realized that the Councilman's words were aimed directly at him. From his post on the parapet, Morgrun could see the tall figure standing at the water's edge. All the sensible citizens of the floating city were long since snug in their cozy nests, Dovirr knew, huddling in safety until the men of the sea had snatched their loot and gone on to their next port of call.

But Dovirr stood his ground. He had done enough huddling for one lifetime. Year after year, as far back as he could remember, he had heard the sound of the trumpets and he had felt the chill of terror descending on Vythain. Even when he was a child, he had not shared the general fear of the Sea-Lords. Dovirr could remember struggling in his father's arms when he was no more than five, crying, "Let me see them! I want to look at the Sea-Lords!"

His father had won that struggle. But now Dovirr was eighteen, and had come to manhood. He had urgent business with the Sea-Lords, and no cowardly man of Vythain was going to force him to share that cowardice.

"Dovirr!" a voice cried.

Dovirr turned slowly. He saw a swarthy man clad in the red robes of a police officer come running toward him across the pier. Dovirr recognized him, of course. When you spent your entire life in one small city, never leaving it, you knew everyone. The policeman was young Lackresh, the son of Vythain's lookout.

Lackresh gestured fiercely. "Dovirr, you madman!" he bellowed. "What do you think you're doing? Get off the pier before the Sea-Lords arrive!"

Dovirr calmly folded his arms. He smiled and said, "I'm staying out here this time, Lackresh. I want to see what they're really like."

Lackresh's eyes widened in amazement. "They'll kill you, idiot! Come on, move along. I have my orders, Dovirr." Lackresh reached into a fold of his uniform, and abruptly he was brandishing a neuron whip. The small gleaming weapon was another legacy from the Dhuchay'y conquerors of the old days. Lackresh jerked his head toward the gray houses of the city. "Hurry it," he snapped. "Get up to your place, fast, and stay there!"

"Suppose I don't go?"

Sweat poured down Lackresh's face. He had never been in a situation quite like this one before, Dovirr knew. Life was very peaceful, here in Vythain. A policeman really had little to do, amid the everlasting calm—the calm that Dovirr hated so passionately. Lackresh's job was mostly ceremonial. It was rare that he had a genuine lawbreaker to deal with, rare that there was any sort of trouble.

"If you don't go—" Lackresh said uncertainly. "If you don't go—"

"Yes?"

The Sea-Lord ship was drawing nearer. It was almost

within the arms of the harbor by now. Lackresh's wavering hand, grasping the compact neuron whip, held its aim unsteadily. The policeman looked at Dovirr with a blank lack of comprehension on his face. He fumbled for words, lips moving in silence a moment.

Then Lackresh burst out: "Why can't you act like a normal person, Dovirr?"

Dovirr laughed harshly. "You'll never get anywhere trying to *reason* with me, you know. You'd better use force, Lackresh."

Lackresh's lower lip trembled. His forehead was glossy with perspiration, beads of sweat rolling into his heavy eyebrows. He raised the neuron whip and trained it square on the center of Dovirr's deep, brawny chest. It was a versatile weapon, Dovirr was aware. A blast from a neuron whip could send a man reeling back stinging with pain, or it could knock him to his knees, or it could leave him unconscious for days, or it could kill him outright. Everything depended on the setting that was used.

Gripping the weapon so hard his knuckles whitened, Lackresh said troubledly, "All right, Dovirr. This is an order, now. Return to your dwelling or I'll fire. I've wasted too much time with you as it is, and—"

Dovirr leaped forward, grinning, and clamped one powerful hand on Lackresh's wrist. The policeman did not fire. Dovirr twisted downward and to one side, bending the older man's slender arm.

"No," Lackresh gasped.

Dovirr reached for the neuron whip with his free hand. Lackresh's fingers strained to hold it, but Dovirr continued to bend the officer's arm until bones began to grind, and the fingers loosed their hold.

"Let go," Dovirr said. "There. That's it."

He grabbed the weapon and shoved Lackresh backward a few feet.

"Go," Dovirr ordered hoarsely, pointing toward the city with the snout of the neuron whip. "Get moving, Lackresh, or I'll whip you right into the water!"

"You're—*crazy!*" Lackresh whispered.

"Maybe so," Dovirr agreed. "But that's not your affair. Go! Get yourself away from here!"

Lackresh hesitated. Dovirr saw him balancing on the balls of his feet, as though readying himself to make some kind of desperate lunge. It was an amusing thing to see. Lackresh was such a peaceful man, and yet here he was, getting poised for a hopeless fight.

"Don't" Dovirr said.

Lackresh could not halt. He came charging forward. Unwilling to hit the man, Dovirr turned the dial of the neuron whip down to the lowest intensity, and flashed a stinging force beam at the officer. It stopped Lackresh in mid-charge and knocked him back a yard or two.

Quivering under the blow, Lackresh rubbed his shoulders where the beam had stung them. He seemed about to burst into tears. Then, recovering some of his self-control, he drew himself up and stared evenly at Dovirr.

"You've beaten me and made a fool of me," Lackresh said. "Very well. You win. I'll leave you here, Dovirr, and may the Seaborn Ones pick your bones!"

"I'll worry about that," Dovirr called out laughingly, as

Lackresh retreated. The officer scrambled without much dignity up the carved stone stairs that led from the pier to the city proper, and vanished into the tumult of winding streets that was Vythain.

Dovirr laughed. He turned his back on the city, and planted one foot on the very rim of the sea wall. Before him, the sea rolled onward to the horizon—the endless sea, the sea that covered all of Earth save where the floating cities constructed by the conquering Dhuchay'y broke the pathless waves. Far below were older cities, the cities of man's past, drowned centuries ago by the invading Star Beasts. Earth was a world of water now, a green ball spinning through the vault of space.

The Sea-Lord ship made for the harbor. It had picked up a good breeze and it came scudding toward Vythain at a steady pace. Dovirr faintly heard the raucous chanting as the rough kings of the sea hove to, drawing back the oars. There were no galley slaves on a Sea-Lord vessel. The Sea-Lords themselves manned the oars, plowing through the unfathomable waters.

Dovirr narrowed his eyes. The black sail billowed in the wind. The ship was close enough now so that he could count the banks of oars. One, two, three, four—a quadrireme, Dovirr saw. Row on row on row on row of oars bristled from the sturdy hull.

He felt a savage throb of excitement. Four banks of oars! That meant that the Thalassarch himself was coming to collect the gold! This was no underling vessel, but the flagship of the fleet!

The tang of sea water stung Dovirr's nostrils. For the

first time, he felt uncertainty. Would they take him on board! Or would they laugh at him and spurn him for the landsman he was?

Dovirr's fists clenched. He was prepared to fight his way on board the Sea-Lord vessel, if he had to. Eighteen years on Vythain—that was enough of a sentence for any man to serve. He was grown, now. He had a dream to follow, and he could not follow it mired here in the floating city. Vythain held no future for him. What was there here? To be a Councilman, to deliberate and ponder and confer, while the years went by and his strong body withered into feebleness? No, Dovirr thought. A Councilman had no power, really. There were the forms of power, yes. The outward trappings. Old Morgrun wore rich robes, he carried the staff of office, he stood grandly on the parapet of the Councilhouse and spoke his words into the microphones left behind by the Star Beasts. And all Vythain obeyed. But was that power?

Was it power to command a single helpless city of weaklings that lay at the mercy of the men of the sea?

No, Dovirr believed. Morgrun's power, such that it was, was hollow indeed. But it was the best that Vythain could offer, and, Dovirr told himself, that best was simply not good enough. He had to escape. He was too big for Vythain, too restless, too strong. Vythain was a city of merchants and craftsmen, and it could not hold him.

Dovirr looked outward. The Sea-Lord flagship was past the breakwater now, heading for the pier. Husky-looking men were reefing the mainsail. Another few minutes, now, and the ship would drop anchor. Boats would put out for the pier, carrying the Thalassarch and his men ashore to wring their tribute from the sniveling leaders of the city. They might stay a day or so, and feast themselves on Vythain's bounty. Then they would leave, making for the vast reaches of the open sea.

And I'll go with them, Dovirr thought. Out into the real world, where a man can show his strength and win some power for himself.

Almost sick with impatience, Dovirr waited for the Sea-Lord vessel to make its landing.

The Thalassarch
Gowyn

THEY CAME ASHORE in solemn procession, one after another, big men, faces toughened by wind and salt water and blazing sun. They climbed from their boats with the bearing of masters, and waited at the edge of the sea in a silent group. Thousands of eyes were trained on them—city-born folk, peering timidly from their windows, watching the Sea-Lords debark. Dovirr watched, too, from closer range.

Where was the Thalassarch, Dovirr wondered? His eyes searched the group of Sea-Lords, and he asked himself if he had perhaps missed the leader.

No. No, here he came now. There was no mistaking the identity of the man who strode onto the pier. It was Gowyn, all right. It could be no one else.

Gowyn, Thalassarch of the Western Sea!

He was a tall, heavy man with the thick, brutal jaw of a ruthless leader, the dark, blazing eyes of a born commander of men. Gowyn wore a tunic of green wool—the precious product of the floating city of Hicanthro, worth its weight and more in gold. The Thalassarch affected a curling black beard that extended from his thin, hard lips nearly to the middle of his chest.

Crouching behind a barrel of whale oil at the water's edge, Dovirr watched the hulking figure come ashore—watched, and felt consumed with envy. This was a man who had attained power. This was a man whose word was law on the sea and in the cities of the world. This was a man who had risen to greatness, who had found purpose for being alive.

The Thalassarch stood nearly six feet six. Around him were underlings, all of them taller than six feet, clad in the tunics and buskins of Sea-Lord dress. They were a proud group. The Sea-Lord vessel lay at anchor in the suddenly quiet harbor of Vythain, which any other day but this bustled with vitality. Tethered to the side of the pier was Gowyn's richly carved dinghy. No ordinary boat for him to come ashore in, not for a Thalassarch! Dovirr, squatting down out of sight, looked at the dinghy, and at the Thalassarch, and then at the black ship of the Sea-Lords. The letters of its name were cut deep on the prow: *Garyun*.

Dovirr smiled. He tried the title on for size in his imagination:

Dovirr Stargan, Thalassarch of the Nine Seas, Master of the ship Garyun. It was a worthy title, a noble ambition. The name itself had a lovely ring to it. *Thalassarch*. It was an ancient title that had come swimming up out of man's remote past. Once there had been a place called Greece and a language called Greek, and there was a word in that language for sea, the word *thalassa*. Other words had grown from that. Panthalassa, the sea that was everywhere. Thalassarch, ruler of the sea. The ancient words had endured, though Greece itself lay under tons of ocean mud.

The Sea-Lords were all gathered on the pier, now. And now the rulers of the city of Vythain, the men of the Council, came in solemn procession to greet the waiting Gowyn. Dovirr watched them scornfully. They were eight doddering oldsters, their wrinkled faces marring the splendor of their robes of office. Councilman Morgrun led the procession. They advanced on unsteady legs, groaning under the coffers that held the tribute.

Gold was the tribute—gold laboriously dredged from the sea by the painstaking hydride process. The yellow metal still kept its value, though the world itself had drowned. The Sea-Lords demanded gold as their price for ridding the seas of pirates. It was a full year's work to reclaim a few handfuls of the precious metal, mining it molecule by molecule from the brine.

Some whispered that there were no pirates at all, that the Sea-Lords had invented them as a convenient fiction for the purpose of keeping the floating cities frightened. That was as it may be. The fact remained that merchant ships *did* sometimes disappear as they journeyed from city to city.

Whether they vanished in pirate raids, as the Sea-Lords claimed, or whether the pirates and the Sea-Lords were one and the same, no man of the cities could tell. But they had no choice; they paid the tribute, and hoped that the Sea-Lords would patrol the waterways. The intercity commerce was vital to the existence of the floating cities.

No city was self-sufficient. Each produced its own special commodity, and traded with the others for the things it needed. From the open fields of Vythain came vegetables; from Korduna, meat. The sheep of Hicanthro yielded treasured wool; Dimnon provided rubber, Lanobul machined goods. Ships of the merchants went back and forth, carrying the wares of one city to the next. Without that trade, all would be lost. Each of the floating communities that drifted on the great panthalassa, each anchored securely to the sunken ancient world beneath the sea, required the aid of the Sea-Lords' services in order to survive.

Hunkered down behind the barrel, Dovirr observed the ceremony of tribute.

Councilman Morgrun came forward. He knelt, dropping to the dirty pavement in his costly robes, while Gowyn the Thalassarch stood before him with a frozen, emotionless expression on his heavily bearded face.

"The tribute, sire," Councilman Morgrun said unctuously.

His seven colleagues bustled toward him. They laid the coffers of gold before the Sea-Lords. With trembling hands they pulled back the lids of the coffers. Dovirr caught his breath at the sight of the golden sparkle. Gold was a useless metal, soft, fit only for women, Dovirr thought. And yet there was no denying that its gleam was splendid to behold.

The Thalassarch peered briefly into the coffers. Then he straightened and made a casual gesture to the men who stood beside him.

"Take the tribute," he growled.

Each of the Thalassarch's lieutenants stopped, easily lifted a heavy coffer, and deposited it in the dinghy. Councilman Morgrun remained where he was, flat on his belly at Gowyn's feet. Gowyn struck a demonic pose, lifting one sandaled foot and resting it none too gently in the small of Morgrun's back.

"For another year," the Thalassarch rumbled dramatically, "I, Gowyn of the Western Sea, do declare the city of Vythain to rest under my protection and care. The gold is solid weight, is it not, Morgrun?"

"Of course," Morgrun mumbled.

"It had better be," the Thalassarch snapped. He kicked the Councilman away from him contemptuously. "Back to your shelter, guppy! Run! Hide! The Sea-Lord will eat you unless you can flee!"

Gowyn roared with laughter. He was obviously enjoying this game, Dovirr thought.

With most undignified haste, Councilman Morgrun scrambled to his feet. He gathered his ornate, richly brocaded robes about him, made a perfunctory bow, muttered his thanks to the Thalassarch for his protection. Then he turned, huffing and puffing and, flanked by the other seven Councilmen, retreated swiftly toward the stone stairs. Gowyn's sardonic laughter echoed through the silent city as the old men ran toward safety.

Smiling, the Thalassarch turned to the comrades who surrounded him. "This city has no fight in it," he complained. "Each year its people hand over the tribute to us like so many frightened fleas. By the stars, I'd love a good fight some year from one of them!"

A deeply tanned, red-bearded man who wore a resplendent jeweled helmet remarked, "They'll never fight, sire. They need your protection too desperately for that."

Gowyn's laughter boomed across the pier. "Protection, Lysigon! Imagine—they *pay* us for what we most dearly love to do!" The Thalassarch looked up at the massed bulk of the floating city, and chuckled in scorn. "Come," he said after a moment. "The smell of cowardice turns my stomach. We have lingered here long enough. Back to the ship!"

The Sea-Lords moved toward the boats they had moored by the pier. Dovirr tensed, clenching his teeth. His nerves twanged in wild excitement. This was the moment. Now—or else he would have to wait in sour disappointment for a full year.

He rose from his hiding place.

"Wait, Thalassarch!" Dovirr shouted.

His voice went echoing through the quiet waterfront. Gowyn had one foot already in the dinghy. He drew it back and whirled around, his face a study in total astonishment as he looked up to see who it was who had dared to hail him so boldly.

Dovirr came forth. The Sea-Lords eyed him, whispered, nudged one another in the ribs. Suddenly Dovirr felt very much alone, with a knot of Sea-Lords confronting him and nothing but the empty stretch of the pier at his back.

He filled his lungs with salty air. He faced the Thalassarch squarely, and tried to speak in a ringing voice that would not betray his inner tension:

"The tribute is yours, mighty Gowyn—but you leave too soon."

"What do you want with us, boy?" the Thalassarch asked coldly.

Dovirr bristled at the offhand, impatient "*boy.*" The word was like a bucket of slops hurled in his face. "No more a boy than any of you, Sea-Lords," he said. "I seek to leave Vythain. Will you take me with you?"

Gowyn's astonishment mounted. He seemed to gape; then he roared with noisy amusement, and clapped one of his companions thumpingly on the back. "Ho! See, a sucker-fish wishes to run with the sharks! Into the water with him, Levrod, and then let's be off for the ship."

The Sea-Lord named Levrod smiled eagerly. He was shorter than most of his comrades, but incredibly thick through the shoulders, so that he seemed almost as wide as he was tall. Muscles rippled against the taut fabric of his woolen tunic. An ugly purplish scar ran lengthwise along one sharp-boned cheek.

"The work of a moment to dump him in, sire," Levrod said. He stepped toward Dovirr, who backed away half a step to give himself clearance, then held his ground. "Come to me, landsman," Levrod crooned in a harsh, rasping bass voice. "Come and taste the sea water!"

"You come to *me*," Dovirr snarled back. "I'll stand my ground."

Anger sizzled in Levrod's eyes at the mocking retort.

The scar on his cheek seemed to blaze. He came rumbling forward over the concrete pier.

Dovirr waited for him, sizing his opponent up. Levrod was strong, beyond a doubt, and from the way he ran it seemed that he was more agile than a man of his build had a right to be. Dovirr guessed that Levrod was planning on a running charge, a quick flip—and a dunking for the rash townsman who delayed the Sea-Lords in their departure. Dovirr had other ideas about the course the contest would take.

The neuron whip that he had wrestled from Lackresh's hand lay in a pocket of his tunic. Dovirr had no intention of using it, though. After all, any child could stop a strong man in his tracks with a neuron whip. If he used it on Levrod, it would save his skin, but it would shame him in the eyes of the very men whose favor he hoped to win. The only tactic, Dovirr knew, was to meet force with greater force.

Levrod reached him. The Sea-Lord's thick fingers, hooked now into grasping claws, clutched for Dovirr's arm and leg, meaning to heave him swiftly into the water. Levrod was fast, but Dovirr was faster. Deftly, the city-dweller stood to one side, stopped, caught the amazed Levrod by the crotch and shoulder.

"Out with you," Dovirr grunted.

In one swift motion he straightened and catapulted the heavy Sea-Lord on a high arc into the water. Levrod hit the sea with a mighty splash. A shower of brine sprayed the men on the pier as Levrod went under.

Dovirr whirled, arms outstretched, ready to parry any new attack. He expected the other Sea-Lords to retaliate for the humiliation he had inflicted on one of their number. But they were holding fast—silent, motionless, grim. They were impressed, Dovirr knew.

As for Levrod, he was surfacing now, and swimming rapidly toward the pier. There was never any telling what lurked in the offshore waters, and Levrod wasted little time quitting them. He clambered up on the pier, cursing explosively and spitting salt water. His magnificent woolen tunic looked sadly bedraggled now, and a puddle began to form where he stood.

Red-faced, Levrod groped for the sword at his hip.

Dovirr stiffened. He had no sword. He still hesitated to draw the neuron whip, a weapon for which the Sea-Lords had no respect. But it was either use the whip, or else turn and flee. Levrod had his sword from the scabbard now, and in another moment—

"No!" Gowyn thundered.

The Thalassarch drew his own sword and brought it crashing down ringingly against Levrod's as the Sea-Lord came toward Dovirr. Stunned by the blow, Levrod let the gleaming sword drop from his numbed fingers. There was a terrible silence on the pier.

Gowyn glanced at Dovirr. "Pick up the sword," the Thalassarch commanded.

Wordlessly, Dovirr obeyed. He scooped the weapon up, gripped the jeweled hilt firmly, and looked at the Thalassarch. The sword was heavier than he had expected it would be. Dovirr felt a chill of cold triumph at the realization that he actually held a Sea-Lord's sword in his hand.

Gowyn was smiling, but it was an icy smile. "Run this

carrion through," he ordered, indicating the dripping, shivering, utterly miserable Levrod.

Dovirr tightened his grip. His mind rebelled at the order. Strike an unarmed man? Why. . . .

He banished the hesitation. No use thinking like a townsman now, not if he wanted to become a Sea-Lord. This was the Sea-Lord way. Life was harsh and brutal among the men of the sea, and there was no room for weaklings. Why hesitate? Only a moment before, Levrod had come charging him, sword on high, murder in his mind. The Sea-Lord would have killed him without an instant's pause.

Besides, Gowyn's orders were orders. The time to begin obeying them was now.

Dovirr looked at Levrod. The Sea-Lord showed no fear. He stood there, wet and sodden, with eyes still defiant. He's daring me to obey Gowyn, Dovirr thought.

Dovirr lunged.

The stroke was true. Levrod crumpled without a word, sprawling face down on the pier with one arm dangling over the side. Gowyn nodded in approval and kicked the corpse over the edge. Slowly, a red trace began to seep out over the oily water of the harbor.

Instantly there was a flutter of fins. The water seemed to boil. Dark, shiny shapes were visible just beneath the surface for a moment, and then the body of the dead Sea-Lord disappeared.

The Seaborn Ones, Dovirr thought moodily. Feeding on their landborn brother.

The Thalassarch watched the grisly scene in the water until Levrod was gone. Then he pivoted, and his eyes came to rest on Dovirr.

He said, "We now appear to have one vacancy aboard the *Garyun*. What is your name, youngster?"

"Dovirr Stargan," he stammered. Could it be possible? Was it really happening?

"Welcome to the *Garyun*, Dovirr Stargan. How old are you?"

"Eighteen, sire."

Gowyn nodded. "Young enough. But I like your spirit and the way you fight. Besides, I long suspected Levrod's loyalty. We're well rid of him." The Thalassarch beckoned to one of his men. "Give him Levrod's berth. Register him in the company. And now, by the stars, let's get ourselves away from this foul place!"

He lowered himself into his dinghy, and the oarsmen seized their oars. The Thalassarch's boat headed bobbingly for the ship anchored further out in the harbor. The other Sea-Lords clambered down into their own boats. Dovirr stood motionless in their midst, hardly believing yet that he had really won a place among them.

A burly Sea-Lord of more than middle years came up to Dovirr. Pale blue eyes stared searchingly at the young townsman for a long silent moment. Uncomfortably, Dovirr met the Sea-Lord's bleak gaze.

Evidently satisfied, the old warrior said, "My name is Holinel. Come in our boat."

"I thank you," Dovirr said.

He followed Holinel to the edge of the pier. A weather-beaten boat waited there, with six men in it already. They glanced at Dovirr without friendship in their eyes, regarding him coolly, as something strange and alien that had unexpectedly been thrust into their midst.

Holinel stepped aboard. Wordlessly, he indicated that Dovirr should get in next to him. Dovirr hesitated. He looked back, over his shoulder, at Vythain. The city rose in tier after gray tier—the marketplace next to the waterfront, the shops a little higher up, then the houses in helter-skelter array, and in each of the houses a wide-eyed townsman who had seen Dovirr slay a Sea-Lord and live.

It was a goodbye to all that, Dovirr thought. Goodbye to friends and family, goodbye to his birthplace, goodbye to his old life. He had said farewell to no one, not even his father, and there was no time for that now. Dovirr regretted that, but there had been no other way, for if he had breathed a word of his plans to anyone, they'd have clapped him in jail until the Sea-Lords were gone. So it would have to be goodbye without saying farewell. Dovirr shrugged. This city had held him prisoner long enough. Out there was the sea, and out there was life and the quest for power.

"Coming?" Holinel asked.

"Of course," Dovirr said.

He jumped down into the boat and found a seat for himself. Moments later the mooring was slipped and the small craft headed across the water toward the dark bulk of the *Garyun*.

The Endless
Sea

THE DECK OF THE SEA-LORD vessel surged with activity. Men were hoisting the sails again, winching in the anchor that had held the ship to the shelf that underlay the shore of the artificial city, hauling the boats on board. Every man seemed to have his specific duty. No one paid attention to Dovirr as he came on board.

He had been to sea before, but not often. Men of Vythian stayed close to land. There were a few fishing boats, of course, that gathered food along the shores of the floating city, but it was a dangerous trade, for the Seaborn Ones, those strange, almost human people of the deeps, often amused themselves by tipping the flimsy boats of the fishermen and dragging their victims to death. Dovirr had gone fishing a few times, and he had seen the Seaborn Ones swimming nearby. That was when he first came to see how fragile human life was, and how close to death men were at any moment. But the Seaborn Ones had not chosen to have sport that day, and Dovirr had returned to Vythain alive.

Other vessels left Vythain, too: the slow-moving merchant ships, bound for neighboring cities. Dovirr had long thought of joining one such ship. But that, too, was an uncertain life. Very often the merchantmen did not return. Dovirr had no fear of death, but he did not want to die pointlessly. And it seemed a pointless death to him to go down aboard a leaky old tub laden with onions and cabbage. If he had to die at sea, he wanted to die fighting, to die among the Sea-Lords.

He was among them now. The *Garyun* had hoisted anchor and had picked up a strong breeze. Men were hauling at the oars belowdecks. Vythain was disappearing from sight.

Holinel, the old warrior who had appointed himself Dovirr's sponsor, let him look around the decks no more than a few minutes. "Come with me," he said brusquely.

Dovirr followed him into the depths of the ship. It was a huge vessel, deck after deck of oars and other levels beneath those. Down Dovirr went, to a realm of darkness. Flickering candles provided a smoky light. Dovirr was astonished at that, but he reminded himself that the lights of Vythain glowed by courtesy of the departed beasts who had conquered Earth long ago. All machinery—all power plants—all that made life soft in the cities—was the heritage of the Dhuchay'y, as were the floating cities themselves. Man's own science and technology had withered away during the centuries when the Star Beasts had ruled Earth.

"Here," Holinel grunted. "This was Levrod's berth. It's yours, now."

It was a little less than magnificent. There was a mattress of straw, loosely bound with cords, for his bed. There were a few crudely carpentered wooden shelves. There was a rack where he could hang his sword—the sword that had once been Levrod's, the sword that now was stained with the dead Sea-Lord's blood. Next to the mattress was a box, a sea chest, that probably contained Levrod's belongings.

Holinel said, "His clothes won't fit you. Get out of those landsman rags and I'll have a decent tunic sent to you."

"That's kind of you."

"No kindness in it, youngster. You can't go about in that kind of costume here. Strip if off."

Shrugging, Dovirr began to remove his tunic. It was half off before he remembered the neuron whip in his pocket. He fished it out and set it carefully on one of the shelves over his berth.

"What's that?" Holinel demanded.

"A neuron whip."

"Which is what?"

"A weapon," Dovirr said. "The Star Beasts left them behind when they went away."

"Hand it here," the Sea-Lord said. "Let's have a look at the thing."

Dovirr was unhappy about surrendering the neuron

whip, but obviously he had no alternative. Holinel thrust one gnarled hand forward. Reluctantly, Dovirr placed the streamlined, mirror-bright weapon in Holinel's palm.

The Sea-Lord stared at it as though it were some particularly unpleasant kind of jellyfish. After a long moment he closed his hand on the butt.

"What does it do?" he asked.

Dovirr groped for words. "It—it does something to a man's brain. If you turn it on low, it just gives you an uncomfortable sting. At the high end, it kills. In between, it can knock a man down, make him unconscious, even paralyze him if he gets a good jolt."

Holinel opened and closed his hand a few times. He looked at Dovirr in a hooded, guarded way.

"Try it on me," he said.

"I don't understand."

"My words were clear, I thought. Show me how the weapon works. Use it. Sting me with it."

"You won't like it."

"Do as I say," Holinel barked, and there was no kindliness in his face as he spoke.

He handed the neuron whip to Dovirr. Feeling queasy about the whole affair, Dovirr checked to make certain that the weapon was down at lowest intensity. Then he trained it on Holinel's left arm and gave him a quick jolt.

Holinel winced for perhaps a fraction of a second. That was the only sign he gave that the neuron whip had caused him any discomfort. He did not rub his arm, he did not hiss in pain, he did not flinch.

"That is the lowest?" he asked.

"Yes," Dovirr said, fearing that now the grizzled old Sea-Lord would want to experiment with the higher intensities of the neuron whip.

"Give it here," Holinel said.

A second time, Dovirr surrendered the weapon. To his surprise, Holinel swung round and carried the neuron whip to the tiny porthole that faced Dovirr's berth. Before Dovirr could move, the Sea-Lord flicked his wrist and the neuron whip disappeared through the port.

"You threw it away!" Dovirr gasped.

"That is no weapon for men to use," Holinel replied evenly. "You have a sword. Use that. This other thing is a sickening toy."

Dovirr shook his head. "You shouldn't have done that. It was a valuable weapon. The Thalassarch might have wanted it. You—"

"We have no need of such things," Holinel said. "Can you use a sword, landsman?"

"I've never been taught."

"You'll learn, then. And you'll fight like a man, or else you'll go overboard, too. None of your Star Beast toys here, boy. Understood?"

"Y-yes."

"Good. Have you any other little trinkets like that one, now?"

"No," Dovirr said.

"Very well. Give me that tunic of yours, then. We'll get you some clothes worth wearing."

Silently, Dovirr finished undressing and handed his thin linen tunic to the Sea-Lord. Holinel crumpled it into a ball and thrust it under his arm. He went away without any further word.

Shivering a little, Dovirr turned to inspect his new home. The loss of the neuron whip still shook him. The cavalier way in which Holinel had disposed of it was even more startling than the fact that it was gone. But this was a harsh society, Dovirr knew. Men acted decisively here. This was what he had wanted, wasn't it? Yes, he told himself. He had ached to leave Vythain, and now Vythain was a dwindling dot on the horizon, and he had to accept Sea-Lord ways. The neuron whip was gone, a plaything for the Sea-born Ones. He would simply have to make do with a sword. No one in Vythain owned a sword, of course, and so Dovirr had little idea of how to wield one. But he would learn, and quickly. Either learn or become food for the Seaborn Ones himself, Dovirr realized.

He bent forward to peer into Levrod's sea chest. It contained some clothing, two stubby, wicked-looking daggers, and a few little statuettes roughly carved from the bones or tusks of some sea animal. Dovirr let the lid drop without inspecting the contents of the chest in any detail. The chest was his, he supposed, by right of inheritance, but he felt ghoulish about prowling through Levrod's possessions just now.

A few moments passed. Holinel returned, a woolen tunic draped over his left arm.

"Try this one," he said.

Dovirr pulled the garment on. A shiver of delight ran down his spine. Wool! He was wearing wool! The warmth of it against his skin was an incredibly exciting sensation. In

Vythain, only the most important men wore wool. Just one city of the world produced the prized fabric, and there was scarcely enough to go around for every jack in Vythain. Yet here he was, the newest of the Sea-Lords, and already he was garbed in fine warm wool!

"Does it fit you?" Holinel asked gruffly.

"It's wonderful."

"It looks all right, yes. All right. Up with you, now. You'll do some pulling on oars before you get a meal on board this ship."

Dovirr scarcely minded. Pull oars? Yes, of course—that and swab decks if he had to, and scrub dishes, and anything else they asked him to do. He was a Sea-Lord now, with a Sea-Lord's work to do.

Holinel led him to the second bank of oars from the top. Sweating, grunting Sea-Lords were seated in parallel rows, hauling at thick handles that jutted through the walls of the ship. No one looked up as Dovirr entered. Holinel took him to an empty seat on one of the front benches.

"This is where Levrod sat," Holinel remarked. "From now on it's yours. You'll have a short shift tonight, but be ready to break your back in the morning. We all row here, all but the Thalassarch."

"I know," Dovirr said.

He took his place on the bench. There were two Sea-Lords there already, and in the faint light Dovirr saw how sweat oiled their bodies. Down here in the galley, it was no place for woolen garments, Dovirr realized. But the Sea-Lords wore their finery no matter what discomfort they might feel.

The huge handle swung toward him. He grabbed it and tried to fit himself into the rhythm of the rowers. His hands were big, but he had to strain to grasp the butt of the oar. It was back-straining work to push it forward, harder work to pull it back.

Holinel vanished. Dovirr glanced at the Sea-Lord immediately to his left—a stocky, dark-haired man with a hook of a nose, full lips, and a sparse, greasy-looking beard.

"My name's Dovirr," he said. "I'm from Vythain."

There was no reply from the Sea-Lord.

Maybe he's deaf, Dovirr thought. He grunted and hauled at the oar. *Stroke! Stroke! Stroke!* The powerful muscles of his back rippled. He was going to have blisters on his hands tonight, he knew. But in a few days, he hoped, he'd be as calloused as the rest of them.

After a moment he tried again, speaking louder this time. "My name's Dovirr!"

"I heard you," the Sea-Lord said curtly. "Don't blast my ear off."

"You didn't answer."

"Why should I?"

"Because—because—" Dovirr stopped, puzzled by that one. He hauled on the oars, three more strokes, before replying. "Because it's a civil thing to do," he said finally.

"Why should I be civil to you? What are you to me?"

"The man at your side, for one thing."

"You're just a stinking landsman."

"Not any more," Dovirr said hotly. "And—"

"Shut up," the Sea-Lord said. He spat in the general direction of Dovirr's feet. "Shut up and row."

For the first time, the man on the far side of the unfriendly Sea-Lord spoke up. In a soft, amazingly deep voice he said, "It costs nothing to give the boy your name, does it? He put Levrod in his place, and maybe he'll put you in yours next. Not a bad idea."

The hook-nosed one shrugged. "I feel no need of his friendship."

"Be civil all the same, Lantise. The boy fought well today. He is one of us now."

Dovirr said, "If you think it's too much trouble to be friendly, forget it."

The Sea-Lord by his side scowled at Dovirr's blunt words. But he said grudgingly, "I am called Lantise, youngster."

"And I am Cloden," said the deep-voiced Sea-Lord on the other side of Lantise. "I watched you handle Levrod. It was well done."

"I feared his sword," Dovirr said. "The Thalassarch saved me, or I would have died instead of Levrod."

"Gowyn recognizes valor," said Cloden softly. "He had little love for Levrod, in any case. Once you threw him in, his life was ended so far as Gowyn cared. Can you use a sword, Dovirr?"

Dovirr paused, wondering if he should tell the truth. It might be unwise to admit to Cloden in the earshot of the unfriendly Lantise that he had no skill in Sea-Lord weapons. But Dovirr decided to take the risk. He would need an instructor, and Cloden seemed an agreeable enough comrade as these rough Sea-Lords went.

He said, "I have never held a sword in my hand before this day, Cloden."

Lantise laughed. "You'll have a short life with us, boy!

Food for the Seaborn Ones!"

"I'll learn," Dovirr shot back at him. "Cloden, will you teach me swordsmanship? I have Levrod's sword, and I'm willing to accept you as my teacher."

"We will both teach you," Cloden said. "Lantise and I. Tomorrow in our free time the lessons will begin."

"Speak for yourself," Lantise snapped. "I'll waste no time teaching city-whelped pups to fight."

Cloden shook his head slowly. "Foolish words, Lantise. You and I and Dovirr must share the pull of this oar. Like him or not, he is your neighbor here. If he is killed in our next combat, two of us must pull an oar meant for the strength of three. Perhaps you feel like doing the work of a man and a half, but not I."

"I hadn't thought of that," Lantise said quietly.

"We'll teach him to fight," said Cloden. "It's in our own best interest. First free time tomorrow, we give him a lesson. And now—pull! Pull! Pull!"

Nightfall came. A gong sounded in the galleys, two short beats and then a long clamorous one. Grunting sounds of satisfaction could be heard as the Sea-Lords docked their oars and rose from the benches.

Cloden said, "Our shift is over. It is time for eating, now."

"Do other men take over our oars while we are eating?" Dovirr asked.

Cloden shook his head. "Not tonight. We have a good wind, so said the signal. We will travel on sail alone until the morning comes. We do not pull oars all the time on this ship, Dovirr."

They got to their feet. Dovirr saw that he stood more than a head taller than the stocky Lantise, but that Cloden was more nearly of a height with him. Cloden was slender, though, with a wiry body that seemed to ripple with strength. It was strange and a little sinister that so deep a voice could come out of so slim a man. Dovirr had not been able to see Cloden clearly in the darkness of the galley, and had guessed that he must have a deep barrel of a chest to produce such a voice. It was not so.

The Sea-Lords were going up a hatchway. Lantise swung himself onto the ladder; Dovirr followed, and then Cloden. They emerged in the uppermost bank of oars, and passed upward another level. Dovirr let Cloden catch up with him. He felt lost here in the inner depths of the giant ship. It was a little like being on a smaller Vythain, Dovirr thought, except that this floating "city" did not anchor itself to one point in the sea, but journeyed freely at the will of its master, the Thalassarch Gowyn. How big was the *Garyun?* Dovirr could hardly guess. It had seemed enormous this morning as it lay off the harbor at Vythain. It was home for several hundred Sea-Lords. Dovirr had seen little of it thus far, only his own berth and the galleys and a passageway or two. He had a sense of cell after cell, stretching out for a vast distance.

They entered a high-ceilinged cabin many yards long. A smoky, acrid-smelling fire lit the room. A long wooden table ran the length of it, and the Sea-Lords at the far end were noisily gulping down bowls of soup. Dovirr caught sight of a few familiar faces. There was the red-bearded one who had stood beside the Thalassarch on the pier at Vythain. What was his name, Dovirr wondered? Lysigon, that was it. Evidently a favorite of Gowyn's, perhaps the Thalassarch's second-in-command. And there was Holinel, near the head of the table, somehow looking sage and dignified even as he held the wooden bowl of soup to his bearded lips. He nodded faintly to Dovirr as the newest Sea-Lord entered.

Dovirr did as Cloden and Lantise did, picking up a clean wooden bowl from a stack near the cabin door, and heading for the great tureen at the opposite end of the room, where a round-bellied man was dishing out the soup.

Cloden said, "That's Marghuin. The cook. Treat him with respect, boy, or he'll poison your broth."

Dovirr held out his bowl. The cook, a fat, sweat-flecked man who hardly looked like a warrior, frowned and said, "This is the new one, eh, Cloden? The demon out of Vythain?"

"You should have seen him on the pier," Cloden said. "He spitted Levrod without a qualm."

There were qualms aplenty, Dovirr thought. He kept the thought to himself and said, "My name is Dovirr. The fame of your cooking reaches even to Vythain, Marghuin."

The cook chuckled. "Such broad flattery will get you no extra meals, boy!" But he did not look displeased at the compliment. He dipped his ladle into the huge, steaming tureen and filled Dovirr's bowl with soup.

Dovirr waited until Cloden had been served, and they took seats at the long table together. There were no spoons or other utensils; Dovirr realized that those were city-dweller luxuries, not to be found in this rougher society. He lifted his bowl to his lips. Before he drank, he looked in it, and wished that he had not. It was a broth of seafood, of course, and he was accustomed to such a diet from Vythain. But great chunks of greasy-looking meat floated in the liquid, and there was some small creature with many legs drifting in the soup. It seemed to Dovirr that the small jointed legs might still be moving, though he insisted to himself that it was only his imagination at work.

Never mind, he thought. This was Sea-Lord fare, and he was of the Sea-Lords now. He put all hesitations from his mind and sipped at the hot broth. It was good, whatever its contents, and he was fiercely hungry. In a few moments, the bowl was empty. He smacked his lips with satisfaction.

Cloden grinned. "We eat well here," he said. "Simple food, but a great deal of it. Gowyn does not believe in starving his fighting men."

He pointed toward the far wall. Marghuin was energetically carving meat from the broiled carcass of some beast of the sea. The Sea-Lords were lining up to be served. Cloden and Dovirr joined the line. The cook smiled as Dovirr extended his plate, and dumped a thick slab of meat onto it. There was something to be said for a compliment at the right time after all, Dovirr thought.

Much later, after the meat was gone and the last cup of wine had been downed, Dovirr and Cloden made their way up one more ladder, emerging on the main deck of the *Garyun*. The night was black. There was no moon, and the stars arching across heaven's vault had a peculiar hard brilliance.

Many times, Dovirr had come down to the edge of the

sea at Vythain and had looked out across the vast expanse of the water. He had dreamed of a day when the Sea-Lords would journey to Vythain and take him away as one of their number, and now that day had arrived. It was not easy to believe.

Starshine speckled the surface of the sea. Wavelets lapped at the *Garyun's* hull. The black sail bellied outward as the strong breeze drove it westward over the endless sea.

Had there once really been a time when the sea covered only part of the world? Dovirr wondered. When cities had held millions of people, when there had been dry land rolling on as far as eye could see? So the old stories said. But the Dhuchay'y, the Star Beasts, had come, and had turned Earth into a planet to suit their own needs, using their scientific skill to drown the continents in an endless sea. They were gone, now, those scaly-skinned invaders, leaving as mysteriously and suddenly as they came, but the sea remained.

Cloden stood silently by Dovirr's side. After a moment Dovirr shook his head and turned away from the view of the sea.

"It's too big," he said. "It baffles me."

"It baffles us all," said Cloden. "We learn to look at one wave at a time. The whole sea is too great for any man to understand."

Dovirr nodded. "Let's go down," he suggested. "It's been a long day for me. I think I had better sleep."

"Can you find your way to your berth?"

"I think so. If I have trouble, I'll ask someone."

He had no trouble, though. Down and down and down

they went, deep into the ship's core, past the banks of oars, along the companionway that led to the berths. He said goodnight to Cloden, and the slender Sea-Lord gravely wished Dovirr a sound sleep. Then Dovirr turned off on the branching passage that took him to his own berth.

Other Sea-Lords had gone to bed already, or lay awake, relaxing on their mattresses. They stared at Dovirr with curiosity, but no one spoke to him. He realized that he had a long way to go before he won many friends aboard this ship. Holinel and Cloden were exceptions, men who recognized that he was one of them now. The greeting he had had from Lantise was more typical. The Sea-Lords were a proud lot who scorned the men of the cities. Dovirr had won a place aboard ship fairly, and they did not grudge him it—but that did not mean they had to like him, or even to speak to him.

He stripped off his woolen tunic and lowered himself to the scratchy, hard mattress. There was an ache in his back and a soreness in his palms from rowing, but he knew that a few days of steady work would spare him from such discomforts. Dovirr closed his eyes. He felt the great ship rocking beneath him. The sea was like a giant cradle, he thought. It was strange here, and different, and hostile. But here was where he wanted to be. The beginning of his path lay with this ship, with this life.

Within moments, sleep took him.

Journey Toward Sunset

NO ONE SLEPT LATE aboard the *Garyun*. It seemed to Dovirr that he had hardly closed his eyes but he felt a savage poke in the ribs, and he awoke, gasping, half doubled up in pain. He gained control of himself in a moment, and even while his eyes were still fluttering open he was reaching for the sword that lay at his side. He was ready to defend himself against whatever enemy might be attacking.

But there was no enemy. Dovirr saw a lanky Sea-Lord going down the rows of berths, nudging each sleeper awake with a thrust of a wooden staff. The Sea-Lords, yawning and grunting, were getting to their feet.

Dovirr rose and dressed. There was no Cloden around to advise him, and he simply followed the nearest Sea-Lord up the ladder. One deck up, there was a barrel of fresh water, and half a dozen Sea-Lords were gathered around it, splashing their faces. Dovirr joined the group. A couple of the Sea-Lords tried to jostle him aside, but he held his ground and was pleased to see that they let him have his turn without further conflict. They were testing him, Dovirr guessed. Trying to provoke him, trying to see where they could master him. It would take patience to live with that sort of treatment—patience and occasionally some strength.

He washed his face in the lukewarm water, dried it Sea-Lord fashion on the sleeve of his precious tunic, and continued on upward for breakfast. No one approached him, no one even smiled at him. It was the silent treatment. Dovirr refused to let it bother him. He knew that he was bigger and stronger than most of these Sea-Lords, and that it would be only a matter of time before he brought his strength to tell against their coldness. He had no fear of them. He was new and did not know the ways of shipboard life, and so for the time being he was vulnerable. But that would pass.

There was no sign of Cloden at breakfast. Dovirr sat alone, munching dried fish and washing the salty meal down with preserved fruit juice. When he had finished, he swung outward from the table and jauntily clambered to his station at the oars. Lantise and Cloden were there. Cloden wished him a good morning; hook-nosed Lantise merely nodded.

Cloden said, "We practice swordsmanship this afternoon, yes?"

"As soon as possible," Dovirr said.

They rowed all morning. The air was calm, it seemed, and all four banks of oars were in operation. According to Cloden the *Garyun* was heading westward, toward the city of Lanobul. The Sea-Lord life, Dovirr was coming to realize, was not entirely one of free roving. There was a definite circuit of visits at each of the cities controlled by the Thalassarch Gowyn. Vythain to Lanobul, Lanobul to Hicanthro, Hicanthro to Vastrok—on through the year the Sea-Lords traveled, collecting tribute from the vassal cities, and also purchasing what was needed to sustain life aboard ship. For food, the Sea-Lords could depend mainly on the bounty of the sea, but not entirely. They needed the meat and vegetable produce of the cities, as well as the manufactured goods of the land-dwellers. So the circuit went, from month to month.

Just now, tugging at the heavy oars, Dovirr did not find much joy in a Sea-Lord's life. From the vantage point of Vythain, he had seen only the swagger and arrogance of the men of the sea, and he had thought of them as wonderfully free in their life of adventure. Now he was seeing the other side—the cramped berth, the itchy mattress, the long hours of toil in the galleys. But at least they were on the move, Dovirr told himself.

The gong sounded. The shift was ended. It was time to eat, once again.

"Get your sword," Cloden told Dovirr when the meal was over. "Meet us on the top deck."

Dovirr hurried downward. One of the first things he had learned, coming aboard the *Garyun*, was that the Sea-Lords did not carry their swords all the time. They wore them when going ashore, of course, to impress the landsmen. And, naturally, they had them handy when they were about to do battle. But there was little room in the narrow companionways for swords, and most of the time the handsome weapons hung in their pegs over their owners' berths.

Brandishing his sword now, Dovirr hurried up toward the top deck. He stepped out into brilliant sunshine. The sky was almost blinding in its blueness, broken only by a few fleecy clouds low on the horizon. There was no land in sight: only the dark sheet of water, running, it seemed, to the rim of the universe.

Cloden and Lantise were waiting for him, swords ready. Stocky Lantise was grinning in an evil way and nervously passing his hands through his sparse, greasy beard. It struck Dovirr that Lantise might easily use the "lesson" as a pretext for running him through. At least, that was what seemed to be on the Sea-Lord's mind right now. But Cloden was nearby, and Dovirr had come to trust Cloden.

"Draw your weapon," Cloden said.

Dovirr pulled Levrod's sword from its sheath. His hand tightened on the hilt. Reflected sunlight sparkled from the broad blade of the impressive weapon.

Cloden said, "What you have here is a saber, Dovirr. It's basically a slashing weapon. You use the edge of it, more than you do the point. A man handling a saber looks crude and oafish, but there's an art to it." He drew his own sword and held it out for Dovirr's inspection. "I use a rapier. It's a subtler weapon. It can be used for cutting or thrusting, as the need arises, but usually only the point comes into play." He brought the tip of his sword forward in a graceful arc, until it rested lightly against Dovirr's chest. Then he pulled it away.

"Which is the better weapon?" Dovirr asked.

"They each have their advantages," said Cloden. "A man of your size and strength is probably better equipped with a saber. You can slash at your enemy and because of your power you can maneuver the heavy weapon quickly enough to parry his thrusts. A man like me does better with a more slender blade, one that can be moved at a great speed."

Dovirr nodded. He glanced at Lantise, whose blade seemed much like his own. Good, Dovirr thought. In the present state of his fencing skill, it was just as well that Lantise had no advantages of speed over him.

Cloden said, "We'll show you some of the basic movements, now. Learn how to hold yourself, first. Sword high. That's it. Right leg forward. Show as little of yourself to the enemy as you have to. Now—"

The lesson lasted an hour. Cloden displayed the essential postures, and then he and Lantise took turns practicing them with Dovirr. For all his evil, glowering expression, Lantise turned out to hold no murderous thoughts. He was nearly as patient as Cloden with Dovirr's early blunders. Half a dozen times, it would have been a simple matter for Lantise "accidentally" to thrust his sword through Dovirr's guard, or to lop off his arm with a sudden chop. At such moments Lantise would laugh and move his weapon lightly through the gap, demonstrating to Dovirr what would have happened if this were not a lesson but a duel.

Dovirr learned quickly. While he fenced with Lantise, Cloden crisply called out suggestions to improve his stance; fencing with Cloden, Dovirr was guided by Lantise's blunt, often insulting, but always useful comments. Sweat rolled in torrents down Dovirr's body. A few of the other Sea-Lords drifted by to watch the lesson. Dovirr forced himself to forget that he had an audience. He concentrated on the words of his instructors, blanking out all else.

The sword was heavy, but Dovirr was strong, and soon he scarcely noticed its weight at all. There was a beauty to the weapon, he thought. It was balanced wonderfully well, and all he had to do was learn to blend with that balance.

"The sword must become part of your arm," Cloden told him. "Flesh and steel, joined without a seam."

The hour ended. Time now to put away the swords, time now to rest. A strong breeze drove the *Garyun* westward. Some of the Sea-Lords put lines and nets overboard, trawling for fish. Others slept in the sun; some played games with gleaming little dice; and a few dueled for their own amusement, sabers ringing and clashing.

The day drew to a close. Far ahead of the ship's prow, sunset purpled the sky. Dovirr ate, a meal much like last night's. He swilled down strong wine, and listened while a Sea-Lord sang an endless ballad of bloodshed and victory. He was singing about the Star Beasts, about the days when the enemies from beyond the heavens came to Earth and conquered her and drowned her cities. And he was singing of the time when the Star Beasts would come back to Earth.

Dhuchay'y blood would stain the sea, the song vowed.

Dovirr was sitting near Holinel. "Do you think the Star Beasts will return?" he asked.

The old Sea-Lord spread his hands wide. "They'll be back," he said. "No man knows when, any more than any man knows why they left."

"And when they return," Dovirr said, "will they conquer us again?"

Holinel laughed harshly. "The world has changed since they were last here. We'll have some surprises for them now, I think!"

Another Sea-Lord stamped his booted feet against the floor in noisy agreement. "We'll show them, Holinel!" he bellowed. "We'll make curtains from their hides!"

The Sea-Lords roared their defiance of the beings from the stars. Silent in the midst of the uproar, Dovirr wondered: if they took our world away from us once, how can we hope to defeat them now? Bombs and guns had been useless against them. Would swords triumph where the awesome weapons of the ancients had failed?

Day after day slid by. Dovirr took his turn at the oars; he sweated in the hot sun, parrying the increasingly more deadly thrusts of Lantise and Cloden; he learned the names of other Sea-Lords; he grew tough and calloused in his new life. He still did not feel welcome aboard the ship. The eyes that turned toward him as he passed down the corridors of the vessel were unfriendly ones. A few Sea-Lords grudgingly nodded to him when they saw him, but he made no new friends.

He lived with the situation. Right now, he needed swordsmanship more than friendship. Whatever free time he had, he spent with his two instructors. His skills were mounting. In three days, he felt able to hold his own in battle. In five, he knew that he was going to be a great warrior, if conflict ever came. The sword had, indeed, become part of him. It was like an extension of his right arm, hooked to his brain and responsive to every command. Even Lantise was impressed by the pace at which he learned. He could handle the heavy saber now as though it were as light and flexible as Cloden's rapier. The daily bouts on the top-deck soon became more nearly a contest of equals, as Dovirr's swordsmanship improved.

Quite often, now, he and Cloden and Lantise had an audience as they drilled. Dovirr was bothered, at first, by these knots of Sea-Lords who gathered around to watch him go through the paces of his practice duels. He felt embarrassed for his clumsiness and his untrained handling of the weapon. But the embarrassment left him as his abilities increased, and he came to realize that the Sea-Lords who formed his audience were genuinely interested in watching his progress. They might not favor him with a friendly smile, but he was not going unnoticed aboard the *Garyun*.

And one day he had a very special observer. Gowyn, the Thalassarch himself, appeared on deck, joined the group of onlookers, stood for a long while watching Dovirr fence. Dovirr did not see him appear. It was only when he turned to catch a moment's rest after a particularly grueling interchange with Lantise that Dovirr saw the bulky figure of the Thalassarch, standing to one side with folded arms, a faint smile on his bearded face. Dovirr's cheeks flamed as he understood that he had been watched by Gowyn. The Thalassarch inclined his head in a quick nod, seemingly telling Dovirr to pick up his sword once again.

"You learn quickly," Gowyn said.

"Thank you, sire."

"We'll see how you do in battle, though. There's the test!"

"I hope to be a credit to the ship," Dovirr said.

"I trust you will be," replied Gowyn. "You have good teachers."

He signaled that the lesson should continue. Dovirr grasped the hilt of his weapon again and swung around to face Cloden. Cloden's rapier dazzled Dovirr's eyes as he wove it through patterns of attack. *Clang!* and Dovirr parried a lightning thrust. *Clang!* and he parried again. *Clang! Clang! Clang!*

Seize the attack, now, Dovirr thought. Show the Thalassarch what you've learned!

He pressed forward. Hefting the massive saber as though it were a stick, Dovirr tried twice to slip under Cloden's guard, and twice was parried. He feinted, whirled, began to slide the edge of his saber across Cloden's arm.

Suddenly Cloden performed an intricate maneuver, and Dovirr's target no longer was where Dovirr had aimed. His saber cut through empty air, and a moment later Cloden drove at him from the side. Dovirr was helpless. The sword spun in his hand, and he had to release it or lose a finger. It described a glittering arc as it flew through the air, landing twenty feet away on the deck. Cloden, laughing, put the point of his rapier against Dovirr's chest.

"You'd be a dead man if we fought in earnest," Cloden said.

"How did you move so fast?"

"Easy when the foe is overconfident, Dovirr."

Dovirr shamefacedly walked over to pick up his sword. His ears burned from the disgrace of it. It was his own fault, he knew: eager to show off before the Thalassarch, he had forced an attack without really having control of the situation. Cloden, still the superior swordsman, had disarmed him without effort. Dovirr saw the jeering faces of the Sea-Lords. No doubt they were happy to see the newcomer taken down a couple of pegs. He could scarcely bear to look toward the Thalassarch.

There was no mockery in Gowyn's eyes, though. His face wore the same faint smile.

He said, "Not everything is learned in a day. There is danger in moving too fast, Dovirr."

Dovirr managed an unhappy smile. His eyes dropped in embarrassment. The Thalassarch, indicating by a gesture that he had been well amused, left them.

That night, as sunset tinged the sea with gold and purple, Dovirr encountered the Thalassarch again. The dinner hour was over, and Dovirr did not feel like joining in the nightly carousing of the Sea-Lords. He came on deck to watch the darkness descend. The warmth of day was still in the air, but a chill was entering it. The wind was turning sharp.

Dovirr stood by the rail. The ship seemed hardly to be moving. The sea lapped at the hull, and there was a dim sensation of motion, but no more than that. Without landmarks, there was no certain way of knowing that they were traveling. Somewhere to the west, in the home of the sunset, lay their next port of call, the city of Lanobul. But in the two weeks that he had been aboard the *Garyun*, Dovirr had seen no sign that Lanobul approached. Only the curving surface of the sea lay before him, whenever he peered outward. How far was Lanobul, anyway? How big was the world? Dovirr had no idea. The journey might take forever. It might take as long as—as the journey to those cold, glittering stars.

Men had gone to the stars once, Dovirr knew. To the close ones, at least, to the stars that were called "planets," because they were solid and did not give off light. Red Mars, and gleaming Venus—the ships from Earth had flown through the darkness to those planets, and to the pockmarked brightness of the Moon. How had they done it? A ship could ride on the waters, yes, but how could it sail to the sky and the planets?

No matter, Dovirr thought. It was not a problem worth pondering for long. The accomplishments of the ancient men of Earth were half mythical, anyway. A thousand years had rolled by since men of Earth had gone to the planets, and much had changed since that day. The Earth of the ancients was gone forever, drowned under the endless sea, and gone, too, were dreams of stars. The stars had come to Earth on wings of flame. The Star Beasts, the conquerors from the darkness, had written finis to the dreams of mankind.

Night had fallen now. The moon was full tonight, cutting a silvery track across the sea. Dovirr peered into the depths. Powerful fins flashed: the Seaborn Ones, he thought, following the ship, swimming along for some scheming reason of their own. Waiting, perhaps, for a man to fall overboard, waiting to carry him down and rend his flesh. And. . . .

Dovirr saw a figure approaching on deck. A big man, bigger even than himself. He emerged out of the darkness. It was the Thalassarch! Dovirr realized.

"Good evening, Dovirr," Gowyn said mildly.

"Good evening, sire. I beg pardon for disturbing you. I ask permission to withdraw."

"Stay," he said. "What brings you on deck?"

"I came to watch the sea. To look at the stars."

"Why not spend the evening with the men? Sing songs with them and pass the wine cup?"

"I felt like being alone, sire."

Gowyn nodded. "They still treat you as an outsider, eh? Well, it's to be expected. It'll pass. The first time we do battle and you draw enemy blood, you'll win yourself a real place aboard this ship."

"I hope so, sire."

The Thalassarch fell silent. He leaned forward over the rail, heavy shoulders hunching. Dovirr stood uneasily at his side, awed by the man. Gowyn was no more than an inch or two taller than Dovirr, no more than ten or twenty pounds heavier. Yet Dovirr had the feeling that the Thalassarch, if the mood took him, could snap him in two like a dried twig. There was strength in Gowyn that went beyond mere physical force. He had majesty. It was almost a mystical thing, Dovirr thought, almost like a mantle of power.

After a while Gowyn said, "Why did you leave Vythain?"

"I was restless. I wanted to find new worlds."

"Have you found them here?"

"Not yet, sire. But my journey's only begun."

"You interest me, Dovirr. I see a hunger in your eyes. You want to rule."

"I admit it, sire."

"Why not stay home, then, and rule Vythain? Someone like you could run that city with ease."

"Vythain wasn't enough," Dovirr said. "To remain anchored to one little city—to live with those people who will not look beyond their next meal—no. No. I had to get away, sire."

"And seek power with us? It's a hard path to take, Dovirr. Sea-Lords die young, and none die more swiftly than those who have the hunger to rule."

"Better a short and honorable life and a quick death than seventy years of boredom," Dovirr said.

"Bravo!" The Thalassarch laughed and clapped Dovirr on the back, a lusty thump that shook Dovirr's teeth to their roots. "You may get your wish," Gowyn said. "The power you crave—or else the quick death. Perhaps both. You have the raw material in you, I think, to be a leader. But you ought to be down below, forming friendships with the men. A leader needs alliances."

"I felt like standing alone on deck, sire."

"Time for that when you're a Thalassarch," Gowyn said. "When you must be aloof, for the sake of your name. You'll hate the loneliness then, and you'll have more than your fill. Take the wine cup now. Sing the songs. Become one of them, Dovirr. Time to set yourself apart after you've won the prize you seek." The Thalassarch turned, looked off into the moonlight-flecked sweep of the sea a moment. "Goodnight, Dovirr," he said abruptly.

"Goodnight, sire," Dovirr muttered. He was alone again. A cold wind came out of the north, suddenly, slicing through Dovirr's tunic like a poniard. A strange conversation, Dovirr thought. A strange man. But his words were not to be ignored. Dovirr moved toward the hatch. Down— down to the songs, down to the laughter, down to the wine cup as it passed from hand to hand.

Pirates of the
Western Sea

THREE WEEKS MORE had passed. Still the *Garyun* pressed
westward through the trackless sea. Day crawled after day.
Dovirr's hands were calloused now, and his arms and shoulders were stronger than they had ever been before, after
these days of hauling at the oars. He was skilled with the
sword now too, a match for Lantise and nearly the equal of
the crafty Cloden. The Sea-Lords were accepting him, without warmth. They greeted him by name; they no longer tried
to jostle him aside; they sometimes favored him with a word
or two of conversation, about the weather, about the prospects of battle, about the talents of Marghuin the cook.

Dovirr welcomed each crumb of friendship. Bit by bit, he was making a place for himself among the Sea-Lords. He still did not really feel one of them, but he was less of a stranger. Even now, he preferred to spend much of his time alone on deck, and sometimes the Thalassarch met him there and talked with him of many things.

Dovirr stood there now. The wide, uneasy sweep of the sea spread out before him as he leaned on the rail near the prow of the *Garyun*. He felt the salty tang blow sharply inward, stinging his nostrils. Though it was only early afternoon, the sky was strangely dark. Overburdened clouds hung low, their bottoms black, threatening cold rain at sea. The golden-brown fins of the Seaborn Ones broke the surface here and there, clearing the waves as they leaped and sported.

Looking outward, Dovirr thought of the Seaborn Ones—those strange once-human things that man had created, centuries ago, in a fruitless attempt to halt the onslaught of the unstoppable Dhuchay'y.

"Thinking again, Dovirr?" a booming voice said, just back of his left shoulder.

He turned. Gowyn stood beside him. Dovirr no longer felt quite the same awe of the Thalassarch as he had at first. Respect, yes. Admiration, certainly. But he had come to see the Gowyn was merely a human being, with hopes, fears, doubts of his own. Gowyn had tasted defeat now and then, and he understood loneliness. Once Dovirr had regarded the Thalassarch almost as a supernatural being, remote from human conflicts. He knew now that it was not so.

Dovirr suspected that he had managed to win a firm place in the affections of the grizzled Thalassarch, in the short time—less than two months—that he had been aboard the ship. Gowyn had no sons. He was near middle age; he had held dominance on the Western Sea for more than twenty years, which was an eternity in the world of the Sea-Lords. Time ran against him. Gowyn must certainly be seeking a successor and, Dovirr hoped, he perhaps had found one. It was a wild hope, Dovirr knew. There was red-bearded Lysigon, the second-in-command. He would succeed to the Thalassarch's title when Gowyn's time had come. Everyone aboard the *Garyun* knew that. And yet . . .

"Thinking, yes, sire. Of the Seaborn Ones."

Gowyn squinted down at the flashing fins. "Thinking of our brethren of the deep, are you? Some day you'll feel their teeth, young one."

"Is it true, sire? That the Seaborn Ones eat men who fall overboard?"

Gowyn shrugged heavy shoulders. "You will find that out the day you topple past that rail," he said. "I've never had cause to know. But beyond doubt a dying seaman will draw them to him within an instant. What they do with him after they've pulled him down, no living man can say."

"Strange," Dovirr said. "Strange that they should prey on us like beasts. They were men once themselves, weren't they, sire?"

"The sons of men only," Gowyn said. Shadows swept the Thalassarch's face. "Years past, hundreds of years gone, when the Earth was dry land, when the Star Beasts first came, men created the Seaborn Ones to fight against the alien conquerors." He chuckled without mirth. "It was a hopeless attempt. The Dhuchay'y defeated the legions of the Seaborn with ease, set a mighty rod in the ocean—and the spreading seas covered the land."

"Men created the Seaborn Ones?"

"In laboratories it was done," said Gowyn. "The scientists took the fertilized eggs of human beings, and changed them. We do not know how it was achieved. Such science has been lost, but the ancients had it. To carve what cannot be seen with the eye—to alter, to shift—it was done. In the laboratories were born creatures fit for life in the sea—creatures who could fight the Star Beasts in their own element. And into the sea they went, but they were defeated. And now they are our enemies, the Seaborn Ones."

"What were the Star Beasts like?" Dovirr asked.

"Amphibians!"

"This word I do not know."

Gowyn laughed. "It means they live part of their lives in the sea, part on the land. They are born in the sea. And so they flooded our world to provide a breeding ground for their spawn, who must live in salt water until they are grown. They used their science to turn air into water—a devil's trick. Of course, flooding our world also served the purpose of cleaning away those troublesome beings who lived on the land. Ourselves."

"And then the Dhuchay'y built the floating cities?"

"Yes," Gowyn said. "They kept little pieces of Earth alive, a forest here, a flock of sheep there, cut them loose, made drifting islands out of solid land. They built the cities, and kept a few of us to serve them." Moodily, Gowyn clenched his fists. "Oh, had I been living then, Dovirr, when they trampled us! To swing a sword and see a Star Beast's blood spurt!"

"What could you have done against them?" Dovirr asked.

"Nothing," said the Thalassarch with sudden bitterness. "No more than the ancients could do. At least I would have tried to strike back. But there was no stopping them, when they came. The sea covered all of Earth except the cities that they built. The world of our fathers lies a thousand fathoms down, Dovirr. The Seaborn Ones sport in the ruins of the drowned cities."

"And then the Star Beasts left," Dovirr said. "Every Dhuchay'y on Earth suddenly left, all at once. They gave no reason for leaving?"

"None."

Heavy clouds seemed to bunch on the horizon. Dovirr shivered as the chill, moisture-laden wind filled the black sails. The rhythmical grunting of the oarsmen on the decks below formed a regular pattern of sound that blended with the steady thumping beat of the sea against the *Garyun*'s stout hull.

"Some day the Star Beasts will return to Earth," said Gowyn suddenly. "Some day—as unexpected as their first coming it will be, and as unexpected as their departure. They will come back." The Thalassarch spun around. His big hands gripped Dovirr's shoulders with fearful strength. "Would that I live to see the day!" he cried.

"Would that you do, sire."

Fierce salt spray shot up the bows. In a lowered voice, the Thalassarch said, "Dovirr, should I die before they come—"

"Sire?"

"Should I die—and mind you that my time is long since overdue—will you swear to destroy them in my place? Will you swear that?"

Dovirr nervously fingered his sprouting black beard. The Thalassarch's eyes glimmered like coals. There was something almost insane about the intensity of his hatred for the Star Beasts, Dovirr realized.

"I swear, sire," Dovirr said huskily.

Gowyn was silent for a moment, his thick fingers digging into Dovirr's shoulders. Gradually he relaxed his grip. His hands fell to his sides.

"It is all we can do, Dovirr, if they come back. We must fight, and fight again, and fight until no strength remains. We cannot surrender to them. Let your friends of Vythain knuckle under to the Star Beasts if they wish. We Sea-Lords will fight them, while a drop of blood remains in our veins. I hope to last till that day. When it comes, Dovirr, you will fight at my side if I am here—or else you will carry the attack in my place."

Dovirr bowed his head. "Thank you, sire."

He sensed that a deep honor had been conveyed, that in some way Gowyn had placed his mantle on him. To fight at the Thalassarch's side—to lead the battle if the Thalassarch no longer lived—what was Gowyn saying, Dovirr wondered, if not that he planned to name him as his successor?

But perhaps Gowyn was simply venting his rage against the Star Beasts, speaking with passion that did not come from the mind but from the heart. Perhaps he had extracted this same vow from a dozen other men of the *Garyun*, from Lysigon and Cloden and Holinel, from thick-muscled Kubril the navigator, from Marghuin the cook. It was too soon to begin calling himself the heir apparent, Dovirr knew.

Yet he could not help but dream of the day when every man on this ship hailed him as the leader. The Thalassarch strode away. Dovirr held his place, looking outward. Somewhere far to the east, far beyond the sight of the keenest eye, was the island city of Vythain. Work and slave, ye landbound lubbers! Dovirr thought defiantly. And don't forget me! You'll pay tribute to Dovirr yet!

The storm broke in all its fury an hour later. The sky turned black as night; blades of yellow lightning crackled across the darkness, and the rumbling boom of thunder echoed from every side. The sea heaved like an angry beast, rising up as though it wanted to hurl the *Garyun* to the stars. Rain pelted down. Great gray waves towered higher than the topdeck, crashing against the hull.

The ship rode out the storm unharmed. It ended swiftly; the rain stopped as if a giant hand had turned a faucet. The sea grew calm, and billowy white clouds floated through a sky cleansed of all its darkness. The sun appeared. Pools of rain and salt water on the deck began to dry. The sails were hoisted once more.

Another hour, and the storm seemed like a happening in a dream. Westward sped the *Garyun*, prow cleaving the waves, and other distractions appeared.

First a merchant vessel came into view. Dovirr, on deck to help swab the flooded flooring dry, stared at the ship in delight. It was the first sign of other human life that he had seen beyond the confines of the *Garyun* since the day he left Vythain.

"An old tub," Cloden muttered. "Out of Lanobul. Heading north to Vostrok, I'd say."

"And flying a flag of distress," said Lantise.

"No," Cloden said. "I don't see—yes! Yes, of course! Your sharp eyes, Lantise . . ."

Dovirr looked westward, shading his eyes from the sinking sun. He could make out the wallowing, slow-moving ship clearly enough, and a flag whipping from its mast, showing the blue and red colors of Lanobul. Suddenly he realized what was awry: the red field was above the blue! They were flying their flag upside down.

"Pirates," Lantise grunted.

Dovirr's pulse raced. "Really? Are you sure?"

"You'll see," said Lantise.

An instant later the cry came from the rigging. Pirates! Pirates attacking a merchant vessel of Lanobul! So then it was true, Dovirr thought. The pirates were not myths fostered by the Sea-Lords. There actually were such rovers, preying on defenseless merchantmen, and the Sea-Lords were genuinely going to give attack.

The *Garyun* heeled around and made for the distressed merchantman. The Sea-Lords moved with precision, some going to battle stations, others vanishing belowdecks to man the oars. Dovirr faltered; this was his first taste of action aboard the ship, and no one had bothered to give him an assignment. He stood motionless in the midst of the swirl.

Someone came by, slapped him on the forearm. It was Kubril, the squat, muscular navigator, who was racing along the deck toward his post on the forecastle.

"Where do you belong?" he shouted.

"I don't know," Dovirr said.

"Get your sword! Join the boarding crew!"

"Where?"

"There!" Kubril cried, already on the move again. He indicated a knot of men lowering a boat on the starboard side. Dovirr nodded and hastened below to seize his weapon. Blood sang in his veins; his chest heaved with excitement; his eyes glowed.

A moment later he was back above. It was easier, now, to see what was happening across the way. The ship of Lanobul, slow-moving and decrepit, was hemmed in by three pirate boats that were attempting to board. The mother ship of the pirates, a dark-hulled pinnace, hung back a short way. The sailors were attempting to defend themselves, probably with neuron whips, and at the moment it seemed that they were making a fair job of it. But the pirates were assailing them on all sides, and in a brief while they'd be scrambling aboard the all but defenseless trader.

Dovirr loped across the deck to the group of Sea-Lords who were lowering the boat. There was no one he knew well in the group, and they looked at him questioningly.

"I'm to go with you," Dovirr said.

"Get in, then!" a one-eyed Sea-Lord cried.

Dovirr hopped over the side. Down the boat went, descending on stout cables until it touched the surface of the water. It held a dozen men. Dovirr found himself in the bow of the boat. He swung around, turning his back on the sweating rowers, and looked toward the scene of action.

The pirates appeared to realize that a Sea-Lord ship was going to intervene. Angry shouts split the quiet air; the three pirate boats were cutting loose from the Lanobul vessel and heading back for their mother ship. Dovirr now came to understand the Sea-Lord strategy. The *Garyun* was heading at a furious rate toward the pirate vessel, moving diagonally between it and the merchantman. The three small boats of the pirates would be cut off, that way, and they could be dealt with by the Sea-Lord boat while the *Garyun* put the mother ship to flight.

"Row, by the stars!" the one-eyed man was booming. "Row! Row!"

The boat sped over the water. Dovirr could see the pirates of the nearest boat now: perhaps a dozen men, thin and haggard-looking, rowing for all they were worth. There was fear in their eyes as they watched the approach of the Sea-Lords. Dovirr unsheathed his sword. The Sea-Lord boat was coming up alongside the priate craft.

"Look sharp!" someone cried. "The other one's coming!"

The pirates, Dovirr realized, had a strategy of their own. Cut off from their mother ship, they were concentrating their attack on the Sea-Lord boat. All three pirate boats were heading toward the small Sea-Lord craft. A second Sea-Lord boat had been lowered, but it was still far away. For at least ten minutes Dovirr and his companions would be outnumbered two or three to one.

"Grapple them!" came the shout from the stern of Dovirr's vessel.

An ugly five-pronged hook passed from hand to hand. A man next to Dovirr took it and hurled it. It cleared the gap of twenty yards separating them from the nearest pirate boat—cleared it, and caught on a gunwale. The boats were linked. A moment later, they were side by side.

Dovirr gripped his sword. There was a flash of metal; he saw a blond-bearded pirate swing at him, and he parried and responded with a tremendous slice of his saber. A sword flew from a pirate hand and vanished into the depths. Dovirr laughed. The swordless pirate fumbled at his belt, drew forth a dagger, leaped into the Sea-Lord boat.

He thrust at Dovirr. Hastily, with hardly room to maneuver, Dovirr caught the descending arm and twisted it. The pirate, insecurely balanced on the gunwale of the boat, toppled backward. He cried out, a single harsh word in a language Dovirr did not understand, and then he hit the water with a great splash.

There was no time to watch his fate. Dovirr swung around and stared into the yellow-rimmed eyes of a wild-faced pirate who hacked at him with a stubby, thick-bladed sword. Dovirr parried. The sea heaved, separating them a moment. The man chopped furiously at Dovirr again. Dovirr leaned back, nearly losing his balance, recovered, used his weapon for a sudden savage thrust that swept the pirate's parry aside and continued on into the man's leather jacket. The pirate screamed and fell back, blood spouting from his chest.

The boats were rocking wildly. There was a dull thunking sound, and Dovirr glanced over his shoulder to discover that the second pirate boat had grappled with theirs on the far side, and that the third was drawing near. So, too, was the other Sea-Lord boat. Dovirr could see Cloden standing tall in the bow of it. But for the moment, the odds were great.

Sweating, shouting, Dovirr fought like a machine of

death. Somehow he had come to take the lead on his side of the boat, and he sent a third and a fourth pirate to destruction. He saw terror in the enemy eyes, now. Two of them were struggling to cut the cord that held the boats grappled.

"They want to run!" Dovirr shouted. "After them!"

Without stopping to ponder strategy, he sprang to the gunwale and vaulted into the pirate boat. Two of the Sea-Lords followed; the rest remained behind to fight off the attackers on the far side.

Only six pirates remained in their boat. Two were taking no risks with Dovirr's sword; they leaped into the water and began to swim desperately toward their distant mother ship. A third pirate threw down his weapon. Dovirr hesitated, seeing an unarmed man before him.

"We need no prisoners," grunted a Sea-Lord at Dovirr's side. His sword flashed. The pirate fell.

It was over a moment later. The remaining three pirates fought fiercely but hopelessly. Dovirr sent one of them overboard, his companions slew the others. It was time now to return to the Sea-Lord boat. Dovirr saw that the pirates were in rout there, too. Cloden had pulled up with reinforcements and the din of battle was ear-splitting, but the pirates were dying.

Dovirr leaned on his sword and tried to catch his breath. He had slain—how many men? Four? Five? The boat ran red with pirate blood. One Sea-Lord was dead, another wounded, but the pirates had had much the worse of it. And now, Cloden and his men were methodically making their way through the other two pirate boats, slashing at the foe, hurling their bodies over the sides.

There was a spreading red slick on the water. Fins could be seen! The Seaborn Ones were gathering for their feast! Dovirr looked for the two men who had tried to swim toward safety. They were nowhere in view. No doubt they had silently been pulled under as they puffed along.

All was tranquil now. The two Sea-Lord boats bobbed cheerfully with the three empty boats of the pirates. Dovirr looked toward the two ships. He saw only the *Garyun*, its huge sail black against the sky.

"Where are the pirates?" he asked.

"Fled," a Sea-Lord by his side answered. "On their way to their base."

"Will Gowyn pursue?"

The Sea-Lord shook his head. "He's content just to drive them off. No use wasting men to hunt down such vermin."

Indeed, the *Garyun* was heading toward them, instead of giving chase. Dovirr thought he saw the pirate ship on the horizon, rapidly retreating without a thought for the men it had sent out in its boats—men who had all perished, anyway. Soon after, the *Garyun* lay alongside, and hauled up the two fighting parties. A carpenter went down to inspect the captured pirate boats. Two of them, he reported, were worthless. The third was hauled aboard.

Cloden came up to Dovirr as he unbelted his sword.

"I saw you swinging that weapon out there," Cloden said. "You give me pride, Dovirr. You handled it well."

"I sent many men to the bottom of the sea," Dovirr said in a husky, strained voice. "It was a kind of fever that came over me, a fever of killing—"

"Better that than a fever of being killed. Sea-Lord lives were at stake. Thanks to you, few of those lives were lost."

Dovirr did not reply. Someone thrust a cup of wine into his hand, and he took it wordlessly, draining it without really tasting the thick, strong drink. Cloden stepped away, and a red-bearded face pushed toward Dovirr. Lysigon, it was, the first mate.

"Here's the hero!" he cried, and it seemed to Dovirr that the note in his voice was as much one of mockery as of praise. "I drink to you, hero from Vythain!"

Lysigon lifted a cup. Dovirr managed a smile. "I thank you for this tribute, Lysigon," he replied thinly.

The first mate looked startled at the retort. "Your first taste of blood, and you think you've slain the Star Beasts, eh? There's battle ahead that'll make this seem like a game!"

"If you had been out in those boats, Lysigon, you would not have thought it a game."

"Why, you landsman pup—"

"Easy, Lysigon. Let the boy have his moment of glory." It was Holinel who was the peacemaker. He stepped between them, pushing the handsome, fiery-eyed Lysigon back a pace or two. "They say you fought bravely, Dovirr."

Dovirr shrugged. "I used my sword. Men died. Is it bravery when your life is forfeit if you don't fight?"

"You used your sword well, though. It's a cleaner weapon than that Star Beast toy of yours, is it not? And you see what good such toys did those men of Lanobul. If we hadn't happened along, they'd be feeding the Seaborn Ones by now."

"They don't know how to fight," Dovirr said. "The

neuron whips alone win no battles. Not without courage."

"Well said!" Holinel boomed. "Wine! Wine for Dovirr!"

"I've had enough," Dovirr said, but his words were lost in the general uproar. He accepted the cup and put it to his lips. Someone clapped him lustily on the back. Word was circulating of his feats in the open boat, and Dovirr knew now that the Sea-Lords would no longer regard him as a stranger.

Figures appeared on the bridge. Gowyn the Thalassarch stood there, with Kubril at his side. They were pointing toward the Lanobul vessel, and Gowyn was conveying some instruction to the navigator. Then the Thalassarch looked up. His eyes met Dovirr's, across a distance of a hundred feet. The Thalassarch was smiling in warm approval.

The Lord of the
Black Ocean

THAT NIGHT THERE was feasting aboard the *Garyun*. The captain of the ship from Lanobul sent over a boatload of provisions, by way of showing his gratitude toward his protectors, and the Sea-Lords were treated to the light white wine of the Lanobul vineyards, and to sweet grapes, and to fresh meat slaughtered no more than three days before. It was pitiful to see the Lanobul captain fall to the deck before Gowyn, thanking the Thalassarch in such an absurdly exaggerated way that even Gowyn seemed embarrassed by it.

It was no way for a man to behave, Dovirr thought.

Especially one who lived by going to sea. But the men who manned the merchant ships of the cities were not Sea-Lords; they went to sea because they had to, because the cities needed to trade in order to survive, but they journeyed in terror, never at home on the sea, fearing death at every moment. The Lanobul captain and the men who came on board with him seemed to be at the very edge of collapse, and here they were only a few days out of their home port. How would they look weeks later, when they reached their destination—*if* they reached it?

The pirates had fled. Dovirr learned that the pirates, men of no flag who swore allegiance to no Thalassarch, operated out of a rooted island midway between Lanobul and Vostrok. There were a few such islands. They had once been the highest mountaintops, before the Star Beasts had drowned the world. Now they jutted above the waves, bare fangs of rock where scattered bands of pirates lurked, preying on merchant vessels, hoping to snatch their cargoes from under the noses of the Sea-Lords. But the pirates, too, were timid men, fleeing when a Thalassarch's flag could be seen.

Dovirr was silent during the revelry that evening. It had been a grim day for him, a day in which he had taken lives without hesitation. He was a hero, now, yes, to all but jeering Lysigon, whose jealousy was obvious. The blood of those pirates stained him, but in a way he was anointed with it, marked now as an important man among the Sea-Lords. They had seen that he could fight, and that he could kill, and that he could inspire other men on to greater effort. He had won a place aboard this ship by killing, and he had made that place secure by killing again. It was a high price to pay,

Dovirr thought, his mind full of death and slaughter.

Faces haunted his dreams that night. The faces of slain pirates came to him, pale, accusing. But in the morning, when he entered the dining hall for breakfast, men called out to him by name, hailing him as they would any valiant comrade, and Dovirr knew now that he was a Sea-Lord beyond doubt.

The wind was strong that day. The *Garyun* held to its western course, making good time. In another day, the city of Lanobul appeared on the horizon; a day more and the Sea-Lord vessel entered its harbor.

It might well have been Vythain, Dovirr thought. He had never seen another city beside his native one, but Lanobul seemed Vythain's twin. There was the same prevailing grayness of the architecture, the same helter-skelter clutter of houses. The Star Beasts had not bothered to introduce much variety into the design, when they built their handful of floating cities. A pier, a residential area, a central plaza for the official buildings, and a zone of production—the formula was the same in each. Lanobul differed from Vythain in being industrial, where Vythain depended on the yield of its farms, but from the sea that difference was scarcely apparent, since Vythain's fields were sheltered and far from the harbor.

Dovirr did not go ashore. He had hoped Gowyn might choose him for the shore party, but somehow he was passed over. Three boatloads of Sea-Lords made the trip from the anchored ship to the pier. Lysigon went, and Cloden, and Kubril, and Holinel, but Dovirr remained on the *Garyun*, annoyed and unhappy. What were they afraid of? Did

Gowyn think that if he saw a city again after all these months, he would desert and take up landlubber life once more? Or had they simply forgotten his name when making up the list of those who were privileged to leave the ship?

Dovirr's resentment did not last. When the shore party had been gone half a day, one boat returned, bearing news: "We're staying here two days. Everybody gets shore leave tomorrow, Gowyn says!"

Dovirr got his chance, then. The Thalassarch had collected his tribute from Lanobul, but apparently he wished to confer with the city's officials, and perhaps to transact some business here. So the next morning the shore leaves began. Roistering, boisterous Sea-Lords erupted into the city of Lanobul.

The city did not seem to welcome the visit. Dovirr was hardly surprised, remembering the terror that a Sea-Lord stay always inspired in Vythain. Shop doors and windows were shuttered; the citizens of Lanobul remained off the streets; fearful eyes peered from windows. Up one street and down the next rampaged the Sea-Lords, breaking into wine shops, rolling barrels along sloping avenues, smashing street lamps and overturning carts.

Dovirr took no part in the vandalism. Such pranks did not come naturally to him. He had lived too long in a city to enjoy destruction for its own sake. His shipmates were letting off steam after months on the *Garyun;* Dovirr was content to stroll through the narrow, winding streets, comparing what he saw here to what he remembered of Vythain.

He did not feel sorry that he had joined the Sea-Lords. Lanobul was much like Vythain, which is to say that it struck him as an intolerably dull place, where little people lived out their little lives and died, finally, of boredom. What did it all mean? What was the point of living such dreary existences, Dovirr wondered? To huddle in fright, to fear a multitude of enemies?

They did it, he told himself, because they knew no other way. They were content. Perhaps they should be envied, then. They were not possessed by the itch to wander, with that restless urge that had so deeply tormented Dovirr. He remembered Lackresh the policeman's puzzled words:

"Why can't you act like a normal person, Dovirr?"

Normal persons were happy. They lived and died in Vythain or Lanobul or Hicanthro, and their children and their children's children did the same, and they were all content. Dovirr flexed his powerful arms, heaved his heavy shoulders. He felt restless again, simply walking the streets of one of these little cities. No, he thought, he was certainly not normal—not by the standards of the city folk. Something drove him, some fierce inner craving that he could not resist.

So now you're a Sea-Lord. Are you happy? he asked himself.

Not really, he knew. There was boredom aplenty aboard the *Garyun*, long hours of drudgery and idleness. But at least he felt that he was finally moving in the right direction. He had been born, he believed, to shape things, to build networks of power, to control events. Only at sea could he hope to fulfill that destiny—only in the brawling world of the Sea-Lords.

Was he ever going to achieve anything? Time alone

would tell him that. But at least he had taken the first steps toward his destiny. At least he had begun.

The *Garyun* put out to sea again the following day. Dovirr had not discovered what had detained Gowyn at Lanobul. Some matter of business, no doubt—of concern only to the men on the highest levels of Sea-Lord power. Dovirr, only a common seaman, had no reason to be taken into Gowyn's confidence on matters of administration.

The next destination of the Sea-Lords was Hicanthro, the city of wool. The only remaining sheep in the world grazed on Hicanthro's hillsides, and the world's most costly fabrics came from Hicanthro's mills. But trouble was in the wind before any sign of Hicanthro could be seen. The *Garyun* was sailing west, and it was coming now into a disputed area of sea that lay between Gowyn's domain and that of the neighboring Thalassarch.

Holinel said it first, looking toward the lee: "We'll have war on this trip, war with Thalassarch Harald."

Dovirr heard it next from Cloden: "Sharpen your sword, friend. There'll be a new struggle soon, and not merely with pirates."

Tension gathered aboard the ship. There were daily battle drills now. Nothing was left to chance. The *Garyun* was preparing for war. On the third day out from Lanobul, sails appeared on the horizon—black sails, friendly ones. Two ships belonging to Thalassarch Gowyn were coming to join the flagship. Dovirr knew that each Thalassarch had not merely his own vessel, but a fleet of eight to ten others; but only in time of war between Thalassarchs did a fleet sail together. Gowyn was clearly expecting trouble.

The two new ships took up positions less than a mile off the *Garyun*'s stern. There was an interchange of semaphored signals. The battle drills became more frequent on board the *Garyun*.

Six nights out from Lanobul, Dovirr stood alone on the topdeck of the ship, mind whirling with unanswered questions. There were footsteps behind him. The Thalassarch appeared. Dovirr had not spoken with him since before the battle with the pirates.

Gowyn said now, "Tomorrow there will be war, Dovirr."

"With Harald?"

"With Harald, yes. It's been a long time in coming, but now it must happen. They told me of him in Lanobul. He's vowed to challenge me."

"We'll send him to the bottom, sire!"

"Perhaps yes, perhaps no." The Thalassarch spoke in a weary tone that Dovirr was not expecting. "One way or another, the time has come. They say you fought well the day we met the pirates, Dovirr."

Dovirr frowned. "I did what I could, sire."

"Tomorrow, if we see action with Harald—do the same again, Dovirr. I want you to fight at my side."

"The honor is too great, sire."

"I need you there," Gowyn said. "We'll fight well together. The men will follow you. Don't you see what a mark you've made on this ship, Dovirr?"

"In a single battle?"

"In everything you've done. Leaving a flabby-bellied

city and winning a place on the toughest ship in the Western Sea. Learning to swing a sword. Taking abuse. The men are awed by you, Dovirr. They'll follow where you lead. They think you have a charmed life. Fight beside me tomorrow, if Harald comes."

Dovirr stared at the older man a moment. Then he dropped to his knees, caught Gowyn's hand, gripped it tight. Gowyn tugged him to his feet.

"Up," he said. "I don't appreciate groveling. Fight well tomorrow, that's all I ask of you."

As Gowyn foretold, the enemy came into view the next day. The flagship of Harald the Thalassarch did indeed come from the leeward early in the afternoon, sailing into the wind. The cry resounded from aloft shortly after midday mess:

"Harald's ship! It comes!"

The *Garyun* readied for war.

There were nine Thalassarchs all told, each of them boasting control over a roughly-hewn section of the globe. Gowyn called his domain the Western Sea; Harald considered himself lord of the Black Ocean, a vague territory lying to the west of Gowyn's waters, and including the floating cities of Dimnon, Ariod, and Hyllimor, among others.

But there were no borders in the ocean. No row of buoys split the seamless sea, marking off Gowyn's dominion from Harald's, and Harald's from that of his neighbor on the far side. Each Thalassarch disputed hotly the extent of his neighbor's sphere of dominance. From time to time, the uneasy jockeying between one Sea-Lord ruler and the next exploded into direct conflict. And the time for conflict between Gowyn and Harald was at hand.

Harald's ship approached. Aboard the *Garyun*, the uppermost bank of oarsmen docked their oars and left their galley. With the wind blowing strongly and in Harald's disfavor, the *Garyun* could maneuver with only three banks of oarsmen at work, thus freeing thirty men and more to bear arms against the foe.

The *Garyun* ran its war flag up the mast—a defiant streamer of red bordered with yellow, in place of the black that was Gowyn's usual sailing color. Dovirr hastened below to get his sword, and returned quickly to the deck. The Thalassarch Gowyn emerged from his own hatch, striding out armed and ready to take his place.

Lysigon appeared. The red-bearded Sea-Lord, magnificent in his jeweled helmet, came forward carrying a shining sword of extraordinary length. He moved to the Thalassarch's right side.

"No, Lysigon," Gowyn said quietly. "You remain in command of the ship. I will lead the boarding party."

"Kubril can maneuver the ship, sire," Lysigon said.

"He will need your help. This is no ordinary battle, Lysigon."

"But at your side—"

"Dovirr will fight beside me," the Thalassarch said. "I think we'll fight well together."

Lysigon turned. His eyes, so intensely blue that at this moment they appeared to be black, fastened on Dovirr's. Dovirr felt a wave of hatred surging from the furious Lysigon. It was out in the open now, and Lysigon knew it; Dovirr, the newcomer from Vythain, had somehow become the Thalassarch's favorite!

Dovirr kept his gaze steady. This was part of his test also, he sensed. If he flinched before the wrath of Lysigon, if he allowed himself to admit for one moment that the red-bearded one had a better claim to the honor Gowyn had conferred—if he weakened at all, he was finished. Gowyn had deliberately arranged this confrontation to see if Dovirr merited the preference, Dovirr suspected.

Lysigon said, "I obey your wishes, sire. But perhaps after the battle you will explain to me why I am pushed aside in favor of this boy."

"Perhaps," Gowyn said. "We will consider it after the battle. To your post, Lysigon."

The first mate nodded. Swinging around on his heel, he stalked away.

Dovirr stationed himself at the Thalassarch's right hand. He saw several of the other Sea-Lords staring at him enviously, but he ignored them, not even bothering to glare. He was Gowyn's chosen man for today's battle, and the others would honor Gowyn's choice—or else!

The enemy ship—there was only one, it seemed—called itself the *Bretwol*. It, too, ran up its war flag, a gaudy ribbon of gold and green, slashed diagonally with a bar of crimson. Gowyn spoke briefly with his semaphore man, who wigwagged instructions to the Thalassarch's two supporting vessels. They were not to enter the battle, Gowyn ordered. This was to be single combat, flagship against flagship, Thalassarch against Thalassarch. Gowyn's strength was greater today, because he happened to have reached the place of battle with three ships to Harald's one—but he declined to make use of that advantage. Sea-Lords, Dovirr thought, fought as their code dictated, and no other way. Perhaps they might take advantage of numerical superiority when fighting with pirates, but not when doing battle with one another. He was reminded of the way Holinel had contemptuously flung the neuron whip into the sea, as a weapon not fit for true men to use. These Sea-Lords were no savages, Dovirr thought, though they might be wild and bloody-minded. They had their honor.

Swords bristled aboard the *Garyun*. The grappling-iron crew readied itself. Steadily, one ship approached the other across a sea whipped to frenzy by a mounting breeze. White-tipped waves lashed the hulls of the two vessels.

It was possible now for Dovirr to see the men on the opposite deck. Gowyn gestured with a sturdy arm, pointing to the figures by the rail.

"See? There is Harald now."

"Which, sire?"

"Short and dark-bearded. With the patch over his left eye; you see?"

Dovirr saw. There was Harald, short and grim-faced, surrounded by his minions, waiting, waiting. The rival Thalassarch was no swaggering giant like Gowyn, but even at this distance Dovirr was aware of an aura of grandeur surrounding him. He looked like a man accustomed to rule over men. Though there were others on the *Bretwol*'s deck who stood a head taller than Harald, the Thalassarch somehow managed to seem the strongest and boldest on board. There was an art, Dovirr thought, to being a leader, and much of it had to do with expression of face and stance of body. No man could lead who did not *look* like a leader.

Another moment and the ships would meet. Dovirr braced himself for the contact. There was the solid thud of wood against wood, and grappling irons fell to before the vessels could separate. Both sides seemed to have the same plan: to put a force of men aboard the other as rapidly as possible, and cut a swath of destruction through the ranks of the enemy.

Gowyn thundered forward and vaulted over the side of the ship, clambering down onto the enemy deck. Moving automatically, Dovirr followed the Thalassarch, keeping Gowyn's right side protected. The *Bretwol* had been breached first!

"Swords! Swords!" roared Gowyn in a voice that carried like a trumpet's blast. "Follow on, men! Follow on! We have them! We have them!"

The *Garyun* had seized the initial advantage. The men of Gowyn swooped down on the dark-clad defenders, swords flashing brightly. Gowyn was left-handed, swinging his mighty weapon with demonic zeal. Dovirr, by his side, shielded him from attack on the right. One of Harald's Sea-Lords came sprinting forward, sword upraised. Gowyn cut him down. Almost at the same moment, Dovirr gripped the weapon he had won from Levrod long before, and drove it through the heart of the first Black Ocean man who challenged him.

"Well struck," Gowyn commented, lashing out at a new opponent and sending him reeling.

Dovirr smiled. He moved closer to the Thalassarch. Together, side by side, they advanced mercilessly across the deck of the *Bretwol*, leading a wedge-shaped force of Sea-Lords that came pouring over from the *Garyun*.

The men of Harald's ship began to deploy themselves for defense. They had no choice but to form ranks and try to defend. Gowyn's sudden charge had left them without an alternative. It was much too late for them to think of mounting an offensive. The first split-second of the battle had shaped its course.

Dovirr and the Thalassarch moved forward on a deck that was suddenly slippery with blood. Their busy swords opened a pathway in the files of the defenders. Here in the initial moments of the battle, the contest was turning into a rout.

"Ah, the pigs!" Gowyn exclaimed suddenly. "The cowardly pigs!"

He pointed to the windward. Dovirr looked, and saw four of Harald's men hacking at the grapples that bound the two ships together. They were trying to cut the *Bretwol* loose, trying to end the contest and gain their freedom. If they succeeded now, Dovirr and Gowyn and the rest of the *Garyun* vanguard would be trapped aboard the enemy ship, where they would eventually be forced to yield from sheer fatigue.

"Cover for me," Dovirr said to the Thalassarch. "I'll deal with them."

Gowyn grunted his assent. He began to raise a fearful barrage of swordplay. His heavy weapon whistled through the air in wild arcs and slashes, driving the men of the Black

Ocean back. Meanwhile Dovirr made his way along the pitching deck to the grapples.

"Away from there, cowards!" Dovirr bellowed.

The four who hacked at the grapples looked up from their work in surprise. Angrily, Dovirr swept into their midst. His sword felled two of them before they could defend themselves. A third sprang back, clutching for his dagger, and scrambled up on the bow to escape Dovirr's blade. He crouched, poised as though to spring on Dovirr, when there was a twang from above, and a bolt from a *Garyun* archer struck him. He toppled headlong between the linked ships, disappearing into the furiously boiling sea.

Dovirr grinned. "I thank you, whoever you might be," he said softly.

Only one foe remained—a hulking brute of a man whose shoulder-length curls, coming unstuffed from his helmet, whipped in the breeze. His long sword rang against Dovirr's. A quick thrust penetrated almost to Dovirr's flesh, but he sidestepped, sucking in his breath as the blade slid harmlessly past him only inches from his ribs. The violent lunge left his opponent off balance. Dovirr brought his own sword around in a determined slash.

He struck home. The man staggered away, dropping his sword and clutching at his belly. Dovirr had nearly cut him in two. After a few steps he fell headlong to the deck, and lay still.

"To me!" Gowyn roared. "To me, Dovirr!"

"Coming!" Dovirr shouted over the clangor of battle. His work done, he raced back to the Thalassarch's side.

He found Gowyn hard pressed, surrounded by enemies

on right and left. Dovirr's sword hewed rapidly through enemy ranks, driving the men of Harald back. Together they cut their way forward once more—until, suddenly, the victorious duo found themselves facing a squat, burly, black-bearded man with close-trimmed hair and a dark patch mounted over his left eye.

Harald himself!

Impetuously Dovirr leaped forward, anxious to be the one to strike down a Thalassarch. It was a mistake, but Dovirr did not realize his error until Gowyn caught him roughly by the shoulder and pulled him back.

"Not you," Gowyn growled.

Dovirr began to protest. Then he realized that Gowyn was right. This particular duel was not his to fight. The honor of taking the life of a fellow Thalassarch belonged rightfully to Gowyn, and Gowyn alone.

Harald nodded. "Welcome, Gowyn."

"My visit is not a friendly one."

"I doubted that it was," Harald said.

There was sudden silence. Then Harald raised his sword and advanced. Blade rang against blade as the Thalassarchs tested one another with probing thrusts not meant to draw blood. They circled warily, the big man and the short. Gowyn had the advantage of size; Harald, that of desperation. He was fighting on home ground, with everything to lose. Nor did Harald look like any weakling. The muscles were thick and corded on the Thalassarch's compact body.

Dovirr watched the contest, tension drawing a tight band across his belly. What if Gowyn were defeated, he wondered? Impossible. Inconceivable. And yet it might happen. Anything might happen when two men faced each other with swords. Dovirr shuddered as a sudden unwanted image blazed in his brain: Gowyn dead on the deck, stretched full length and weltering in his own gore. It seemed to Dovirr that the world itself would totter if Gowyn perished here today.

But Gowyn appeared to have the upper hand. Step by step, Harald was yielding ground. Gowyn's sword hammered against Harald's, and the smaller man was hard put to meet and deflect each slashing thrust. Harald was a formidable opponent, but he seemed tired and sick at heart, perhaps discouraged by the utter failure of his assault on the *Garyun*. Although he was putting up a fearsome defense, Gowyn's greater size appeared to be telling. Harald was visibly losing strength from moment to moment.

Suddenly Gowyn's sword went high and beat Harald's down. An onlooker gasped, and the gasp was hardly past his lips when Gowyn drew back his blade and spitted his rival with a single stroke.

He pulled the weapon free. Harald's eyes were already glazing. He toppled and fell.

"Harald lies dead!" Gowyn bellowed.

Instantly all action ceased. Fighters of both ships put down their swords, standing as in a tableau, frozen, staring at the fallen figure of Harald. Harald did not move. Gowyn rested on his sword.

The battle was over.

Unaccountably, Dovirr found himself trembling, not with fear so much as with awe. A Thalassarch lay dead practically at his feet. Gowyn now was ruler of two seas. Hardly ever had such a thing happened before.

Harald's men were kneeling to Gowyn, now. First one, then several, then the entire company of the *Bretwol* cast down their swords and sank to the deck.

Overhead, a yellow sea-bird flew screaming through the air, laughing raucously at the solemn scene. Around the ship, the threshing Seaborn Ones swam for the bodies of the fallen warriors. Gowyn remained unmoving, the target for all eyes, a powerful figure whose head now was bowed.

"I proclaim myself Thalassarch of the Black Ocean and of the Western Sea," he said slowly. "Does anyone here dispute that claim?"

There was silence.

Gowyn pointed toward the body of Harald. "We will bury him with all proper honors. A good man has died today."

Dovirr the Thalassarch

THERE WAS STRICKEN SILENCE still as Gowyn and Dovirr returned to the *Garyun*, followed by Gowyn's other men. The ships remained grappled. Dozens of Harald's Sea-Lords had perished in the fight; the casualties on Gowyn's side had been no more than a handful.

Holinel, who had not crossed over to the *Bretwol* during the brief encounter, came up to Dovirr now.

"Well fought," he said. "You served Gowyn well today, Dovirr."

Dovirr nodded. He had little to say. He had seen too

much violent death today to feel cheerful or talkative even in victory. There were now but eight Thalassarchs, and the framework of the watery world had been altered. The death of Harald remained uppermost in Dovirr's mind.

As in Gowyn's. "Holinel!" the Thalassarch called. "Look after Harald's funeral."

"I will, sire."

"Bury him with full honors, as befits his rank. Let there be a service, too. Find his officers, if any survive—let them be his honor guard."

"It will be done, sire," Holinel said gravely, saluting and departing.

"Kebolon!" Gowyn called. "Where is Kebolon!"

Kebolan came forward. He was the second officer of the *Garyun,* third in command behind Gowyn and Lysigon—a tall, hawk-faced man who believed in wasting few words. He nodded to the Thalassarch.

"You will be captain of the *Bretwol,*" Gowyn declared. "Take command in the morning. Enter the Black Ocean and find Harald's other ships. Let them know now that they owe fealty to Gowyn."

"Yes, sire," Kebolon said.

Lysigon moved toward the Thalassarch. His face looked taut; a muscle quivered tensely in his cheek. He was still angry, Dovirr thought, at being forced to miss the action and hang back aboard the *Garyun.*

Lysigon said, "Sire, we now need a second officer in Kebolon's place. I propose—"

"Dovirr," Gowyn said swiftly. "Time to let him taste responsibility. Post the notice, Lysigon. Dovirr is our new second mate."

Lysigon's ruddy face seemed to purple. He sputtered for words, without managing to utter any. Dovirr remained calm, at least outwardly, though he felt a surge of excitement at the Thalassarch's words. Second officer! To dine with the Thalassarch instead of at the common table—to hold authority aboard ship by virtue of rank, and not merely by virtue of strength and size—to have risen in a few short months from lowly newcomer to second officer—!

"The notice will be posted," said Lysigon darkly. The glance he shot at Dovirr was tipped with venom.

At nightfall, Harald was put to rest. Holinel spoke the words. The surviving officers of the *Bretwol* stood to one side, those of the *Garyun*, including Dovirr, to the other. Throughout the ceremony, Gowyn remained in silence, staring at the deck. The moment came when Holinel gestured toward the sea, and the shrouded body of the dead Thalassarch was cast to the waves, and was swallowed up in darkness.

Gowyn lifted his head. "Tonight we feast!" he cried. "Tonight we celebrate victory! Break out the rum! Rum for everybody!"

The men of the *Bretwol* returned to their ship, and the grapples were lifted. Tonight the two vessels would ride side by side; at sunrise, under her new captain, the *Bretwol* would set sail for Gowyn's newly won domain.

Gowyn now was master of two seas. The men of the *Garyun* were still talking about it. It was rare for one Thalassarch ever to attack the flagship of another, and not in any man's memory had a Thalassarch slain a Thalassarch in open combat as had happened today. What had provoked Harald to make his suicidal attempt? No one knew, and probably no one ever would know. Some inner prod, perhaps, some raging force that drove him to challenge Gowyn and meet his doom. The victors, endlessly discussing the contest, agreed that Harald's bold move, while it had brought him only death, had been nobly conceived. He had died well. What more, perhaps, could a man hope for?

The rum was passed. Marghuin the cook began to prepare the victory feast. In the hearts of the men of the *Garyun* there was rejoicing—but no heart leaped higher than that of Dovirr, landsman turned Sea-Lord, whose blade had drawn blood in Gowyn's service and who had been richly rewarded for his valor.

Dovirr stood alone on the deck, his body warmed by the fiery rum in his stomach. He had not yet eaten. He gripped the rail, listening to the sea hammering the keel of the *Garyun*, booming dully as it splattered the sides.

Far in the distance, the flickering light of a laden merchantman bound from Dimnon to Hicanthro with a cargo of rubber broke the darkness. The coded light flashed red; should it become suddenly green, the lookout would call, and the *Garyun*'s oarsmen would heave to, as the Thalassarch came to the merchantman's rescue. Even now, with a day of battle behind them, the Sea-Lords would fight again if a pirate vessel appeared.

That was part of the contract. The cities paid tribute to the Sea-Lords, but the Sea-Lords provided services in return. When he had lived in Vythain, Dovirr had seen the Sea-Lords as other city-dwellers did, viewing them as barbaric villains who exploited the helpless men of the land.

Dovirr had joined them, all the same, but now that he was among them he knew that the Sea-Lords were bound by their oath, and did not exact tribute idly. A man had died to save that ship of Lanobul the week before, and other Sea-Lords no doubt would perish in the days to come on behalf of the city folk.

Dovirr watched the steady progress of the Dimnon vessel in the distance. The vast bulk of the sea separated them, and the red light grew faint.

Thalassa. Sea. The ancient word, that came from a language long drowned with the rest of Earth. It conveyed the majesty and the awesomeness of the sea. *Thalassarch—* sea king. The word rolled well on the tongue.

Dovirr Stargan, Thalassarch of the Nine Seas. . . .

Now *there,* Dovirr thought, was a sentence that fell smoothly from the tongue!

He smiled at his own foolishness. First get one kingdom, he told himself, before you dream of mastering them all. But it cost nothing to dream. If he had never allowed himself the luxury of dreaming, he would still be back in Vythain, living in a clammy stone-walled room and going through the dreary round of daily chores. He had come a long way. Dovirr Stargan, Second Officer of the *Garyun!* Who was to say what titles might not be his one day?

Gowyn, too, had gained a title today, Dovirr thought. Now Gowyn had mastered two empires, something few if any Thalassarchs had done. Tonight was a proud one for Gowyn. But someday Gowyn would lie with the Sea-born Ones, and a new Thalassarch would be needed for those two empires. That would be Dovirr's opportunity for greatness.

It was this he had dreamed of—this, all the long landlocked years in Vythain while he had watched the far-off dots of ships against the blue curtain of the sky, and waited with seething impatience to grow to manhood's estate.

He turned to go belowdecks. Dovirr enjoyed coming here to brood over the vastness of the sea, to sort out his thoughts in solitude. But he knew that on a night of celebration such as this one, his place was below, with the gay throng of roisterers.

Making his way over the rolling deck, he found the hatch and headed below, to the main hall. The lights glowed brilliantly; the ship's stewards had spared no expense to kindle the whale oil tonight. Rum, fierce and fiery, flowed as freely tonight as mere wine did on other nights. The Sea-Lords were singing with free abandon, bellowing songs of triumph at the tops of their lungs. It was hardly every night, after all, that a rival Thalassarch fell in battle.

Dovirr entered the big cabin and halted just within the doorway. He saw Gowyn, standing near the head of the long table. The Thalassarch was draining a cup of rum and holding it out for a fresh supply, and it did not seem as though it were his first drink of the evening, either. The crewmen about him were laughing with a violence that threatened to shake the ship to shivers.

Dovirr stiffened as he discovered what was causing their mirth. It was not just the joy of victory, he realized, or the influence of the rum. He stepped forward. A knot of seamen standing around Gowyn parted, to reveal something wet and dark lying on the deck, wriggling in obvious torment, beating its great fins thumpingly against the wood in an agony of death. The creature was uttering hoarse, desperate barks of pain.

Gowyn spied Dovirr and beckoned him. "Ho, there, Dovirr! We've brought up another prize! Two catches on one day, lad—first Harald, and now this!"

Dovirr made his way to the Thalassarch's side. Gowyn's eyes were glossy with drunkenness, Dovirr saw. Sweat beaded the older man's face. Dovirr glanced at the creature at their feet.

"What may that be, sire?" he asked.

"Dovirr, I sometimes forget you were a landsman but a few brief months ago," Gowyn rumbled. "Do you not know the Seaborn Ones when you see one beached?"

"The Seaborn—!"

"Marghuin the cook was trawling to catch us some fine prize for our dinner—and netted this!"

Of course, Dovirr thought. Many times he had watched the flashing fins, the lithe bodies coursing through the sea. Now, for the first time, he saw a Seaborn One out of its native element. With raw curiosity Dovirr studied the writhing creature that lay in a pool of moisture on the floor of the cabin.

The Seaborn One was about the size of a man, but its unclothed body terminated in powerful flukes rather than in legs. It was still possible to see the outline of the past in the creature's tail, though. It seemed to Dovirr that he could make out the muscular and bony structure of two legs that had been fused into the tail by the cleverness of the genetic engineers of long ago. Beneath the fishy exterior, the human ancestry of the Seaborn One was evident. But there had been centuries of change at work. The creature was a golden brown in color, its hide thick and tough, shiny with tiny scale-like coverings.

And the face—the face was that of a man, Dovirr saw in shock. A man in death agonies, a man strangely transformed—but there was a kinship. The eyes were shielded by transparent lids, the nose was a mere dotted pair of nostrils—but the mouth was a man's mouth, with human pain expressed in the tortured appearance of the lips. Slitted gills flickered rapidly where ears might have been.

The transparent lids peeled back momentarily, and Dovirr clearly saw the eyes—the eyes of a man. A dark intelligence lurked in those eyes. Mighty flukes thumped angrily against the floor.

"How long can the Seaborn One live when taken from the water?" Dovirr asked.

The Thalassarch answered, "They're pretty sturdy beasts. Five minutes, maybe ten."

"And you're just going to stand here and watch it die, sire?"

Gowyn shrugged and swilled rum around in his cup. "It amuses me to watch, Dovirr. And I hunger for amusement this night. Why do you ask? I have little love for the Seaborn Ones—or they for me."

"But—but, sire—they were once *men*," Dovirr said in a low, troubled voice.

The Thalassarch gave him a curious look. "The creatures you were killing this afternoon still *were* men, Dovirr. Yet I noticed little hesitation in the strokes of your sword."

"That was different, sire."

"How so?"

"I was fighting them in fair combat," Dovirr said. "My life staked against theirs. And I was giving them a man's death. This is something I wouldn't do to a beast—and the Seaborn One seems much more than a beast."

Gowyn scowled and took a deep draft of his rum. Dovirr wondered if his words, carrying such harsh criticism of the Thalassarch's amusement, had offended Gowyn. The older man did indeed seem stung. He's drunk, Dovirr thought. Be careful not to push him too far.

The Thalassarch took a few steps forward, to the long table. He planted his thick legs astride it and shouted, "A sword! Bring me a sword!"

Out of the hubbub and confusion a man emerged carrying a scabbarded sword. The Thalassarch seized it and unsheathed the blade. He gave Dovirr a sour glance.

Gowyn approached the writhing Seaborn One. The creature from the sea seemed to be clinging to life with furious determination, but its strength was clearly ebbing. Gowyn looked down at it and said, "Our friend Dovirr claims that you are a man. Very well. A man's death you shall get, quick and honorable."

He plunged the sword downward.

The Seaborn One quivered and was still. A moment later, its agonies ceased forever.

Gowyn handed the sword to its owner. He gestured at the dead Seaborn One. "Overboard with him!" Gowyn cried. "Let his brothers pick at his flesh!"

Two Sea-Lords gathered the body up and carried it away. Gowyn took a seat at the head of the table. Dovirr saw that the Thalassarch's face was pale. I gave him offense, Dovirr thought. But I couldn't stand by and watch him torturing the beast.

Beast or man, Dovirr wondered? Or something not quite part of either realm? He shook his head. There was a fishy reek in the cabin that did not come entirely from Marghuin's stew.

Gowyn slammed his palm against the table. "Food!" he roared. "I famish!"

A platter was put before him on the wooden bench. A fish, new from the kettle, lay in a pool of savory juice. It was a rare thing for a Thalassarch to dine with his men in the great hall, Dovirr knew. Gowyn was showing, by his presence here tonight, his gratitude for the services of battle that had been rendered against Harald that afternoon.

The Thalassarch scooped the fish from the platter. Before he put it to his mouth, he looked up, glowering, at Dovirr. "You've had your wish," he said. "I gave it a decent death. Are you content, Dovirr?"

"Sire, I did not mean—"

"Enough," Gowyn snapped. Angrily, he seized his fish with both hands and bit into it.

He'll forget all this in the morning, Dovirr thought. I helped him win an empire today. He won't hold a grudge because I dared criticize him tonight.

Dovirr stood to one side, watching the Thalassarch fiercely attack his dinner. Gowyn seemed to be venting all his anger on the hapless fish, taking bite after savage bite. His head was thrust forward, almost into his platter. His huge shoulders were hunched.

Suddenly Gowyn paused. He lowered the fish to the platter and grabbed desperately for the water cup that stood nearby.

Choking and gasping, the Thalassarch drained it—and continued to gag.

"Water!" he cried, his voice thin and strange.

In the general merriment and confusion, hardly anyone seemed to be noticing that the Thalassarch was in distress. Dovirr rushed to his side, pounded on Gowyn's back. It did not seem to help. The situation seemed to be growing worse by the moment. The Thalassarch was unable to speak; he rose from his seat, clawed at his throat, emitted little strangled gasps. His tanned, leathery face turned a ghastly scarlet color.

"Get the surgeon!" Dovirr shouted at a man to his left. "Hurry, idiot!"

The man sped away. Dovirr tried to seize Gowyn, who was staggering around in great lurching strides. The Thalassarch brushed Dovirr away with a push of his arm. Then he sank to the floor.

"Sire!" Dovirr said in alarm. "Here, give me some water—"

Too late for water, he realized. Too late for the surgeon. The Thalassarch was dying!

It was over almost in a moment. Gowyn writhed, as the Seaborn One had writhed. Gowyn's feet thumped against the floor, as the flukes of the dying Seaborn One had thumped against the floor. Gowyn's face became a mask of pain. He struggled for breath, but he was choking. The great chest heaved as the lungs fought for air.

Stunned, cold with horror, Dovirr still was able to appreciate the irony of it: mighty Gowyn, Thalassarch for two decades, ruler now not only of the Western Sea but of the Black Ocean as well, choking to death on a fishbone. On a *fishbone!*

Dovirr's numbed mind took in the information his eyes conveyed, and reluctantly accepted it. The powerful form of Gowyn lay sprawled on the cabin floor, his face a mottled purple color, his eyes open and bulging horridly. The other Sea-Lords ringed around were beginning to realize what had happened, but their minds did not work as swiftly as Dovirr's, it seemed. They gaped, stupefied by the fact of Gowyn's sudden death.

With strange clarity Dovirr realized, even in this moment of almost crushing grief, what it was that he had to do at once.

He leaped to the tabletop.

"Silence!" he roared.

The hubbub died away. All eyes turned to him. Dovirr cast his glance from one shocked, frozen Sea-Lord face to the next. Then he pointed to the floor, to the fallen form of Gowyn.

"Not one but *two* Thalassarchs have died today, Sea-Lords," Dovirr said loudly. "Gowyn, whose sword smote all that opposed him, has been slain by the bone of a fish."

His eyes scanned the taut faces again. Dovirr saw some of his fellow officers staring at him intently. There was Holinel, and there Lysigon, and there the navigator Kubril—and not one of them spoke.

Seize the moment, Dovirr thought.

"This morning," Dovirr said, "as if foretelling his death, Gowyn named his successor. We met on the top deck, Gowyn and I, and he spoke of a possible end to his days, and he told me to take over his responsibilities when he was no longer here. Friends, I call upon you now to offer allegiance to your new Thalassarch—Dovirr of Vythain!"

The hall was so silent that his words echoed from the rafters. There was a long, strange moment without a response from anyone.

Then it was Holinel who first took up the cry: "Long live the Thalassarch Dovirr!"

"Long live Dovirr!" cried Cloden and Kubril. "Long live the Thalassarch!" bellowed Lantise. "Dovirr! Dovirr! Dovirr!"

The Challenge from Lysigon

IT HAD ALL HAPPENED SO swiftly that the mind had difficulty encompassing it. One moment, Gowyn had stood jeering at the sufferings of the Seaborn One. The next, he and Dovirr had quarreled, the Seaborn One had been slain, and Gowyn was angrily tearing at his dinner. An instant later, the Thalassarch writhed on the floor inches from the place where the Seaborn One had perished—and then Gowyn was dead, and the hall was ringing with cries acclaiming the new Thalassarch, Dovirr of Vythain.

Dovirr had applied a valuable lesson that he had

learned that day during the battle with Harald's ship: act quickly, seize the initiative, and let the slower thinkers be content with second best.

The excitement caused by the sudden snuffing out of the Thalassarch's life had served as fit frame for the young ex-landsman's ascent to power. He had stated his claim, and Holinel had backed him, and in the frenzy of the moment the Sea-Lords had shouted him into office.

Dovirr clambered down from the tabletop. He turned slowly, eying every man in the hall. He found Lysigon and looked toward him. If a challenge was going to come, Dovirr thought, it would come from Lysigon. The red-bearded one was first officer; he was the natural successor to Gowyn, in the normal course of events. But Lysigon had moved too slowly. He had been silent while Dovirr put forth his claim. And the men of the *Garyun*, remembering that Gowyn had chosen Dovirr and not Lysigon to fight at his side today, obviously were willing to believe that the dead Thalassarch preferred the younger man as his successor.

Lysigon remained silent now. His eyes were glittering as though in shock. Was he more stunned, Dovirr wondered, at the death of the Thalassarch, or at the rapid seizure of power that had followed?

Dovirr said, "Well, Lysigon? Will you serve me as my first officer?"

He waited for the scornful reply, for the challenge to his coup. It did not come. Lysigon's scowl deepened; he tugged at the flame-colored curls of his beard, pulled at his lower lip. After a long moment he said in a voice that could hardly be heard, "We will talk of this another time, Dovirr."

"Talk now, Lysigon! Will you stay in your post?"

"I want no share in your glory, Dovirr." Lysigon stretched forth his hands, touched the arms of three Sea-Lords by his side. "I am done with feasting for tonight. If you are my friends, come with me."

He stalked out of the banqueting hall. The three men he had tapped followed him.

Holinel moved to Dovirr's side. His face was pale, and his light blue eyes held the gleam of shock. He murmured, "There will be trouble from that quarter, Dovirr. He's a bitter one."

Dovirr nodded. "When trouble comes, I'll deal with it. Cloden—"

"Sire?"

Dovirr shivered as he heard the Thalassarch's title of honor rendered to him for the first time. "Cloden, go after Lysigon. Keep watch on him. He may plan some mischief tonight."

Cloden nodded and went out.

Dovirr looked toward Gowyn once more. The surgeon had been working on him for minutes, now, but without result. The man got to his feet, shaking his head in disbelief.

"Gowyn is dead," the surgeon said hoarsely.

"The feast is at an end," Dovirr said. "There will be no more drinking tonight. Kubril, see to it that word is sent to the other ships of what has happened. Ask all the captains to come aboard the *Garyun* in the morning. Holinel, make preparations for the burial of Gowyn. We will hold the ceremony in an hour. Lantise, be my companion now, as I move my belongings to Gowyn's cabin."

Three men lifted Gowyn's body and carried it from the room. Dovirr placed Marghuin in charge of keeping order in the dining hall, and went out, followed by Lantise. The sturdy, hook-nosed man seemed dazed at the thought that the impudent boy he had helped teach to fence was now a Thalassarch twice over. But Dovirr knew that Lantise would be loyal. He had won the Sea-Lord's grudging respect. And, right now, he needed a loyal companion to walk by his side as he moved about the ship in darkness. There was a very real possibility that Lysigon was scheming an ambush.

Dovirr went down to his old berth, and he and Lantise collected Dovirr's possessions. Dovirr strapped on his sword. Lantise hoisted the sea chest. The chest had once been Levrod's. I'm collecting the property of dead men, Dovirr thought.

"Is that everything, sire?" Lantise asked.

"I think it is."

They went up. Never again did Dovirr expect to set foot down here, it was not a Thalassarch's place to enter the lower levels of the ship. They made their way to the top deck, and down the other side, to the cabin of the Thalassarch. Dovirr had never entered it before—not until this moment when he came to claim it as his own.

It was startling in its austerity. The room was perhaps ten feet on each side, and its dark-beamed ceiling was so low Dovirr had to stoop; Gowyn, who had been even taller, must have been forced to crouch in his own cabin. Nor were the furnishings particularly regal. The straw mattress looked no more comfortable than the one Dovirr had left behind. There were a few shelves, a pair of swords, a rack of handsome daggers. Otherwise, the room was bare.

"Wait outside," Dovirr said. "Stand guard a while."

Lantise saluted and went out. Dovirr belted his sword in place—on this night of strangeness, it was best to go armed—and stood for a moment in the middle of the room, thinking of what had occurred. He could not yet fully believe that he was master of this ship now, indeed, master of two-ninths of the world. Was it so, or only a dream? Morning would tell the answer, Dovirr thought. If sunrise still found him hailed as Thalassarch, he would know it really had happened.

It was a busy night for Dovirr. First, there was Gowyn's burial to attend to. Dovirr took no active part in the ceremony. That was Holinel's task, as the oldest and wisest of the Sea-Lords. He spoke the words while the men of the *Garyun* stood stiffly at attention, and then Gowyn's body was tenderly committed to the darkness of the deep.

Afterward, Dovirr held conferences with the men he regarded as most trustworthy—Holinel, Kubril, Cloden, Lantise. They discussed many things: the dangers of Dovirr's position, the possibility of an uprising by those who favored Lysigon, the problems of unifying the two Thalassarchies that Gowyn had joined in one.

Lysigon was the chief worry. Cloden said, "He's plotting something, Dovirr. I left men guarding his cabin. He's got his three cronies in there, and they're scheming a revolt, I'll wager."

"The men won't follow him," Holinel said. "They've never liked him. He was too proud, too cruel."

"Why did Gowyn make him first officer, then?" Dovirr asked.

"Because of his blood," Kubril said. "He's got Sea-Lord

blood for ten or twenty generations. His people once were Thalassarchs. Gowyn did it for political reasons."

"But he was considering replacing Lysigon," Holinel said. "Even before you came, he talked of it with me. He never wanted Lysigon to succeed him. And the men know that. That's why Lysigon was afraid to challenge you in the hall tonight. He knew he wouldn't swing the tide in his favor."

"But a direct challenge," Cloden said. "A duel—"

"Let him challenge," said Dovirr. "I'll fight him any time!"

"Or an ambush," said Kubril. "He might try to get rid of you in a cowardly way, and then to seize control before anyone could object. I say kill him, Dovirr. Haul him out of that cabin and hurl him overboard tonight."

"No." Dovirr's answer was emphatic. "I won't begin my reign treacherously. Until he tells me otherwise, Lysigon is my first officer. Perhaps I can win his allegiance."

"Impossible, sire!" Kubril blurted.

Dovirr smiled. "It was impossible for me to become Thalassarch only a few months after I left Vythain, was it not? Maybe I'll have the same luck winning Lysigon!"

Brusquely, he changed the subject, asking that charts be brought to him, the ship's log, any records that would help him understand his role as Thalassarch. Dovirr was aware of how little he really knew about the part he had insisted on playing. There was almost everything to learn.

He got no sleep that night. He conferred with his little band of loyal supporters well past midnight; then they left him, and he sat alone in the Thalassarch's cabin, studying maps, familiarizing himself with the location of all of the floating cities, marking off the domains of his seven rival Thalassarchs, planning, thinking. The logbooks were piled high on his table. He glanced at them, but there was no time now to read them in detail.

Morning came—a pale dawn and chilly winds. Dovirr emerged on the deck, and saw the other ships flanking the *Garyun*—close by, the captured *Bretwol,* and at a slightly greater distance the two ships of Gowyn's own fleet. Boats were putting forth; the officers were coming to greet the new Thalassarch.

Dovirr met them. He spoke briefly, taking care to act every inch the Thalassarch. He knew that the future of his rule was largely in their hands. If they respected him, they would recognize him as their Thalassarch. Otherwise, they might go their own ways, and his power would disintegrate. Aboard the *Garyun,* Dovirr could enforce his authority by the strength of his own right arm. But some higher bond was needed to hold the other ships to his flag.

They seemed impressed. They were men twice his age and more, and in turn each knelt before him to pay homage that was due. Dovirr bade them rise.

"Carry the word," he said. "We will gather near Korduna—every ship of the Western Sea, and all those of the Black Ocean. We will hold the ceremony of my coronation there, in a month's time."

The vassal captains returned to their ships. The day brightened. Dovirr sent word to Kubril to plot a course that would carry them toward Korduna, one of the largest of the floating cities. He returned to his cabin and spread the maps before him.

Shortly before midday, Cloden came to him. "There

will be trouble with Lysigon soon," the slender Sea-Lord said.

"What kind of trouble?"

"The guard I posted on his cabin says he's donning full battle armor. He's getting ready for some kind of uprising, that's obvious. Shall I have him put in chains, sire?"

"Not. Let him do as he pleases."

"But—"

"I won't clap him in irons until he gives me cause, Cloden. Simply putting on his armor isn't good enough cause. Tell him I want to see him. Tell him I want to find out if he has any grievance against me."

"Yes, sire," Cloden said stiffly.

"And remember, he's still the first officer of this ship, until I say otherwise!"

Cloden went out, returning in a few moments. "I spoke to him," Cloden reported. "He says he'll see you in due time. There was insolence in his voice."

"We'll be patient with him," Dovirr said. "Give him every chance to calm down. I think I'll go up on deck—and he can come to me in the open, if he cares to."

At Dovirr's orders, a broad table was carried to the top deck, and the new Thalassarch took his place behind it, poring over his charts. It was while he was occupied with his studies in this way that Lysigon came to him. An hour had passed since Cloden had spoken with the surly first officer. Lysigon came before Dovirr in full battle rig, his red beard curling lushly down over shining, freshly polished armor.

"What does this outfit mean, Lysigon?" asked Dovirr

casually, glancing up at the proud Sea-Lord and quickly back again to his charts.

"You know well enough what the wearing of battle clothes means, Dovirr."

Dovirr kept his voice mild. "Surely no trouble beckons, Lysigon. Or do you have some witchcraft way of knowing of impending battle before my lookout sees ships approaching?"

"The battle is here, landworm. Look out for your own safety!" Lysigon crashed a heavy fist down on the table, disturbing the charts.

Dovirr rose instantly. He drew himself up to his full height, an inch above his rival's. But he kept his voice still in check as he said, "What do you want, Lysigon?"

"*Lord* Lysigon. *Thalassarch* Lysigon."

"Bold titles. But all you can lawfully call yourself is first officer of the *Garyun*."

"I've stood your usurpation long enough, man of Vythain!" said Lysigon in an ugly, menacing tone.

Dovirr fingered the rough edge of the table before him. He flicked a quick, thoughtful glance behind the angry Sea-Lord, and saw a handful of Lysigon's comrades skulking in the background near the rigging. All of them, Dovirr knew, were full-blooded Sea-Lords of old families, whose sympathies were likely to lie with Lysigon. Dovirr's flesh grew cold. Was this a carefully nurtured assassination plot? Where was Cloden, where was Lantise, where was Kubril? Had they left him alone to deal with the rebels?

No, he realized. He caught sight of his loyal men gathering now. But they hung back. They would not interfere unless Lysigon attempted to bring him down unfairly. At the moment, this was a quarrel between one man and another, with the Thalassarchy at stake. Dovirr would not have had it any other way.

He said evenly, "Do you refuse the title of first officer, Lysigon?"

"I refuse it and hurl it in your face, usurper! I am the Thalassarch!"

"I strip you of the title you refuse, then. Cloden henceforth is first officer on this ship. I order you to remove armor, Lysigon. The *Garyun* is not threatened with attack at this moment. And I'll thank you to keep a civil tongue to me, or I'll have you flayed and your flesh rubbed in salt!"

Lysigon smiled coolly. "Strong words, boy. Words worthy of Gowyn himself! But I think you lack some of Gowyn's strength, and I think you have overreached yourself, landsman. Tonight the Seaborn Ones feast on your flesh. Tomorrow, I give the orders on the *Garyun*."

He unsheathed his sword. The weapon hung shimmering in the air for an instant; then Lysigon lunged. Dovirr was ready for the thrust. His hands had been gripping the edge of the table for some moments. Now he smoothly up-ended it, ducking down so that the table top acted as his shield.

Lysigon's keen sword splintered wood. So great was the force of his murderous thrust that the weapon embedded itself deep in the table. Cursing, Lysigon struggled to extricate it from the wood and strike again.

Dovirr was unarmed. He laughed as Lysigon fought to free his blade, and, scooping up the ink pot that had rested on the deck beside his chair, Dovirr flung its contents into the Sea-Lord's face. Lysigon fell back, hands clutching for his eyes. The sepia ink, extracted from the pouches of squid, stained the proud Sea-Lord's fiery beard and trickled down onto his armor.

Bellowing with rage, Lysigon abandoned his blade and charged blindly forward, hands groping for Dovirr's throat.

"Where are you?" Lysigon boomed. "By the stars, when I can see you again . . . !"

Dovirr deftly side-stepped around the table as the maddened Lysigon clanged against it. The Sea-Lord rebounded and staggered back a few paces, nearly toppling. Dovirr was waiting for him. Without sword, without armor, Dovirr stood in readiness by the bowsprit.

"Here I am, Lysigon," he sang softly. "Come and do your worst."

Lysigon paused. He blinked, getting the last of the ink from his eyes. Like a furious beast he came rumbling forward in another wild charge.

Dovirr absorbed the impact by rolling with it as Lysigon hit him. He stepped back, stooped, seized one of Lysigon's legs, and gave it a sharp yank. The Sea-Lord toppled heavily to the deck, landing with a crash that brought men running topside to see what was going on.

"Enough, Lysigon?" Dovirr asked.

Lysigon spat. His face was dark with ink and flushed with shame. The humiliated Sea-Lord crawled belly-first on the deck toward Dovirr, still too dazed by his thumping fall to rise. His hand clutched at Dovirr's tunic.

With a mocking laugh, the Thalassarch trampled on the outstretched hand. Lysigon hissed and pulled it back. He tried to stand. Dovirr did not attempt to seize him. He was biding his time, waiting for word to travel through the ship that he and Lysigon were fighting on topdeck. The crew was gathering, Dovirr wanted the largest audience he could get for this. Lysigon's three cohorts held back, eying one another uneasily, afraid to interfere.

"What do you ask of me, Lysigon?" Dovirr demanded. "That I appoint you Thalassarch in my place?" His foot thumped ringingly against the Sea-Lord's armor. Lysigon, who had been slowly gathering his strength, responded by uttering a strangled roar and leaping to his feet.

He charged a third time. Once more, Dovirr met the charge evenly, taking Lysigon's weight with a smooth roll of his body, and smashed his fist into the Sea-Lord's face.

Lysigon grunted with pain. He went stumbling backward. Dovirr followed after him and hit him again, knocking him up against the railing. Lysigon was groggy now. He swayed uncertainly, hands raking the air.

"To your kingdom, Lysigon!" Dovirr yelled, seizing the Sea-Lord's feet. Dovirr straightened. A quick upward flip and the hapless officer vanished over the *Garyun*'s side.

There was a howl—a splash—and silence.

In full armor, Lysigon sank like a stone weight. Dovirr, unscratched, turned to the onlookers.

"Lysigon desired to rule the sea," he said. "He now has his opportunity—at close range."

No one smiled. No one spoke. Dovirr looked toward Lysigon's three supporters.

"Will you challenge me now, you three? Does one of you hunger to be Thalassarch?"

They shook their heads. The deck was silent. It was the total hush of utter and complete awe and, from that moment, Dovirr Stargan was the unquestioned and unchallenged Thalassarch of the Western Sea and the Black Ocean.

Return to
Vythain

THE CYCLE OF DAYS rolled on, filling out the year. With the death of Lysigon, there were no further challenges to Dovirr's supremacy, and after a while it began to seem as though it had been perfectly natural for a youthful stranger to seize control of the ship. The men were behind him all the way—the same men who had treated him so coldly when he first joined the crew.

Dovirr knew why they backed him. He had convinced them that he was fit to be their leader. Holinel was too old; Lysigon had been too rash; Kubril, though he was a prince among navigators, lacked the spark that could make him a leader of men. Each of the other likely candidates to succeed Gowyn was flawed in some similar way. Only Dovirr had both the strength of body and the intensity of purpose to hold the title, and he had made good his claim.

Now that he was Thalassarch, Dovirr had taken over Gowyn's logbooks, and in the quiet hours of the night he read by a flickering candle, reliving triumphs of the late Thalassarch that had been recorded before Dovirr was born. Gowyn had filled a long row of books with the records of his reign. The last of them was only barely begun, and already a new hand had entered much, starting on a fresh page after Gowyn's last entry. There was the death of Harald to report, and the death of Gowyn himself, and the conflict with Lysigon, and the wanderings of the *Garyun* in the first months of Dovirr's reign.

They were active months. The ship went first to Korduna, the large city that the Star Beasts had stocked with cattle; the Kordunans supplied meat to the world. It had been Gowyn's practice to exact tribute from Korduna in meat, rather than in gold, and Dovirr saw the wisdom of continuing that system. A year's supply of barreled pork and salted beef and other meats came aboard, to be stored in the *Garyun*'s capacious hold.

Off Korduna, too, was held the ceremony of coronation by which Dovirr officially assumed the title of Thalassarch. All his ships and all of Harald's attended, meeting and anchoring in shallow water, the captains kneeling to Dovirr and proclaiming their loyalty. As was traditional, Dovirr distributed merchandise and wealth to each of his vassals, presenting the officers of the other ships with gold and meat, with fine robes and shining swords.

Then it was onward again on the ceaseless round. The *Garyun* passed through a zone of tiny pirate-infested islands, and rescued a ship of Vostrok one day simply by giving chase; the pirates fled in panic at the Sea-Lord's approach, and no lives were lost.

Another time, the *Garyun* helped a merchant ship bound for Vythain, out of Hicanthro. The traders were being badly plagued by a school of playful whales. Dovirr, vastly amused by the difficulties that the nervous merchants were encountering, answered the distress call and drove the whales off. The *Garyun* put out a boat that harpooned one of the great beasts, and the Sea-Lords dined on fresh meat for a while.

Onward—across the trackless sea. They came to the westernmost verge of what had been Harald's domain, and pulled back without trespassing. Dovirr was not ready yet to challenge another Thalassarch. He headed northward into the zone of short days and long nights, and the *Garyun* paid calls on several of the tributary cities that once had belonged to the dead Thalassarch of the Black Ocean.

It was difficult for Dovirr to convince himself that it was only twelve months since that day when he had huddled hesitantly at the pier of Vythain. It seemed like decades. But it was only a year, and in that time three of the mocking Sea-Lords who had called on Vythain that day lay at the bottom of the sea. Two of them, Levrod and Lysigon, had been sent there by Dovirr's own hand; the third was Gowyn.

Dovirr, who had never left the city of Vythain once in

all his first eighteen years, now roamed two seas. He wore the gaudy title of Thalassarch. Nine ships of his own and eight that had been Harald's claimed their allegiance to him. It had been a strange and wonderful twelve months.

The year had changed him. His body had grown hard at sea, his muscles quickening to split-second responses, his skin toughening. Even now, though he was hailed as Thalassarch, he sometimes took a hand in the galleys, tugging at his oar next to some sweating sailor. It was an unheard-of thing for a Thalassarch to do, but Dovirr did not consider himself bound by all the ancient traditions.

He had changed in other ways, too, beside growing callouses on his palms and learning to swing a sword. A year ago he had been a raw boy, uncertain, unsure of himself, knowing only that there was great strength in him but not knowing how to put that strength to work. Now he was a man. He had watched and listened and learned, and he could deal with men now as a leader. Gowyn had taught him much. So had Holinel and Cloden and Kubril. Dovirr was never too proud to learn. And at night he lay awake in the Thalassarch's lonely cabin, wondering about the things he still needed to know.

He wondered, too, about Gowyn's belief that some day the Star Beasts would come back. "Should I die before they come," Gowyn had said that night long ago, "will you swear to destroy them, Dovirr?" And Dovirr had sworn.

Dovirr tried to imagine what the world had been like in the days before the Dhuchay'y came. What kind of a world could it have been, he asked himself, with its vaulting cities and lofty mountains, with all the majestic land now slimy with crawling sea-things? He envisioned the people of that remote time as a race of golden giants, each man strong as a Sea-Lord, heroic and mighty.

And then Dovirr saw that he had to be wrong. The Star Beasts could never have conquered such a race of heroes. No: the Earthmen must have been meek landworms of the sort that thrived in Vythain and Hicanthro and Dimnon and the rest, or else the alien invaders would have been thrown back in shameful rout.

Anger rose fiercely in him as he thought of the conquest, and of the cruel drowning of Earth. At nightfall he often stared upward, sometimes shaking his fist at the unblinking stars.

Somewhere among those brilliant dots of light and color dwelt the Dhuchay'y. Dovirr, wearing the mantle of the dead Gowyn, would scowl at the stars with bitter hatred, feeling some of the rage that Gowyn had felt. By whose right had they taken this world? How had they dared to rob mankind of its home?

Come back, Star Beasts! Dovirr begged silently. Come back and give me a chance to destroy you!

But the stars made no reply.

Dovirr would turn away wearily, and return to his charts. Now, his task was to learn the way of the sea. Later, perhaps, the Dhuchay'y would return, and he would be ready for them. His year at sea had taught Dovirr some patience. He was growing used to waiting long for what he most desired, knowing that in time his chance would come.

The twelfth month drew to its end. A pleasant task had arrived for Dovirr. According to Gowyn's logbook, the time had come to return to Vythain for the collection of the annual tribute. This would be sweet, Dovirr thought. This would be delicious!

He gave the orders: head for Vythain. Dovirr spent a cheerful moment studying Gowyn's log entry for this date a year earlier:

Fifth of Eighthmonth, 3261. Today we return to Vythain to receive our gold. The wind is good: course holds true. Belowdecks all is not so well. Levrod has been murmuring against me, stirring up trouble. To my face he acts loyal, but I think it is otherwise in his heart. I must watch him closely. . . .

Sixth of Eighthmonth, 3261. Collection of tribute without difficulty at Vythain, as usual. Those people have no spirit—though there is at least one exception. As we were leaving, we were accosted by a good-looking Vythainan boy. He asked to join us. I set Levrod on him. The boy humiliated Levrod in hand-to-hand combat, and killed him at my orders. It was well done, and I am rid of that troublemaker. I took the Vythainan aboard ship. He is strong and clever and I like him greatly . . .

Smiling at Gowyn's words, Dovirr looked up from his reading of the dead Thalassarch's log. Ahead, on the horizon, he could see the growing dot that was Vythain. Even now, perhaps old Lackresh was calling out the news that the Sea-Lords approached; even now, terror would be sweeping through the city as the poor landworms hurried to hide before the *Garyun* docked.

How they dreaded it! How they feared that the Sea-

Lords would, for sport, sack the city while they were in harbor there!

Dovirr chuckled. Perhaps the people of Vythain had heard of the new Thalassarch's rise; perhaps not. News traveled slowly on the water-covered world. But it will be good to see Councilman Morgrun's expression, Dovirr thought, as he hands over this year's tribute—to me!

The *Garyun* drew into the harbor of Vythain early the next day. Dovirr did not intend to send a large party ashore this time. A single dinghy would do—the ornately decorated one that was used by the Thalassarch. He chose six men to accompany him—Cloden, Lantise, and four ordinary seamen. Holinel was put in command of the *Garyun* during the Thalassarch's absence.

They set out for shore. Dovirr stood, one foot on the seat, in the prow of the little craft, peering with strange fascination at the city of his birth. He could see tiny figures moving with great haste on the pier. The police officers were clearing away the passersby, no doubt, Dovirr guessed.

The sea was calm; tiny wavelets licked at the dinghy's sides as it slid through the water to the pier. They drew up slowly, and Lantise gathered the rope in his hand, swung it out to loop it over the mooring. Dovirr grinned at the sight of the familiar stone steps, the pile of buildings set back from the water and rising to the bright summit of Lackresh's lookout tower.

Dovirr was the first one over the side and onto the pier when the dinghy docked. His six men arrayed themselves at his side, and they waited in awesome majesty for the bringers of the tribute.

"A day of homecoming for you, eh, sire?" Cloden asked.

Dovirr shrugged. "I was glad enough to clear out of this place. It brings me little joy to come back."

"But when the citizens see you—"

"Here they come!" cried Lantise.

With faltering step, the eight old men of Vythain's Council began their annual procession down the rough-hewn steps to the pier, groaning under the weight of coffers as they advanced.

Dovirr folded his arms and waited for them.

Leading the procession was Councilman Morgrun, looking even older and more shrunken that Dovirr remembered him. Morgrun's eyes, deep-set in a baggy network of wrinkles, were filmed over with the rheum of age. He was staggering beneath the heavy coffer, barely able to manage. Dovirr doubted that Morgrun's ancient eyes would manage to recognize him at this distance. Step by step by step the tribute-bearers tottered forward.

When Morgrun was no more than twenty paces away, eyes to the ground so he would not stumble, Dovirr called out to him loudly:

"Ho there, Morgrun! Scuttle forward faster and greet your new Thalassarch!"

He laughed. Morgrun hesitantly lifted his head.

The aged Councilman emitted a tiny gasp. He nearly dropped the coffer of tribute in his astonishment. *"Dovirr!* You?"

"Your memory has not failed you yet, I see. Yes, old one—Dovirr!"

Morgrun gaped. The other seven Councilmen gathered

around him, lowering their coffers to the ground. They huddled together in a puzzled clump, whispering and murmuring in anguished tones.

Finally Morgrun said, his voice quavering, "This is some joke of Gowyn's. He seeks to humble us by sending this runaway boy in costly robes."

Dovirr spat. "I should have you hurled into the sea for those words, Morgrun. Gowyn lies dead off the edge of Harald's realm. Harald lies beside him. *I* rule both Thalassarchies!"

The Councilman stared at him. The sneer of disbelief remained on his face an instant more. Then, seeing the unquestionable look of authority in Dovirr's eyes, Morgrun muttered, "I—I beg forgiveness, sire."

He sank to his knees. One by one, the other Councilmen followed his example. Dovirr looked down at them, smiling broadly as he relished the moment.

"Into the dinghy with the tribute," he ordered. "No. Wait—open the nearest coffer."

A Sea-Lord pried back the coffer lid. Dovirr snatched up an ingot, studied it, pressed his thumbnail into the soft metal, mockingly sniffed it. He casually tossed the block of gold back with the rest.

"Morgrun, is the gold pure?" he asked.

"Of course, Dov—sire."

"It had better be." Shading his eyes, he looked upward at the city. "I have never much liked Vythain," he said thoughtfully, trying to hide his smile. "Should there be a single ounce of dross in these coffers, Morgrun, I think I shall raze the city."

"The gold is pure, sire!" Morgrun groaned.

"Let us hope so, Morgrun." It was pleasant to tease the old man this way, Dovirr thought. After all the years that he had spent simmering with impatience in Morgrun's city, Dovirr felt that he was entitled to have some fun at the Councilman's expense.

Morgrun remained crouched at Dovirr's feet. Gently, Dovirr lifted Morgrun's bowed head with the tip of his boot. "Tell me, Councilman—how goes it in Vythain? I have been somewhat out of touch, this past year. Is my father in good health?"

"He is fine, sire. He will be amazed to see what has become of you."

"I'm sure he will, Morgrun. Have him sent to me. And what of old Lackresh, the spyman?"

"Dead, sire."

"Dead, at last? Too bad; I would have enjoyed watching his face as he discovered who had succeeded Gowyn. Has the dredging gone well this year?"

"Poorly," Morgrun said. "You have taken nearly all our gold in the tribute, sire."

"A pity, I suppose. You'll simply have to squeeze some unfortunate neighbor city of yours to make up the loss, won't you? But you Vythainans always were sharp traders. You'll manage to come out ahead."

A chill wind swept suddenly over the pier. Dovirr gathered his cloak about him. It was almost time to return to the ship, he thought. The fun here had been about wrung dry. He wanted to speak with his father, and then he would depart.

Morgrun glanced up. "Sire, may I ask a question?"

"What is it, Morgrun?"

"Sire, have you heard any news out of Vostrok as you traveled around?"

Dovirr frowned. Vostrok was a northern city, and next to Korduna it was the largest on the surface of the sea. Vythain depended on it for its supply of wood; Vostrok had Earth's finest forest, and from its trees had come most of the planet's ships.

"We were expecting a shipment of wood from Vostrok," Morgrun continued. "It has not come, and many weeks have passed. We pay our tribute, sire, and—"

"We do our job," Dovirr said coldly. "I give you my word on that. But there have been no distress signals coming from Vostroki vessels. We have heard no reports of pirates intercepting ships from that city. Have you called them?"

"We have," Morgrun said. Subradio channels established by the Star Beasts were still in operation, linking the floating cities. "Sire, there is no answer from Vostrok. *There is no answer!*"

"The equipment may have broken down, then."

"Our tests show that the lines are open," said Morgrun. "But they will not reply."

Dovirr glanced warily at Cloden. "Very strange," the Thalassarch muttered. "Perhaps Vostrok is planning some rebellion against us. It might bear investigation."

"We're bound there in a month's time," Cloden said. "After our call on Lanobul."

"We'll go to Vostrok first," Dovirr said. To Morgrun he added, "Don't fear for your wood, old one. We'll do what needs to be done."

The Sea-Lords left Vythain an hour later, with Vostrok their destination. But before they departed, Dovirr was paid a visit by his father. The elder Stargan came down to the pier, since Dovirr did not think it was wise for him to enter the city; it might create a disturbance that was best avoided if they hoped to make a quick sailing. For the first time since his return to Vythain, Dovirr felt uneasy and uncertain of his words. It was simple enough to play the role of Thalassarch before Morgrun, but how did he do it in front of his own father?

The passage of a year had aged his father more than Dovirr expected. Once, the elder Stargan had been tall and straight-backed; not nearly as powerful of body as his son, but big enough as Vythainans went. Now he looked stooped and shrunken. He hobbled a little as he crossed the gray expanse of pier. His hair, once deep black, was whitening.

Dovirr hurried to him, stretching out his hands.

"Father!"

He reached to embrace the older man. But his father shied away and fell to his knees. There was a long wordless moment, awkward and endless.

Dovirr said finally, "Rise, father. You should not kneel before me."

"You are the Thalassarch. That is what they told me, Dovirr, and men of Vythain bow the knee to the Thalassarch when he summons them. Is it true, Dovirr? Or is this all some strange dream?"

"It's true, father. But rise and look at me!"

The elder Stargan came unsteadily to his feet. His eyes met Dovirr's. They had quarreled interminably, Dovirr remembered, in the old days. Dovirr would talk of his rest-

lessness and of his ambitions to be something more en-
thralling than a merchant of Vythain, and his father would
laugh, or mock, or speak in angry tones of Dovirr's non-
sense. All that was done with now, Dovirr realized. He had
run away, and somehow he had turned his crazy dreams into
realities, and it would only seem cruel and boastful to re-
mind his father that he once had looked with scorn on those
dreams.

The two men embraced. Dovirr held his father tight,
gripping him now with a warmth that he hoped would make
up for his failure to have said farewell a year before. At length
Dovirr released him. The older man gazed blankly into
Dovirr's eyes.

"How did it happen, Dovirr? How could you have
become what you are?"

"A long story, father. There was luck in it, and some
bloodshed, and perhaps even some valor. Mostly I think it
was a great deal of luck."

"Luck does not make a city man a Thalassarch!"

"Not luck alone, maybe. But it helps, father. It helps
greatly!"

"Have you fought much?"

"Some." Dovirr nodded toward Cloden. "This man
helped to teach me to swing a sword. A good teacher,
indeed. But for him I'd have been food for the Seaborn Ones
a long time ago, father."

"You kill when you fight?"

"When necessary. A Sea-Lord lives in constant warfare," Dovirr said. "I haven't learned to like killing yet, and I
never will."

The conversation faltered. They had run out of things to

say to one another, though they had only been speaking a few moments. Dovirr realized that he had little in common with this aging man who wore his name and had given him life. His father was a merchant, a timid man who hated the sea. Through some miracle he had brought a Thalassarch into the world—but merchant and Thalassarch had no meeting ground on which they could talk.

His father broke the uncomfortable silence after a while. "Will you come to our house, Dovirr?"

"No, father. It would not be right."

"We'd have a feast in your honor."

Dovirr shook his head. "Sea-Lords don't accept the hospitality of city folk. I'm sorry, father. It would cause confusion in the city if I entered. I would have to bring my men—there might be fights and revelry—"

"You think of yourself as a Sea-Lord now, Dovirr?"

"I am one, father. Sea-Lord and Thalassarch."

"My mind finds trouble accepting this, Dovirr."

In a low voice Dovirr said, "Don't tell this to anyone, father. But my mind finds trouble accepting it too, in the darkest hours of the night. I keep fearing that when I wake it will all vanish."

They fell silent again. Then his father said, "When will you return to Vythain?"

"Next year, at tribute time."

"Not before?"

"Not before, father."

His father sighed. "I'll pray to see you again at tribute time, then. Be careful, Dovirr. You live with danger all about you. Be careful!"

"I will," Dovirr promised. He clasped his father's hand

a moment, and then stood watching until the elder Stargan had mounted the steps and begun his climb back toward the heart of the city. Dovirr gestured to his men. "Into the boat," he said. "We sail for Vostrok tonight!"

The Star
Beasts

VOSTROK WAS THE NORTHERNMOST city of those that Dovirr had inherited from the late Thalassarch Gowyn. It floated in high, choppy seas more than a week's journey from Vythain. Dovirr had seen it only briefly the year before on the tribute call; he had not been one of those who went ashore in Gowyn's retinue.

The course called for the *Garyun* to make the tribute call at Lanobul first, far to the west, and then to circle back to reach Vostrok many weeks later. But in view of the mysterious silence out of the northern city, Dovirr decided to make for Vostrok at once. Leaving Vythain, he encountered the *Ithamil*, one of his second-line ships, and sent it to Lanobul to make the scheduled tribute pickup there as his representative. The Councilmen of Lanobul would simply have to wait another year to meet their new Thalassarch.

The *Garyun* proceeded steadily northward through waters that grew increasingly rough. Crowds of the Seaborn Ones attended the ship. Dovirr moodily watched the flukes of the once-men churning in the dark waters, and remembered the Seaborn One that had perished so dreadfully aboard the *Garyun* a few minutes before the death of Gowyn.

As always, the presence of the sleek-bodied creatures of the sea stirred Dovirr's imagination. He thought of the Earth that once had been, and of the valiant days of the defense against the Star Beasts. He thought of the ancient scientists who had—by what strange magic?—created a breed of men fit to live and do battle in the seas.

On the fourth day out of Vythain, an off-duty deckhand harpooned one of the Seaborn Ones. Dovirr had given orders long before that the sea-creatures were not to be harmed: no one was to hunt them, and if one should get caught in the nets that trawled for fish, it was to be released. The seaman who had disobeyed Dovirr's orders was brought before the Thalassarch trembling with fear.

"I thought it was a dolphin, sire!" the man babbled.

"He lies!" declared Lantise. "I heard him talking! He knew what he was aiming at, and he wanted to kill it!"

"Is this true?" Dovirr asked.

The prisoner hung his head. "I thought it was a dolphin, sire," he repeated weakly, but it was obvious that he was lying.

Anger surged in Dovirr. For no reason at all but sport, this man had taken the life of an intelligent creature. "Let him be flayed," Dovirr said. "Then throw him overboard and let the Seaborn Ones take their vengeance."

"No, sire! No!"

The man was dragged away, screaming in terror. But before the sentence could be carried out, Dovirr relented. The sentence was a harsh one, and might stir resentment among the crew. Slay a man for killing a Seaborn One? The man had disobeyed Dovirr's orders, but it was not likely that he would do so again. Dovirr ordered the man brigged and put on half rations for a few days. He let it be known that there would be no mercy for the next man who did the same.

There was, it seemed, a raw, deep-lying hatred between the men of the *Garyun* and the Seaborn Ones. The Sea-Lords detested the shining creatures of the water, and the Seaborn Ones seemed to lie in wait to make certain that no man who fell into the water would leave it.

Dovirr felt none of that hatred himself. When the Seaborn One had been brought on deck at Gowyn's victory feast, Dovirr had been completely unable to share in the general merriment over the creature's torture. He had felt only sympathy for an unhappy animal out of its element. Dovirr realized that, Thalassarch or not, he was actually still a landsman at heart. By sheer strength, luck, and determination, he had bulled his way to his present high rank. Still the men of the *Garyun* sometimes seemed as alien to him in way and thought as the flashing creatures of the deep.

Dovirr turned toward the water again, and watched the heaving flukes. The Seaborn Ones were sporting like playful porpoises today. That was an evil omen, some were saying aboard the ship, foretelling, perhaps, a deadly fate for the Sea-Lords in Vostrok.

The sea grew steadily rougher, and cold squalls began to blow. Heavy clouds lay like sagging balloons over the water, dark-bellied, shot through with gray. Dovirr bided his time as the *Garyun* sailed northward. Vostrok had broken off subradio contact with Vythain, eh? Why? Why?

It was strange, Dovirr thought. It could mean many things.

Eight days out from Vythain, Vostrok appeared, and early the following morning the *Garyun* sailed into Vostrok harbor. The city was larger than Vythain, and wealthier looking; where Vythain's houses, built without plan over hundreds of years, were higgledy-piggledy in their confusion, Vostrok had elegant towers that rose in neat ranks. According to information that Dovirr had found in Gowyn's logbooks, Vostrok had been the central base of the Dhuchay'y during the Star Beasts' occupation of Earth centuries ago.

Dovirr ordered the anchor dropped half a league off shore. Calling his officers about him, he stared uneasily toward the waiting city, which looked strangely quiet, with no trace of activity.

"Well, sire?" Kubril asked. "Shall we break out the boats and go ashore?"

Dovirr frowned. He wore his finest cuirass and a bold red-plumed helmet; his men likewise were armored today.

"I don't like the looks of this city," the Thalassarch said. "I see no men on the pier and no one moving in the streets. Hand me the glass, Liggyal."

A seaman passed a telescope to Dovirr, who trained it on the distant shore. Tensely he studied the area about the pier. Finally he lowered the glass.

"No one is there."

"Perhaps they don't recognize us," Cloden suggested. "The tribute isn't due for another month."

"Even so, when the *Garyun* casts anchor in their harbor it should cause some excitement over there! Where are they? All hiding so quickly?"

"What will you do?" Kubril asked.

"Let's land three boatloads of men on their pier, and find out why they're so shy."

Holinel said, "Will you go with the party, sire?"

"Of course."

"But the danger—"

Dovirr scowled bleakly. "Am I to sit here, then, like a woman, and watch you fight? Go on, Holinel. You insult me with your fears!"

Dovirr gave orders for three of the *Garyun*'s boats to be unshipped. He named thirty of his best men, sparkling in their burnished armor, to man them; the sturdy boats groaned under the weight, and the sea water licked high near the gunwales, but the boats held fast.

Oars bit water. Standing in the prow of the leading boat, Dovirr peered landward, feeling troublesome premonitions of danger and hazard.

The pier was still empty of men when the three boats pulled up and moored. Dovirr sprinted over the side of his boat to the pier, followed by a brace of his men. Cautiously they advanced as the other boats unloaded.

The Vostrok pier was a long, broad expanse of concrete, an apron extending triangularly out from the city proper into the sea. Beyond it lay the buildings of Vostrok. The windows seemed shuttered, the streets deserted.

"Should we enter the city?" Kubril asked.

"This may be a trap," said Cloden warily.

"Wait," Dovirr said. "Someone's coming!"

A figure could be seen, now—the first sign of life since the *Garyun* had arrived. An old man, a graybeard, had emerged from a customs-house at the far end of the pier, and was coming slowly toward the Sea-Lords.

"Do you know him?" Dovirr asked.

"One of the city fathers, no doubt," said Kubril. "They all look alike at tribute time."

The old man drew near. He was pale and wizened, so ancient that the whites of his eyes were yellowed with age. Strain was evident on his withered face. His thin lips trembled uncontrollably, and lines creased his forehead. Though the weather was cold, beads of sweat glittered on his face, pasting the gray wisps of his hair to his skull.

"The tribute is not yet due," he began in a small voice. "We did not expect you for another month. We—"

"That is understood," Dovirr said. "We have not come here for the tribute. The city of Vythain reports that you have failed to deliver agreed-upon shipments of wood, and that you refuse contact by radio with them. Can you explain this?"

The oldster shivered. He tugged at Dovirr's cloak with clawlike hands. "There are reasons," he husked. "Please, sire, go away. Leave!"

Startled, Dovirr drew back from the old man's grasp. He heard Kubril gasp in sudden surprise. And then a curious stale odor drifted to Dovirr's nostrils, an odor much like that of dried, rotting fish spread out on a wharf in the sun. Dovirr glanced up the pier toward the city. The old one turned too, and uttered a groan of wrenching despair.

"They come, they come!"

Dovirr stiffened. The old man broke away and dashed out of sight. Advancing across the bare pier toward the little group of Sea-Lords were eight *things*. Horror grasped Dovirr as his eyes took in the bewildering sight of the creatures. Eight feet tall or even taller, with bony scaled skulls and gleaming talons, they were beasts out of a nightmare. They advanced at a deliberate pace, each sweeping a long, thick tail behind. Dovirr remained transfixed.

He recalled what Gowyn had told him once about green-fleshed, evil-smelling demon-creatures, their bright eyes like yellow beacons of hatred, their jaws burgeoning with knifelike teeth, their naked hides scaly and metallic-looking. And now eight of them came, moving in a solemn phalanx.

A sudden surge of mingled fear and joy shivered through him. Dovirr whirled around to face his men, who stood numbed with astonishment. He yanked his sword from its scabbard and waved it aloft.

"Forward!" he shouted. "Forward and attack! The Star Beasts have come back!"

Indeed, it was so.

The gruesome creatures that now were slinking from

the heart of the city of Vostrok could only be Dhuchay'y, come to reclaim the world that they first had transformed into a globe of water, then had abandoned.

Their musty, sickening odor preceded them along the pier. The Star Beasts walked erect; including their tails, they measured twice the length of a man, Dovirr guessed. Their hind feet were thick and fleshy, terminating in ugly webbed claws. Their hands, curiously manlike, were poised for combat, gripping wedge-shaped knives of some dull grayish metal. The Star Beasts began to move faster now as the distance between them and the Sea-Lords narrowed. Dovirr led his men forward to them in desperate haste.

As he drew near, he saw the delicate fringe of gills near the blunt snout. The creatures, then, were equipped for action on land or on sea, breathing just as well in either medium. A chilling thought struck Dovirr: what if a swarm of the Dhuchay'y were to force him and his men into the water, then follow after as they flailed helplessly in their heavy armor, slaying them even as they sank?

Dovirr closed with the Star Beasts, Kubril and Cloden flanking him, the rest of the Sea-Lords around them. Dovirr shook with excitement. This was the true enemy! These were the destroyers of Earth!

His voice rose to a piercing battle-shriek. "Kill them! Kill!"

Ah, poor Gowyn, he thought. If you had only lived to strike a blow against them!

Leather-webbed feet thumped concrete around him as Dovirr drove headlong into the midst of the alien horde. His sword flickered overhead, chopped downward, and sliced through a Dhuchay'y arm. The severed member fell; the knife it had held clinked against the pavement. The Star Beast uttered a whistling scream of pain. There was a spurt of golden-green blood.

"First blood!" Dovirr yelled.

In fear-maddened rage, Dovirr's men charged the invaders from space. Dovirr smiled at the sight of a javelin, hurled by a towering Sea-Lord named Zhoncoru, humming into a scaly bosom. A Star Beast fell back, clawing at the weapon. Dovirr's own sword bit deep into a meaty flank. At his side, Cloden struck a telling blow, cleaving Dhuchay'y flesh.

Once again, the teachings of Gowyn had served Dovirr in good stead. Without waiting to judge the intentions of the enemy, the Sea-Lords had leaped to the immediate attack. Taken by surprise, the aliens were dropping back. Already one bloody form lay sprawled on the pier, kicking feebly in the death-throes, its life escaping through the wounds of thirty Sea-Lord thrusts. Another mighty bulk was toppling under determined assault. At Dovirr's left, Kubril thrust a ceremonial spear into the falling creature and hastened its descent. Cloden's sword crashed into the thick throat. The heavy tail writhed momentarily, slammed twice against the pier, then ceased to move.

Another Star Beast swept toward Dovirr. It reared up high, and he swung round to deal with it, realizing that he would not have time to protect his left side against the alien's attack. Holding his sword like a lance, Kubril thrust it into the Dhuchay'y that menaced Dovirr. A torrent of blood issued from the torn belly, and the alien creature fell back.

"Thanks," Dovirr murmured, and celebrated his rescue by slicing into an alien eye with a tiptoe thrust. The pier was covered now with mingled red and golden-green blood; the footing was slippery and treacherous. Dovirr within his armor was bathed in sweat.

The Star Beasts were yielding, though.

Three of them now lay dead on the pier. A fourth was staggering from its wounds, and would fall in another moment. Of the remaining four, not one had escaped some damage. Dovirr himself, weaving in and out of the struggling group to strike a blow here and there, had so far evaded all harm. Kubril had been struck by raking talons, but seemed little the worse for it. Javelin-wielding Zhoncoru bore a ragged cut down his tanned cheek.

Glancing quickly to one side, Dovirr saw three of his men lying dead in a welter of blood. He regretted it; but there was little time for the luxury of sorrow just now. The battle was still a bitter one. Dovirr's sword slashed through a Star Beast's gills, bringing forth a shrill shriek of pain that caused Dovirr momentarily to feel pity for the wounded invader. Then the Star Beast, cutting savagely, slicked the plume from Dovirr's helmet. Dovirr's newfound pity melted as quickly as it had come, and with a laugh of triumph he thrust his sword through the creature's exposed throat.

Now Dovirr drew back, gasping for breath. The stink of the dying monsters was overpowering. Rivers of sweat poured down his body; the perspiration ran out from under the band of his helmet and into his eyes. Writhing or dead Star Beasts lay everywhere. Of the eight that had come out to challenge the Sea-Lords, only two still lived, and those two had leaped into the water to hide from the flashing swords.

The first skirmish between Earthmen and Star Beasts in centuries had brought victory for the Earthmen. It had been clear and decisive, Dovirr thought. But—

"Ho there!" he cried with sudden hoarseness.

He caught Kubril's arm. The navigator had been striking a vicious blow at a dying Dhuchay'y. He faced Dovirr, puzzled.

"What's the matter?" he asked.

"Use your eyes!"

Dovirr pointed toward the distant city. The other Sea-Lords saw, too, and gaped in shock. The Star Beasts were sending reinforcements. Coming toward the Sea-Lords, talons thundering against the pavement, were more Dhuchay'y—

Hundreds of them!

Battle at
Sea

"TO THE SHIP!" Dovirr called. "Retreat! Retreat!"

It was the only possible step that could be taken. Even in the flush of their first triumph, the Sea-Lords would have to give ground. Twenty-five Terrans could never hold the pier against an uncountable multitude of the alien invaders, and it was suicide to make the attempt.

Dovirr led the retreat. The surviving Sea-Lords dragged their dead and wounded comrades into the boats, and they struck out for the waiting *Garyun*.

The ship had not been sitting by idly during the brief,

fierce combat with the Star Beasts. Holinel, whom Dovirr had left in command, had obviously seen what was taking place, and he had already struck anchor. The *Garyun* was coming as close to shore as it dared, to pick up the survivors of the frantic melee.

But would they make it to safety?

Abruptly it began to seem as if they would not. "They're coming after us, sire," Cloden muttered.

"Row for all you're worth!" shouted Dovirr.

With cold horror he saw the legions of Dhuchay'y reach the end of the pier. The Star Beasts were not stopping there. They were marching straight ahead, right over the hacked bodies of their fallen comrades, and were plunging into the water! Dovirr could see them swimming with powerful strokes toward the rapidly retreating Sea-Lord boats.

Around the boats in the water, the flukes of the Seaborn Ones were becoming visible. The water churned and seemed to boil. The Seaborn Ones were going to eat well tonight, Dovirr thought grimly.

"Pull those oars!" he urged his straining men. "They're gaining on us!"

But it was a useless effort. The amphibious Dhuchay'y moved easily in the water, and they were converging on the three fleeing boats in a milky rush of foam. Dovirr glanced back and saw the blunt, scaly heads ominously breaking the waves in their inevitable advance.

Suddenly a taloned claw appeared at the edge of the boat. They were trying to board!

Dovirr instantly hacked downward with his sword. The severed claw dropped into the boat, and the Star Beast's arm withdrew. But at once four more appeared. The Dhuchay'y had caught them—and the mother ship was still a good distance away.

The boat began to rock as the Star Beasts tried to tip it. Glancing toward Kubril's boat, Dovirr saw that its occupants were similarly beset by the swarming aliens, while the third boat seemed to be on the verge of capsizing from the weight of its attackers.

Dovirr knew what had to be done. Stripping off his breastplate, he flung the costly polished cuirass at the bare skull of a Star Beast who was grasping the gunwale. It was fine armor—armor to be prized—but it was worse than useless now.

"Out of your armor!" Dovirr ordered. "They're going to capsize us! We'll have to swim for it!"

There was no way to prevent the boats from over-turning. The bulky beasts were rocking the flimsy dinghies, which were heavily loaded with men to begin with. The only hope now—and it seemed like an impossible one—was to outswim the creatures.

The boat rocked dizzyingly as Dovirr and his men stripped down to their tunics. They hurled the useless armor at the bobbing Star Beasts, beat at them with oars, slashed with swords—to no avail. The creatures clung fast, tipping the boat to and fro.

Already, Dovirr saw, Kubril's boat had been over-turned, and he and his men were splashing in a wild tangle of aliens. He could not see what had happened to the third boat. In a moment more, the turn of his dinghy came.

The boat went over. Its eight occupants leaped free. Two dead Sea-Lords had been aboard the boat, but there was no way of rescuing their bodies now; they would go to their burial in the sea a little early, that was all.

As Dovirr sprang, he caught sight of the *Garyun* looming above. Crossbowmen lined its decks, ready to fire if only they could be sure of hitting none but aliens. Already, they had loosed a few hesitant bolts, and the shrieks of wounded Star Beasts resounded.

The water, in this northerly latitude, was icy. Dovirr hit the waves and went under, shivered, clawed his way forward. He opened his eyes and peered ahead as though looking through a window of badly blown green glass. He could see aliens swimming all about him. Choking, he broke the surface, sucked in a lungful of air, and submerged again, swimming toward the ship. He hoped that the *Garyun* would lower lines to pick up the survivors. Surely Holinel would have the good sense to do that!

A bolt from the ship thudded into the water above him. The idiots! he thought. They're just as likely to kill me as the Star Beasts. He came to the surface again, hoping that his men would get a good look at him before they aimed their bolts the next time. He grabbed air and went under.

Dovirr swam on. Suddenly he felt the blazing pain of claws raking his back. Dovirr wriggled away, escaping the grasp of his foe, and grabbed for the dagger at his belt. A Dhuchay'y swam between him and the ship.

The Star Beast seemed gigantic. It moved confidently, at home in this element where Dovirr was a stranger. Gasping for breath, Dovirr sensed that there was no way to swim round the alien, no way to elude it. He would have to rely on a direct attack, and on luck.

He jabbed the dagger upward and felt it strike home in

the creature's belly. The powerful, wiry arms of the Star Beast gripped him anyway, and drew him below the surface. Dovirr had just time to get a mouthful of air before he went under. Frantically, he sliced downward and across with his knife, cutting a ragged trail through the thick-hided body; even with that terrible wound, the squirming alien refused to let go of him, and held him under the waves. Dovirr thought that his lungs would burst in a moment more.

He worked an arm free and groped for the creature's throat. His hand closed on something smooth, a trinket, some sort of amulet, perhaps. Blindly, Dovirr ripped it away and thrust his dagger toward the place where the amulet had been. The blade went deep.

The alien abruptly relented. The clutching arms released Dovirr, who shot to the surface. His head bobbed into the air, and, gratefully, he let himself breathe. The Star Beast was somewhere nearby, a greenish shape dimly visible a few feet down. Still somehow clutching the amulet in his clenched fist, Dovirr stabbed down again and again into the bloodying water, until the Star Beast, with a mighty lash of its tail, went veering away from its tormentor.

"Sire!" someone called. "Here!"

Dovirr, alone in the water now, looked up. He was amazed to find the *Garyun* virtually on top of him, its dark hull rising from the water only a few yards away. A line dangled invitingly nearby. He saw a few of his men, bloody and torn, climbing other such lines to safety. In one case, a wounded alien still clung to a Sea-Lord's legs.

Choking, gasping, Dovirr seized the sturdy line and pulled himself up, past bank after bank of oars. He felt strong

hands clutch at him and ease him over the railing onto the
deck. He swayed uncertainly and fought to keep from falling. Blood poured from a dozen wounds. The open places
were fiery with salt water.

"Let me help you, sire," a seaman offered.

"I'm all right," Dovirr grunted. Disdaining all support,
he gathered his strength, strode to the bow, looked down at
the scene of battle. A blood-slick covered the sea, and the
preying creatures of the deep were beginning to gather for
their meal. The battle was over. Wounded aliens drifted like
rotting hulks in the water, their bodies strangely buoyant.
The overturned boats bobbed untended a hundred yards
away. Dovirr saw none of his own men except those few who
had already clambered aboard.

He gripped the rail. His legs felt shaky, and there
seemed to be a dozen gallons of salt water in his belly.
Numbly, his voice a harsh croak, the Thalassarch shouted:
"Full speed out to sea! Let's get out of here!"

"The boats, sire—"

"Leave them! We'll have Star Beasts aboard in another
moment!"

Dovirr could see the aliens still massing on the pier,
leaping one after another into the water. A dozen of them
clustered around the *Garyun*. Sudden dizziness struck him.
He started to topple forward, checked himself, and snatched
a javelin from a man standing nearby. With a vicious thrust
he hurled it downward at a dying alien threshing in the sea.
The weapon struck; the Star Beast quivered and began to
sink.

Wind caught the sails. The Sea-Lords manned the cars.

The *Garyun* fled the scene of slaughter hurriedly, and by nightfall Dovirr had put leagues between himself and Dhuchay'y-infested Vostrok.

There came a time for licking of wounds, a time for drawing back into the open sea and drifting broodingly while strategy was formed. For the next few days Dovirr kept mostly to himself, remaining alone in his cabin, going over and over in his mind the events of the battle.

The Star Beasts had returned, as men had for so long feared would happen. That much was clear. The Dhuchay'y had silently slipped down from the sky and retaken Vostrok, and now a countless horde of aliens once again abounded in the former Star Beast capital.

They held one city now. Judging by the ease with which they had made themselves masters of Vostrok, it would not be long before the Star Beasts held all the other cities as well. And what could be done to stop them? In anger, Dovirr clenched his fists and pounded them against the table while he cursed his own helplessness. How could men of flesh and blood defeat those monsters?

Thirty Sea-Lords had gone ashore at Vostrok that gray morning. Six of the thirty had returned alive to the *Garyun*, every one of those six bearing severe wounds. One of those who had not returned was Cloden. Dovirr felt the loss of the slender, deep-voiced Sea-Lord even more keenly than he felt the slashes of the Star Beasts on his own body. Cloden had been the first to show friendship toward him aboard the *Garyun*, and had been a wise and crafty counselor. Now he was gone. Other good men had died with him that day, in the brief, frenzied battle.

Three boats had been abandoned; twenty-four lives had been lost; thirty good suits of armor had gone to the bottom of the sea. Dovirr scowled. New armor could always be forged, new boats built; but men were irreplaceable, especially valiant men like those. And, now that the Star Beasts again gripped Earth in their clammy grasp, Dovirr knew he would need every man he had.

Hatred surged through him—hatred for the cruel alien overlords. Once he had thought it strange that Gowyn should be so driven by the need to do battle against the Star Beasts, but now that he had seen them, now that he had felt their might, the same need drove Dovirr as well. Long ago, they had stolen a world from its rightful owners, and now they were here to reclaim their possession. Not if I can help it, thought Dovirr. For the thousandth time he relived that struggle beneath the seas, where, tangled in a wreath of brown kelp and choking for breath, he had drawn the life of a Dhuchay'y and had saved his own.

Dovirr still had souvenirs of that encounter, eight of them: seven claw marks down his back, beginning now to form scabs and heal—and one amulet, wrenched from a Star Beast as they fought.

Dovirr looked at that amulet now. It had still been in his hand when he came aboard the *Garyun*, tucked in a fold of his palm. He had not really meant to bring it with him; it had simply been clenched there, and in the fury of the battle he had not bothered to release it. The amulet was small, made of polished onyx or some mineral much like onyx; a lambent flame glowed in its heart, a tiny worm of fire that danced dizzily without tiring. It was a pretty thing, Dovirr thought. He had not looked at it at all since the moment he entered his cabin to rest, on the day of the battle.

He fingered the smooth trinket. There was a knock at the cabin door.

"Who's there?" Dovirr called.

"I, sire," said a hoarse voice.

"Come in, Kubril."

The burly officer entered, limping from the wounds he had suffered. With Cloden dead, Kubril now was first officer of the *Garyun*, and Dovirr's most trusted companion. He lowered himself heavily into a seat opposite Dovirr, and jerked a finger at the stone in Dovirr's hand. "Fondling your pretty toy, Dovirr?"

The Thalassarch rolled the amulet idly over the table. "A souvenir of battle," he said. "Tell me, Kubril—do we dare attack Vostrok, do you think?"

Kubril stared at him. A raw, livid wound ran down one side of his face; a thick lock of his beard had been ripped away in the strife. Kubril began to chuckle. "Attack Vostrok? I'd sooner attack the sea itself."

"How do you mean?"

Kubril spread his stubby fingers on the table. "Sire, we have seventeen ships to our fleet. We might be able to gather them all for the attack, but there could be some laggards—or some cowards. Say we have fifteen ships. Who knows how many of the Star Beasts there may be in Vostrok? We can count on no more than five hundred swords."

"In our fleet alone. But if the other Thalassarchs co-operate with us?" Dovirr asked.

"Four thousand, then. Though I hardly think the Thalassarchs will join our banners gladly."

"Say that they will," Dovirr pressed. "This is Earth they're fighting for. They'll be able to rise above their petty squabbles for once!"

"Perhaps so. Four thousand men, then—but even so, we couldn't get close to the city."

"Why?"

"The Star Beasts are on the alert now. They've felt our swords and they know we can fight. They'll guard Vostrok well, now that they understand that they have more to cope with than yellow-bellied city folk. They live in the sea as well as on the land; the seas will be thick with them as our boats approach." Kubril shook his head. "It's too soon for you to have forgotten what happened to us when they caught us in our boats."

Dovirr scowled and tugged angrily at his beard. "Aye. They would tip our boats as soon as we drew close to shore. And the harbor is too shallow to allow bringing the *Garyun* near enough."

"If we could ever land our men—" Kubril said.

"The Star Beasts will have a cordon of swimmers surrounding Vostrok the instant that our ships appear on the horizon. We could neither get boats through to shore nor land men. Then how are we to attack?"

"They say that in the old days men had machines that could fly," Kubril observed.

Dovirr chuckled harshly. "So they say, indeed. But the old days are gone, Kubril—and with them, the flying machines." Holding forth his calloused hands, Dovirr said, "We shall have to rely on *these* to win our battles. We have no flying machines."

"What about the weapons of the Star Beasts?" Kubril asked. "They came at us with daggers, but they have greater weapons than those. The next time—"

"I had overlooked that," Dovirr said. He remembered the neuron whips, and what they could do to men. How could he hope to stand against these conquerors with nothing but swords and javelins?

He walked toward the port and peered at the unbroken stretch of sea. Gloom enveloped him. It was hopeless, hopeless, hopeless!

Bitterly he said, "The aliens have Vostrok, and we cannot take it from them. And when they realize that we are powerless, they will take the rest of their cities back, and hunt us down and slay us."

"I see now why the men of old created the Seaborn Ones," said Kubril. "The only possible way to attack the Dhuchay'y is in the sea, where they breed. Strike at them where they're most vulnerable. Knock out their main line of defense. Then march to the city!"

"The Seaborn Ones failed," Dovirr pointed out. "Else mankind would not have fallen to the Star Beasts."

"The Seaborn Ones failed because they came too little and too late; The world was already on the edge of defeat when the Seaborn Ones were loosed against the Dhuchay'y. If—"

"Enough," Dovirr said wearily. "This talk makes my head throb."

He leaned on his arms. The encounter off Vostrok had been his first and only taste of defeat; up till now, his rise had been straight and spectacular, from city boy to Thalassarch.

Now his way seemed utterly blocked. Dovirr was not accustomed to defeat. It rankled within him, leaving him harsh and sour.

Kubril said, "If we could find a way to ally ourselves with the Seaborn Ones . . ."

"You talk of miracles, Kubril. Miracles are hard to accomplish. Leave me."

"Sire—"

"*Leave me!*" It was practically a scream. Dovirr's nerves were raw and throbbing.

"Very well," Kubril said quietly. "I would not wish to disturb you."

The hulking first mate rose, looked pityingly at his captain, and left the cabin.

Dovirr watched the door close. Dovirr scooped up the alien amulet, gripping it tightly in his hand. A paroxysm of frustration racked him.

I've defeated all who ever stood in my way, he thought. But I've met my masters now. The Dhuchay'y, the Star Beasts—what can I do against them?

Dovirr raised the amulet on high, lifting his hand as though meaning to dash the stone to powder against the cabin wall. It was a meaningless gesture, Dovirr knew. Destroying the trinket would not crush the race that had polished and set it.

Suddenly, the amulet seemed to burn against his palm. It was a cool sensation, and yet oddly like flame. Dovirr gasped. He closed his eyes. He swayed dizzily, trying to understand the strange thing that was happening to him. His brain throbbed. His head reeled.

There seemed to be a shroud around his mind, keeping him from seeing—from seeing *what?* The hand clutching the amulet tightened all the more. The murky shroud appeared to yield, to open.

Dovirr sucked in his breath in amazement.

He saw the bottom of the sea.

Into the
Depths

DOVIRR SAW TOTAL BLACKNESS begin to give way to faint light. Strange creatures were moving with stately grace through the deep. The effect was a vivid one; it was as if he himself were below the waters, not just seeing into the depths through some unknown magic.

In the distance were towers springing from the ocean floor—incredibly lofty towers, grotesquely festooned with the clinging vegetation of the sea. They were enwrapped with streamers of brown kelp and crusted over with anemone and budding coral, bright with glaring reds and greens and astonishing iodine-purple. No human eye had beheld those wondrous towers since the sea had engulfed them.

None but Dovirr's, and Dovirr was not sure whether he woke or dreamed. For a long while he stared at the towers, and then he began to approach them, moving without effort, as if floating.

He knew now that he was looking at a city—a city of the ancients, a city that once had known bright sunlight and the sting of a winter wind. Now, disinterested fish flitted through the smashed windows of the dead buildings, gaping open-mouthed, goggle-eyed, displaying a surprise that they could not possibly feel. Coiling moray eels wound themselves around what had been television antennas and yawned, baring their myriad tiny, razor-sharp teeth.

Dovirr drifted upward along the wall of a building and peered through a window. An enormous turtle sprawled on the sagging floor of someone's room. Its soft green flippers idly scuttled back and forth, disturbing the thick layer of silt that had formed through the ages.

This was a dead world. This was a city of the departed ones, a ghostly fossil of a lost civilization.

Looking up, Dovirr saw the black curtain of the water's top cutting off the sea from the sky. He fancied that he could see the glimmering sun penetrating the depths, but he suspected that it was only a trick of the upper water. At this depth he could see no sun. He moved on, stalking silently.

In the sunken street, coral-covered automobiles stood waiting for their owners to turn over their motors. Those owners would not come. Bright bones lay strewn at random, gleaming against the silty bottom. Dovirr shuddered, and continued.

Sea spiders twice the height of a man crawled over the faces of the buildings, moving unhurriedly and confidently. Barnacles sprouted on walls and streets. A golden-yellow starfish stretched its legs and seemed almost to yawn. Dovirr saw that in some places there were merely low mounds of sand where buildings once had been. The sea was reclaiming, concealing, reshaping. Strange new forms were emerging as the encrusted sea-things hid the works of man. In a thousand years more, no one would ever know there had been a city here at the bottom of the sea.

And the endless sea would roll on, over the lost cities of mankind.

Dovirr shot forward through the water, traveling with the easy grace of a disembodied spirit. He came to an anchor—a huge staple of some glittering white metal, fastened to the bottom. A mighty chain, each of its links many feet thick, stretched upward to a cloudy bulk far above. At first the anchor and chain puzzled him, and then he realized what it was. He had reached a city-anchor. He stood by one of the powerful guy-wires that held some floating city in place. Dovirr rose along the anchor, heading toward the surface.

In a moment, he was no more than thirty feet beneath the surface of the sea. He saw the Dhuchay'y, suddenly. There were ten or twelve of them, wading on the shallow, artificial shelf of sand that lay just off the city. The city was Vostrok, Dovirr realized. With the curious clarity of a dreamer he saw what the Star Beasts were doing. They were burying things in the sand. White round things.

He felt a chill of revulsion. The white things were eggs. Star Beast eggs!

The Dhuchay'y were breeding! The eggs would hatch, and tiny swimming creatures would come forth and grow to adulthood, and the numbers of the aliens would increase. The seas would swarm with them!

Hastily Dovirr pulled away, struck out for mid-sea before the Star Beasts could become aware that he had spied on them. His mind, guided by the little amulet, slid smoothly through the waters. He caught sight of another sunken city and dipped to inspect it.

Mighty flukes passed him: a ponderous right whale, moving massively through the sea on some private journey of its own. Dovirr paused to admire the whale's awesome bulk, which traveled with an odd buoyant agility here. The whale did not appear to notice him. Dovirr continued onward.

Fingers brushed his mind.

Thoughts came, unbidden:

Who are you, intruder? What do you want?

Dovirr froze, letting his mind range in all directions about him until he found what he wanted to see. One of the Seaborn Ones hovered some fifty yards above him, body suspended in alarm.

Who are you? the Seaborn One challenged again.

A friend, Dovirr replied. *I am a friend. I mean no harm, Seaborn One.*

What do you seek in our world?

I will explain. Come down to me, Dovirr's mind said, *and let me explain to you.*

And the Seaborn One came. Dovirr watched the lithe creature flick its tail and descend, heading toward the point from which Dovirr's thoughts radiated.

Suddenly the Seaborn One stopped short. Its mind was emanating thoughts of perplexity.

Where are you, stranger? I detect your mind but I do not see you anywhere about.

Tensely, Dovirr thought: *I am above the sea. Only my mind roves in the depths.*

How can this be?

Dovirr answered, *I use an amulet taken from the alien invaders. I have no idea how it works, but it sends my mind down to the deeps.*

The Seaborn One was silent a moment. Dovirr felt pressure, as though the sea creature were probing at the innermost chambers of his mind. Then came a new message: *You are born of Earth, and no Star Beast.*

Yes, Dovirr answered. *I stole the device from them in combat.*

There was the equivalent of a chuckle. *The Star Beasts, then, must manufacture artificially what we have been granted by our creators*, the Seaborn One said.

What do you mean?

What you call an amulet is a device for linking mind and mind, came the silent reply. *There is no way to speak with voices beneath the sea. The sounds are blurred and lost. My people communicate with mind to mind. But the Star Beasts need toys like your amulet to help them focus their mind powers beneath the seas, it seems.*

Dovirr understood now the nature and purpose of the amulet he had snatched from the dying Star Beast. It was a communication device. His quick mind guessed at its use. The young of the Dhuchay'y were born in the sea, and lived in the sea, and spoke the mind-to-mind language of the sea. When the amphibious creatures grew older, they came up from the water to dwell on land. In order to communicate with their sea-dwelling young, the land-dwelling adult Star Beasts needed such amulets. Perhaps the ability to link mind and mind withered away at the end of childhood for the Star Beasts, when the lungs developed.

The amulet could link any minds, evidently—not just those of Star Beasts. For Dovirr, gripping the amulet, had somehow activated it, had somehow reached down into the sea to interchange thoughts with a Seaborn One.

Looking through the eye the amulet gave him, Dovirr studied the Seaborn One closely. Here, in his natural element, the mutant man was the embodiment of grace. The feathery gills flickered in and out with dizzying speed, while the Seaborn One's heavy tail-flukes kept him serenely stabilized in the water. He was a magnificent creature, superbly designed for underwater swimming.

The Seaborn One stared in deepest concentration at the place in the water from which Dovirr's thoughts seemed to be coming. There was an undercurrent of hostility in the sea-creature's mind. Dovirr picked up the thought: *Your people have killed many of mine, man of the upper world. If you yourself were here, and not just your thought-shadow, perhaps I would kill you.*

Your people and mine have fought long, and for foolish reasons, said Dovirr. *We are all men. We are like brothers who have gone different ways.*

Yes, agreed the Seaborn One. *But your people hate my people. You torment us and kill us. Are we fools to hate you in return? If you had the chance, man of the land, you would slay me without pause. I know you would.*

Not I, answered Dovirr.

He strained to open his mind to the Seaborn One, to knock down all barriers and let the man of the sea read clearly what was there. Vividly, Dovirr transmitted the image of that long-ago scene when Gowyn the Thalassarch had uproariously watched the agonizing death of a captive Seaborn One. Dovirr's own land-nurtured emotions came through: his feeling of sharp horror at the cruel act, his insistence that Gowyn put a stop to the atrocity.

There was a long silence.

Then the Seaborn One's thought returned: *You are not like the others, then.*

No.

I believe in what your mind says. I see you are different, that you do not have hate in your heart. I am called Halgar, land-brother.

And I am Dovirr.

What do you seek here? Why do you search us out?

Dovirr replied: *I have a common cause with you. We have need for one another.*

How, land-brother?

Dovirr felt confidence rising in him. *Long ago, men from the skies came to our world as conquerors. My people—the land people—created yours then, to help in the struggle against the invaders.*

I know, Halgar said. *We have stories of those old days. Legends of our creation. The wise ones made us and put us in the sea.*

Even so, the Star Beasts triumphed, Dovirr said.

Yes, Halgar agreed. *We failed. There were but a hundred of us. It was not enough.*

How great are your numbers now?

There are many millions of us, Halgar replied. *We cover the seas thickly, land-brother.* An image came with the thought: Seaborn Ones in great throngs, gliding through the cool waters of the panthalassa.

Dovirr felt his mind growing weary under the strain of this mental communication. He knew that he could not keep the contact for long. Gathering all his strength, he projected a vehement thought:

Know, then, that the aliens have come again! The Star Beasts have taken Vostrok and they are planting their eggs in the sea. Soon they'll swarm everywhere. We both are threatened, Halgar—your people and mine!

What is to be done, Dovirr?

We must fight! Seaborn and landborn together! There is no other way, but defeat! Will you give your help? Will you end the hatred between us? The real enemy comes from another world. We are all Earthmen, Halgar!

The Seaborn One's response came slowly. *I will take your words to my people, Dovirr.*

There was silence, the deafening silence of the depths. Dovirr hovered, mind suspended in the sea. Tension enfolded him as he waited for the word of Halgar. Dovirr wondered what strange event was happening now, what unimaginable linking of mind and mind throughout the domain of the Seaborn Ones, as Halgar consulted his people. Were they debating? Were they voting to accept or reject? Would they join forces with the land-dwellers who had been their enemies so long?

Silence was the only answer.

Then:

We will help you, Dovirr of the land world!

The contact broke. The amulet fell from Dovirr's quivering hand, dropped to the cabin floor, and skittered up against the wall. Dovirr stood for a moment like a man who has been struck by lightning; the impact of what he had seen and done buffeted him, and knocked him to his knees.

He made no attempt to rise. He splayed his hands out against the rough wood of the floor, holding tight as though he expected to soar away if he did not. His head throbbed. His eyeballs ached. His mind was whirling.

He had gone down into the world of the Seaborn Ones. He had seen the slime-shrouded towers of Earth's lost cities. He had spoken with a Seaborn One—

And had returned with a treaty of alliance.

Had it been a dream, Dovirr wondered? Some hallucination, some wild fantasy of a fevered brain?

No. No, he insisted, he had not dreamed it.

Strength flowed back into him. It had been a fierce drain, communicating with the Seaborn One, and he was still weak and shaky, but slowly his vitality asserted itself. He struggled to his feet. Where was the amulet? There. He seized it, snatching it up.

"Kubril!" he roared, running to the door of his cabin. "Kubril, come here!"

It was a bellow that could be heard everywhere on deck. The first officer appeared, wearing a frown of concern.

"Sire? You look so pale—"

"Never mind that. Come in, and sit down."

Kubril entered the cabin. Dovirr slammed the door shut. The stocky first officer, looking more puzzled with each moment, pulled out a chair for himself.

Dovirr said, "How long has it been since you left here, Kubril?"

"How long?"

"How many minutes?"

"Why, no more than three or four, sire. You ordered me to get out, and I did, and I went updeck and spoke to Holinel, and—"

"Enough," Dovirr said. "Only a few minutes, then? It seemed like hours to me." Dovirr crossed the cabin and leaned forward so that his face was only inches from Kubril's. His eyes locked on those of the first officer. "I'm going to tell you a story, Kubril. Just listen to it, and don't interrupt. You'll think I've gone crazy, and I won't blame you for thinking it, but don't say it. Sit. Listen. Don't even think."

"Sire, I don't understand—"

"You don't need to understand. Do as I say. Listen!"

"I'm listening, sire."

Dovirr took a deep breath. "After I ordered you out of here, Kubril, a strange thing happened to me. I was holding this Star Beaşt amulet tight in my hand, really gripping it, you understand. And a vision came to me. A vision of the bottom of the sea and of a city that was down there."

Quickly Dovirr told his tale: he described the ruined city, gave a concise account of his encounter with the Sea-born One, repeated as much of the silent mental conversation as he could, and ended by telling Kubril of the Seaborn One's promise of cooperation in the war against the Star Beasts. Kubril's face was a study in restraint. It was quite obvious that he wanted to burst out laughing at this wild narrative of his Thalassarch's, and just as obvious that he believed Dovirr had lost his mind. But Kubril kept his feelings in check.

When he had finished, Dovirr said, "What I want to do now is gather every Sea-Lord fleet together. I want to send out word to all the other Thalassarchs. We'll meet and make a concerted attack on Vostrok. The Seaborn Ones will help us by attacking the Star Beasts underwater and interfering with their front line of defense. If thousands of swordsmen come ashore and attack in one body, the Dhuchay'y won't have a chance to get organized. Their fancy weapons won't be of any use, because we'll be fighting in such close quarters that they'll have to kill their own men off to get at us. We'll drive them out of Vostrok and slaughter them in the sea." Dovirr paused and smiled. "You think I'm insane, don't you?"

Kubril cleared his throat and tugged uneasily at the collar of his tunic. "Sire, I don't go so far as all that. But this talk of making contact with the Seaborn Ones—of an alliance—frankly, sire, it's a little hard to buy."

"It certainly is," Dovirr agreed. "It's utterly preposterous, as a matter of fact. Sheer raving madness." He tossed the amulet suddenly to Kubril. "Here. Take that. Hold it in your hand, Kubril. Grip it. Tight. *Tight*."

The first officer held the Star Beast amulet as though it were a poisonous insect. He darted an unhappy glance at Dovirr, wordlessly begging him to take the thing away.

"Tighter, Kubril. Now concentrate. Blank everything out of your mind and see what happens to you."

Dovirr turned his back. A long moment went by, and then the Thalassarch turned. Kubril's eyes were closed and his face was contorted into a grotesque grimace. His head lolled forward onto his chest. His right fist was tightly clenched about the amulet. He seemed to be in another world.

A minute passed, and a second one, and a third. Then Kubril's hand opened, and the amulet rolled free. Dovirr picked it up. Kubril's eyes were wide with shock; his face was fishbelly white.

"Sire," he muttered. "*Sire!*"

"Did you see, Kubril?"

"I saw—the sea and all that's in it. I saw a Seaborn One, and spoke with him. I— I—" The burly first mate's voice dropped. He was trembling uncontrollably. "This is witchcraft, sire!"

"Perhaps. But useful witchcraft, Kubril."

"The Seaborn One spoke, sire! I understood his words and he understood mine!"

"Do you still think I'm a madman now?" Dovirr asked.

Kubril managed a faltering grin. "No, sire. Unless— unless we both have the same insanity."

"This Star Beast toy has opened the way for us, Kubril. We have allies now, beneath the waves. We'll have to get the word around. The cities will do it for us. They'll radio messages around the world, telling the Thalassarchs to meet us at a chosen point. And we'll spread the word too, with our own ships."

"Will they come, sire?"

"They'd better!" Dovirr said. "Unless they want to hand the world back to the Star Beasts without a struggle. Get to your feet, Kubril. There's plenty of work to be done. We'll have little sleep till the last of the Dhuchay'y has been slaughtered."

The Armada of
Earth

THE SHIPS GATHERED.

Slowly, the Sea-Lords of Earth gathered their might, massed their armada in the heart of the roiling ocean. United for the first time in the ten centuries since the world was drowned by enemies, the Thalassarchs mustered their united power in the common defense.

They came. Thousands strong, the warriors of the sea came.

They met in the Western Sea, in Dovirr's territory, at Dovirr's call. Suspiciously at first, then open-heartedly as they learned that the tale of the Dhuchay'y return was true, the Sea-Lords came, thirsting for battle, longing to bury their keen swords in alien hide, hungry for the spurt of the alien golden-green blood.

They came from every region of Earth:

Duvenal the Red, from far Northland Sea. Cromhargan, of the East. Jholain of the Southland came, and Bramonan of the Yellow Waters.

These Thalassarchs also came:

Fiery Murduien, of the raging Sea of Night. Quirotha, from the Utmost Deeps. Log-probek, Thalassarch of the Sea of Blood.

They were bold and bloody men, men who had ruled their zones of the globe for years, men who jealously guarded their rights and boundaries. Yet all these Thalassarchs acclaimed another as their leader. At the head of their league they placed the youngest of the eight monarchs, the newest to call himself Thalassarch:

Dovirr Stargan, Thalassarch of the Western Sea, Lord of the Black Ocean.

Dovirr Stargan, Thalassarch of Thalassarchs, Thalassarch of the Nine Seas!

There was no need for him to have won that title by conquest. It was enough that he had succeeded both Gowyn and Harald, and that he had slain Star Beasts in open combat off the shore of Vostrok, and that he held an amulet that allowed him to send thoughts down into the realm of the Seaborn Ones. The other Thalassarchs solemnly considered those qualifications, and whispered among themselves, and then they yielded their rights to Dovirr and named him as their commander for the battle that lay ahead.

The fleets of the Thalassarchs massed in mid-ocean, some seventy ships in all, nearly four thousand swords. They readied themselves for the assault on Vostrok. The ships raised their war flags as sweating seamen labored to put them in battle trim.

In Vythain, in Dimnon, in Lanobul, in Hicanthro, in all the fifty floating cities of the sea-world, the landsmen cowered, asking each other in hushed whispers what strange compulsion had brought the eight Thalassarchs together in one sea, what awesome battle was about to be fought. Snug in their landbound homes, they wondered fearfully why Dovirr had asked them to call the Sea-Lords together. The men of the land little dreamed that the aliens from the stars had come to Earth again, had taken back the proudest of the cities they had built long ago.

Earth had been forgotten by the beings of the stars, and during the time of Earth's abandonment the Sea-Lords had flourished and grown strong. Now, the aliens had remembered. They had come to reclaim their conquered world.

But now, things would be different.

The time of battle was at hand. The sea seemed to boil with life. Flukes broke the surface, slipped down into the depths again, rose, flashed brightly in the sunlight, slid beneath the white crests. The war fleets of the Thalassarchs watched; the Seaborn Ones were on the march!

No man had ever seen so many of them before. From the corners of the water-covered world they came, thousands upon thousands of them, swimming easily and powerfully toward the place of gathering. Dovirr stood at the prow of the *Garyun*, now the flagship of the Sea-Lord fleet, and looked down on a sea that was thick with the mutants that had sprung from the line of men. Like so many logs, the Seaborn Ones clustered about the ships. Their horde spread out for miles.

Over the centuries, the hundred original Seaborn Ones had grown into a vast population. They had bred—and they had had an entire fertile world of water in which to breed. The fastest moving and most intelligent creatures of that world, the Seaborn Ones had doubled and redoubled many times over. Just as once the landsmen had numbered in the billions, now the Seaborn Ones, beginning with the mere hundred created by the genetic scientists of the land, had proliferated, had been fruitful and multiplied.

Now an incredible number of them sported in the sea before the Terran armada. Dovirr waited while the legions of the Seaborn Ones assembled. Clutching the precious amulet in his hand, the Thalassarch let his mind rove out among theirs to make contact, to welcome them, to feel and share in their joy of the sea.

He spoke with Halgar the Seaborn, who led the legions of the sea as Dovirr did those of the air-breathing ones.

We are coming, Halgar said. *The Star Beasts shall not survive this day, eh, Dovirr?*

Dovirr replied, *We'll wipe them out and Earth will be free. They will never come here a third time. How great is your army, Halgar?*

There are millions of us. Ready yourself for battle, land-brother. When you give the command, we make for Vostrok!

The command will not be long in coming, Dovirr declared.

Tension rippled through him. His eyes swept over the gathered armada. The sea was full of ships, and aboard each could be seen strapping Sea-Lords making the last preparations for battle.

Dovirr beckoned to Kubril. The first officer came to the rail and looked down at the tight-packed phalanxes of Seaborn Ones. His expression was one of mingled disgust and awe. Like most of the other Sea-Lords, Kubril had not fully been able to overcome his hatred of the mutant waterbreathers—not even now, when he was locked in alliance with them.

"Sire?" Kubril said.

"Send the word," Dovirr ordered. "To Duvenal, to my left, and Murduien at my right. We sail in an hour. Be ready to lift anchor."

"Aye," Kubril said. Swiftly he set to the task.

Dovirr grasped his amulet.

Halgar?

I hear you, land-brother.

We sail in an hour. The time has come for you to begin the journey to Vostrok.

I hear, Halgar said. *We are ready.*

Flukes glistened in the sunlight. The Seaborn Ones swept their mighty arms forward; the army of swimmers began to draw away from the anchored ships.

The assault on Vostrok was beginning.

The Sea-Lord armada followed in the wake of the

waterborn allies, northward toward Vostrok. The *Garyun* led the way, with the other vessels forming a great wedge-shaped array to the right and left of the flagship.

They held the formation even when drawing near to Vostrok. The fast-moving Seaborn Ones had easily out-distanced the ships, and when the *Garyun* dropped anchor, about a league off the shore of Vostrok, the beings of the sea had not been seen for several days. The Sea-Lords moved into position, setting up their formation as a circle ringing the occupied island city.

Dovirr looked toward Vostrok—and saw the clustering Seaborn Ones.

Holinel and Kubril stood beside him on the bridge. Dovirr pointed toward the water. "Look at them," he whispered. Pride choked his voice—pride in his allies, the sleek men of the sea, and pride in those ancient wizards who somehow had altered the body of man so he could breathe the ocean.

The sea bubbled with their numbers.

"They're attacking!" Holinel cried.

"Yes," Dovirr said. "The battle has started."

Through his glass, Dovirr watched the encounter between the Star Beasts and the Seaborn Ones. Massed forces of the Seaborn swarmed toward Vostrok on all its sides, forming a ring almost a mile deep, a brown carpet threshing in the water. Dovirr's heart rose as he saw the young Dhuchay'y being hauled from their nests beneath the surface, being ripped to pieces in the shallow water. He saw eggs, golden-green blood, the upturned bodies of dead Star Beasts.

A dull boom resounded. The shore installations of the Star Beasts were gunning the Seaborn Ones. At this distance, such subtle weapons as neuron whips could not be effective. The aliens were using cannons. A shower of blue spume went up as the cannons barked, and the shells, landing in the close-packed ranks, took many lives. But as the alien shells landed, as the ranks of Seaborn Ones were thinned, other warriors came surging up from the depths to take the places of the casualties in the front line.

"Down boats!" Dovirr shouted.

The cry was taken up by ship after ship through the armada. "Down boats! Down boats!"

The men leaped into action. There was the thumping sound of boats hitting the water, as the Sea-Lord fighting teams headed toward battle. Dovirr led one boat; Kubril commanded one just to his left, and hook-nosed Lantise the boat rowing at the Thalassarch's right. Further along, Dovirr could see the boats of the other Thalassarchs. Oars dug the waves. Fifty, a hundred, two hundred Terran boats sped forward to the scene of battle, each manned by a small, eager crew of battle-hardened veterans.

The boats were beginning to reach the edge of the ring of Seaborn Ones. Although he had helped to plan the strategy himself, Dovirr could not hide his astonishment at the way the sea creatures had arrayed themselves. They were shoulder to shoulder a few inches beneath the surface of the water, forming a solid barrier of living flesh.

And now the strategy devised by Dovirr and Halgar the Seaborn went into effect.

Four thousand Sea-Lords, in full armor, left their boats

at the outer edge of the Seaborn ring. They were barefoot. Led by Dovirr they advanced over the massed ranks of the Seaborn Ones, walking on their shoulders, running and leaping over the shifting floor of slippery bodies.

"Follow me!" Dovirr cried. His weight came down on a glossy Seaborn back, but the water-being bore it without effort. The Thalassarch plunged forward, keeping his sword high as a gleaming banner.

The Seaborn Ones maintained a steady support. Here, there, Dovirr saw one of his men lose his footing and slip, and saw webbed hands reach up to steady the fallen Sea-Lord and help him to rise.

Occasionally, as he ran, Dovirr would look down and see the grinning face of a Seaborn One just below the water's brim. The Seaborn Ones seemed gleeful now that they were allied with their old enemies and at war with an even more ancient foe.

The shore battery of the Dhuchay'y kept up a constant barrage. But the marksmanship of the aliens was not very good, it appeared. More than half their shots sailed far beyond the encircling ring of Seaborn Ones and splashed in the open sea without doing harm. Yet often they struck direct hits. Again and again the big guns barked, and ten square feet of Seaborn Ones would vanish, cutting a gaping hole in the living bridge. But instantly a hundred more would surge from below, filling the gap. Dovirr knew that countless reinforcements lurked beneath the sea.

Now he was close enough to see the Star Beasts on the shore of their captured city. A few of them were rash enough to venture out into the water—and were dragged under instantly, to be ripped apart by the waiting hordes of Sea-born Ones. They carried not only daggers but neuron whips and small arms, but they were able to fire no more than a couple of blasts before the Seaborn Ones seized them. For every Star Beast there were hundreds of attackers. The Dhuchay'y were beginning to see how futile it was to try to carry the war into the water, and the more cautious ones were hanging indecisively back, grouping themselves on the pier.

Dovirr was the first Sea-Lord to make it all the way across the living bridge to the pier. He sprang onto it, and in the same moment lashed out with his sword, ripping upward into an alien belly. A steaming torrent of greenish-gold blood poured forth.

"Onward!" Dovirr yelled to his men. "Onward!"

He cut a swath through the aliens and looked back, seeing the Sea-Lord swordsmen advancing grimly over the packed sea. The defense of the Star Beasts had been completely canceled out; their hopes of keeping Sea-Lord invading parties away from Vostrok by means of an underwater network of defenders had vanished under the vast counterattack by the Seaborn Ones. And in the turmoil and tumult of the onslaught, the Dhuchay'y were unable to use their superior weapons to their advantage. Force of numbers was what counted now, and determination to win. For all their fierce appearance, the Star Beasts were fighting in a muddled, confused, bewildered way.

They've gone soft, Dovirr thought. They didn't expect any real trouble from us, and they aren't very good fighters any more.

His sword flashed in stroke after furious stroke. Even as Dovirr brought death on all sides, though, his heart was sad for the dead Thalassarch who would have so keenly relished this moment of triumph for Earth. Ah, Gowyn, Gowyn! Dovirr thought. What a great day this would have been for you!

The Sea-Lords were packed shoulder to shoulder now on the pier, just as the Seaborn Ones had been in the water. Dovirr's swordsmen were advancing in a solid troop, their weapons held before them as a wall of death. The Star Beasts, hardly prepared at all for such a vigorous assault by a foe they had held in such contempt, gave ground.

"They're running away!" Lantise shouted.

"Corner them!" cried Dovirr. "Pen them up!"

Dovirr and his men isolated a pocket of perhaps fifty of the Star Beasts, fencing them in with a line of flashing steel. The aliens milled uncertainly about, shrinking back from the shining blades.

"To the sea with them!" Kubril boomed suddenly. "To the sea with them! Drive them in!"

It was a fitting doom. Dovirr joined the shout.

"Aye, to the sea!"

The Sea-Lords drove the panic-stricken band of aliens before them to the edge of the pier. Step by step, the Star Beasts fell back from the advancing swordsmen, and each step took them closer to the water. The Seaborn Ones, realizing what was being done, leaped up from the water in delight, seizing the huge amphibians. The Star Beasts were dragged down into the element of their birth—the element that now would bring them death. Onward, onward the

Sea-Lords forced the aliens, who one by one dropped into the clutches of the waiting, jubilant Seaborn Ones.

From the heart of Vostrok now poured Star Beast reinforcements—the rest of the Dhuchay'y occupation force, no doubt. Dovirr smiled grimly. The aliens had returned to their abandoned province expecting to find a world of crushed serfs; instead, they were getting a most unexpected sort of welcome from Earth.

The Star Beasts who advanced were bristling with weapons. Hand cannons sent waves of heat skimming toward the Earthmen. Thermal vibrators! The Sea-Lords in their armor poured forth rivers of sweat as heat rose around them. Dovirr saw some of his men falter and drop. He hesitated himself. They're frying us, he thought.

They were frying their own wounded too. But that didn't seem to matter to the Dhuchay'y now. This was a last-ditch defense, and the fallen were expendable.

The heat became unbearable. The Sea-Lord line of attack was ragged; some men had collapsed, others were struggling on into the Star Beast party despite the searing temperature. No use, Dovirr thought. It was suicide to press onward. For one bleak moment it seemed to him that his plan of direct assault had been absurd; the Dhuchay'y were going to drive them off and the war would turn into a campaign of attrition, with Seaborn Ones waiting in the offshore waters to catch unwary Star Beasts and pick them off one by one.

It could never have worked, Dovirr thought. Swords against cannons and thermal vibrators? The Dhuchay'y had all the advantages except that of mere numbers. And—

And something totally unexpected happened.

Dovirr heard a shout erupt from hundreds of throats—in back of the Star Beast force.

The city people! The people of Vostrok were joining the battle!

It was hard to believe. They were racing forward, thundering down out of the city by the hundreds. They carried kitchen knives, benches, the legs of chairs, any improvised weapon at all. And they fell on the doomed aliens with murderous anger.

The Star Beast file was broken. As they turned to deal with this new attack, the waves of sizzling heat that had held Dovirr's forces back no longer were a barrier. Dovirr shouted to his men to resume the attack, and rushed forward. He was like a demon, fighting everywhere at once on the blood-soaked pier. The Star Beasts, attacked in front and rear, were in dissarray. Dovirr let nothing dismay him now. Once, razor-sharp Dhuchay'y talons raked his shoulder; he retaliated with a swift, deadly thrust, and saw the Star Beast fall.

"On! On!" Dovirr called. "They're dying fast now!"

The Dhuchay'y reinforcements were being driven into the sea as remorselessly as the first wave. The thunder of cannons came less frequently as Star Beast ranks were thinned. Battalions of Seaborn Ones swarmed everywhere, even climbing up onto the pier to engage in combat for a few moments until, gasping, they were forced to slip back into their own medium.

Gold-green blood stained the water. Scaly alien bodies lay strewn like pebbles.

Red-maned Duvenal, the Thalassarch of the Northland Sea, appeared suddenly at Dovirr's side. His chain-mail had been rent by the claws of Star Beasts, and his blood-streaked bare chest was visible. But Duvenal managed to grin at the sight of Dovirr.

"Ho, young Sea-Lord! *This* is battle, eh?"

"Indeed it is, Duvenal. And guard your left!"

The Northerner whirled and sank his mace deep into a Dhuchay'y skull; at the same moment, another alien appeared from nowhere and sent the Thalassarch reeling with a backhand swipe of a taloned arm. Dovirr sprang to Duvenal's aid, felling the Star Beast with a thrust through its beady eye.

"Duvenal?"

The red giant staggered to his feet. "Have no fears for me! Attend to yourself."

Dovirr ducked as an alien scimitar whistled over his head. A javelin hummed past and buried itself in the thick scales of the creature's throat; it tottered and Dovirr applied the coup de grâce with a two-handed swipe.

He looked around. There were few Dhuchay'y to be seen. Dovirr's muscles throbbed with excitement, and he urged his men onward to finish the job, shouting to them with a roar that could have been heard clear to Vythain.

Warm blood trickled over the pavement, tickling his bare feet. The sea heaved in tumult. Overhead, sea birds wheeled and screamed, spun in the air, shouted a raucous commentary on the frenzy beneath them.

And everywhere the Star Beasts perished.

The frightful carnage continued for more than an hour.

At last, hanging on his sword, gasping for breath, covered from head to foot with sticky, slimy alien gore, Dovirr paused, for there was no enemy left to smite.

The invaders from the stars lay dead to the last of them. The day was a triumph for Earth. Gradually the sea returned to calmness as the Seaborn Ones dispersed, spreading out loosely and slipping away to their deep homes.

Dovirr groped in his tunic for the amulet of the Dhuchay'y. His thought went out:

Halgar?

As if from a great distance came the weary voice of the Seaborn leader. *I hear you, Dovirr.*

The battle has ended. How has it gone with you?

There are no Star Beasts alive in the water, Halgar reported. *We are still searching the floor of the sea for their eggs.*

It was a great day, Halgar.

It was a day never to be forgotten, Dovirr.

Dovirr asked Halgar to have his men bring the Sea-Lords' boats to shore. The Seaborn Ones towed to the pier the flotilla of boats that the Sea-Lords had left at the edge of the battle zone. Those who had survived carried the bodies of the dead and wounded into the boats, seized the oars, rowed out to the waiting mother ships a league away.

Dovirr was the last to leave the pier. He stood ankle-deep in alien blood, looking around, feeling sorrow that Gowyn had not been with him on this day of Earth's greatest triumph.

Night was settling over the now-peaceful scene. The

moon glistened in the sky, and faint sprinklings of stars appeared against the black bowl of the heavens. Leaning on his sword, Dovirr looked upward.

Somewhere out there was the home world of the Star Beasts. Somewhere deep in the blackness dwelled the Dhuchay'y.

Dovirr smiled. Perhaps it was not for him, nor for his children, nor for his children's children—but the ultimate battle was yet to be fought. Up there—on the home world of the star marauders.

Some day, he thought broodingly. Someday Earthmen would carry the battle to the stars, and insure a secure and peaceful universe forever.

In the meanwhile, much remained to be done on Earth. The alliance between Seaborn and landsman would have to be strengthened. It had been forged in a time of peril, but it would have to endure even with the immediate danger gone. Neither could have thrown back the alien horde without the other; together, they had been triumphant.

Then, too, the feuding Thalassarchs would have to be joined in harmony. They had united behind Dovirr's flag, but would that unity last now that the Dhuchay'y were again gone from Earth? It would have to, Dovirr thought.

He saw now the purpose toward which his life had been shaped. He had sought power over men, not knowing why. Restlessly, blindly, he had left his home to look for adventure at sea, and had catapulted himself into authority before his time. He had not known what force drove him; he had simply known that he could not live the sheeplike life of an ordinary man.

Now he knew. Power, he saw now, was meaningless when acquired for its own sake. A man made himself Thalas- sarch, and other men bowed to him—what of that? Someday he would be dead, and all his power would count for nothing. Titles alone were hollow noises. Even the allegiance of men was a pointless thing to win unless some higher end were served. Power meant nothing unless it was put to real use.

What use, then?

The building of a new union of men. *That* would live on, even when Dovirr the Thalassarch slept the long sleep. He had drawn together the scattered remnants of Earth's popu- lation. He had temporarily broken down the walls of fear and mistrust that separated Sea-Lord from Seaborn, Sea-Lord from Sea-Lord, city-dweller from Sea-Lord and Seaborn. Would the new harmony last? It must, Dovirr knew, for the Star Beasts would return, perhaps in a year, perhaps not for a thousand years, and Earth would have to be ready. He saw himself as the one man who could lead that reunited Earth.

I'm young. I have much to learn. But I've made a good start, he thought. I have strength in me. I owe it to myself and to my world to use that strength wisely.

Kubril appeared at his side. The first officer said gently, "The boat is waiting, sire."

"Very well."

Limping, for an alien blade had dug into the flesh of his calf late in the battle, Dovirr walked toward the boat, dreaming of a bright world of tomorrow.

He cupped his hands. "Row to the *Garyun* for all you're worth! The battle's over; there's tribute to be collected!"

Master of Life

and Death

For Antigone—
Who Thinks We're Property

Introduction

MY CAREER WAS FAIRLY WELL launched by the time I began *Master of Life and Death* in February, 1957. I had already published one novel for young readers (*Revolt on Alpha C*, 1955, still in print!) and one novel allegedly for adult readers (*The Thirteenth Immortal*, 1957, out of print and likely to stay that way if I can help it), and, in collaboration with Randall Garrett, the magazine serial "The Dawning Light." And, in the two years since I had settled into full-time production of fiction, I had also published several dozen short stories, some magazine articles, and assorted other odds and ends. I was earning a comfortable living, back there in my early twenties, and I had already won a Hugo award. (As the most promising new writer of 1956.)

But *Master of Life and Death* now seems to me to mark a sort of beginning in that career. Except for a handful of short stories, it is the earliest work of mine that I can bear to have republished without embarrassment. Although it's far from a perfect novel, it seems to me to be a pretty impressive job for a writer who was barely old enough to vote, and there are clear foreshadowings in it of the kind of fiction I would write a decade later.

The title, incidentally, is not my doing. Usually I've had a clear notion of each book's title before beginning to write it; on a couple of occasions (*Thorns*, *Tower of Glass*) the title came to me before I had any idea of the plot, and I worked backward from there. I have a theory, which at any rate applies fairly accurately to my own work, that when a writer doesn't know what to call a story, he generally doesn't have complete insight into what his story is about, and there's likely to be some failure of focus about the work. In the case of the book now known as *Master of Life and Death*, though, I had a pretty good idea of what my theme was, but somehow couldn't put a title to it. So when I submitted a preliminary proposal to Donald A. Wollheim, the editor of Ace Books, in the winter of 1956–57, I called it *Gateway to Utopia* for lack of anything better. Wollheim instantly scrapped that vague and blurry label, and when the book appeared a few months later it was emblazoned with a resonant tag of Wollheim's own invention: *Master of Life and Death*. I didn't like it much—it sounded very 1934-pulp-magazine—but it was certainly an improvement over the nowhere *Gateway to Utopia*, and it did fairly well describe the role my protagonist must play. I've had twenty years to consider it, now, and it seems to fit the book well enough.

What I was trying to do in *Master of Life and Death*, aside from giving the old overpopulation theme one more run-through, was to produce a masterpiece. I know, that sounds awfully pretentious to you, but only because you aren't yet aware that I'm using "masterpiece" in its medieval sense: not a sublime work of genius, but merely the piece of work which a craftsman presents by way of proving that his apprenticeship is over, that he has passed beyond mere journeyman status as well, that he is ready to join the guild of masters—the big-time pros. To me, at that stage of my career, the essential craft of fiction involved the manipulation of plot elements, primarily, with such things as style and characterization taking a secondary place. The style I used was simple, direct, unadorned magazine-speak: I tried to tell my stories clearly and without fancy flourishes of prose. As for characterization, I aimed to keep my heroes from becoming unduly heroic and my villains unduly villainous, and I suppose I managed to create characters that seemed fairly complex and realistic in the context of the science fiction of the era, but it would never have entered my mind to populate one of my books with *Dying Inside*'s David Selig or *Shadrach in the Furnace*'s Shadrach Mordecai back then—he would have been too conspicuous a figure, too intense for the proper flow of the plot.

But the plot, the plot, ah, the plot! The meshing of character and incident, of desire and obstacle, of thrust and counterthrust! That was what fascinated me; that was what I knew I must master. My early books suffered from an inability to tie up loose ends; in the first draft of my first novel, the plot had depended on the selection of one cadet out of a group of four for special honors, but when I reached the climax of the book, or the place where the climax ought to have been, I found I had no idea why any of my four cadets was more deserving of the accolade than the others, and I had to rewrite half the book to eliminate that mechanism. So I studied my elders, I analyzed the means by which the science-fiction writers I admired wove the strands of their stories, and I took instruction from higher authorities even than they, going all the way back to Sophocles and Homer for deeper understanding of the mechanics of story. (A book by H. D. F. Kitto, *Greek Tragedy*, was my chief guide, and to this day I have recommended it, probably fruitlessly, to all young writers who want to learn the technique of plotting.) I studied and I imitated and I codified and finally, in *Master of Life and Death*, I let loose with all my thunderbolts.

  Master of Life and Death is a demonstration of plot. In a breathless way I piled one complication on another, trying to keep at least three major plot tangles going at once. The world is overpopulated already? Good: let's have someone invent an immortality serum, too. Is Earth trying to colonize a habitable but uninhabited planet of another solar system? Then have an ambassador from an alien species arrive on Earth to veto the scheme. And so on—one damned thing after another, all packed into some 50,000 words, and everything tied together in the final few pages. It makes for a hectic kind of prose, I guess, but it came off fairly successfully for the stunt that it was. Anthony Boucher, bless him, reviewed it in the summer of 1957 in *Fantasy & Science Fiction*, saying, "Silverberg's success in maintaining complete clarity and strong narrative drive while manipulating unnumbered plots and complex concepts is a technical triumph, and results in a lively and enjoyable book." It was the nicest thing anyone had ever said about my work.

The first edition of *Master of Life and Death* was an Ace Double Novel, published in August of 1957; the two-novel package also included James White's novel *The Secret Visitors*, and when I met White a few weeks later at the World Science Fiction Convention in London we posed for a back-to-back photograph, though neither one of us cared to do a handstand so that the photo would duplicate the up-and-down format of the double novel. When that edition went out of print, the book was issued in single format by Avon Books—that was March, 1968—and, another decade having gone by, here is my old novel finding its way home to Ace once more.

—Robert Silverberg
Oakland, California
February 1978

One

THE OFFICES of the Bureau of Population Equalization, vulgarly known as Popeek, were located on the twentieth through twenty-ninth floors of the Cullen Building, a hundred-story monstrosity typical of twenty-second-century neo-Victorian at its overdecorated worst. Roy Walton, Popeek's assistant administrator, had to apologize to himself each morning as he entered the hideous place.

Since taking the job, he had managed to redecorate his own office on the twenty-eighth floor, immediately below Director FitzMaugham's—but that had created only one minor oasis in the esthetically repugnant building. It couldn't be helped, though; Popeek was unpopular, though necessary; and like the public hangman of some centuries earlier, the Bureau did not rate attractive quarters.

So Walton had removed some of the iridescent chrome scalloping that trimmed the walls, replaced the sash windows with opaquers, and changed the massive ceiling fixture to more subtle electroluminescents. But the mark of the last century was stamped irrevocably on both building and office.

Which was as it should be, Walton had finally realized. It was the last century's foolishness that had made Popeek necessary, after all.

His desk was piled high with reports, and more kept arriving via pneumochute every minute. The job of assistant administrator was a thankless one, he thought; as much responsibility as Director FitzMaugham, and half the pay.

He lifted a report from one eyebrow-high stack, smoothed the crinkly paper carefully, and read it.

It was a despatch from Horrocks, the Popeek agent currently on duty in Patagonia. It was dated *4 June*, 2232 six days before, and after a long and rambling prologue in the usual Horrocks manner it went on to say, *Population density remains low here: 17.3 per square mile far below optimum. Looks like a prime candidate for equalization.*

Walton agreed. He reached for his voicewrite and said sharply, "Memo from Assistant Administrator Walton, re equalization of . . ." He paused, picking a troublespot at random, ". . . central Belgium. Will the section chief in charge of this area please consider the advisibility of transferring population excess to fertile areas in Patagonia? Recommendation: establishment of industries in latter region, to ease transition."

He shut his eyes, dug his thumbs into them until bright flares of light shot across his eyeballs, and refused to let himself be bothered by the multiple problems involved in dumping several hundred thousand Belgians into Patagonia. He forced himself to cling to one of Director FitzMaugham's oft-repeated maxims: *If you want to stay sane, think of these people as pawns in a chess game—not as human beings.*

Walton sighed. This was the biggest chess problem in the history of humanity, and the way it looked now, all the solutions led to checkmate in a century or less. They could keep equalizing population only so long, shifting like loggers riding logs in a rushing river, before trouble came.

There was another matter to be attended to now. He picked up the voicewrite again. "Memo from the assistant administrator, re establishment of new policy on reports from local agents: hire a staff of three clever girls to make a précis of each report, eliminating irrelevant data."

It was a basic step, one that should have been taken long ago. Now, with three feet of reports stacked on his desk, it was mandatory. One of the troubles with Popeek was its newness; it had been established so suddenly that most of its procedures were still in the formative stage.

He took another report from the heap. This one was the data sheet of the Zurich Euthanasia Center, and he gave it a cursory scanning. During the past week, eleven substandard children and twenty-three substandard adults had been sent on to Happysleep.

That was the grimmest form of population equalization. Walton initialed the report, earmarked it for files, and dumped it in the pneumochute.

The annunciator chimed.

"I'm busy," Walton said immediately.

"There's a Mr. Prior to see you," the annunciator's calm voice said. "He insists it's an emergency."

"Tell Mr. Prior I can't see anyone for at least three hours." Walton stared gloomily at the growing pile of paper on his desk. "Tell him he can have ten minutes with me at—oh, say, 1300."

Walton heard an angry male voice muttering something in the outer office, and then the annunciator said, "He insists he must see you immediately in reference to a Happysleep commitment."

"Commitments are irrevocable," Walton said heavily. The last thing in the world he wanted was to see a man whose child or parent had just been committed. "Tell Mr. Prior I can't see him at all."

Walton found his fingers trembling; he clamped them tight to the edge of his desk to steady himself. It was all right sitting up here in this ugly building and initialing commitment papers, but actually to *see* one of those people and try to convince him of the need—

The door burst open.

A tall, dark-haired man in an open jacket came rushing through and paused dramatically just over the threshold. Immediately behind him came three unsmiling men in the gray silk-sheen uniforms of security. They carried drawn needlers.

"Are you Administrator Walton?" the big man asked, in an astonishingly deep, rich voice. "I have to see you. I'm Lyle Prior."

The three security men caught up and swarmed all over

Prior. One of them turned apologetically to Walton. "We're terribly sorry about this, sir. He just broke away and ran. We can't understand how he got in here, but he did."

"Ah—yes. So I noticed," Walton remarked drily. "See if he's planning to assassinate anybody, will you?"

"Administrator Walton!" Prior protested. "I'm a man of peace! How can you accuse me of—"

One of the security men hit him. Walton stiffened and resisted the urge to reprimand the man. He was only doing his job, after all.

"Search him," Walton said.

They gave Prior an efficient going-over. "He's clean, Mr. Walton. Should we take him to security, or downstairs to health?"

"Neither. Leave him here with me."

"Are you sure you—"

"Get out of here," Walton snapped. As the three security men slinked away, he added, "And figure out some more efficient system for protecting me. Some day an assassin is going to sneak through here and get me. Not that I give a damn about myself, you understand; it's simply that I'm indispensable. There isn't another lunatic in the world who'd take this job. Now *get out!*"

They wasted no time in leaving. Walton waited until the door closed and jammed down hard on the lockstud. His tirade, he knew, was wholly unjustified; if he had remembered to lock his door as regulations prescribed, Prior would never have broken in. But he couldn't admit that to the guards.

"Take a seat, Mr. Prior."

"I have to thank you for granting me this audience," Prior said, without a hint of sarcasm in his booming voice. "I realize you're a terribly busy man."

"I am." Another three inches of paper had deposited itself on Walton's desk since Prior had entered. "You're very lucky to have hit the psychological moment for your entrance. At any other time I'd have had you brigged for a month, but just now I'm in need of a little diversion. Besides, I very much admire your work, Mr. Prior."

"Thank you." Again that humility, startling in so big and commanding a man. "I hadn't expected to find—I mean that you—"

"That a bureaucrat should admire poetry? Is that what you're groping for?"

Prior reddened. "Yes," he admitted.

Grinning, Walton said, "I have to do *something* when I go home at night. I don't really read Popeek reports twenty-four hours a day. No more than twenty; that's my rule. I thought your last book was quite remarkable."

"The critics didn't," Prior said diffidently.

"Critics! What do they know?" Walton demanded. "They swing in cycles. Ten years ago it was form and technique, and you got the Melling Prize. Now it's message, political content that counts. That's not poetry, Mr. Prior—and there are still a few of us who recognize what poetry is. Take Yeats, for instance—"

Walton was ready to launch into a discussion of every poet from Prior back to Surrey and Wyatt; anything to keep from the job at hand, anything to keep his mind from Popeek. But Prior interrupted him.

"Mr. Walton . . ."

"Yes?"

"My son Philip . . . he's two weeks old now . . ."

Walton understood. "No, Prior. Please don't ask." Walton's skin felt cold; his hands, tightly clenched, were clammy.

"He was committed to Happysleep this morning—potentially tubercular. The boy's perfectly sound, Mr. Walton. Couldn't you—"

Walton rose. "*No,*" he said, half-commanding, half-pleading. "Don't ask me to do it. I can't make any exceptions, not even for you. You're an intelligent man; you understand our program."

"I voted for Popeek. I know all about Weeding the Garden and the Euthanasia Plan. But I hadn't expected—"

"You thought euthanasia was a fine thing for *other* people. So did everyone else," Walton said. "That's how the act was passed." Tenderly he said, "I can't do it. I can't spare your son. Our doctors give a baby every chance to live."

"*I* was tubercular. They cured me. What if they had practiced euthanasia a generation ago? Where would my poems be now?"

It was an unanswerable question: Walton tried to ignore it. "Tuberculosis is an extremely rare disease, Mr. Prior. We can wipe it out completely if we strike at those with TB-susceptible genetic traits."

"Meaning you'll kill any children I have?" Prior asked.

"Those who inherit your condition," Walton said gently. "Go home, Mr. Prior. Burn me in effigy. Write a poem about me. But don't ask to do the impossible. I can't catch any falling stars for you."

Prior rose. He was immense, a hulking tragic figure

staring broodingly at Walton. For the first time since the poet's abrupt entry, Walton feared violence. His fingers groped for the needle gun he kept in his upper left desk drawer.

But Prior had no violence in him. "I'll leave you," he said somberly. "I'm sorry, sir. Deeply sorry. For both of us."

Walton pressed the doorlock to let him out, then locked it again and slipped heavily into his chair. Three more reports slid out of the chute and landed on his desk. He stared at them as if they were three basilisks.

In the six weeks of Popeek's existence, three thousand babies had been ticketed for Happysleep, and three thousand sets of degenerate genes had been wiped from the race. Ten thousand subnormal males had been sterilized. Eight thousand dying oldsters had reached their graves ahead of time.

It was a tough-minded program. But why transmit palsy to unborn generations? Why let an adult idiot litter the world with subnormal progeny? Why force a man hopelessly cancerous to linger on in pain, consuming precious food?

Unpleasant? Sure. But the world had voted for it. Until Lang and his team succeeded in terraforming Venus, or until the faster-than-light outfit opened the stars to mankind, something had to be done about Earth's overpopulation. There was seven billion now and the figure was still growing.

Prior's words haunted him. *I was tubercular. . . . where would my poems be now?*

The big humble man was one of the great poets. Keats had been tubercular too.

What good are poets? he asked himself savagely.

The reply came swiftly: *What good is anything, then?*
Keats, Shakespeare, Eliot, Yeats, Donne, Pound, Matthews
. . . and Prior. How much duller life would be without
them, Walton thought, picturing his bookshelf—his one
bookshelf, in his crowded little cubicle of a one-room home.

Sweat poured down his back as he groped toward his
decision.

The step he was considering would disqualify him from
his job if he admitted it, though he wouldn't do that. Under
the Equalization Law, it would be a criminal act.

But just one baby wouldn't matter. Just one.

Prior's baby.

With nervous fingers he switched on the annunciator
and said, "If there are any calls for me, take the message. I'll
be out of my office for the next half-hour."

Two

HE STEPPED out of the office, glancing around furtively. The outer office was busy: half a dozen girls were answering calls, opening letters, coordinating activities. Walton slipped quickly past them into the hallway.

There was a knot of fear in his stomach as he turned toward the lift tube. Six weeks of pressure, six weeks of tension since Popeek was organized and old man FitzMaugham had tapped him for the second-in-command post . . . and now, a rebellion. The sparing of a single child was a small rebellion, true, but he knew he was striking as effectively at the base of Popeek this way as if he had brought about repeal of the entire Equalization Law.

Well, just one lapse, he promised himself. I'll spare Prior's child, and after that I'll keep within the law.

He jabbed the lift tube indicator and the tube rose in its shaft. The clinic was on the twentieth floor.

"Roy."

At the sound of the quiet voice behind him, Walton jumped in surprise. He steadied himself, forcing himself to turn slowly. The director stood there.

"Good morning, Mr. FitzMaugham."

The old man was smiling serenely, his unlined face warm and friendly, his mop of white hair bright and full. "You look preoccupied, boy. Something the matter?"

Walton shook his head quickly. "Just a little tired, sir. There's been a lot of work lately."

As he said it, he knew how foolish it sounded. If anyone in Popeek worked harder than he did, it was the elderly director. FitzMaugham had striven for equalization legislation for fifty years, and now, at the age of eighty, he put in a sixteen-hour day at the task of saving mankind from itself.

The director smiled. "You never did learn how to budget your strength, Roy. You'll be a worn-out wreck before you're half my age. I'm glad you're adopting my habit of taking a coffee break in the morning, though. Mind if I join you?"

"I'm—not taking a break, sir. I have some work to do downstairs."

"Oh? Can't you take care of it by phone?"

"No, Mr. FitzMaugham." Walton felt as though he'd already been tried, drawn, and quartered. "It requires personal attention."

"I see." The deep, warm eyes bored into his. "You ought to slow down a little, I think."

"Yes, sir. As soon as the work eases up a little."

FitzMaugham chuckled. "In another century or two, you mean. I'm afraid you'll never learn how to relax, my boy."

The lift tube arrived. Walton stepped to one side, allowed the director to enter, and got in himself. FitzMaugham pushed *Fourteen;* there was a coffee shop down there. Hesitantly, Walton pushed twenty, covering the panel with his arm so the old man would be unable to see his destination.

As the tube began to descend, FitzMaugham said, "Did Mr. Prior come to see you this morning?"

"Yes," Walton said.

"He's the poet, isn't he? The one you say is so good?"

"That's right, sir," Walton said tightly.

"He came to see me first, but I had him referred down to you. What was on his mind?"

Walton hesitated. "He—he wanted his son spared from Happysleep. Naturally, I had to turn him down."

"Naturally," FitzMaugham agreed solemnly. "Once we make even one exception, the whole framework crumbles."

"Of course, sir."

The lift tube halted and rocked on its suspension. The door slid back, revealing a neat, gleaming sign:

FLOOR 20
Euthanasia Clinic and Files

Walton had forgotten the accursed sign. He began to wish he had avoided traveling down with the director. He felt that his purpose must seem nakedly obvious now.

The old man's eyes were twinkling amusedly. "I guess you get off here," he said. "I hope you catch up with your work soon, Roy. You really should take some time off for relaxation each day."

"I'll try, sir."

Walton stepped out of the tube and returned FitzMaugham's smile as the door closed again. Bitter thoughts assailed him as soon as he was alone.

Some fine criminal you are. You've given the show away already! And damn that smooth paternal smile. FitzMaugham knows! He must know!

Walton wavered, then abruptly made his decision. He sucked in a deep breath and walked briskly toward the big room where the euthanasia files were kept.

The room was large, as rooms went nowadays—thirty by twenty, with deck upon deck of Donnerson micro-memory-tubes racked along one wall and a bank of microfilm records along the other. In six weeks of life Popeek had piled up an impressive collection of data.

While he stood there, the computer chattered, lights flashed. New facts poured into the memory banks. It probably went on day and night.

"Can I help—oh, it's you, Mr. Walton," a white-smocked technician said. Popeek employed a small army of technicians, each one faceless and without personality, but always ready to serve. "Is there anything I can do?"

"I'm simply running a routine checkup. Mind if I use the machine?"

"Not at all, sir. Go right ahead."

Walton grinned lightly and stepped forward. The technician practically backed out of his presence.

No doubt I must radiate charisma, he thought. Within the building he wore a sort of luminous halo, by virtue of being Director FitzMaugham's protégé and second-in-command. Outside, in the colder reality of the crowded metropolis, he kept his identity and Popeek rank quietly to himself.

Frowning, he tried to remember the Prior boy's name. Ah . . . Philip, wasn't it? He punched out a request for the card on Philip Prior.

A moment's pause followed, while the millions of tiny cryotronic circuits raced with information pulses, searching the Donnerson tubes for Philip Prior's record. Then, a brief squeaking sound and a yellow-brown card dropped out of the slot:

3216847AB1
PRIOR, Philip Hugh. Born 31 May 2232, New York
General Hospital, New York. First son of Prior, Lyle Martin and Prior, Ava Leonard. Wgt. at birth 5 lb. 3 oz.

An elaborate description of the boy in great detail followed, ending with blood type, agglutinating characteristic, and gene-pattern, codified. Walton skipped impatiently through that and came to the notification typed in curt, impersonal green capital letters at the bottom of the card:

EXAMINED AT N Y EUTH CLINIC 10 JUNE 2232
EUTHANASIA RECOMMENDED.

He glanced at his watch: the time was 1026. The boy was probably still somewhere in the clinic lab, waiting for the axe to descend.

Walton had set up the schedule himself: the gas chamber delivered Happysleep each day at 1100 and 1500. He had about half an hour to save Philip Prior.

He peered covertly over his shoulder; no one was in sight. He slipped the baby's card into his breast pocket.

That done, he typed out a requisition for explanation of the gene-sorting code the clinic used. Symbols began pouring forth. Walton correlated them with the line of gibberish on Philip Prior's record card. Finally he found the one he wanted: *3f2, tubercular-prone.*

He scrapped the guide sheet he had and typed out a message to the machine. *Revision of card number 3216847AB1 follows. Please alter in all circuits.*

He proceeded to retype the child's card, omitting both the fatal symbol *3f2* and the notation recommending euthanasia from the new version. The machine beeped an acknowledgement. Walton smiled. So far, so good.

Then, he requested the boy's file all over again. After the customary pause, a card numbered 3216847AB1 dropped out of the slot. He read it.

The deletions had been made. As far as the machine was concerned, Philip Prior was a normal, healthy baby.

He glanced at his watch. 1037. Still twenty-three minutes before this morning's haul of unfortunates was put away.

Now came the real test: could he pry the baby away from the doctors without attracting too much attention to himself in the process?

Five doctors were bustling back and forth as Walton entered the main section of the clinic. There must have been a hundred babies there, each in a little pen of its own, and the doctors were humming from one to the next, while anxious parents watched from screens above.

The Equalization Law provided that every child be presented at its local clinic within two weeks of birth, for an examination and a certificate. Perhaps one in ten thousand would be denied a certificate . . . and life.

"Hello, Mr. Walton. What brings you down here?"

Walton smiled affably. "Just a routine investigation, Doctor. I try to keep in touch with every department we have, you know."

"Mr. FitzMaugham was down here to look around a little while ago. We're really getting a going-over today, Mr. Walton!"

"Umm. Yes." Walton didn't like that, but there was nothing he could do about it. He'd have to rely on the old man's abiding faith in his protégé to pull him out of any possible stickiness that arose.

"Seen my brother around?" he asked.

"Fred? He's working in room seven, running analyses. Want me to get him for you, Mr. Walton?"

"No—no, don't bother him, thanks. I'll find him later."

Inwardly, Walton felt relieved. Fred Walton, his younger brother, was a doctor in the employ of Popeek. Little love was lost between the brothers, and Roy did not care to have Fred know he was down here.

Strolling casually through the clinic, he peered at a few plump, squalling babies, and said, "Find many sour ones today?"

"Seven so far. They're scheduled for the 1100 chamber. Three tuberc, two blind, one congenital syph."

"That only makes six," Walton said.

"Oh, and a spastic," the doctor said. "Biggest haul we've had yet. Seven in one morning."

"Have any trouble with the parents?"

"What do you think?" the doctor asked. "But some of them seemed to understand. One of the tuberculars nearly raised the roof, though."

Walton shuddered. "You remember his name?" he asked, with feigned calm.

Silence for a moment. "No. Darned if I can think of it. I can look it up for you if you like."

"Don't bother," Walton said hurriedly.

He moved on, down the winding corridor that led to the execution chamber. Falbrough, the executioner, was studying a list of names at his desk when Walton appeared.

Falbrough didn't look like the sort of man who would enjoy his work. He was short and plump, with a high-domed bald head and glittering contact lenses in his weak blue eyes. "Morning, Mr. Walton."

"Good morning, Doctor Falbrough. You'll be operating soon, won't you?"

"Eleven hundred, as usual."

"Good. There's a new regulation in effect from now on," Walton said. "To keep public opinion on our side."

"Sir?"

"Henceforth, until further notice, you're to check each baby that comes to you against the main file, just to make sure there's been no mistake. Got that?"

"*Mistake?* But how—"

"Never mind that, Falbrough. There was quite a tragic slip-up at one of the European centers yesterday. We may all hang for it if news gets out." *How glibly I reel this stuff off,* Walton thought in amazement.

Falbrough looked grave. "I see, sir. Of course. We'll double-check everything from now on."

"Good. Begin with the 1100 batch."

Walton couldn't bear to remain down in the clinic any longer. He left via a side exit, and signaled for a lift tube.

Minutes later he was back in his office, behind the security of a towering stack of work. His pulse was racing; his throat was dry. He remembered what FitzMaugham had said: *Once we make even one exception, the whole framework crumbles.*

Well, the framework had begun crumbling, then. And there was little doubt in Walton's mind that FitzMaugham knew or would soon know what he had done. He would have to cover his traces, somehow.

The annunciator chimed and said, "Dr. Falbrough of Happysleep calling you, sir."

"Put him on."

The screen lit and Falbrough's face appeared; its normal blandness had given way to wild-eyed tenseness.

"What is it, Doctor?"

"It's a good thing you issued that order when you did, sir! You'll never guess what just happened—"

"No guessing games, Falbrough. Speak up."

"I—well, sir, I ran checks on the seven babies they sent me this morning. And guess—I mean—well, one of them shouldn't have been sent to me!"

"No!"

"It's the truth, sir. A cute little baby indeed. I've got his card right here. The boy's name is Philip Prior, and his gene-pattern is fine."

"Any recommendation for euthanasia on the card?" Walton asked.

"No, sir."

Walton chewed at a ragged cuticle for a moment, counterfeiting great anxiety. "Falbrough, we're going to have to keep this very quiet. Someone slipped up in the examining room, and if word gets out that there's been as much as one mistake, we'll have a mob swarming over us in half an hour."

"Yes, sir." Falbrough looked terribly grave. "What should I do, sir?"

"Don't say a word about this to *anyone*, not even the men in the examining room. Fill out a certificate for the boy, find his parents, apologize and return him to them. And make sure you keep checking for any future cases of this sort."

"Certainly, sir. Is that all?"

"It is," Walton said crisply, and broke the contact. He took a deep breath and stared bleakly at the far wall.

The Prior boy was safe. And in the eyes of the law—the

Equalization Law—Roy Walton was now a criminal. He was every bit as much a criminal as the man who tried to hide his dying father from the investigators, or the anxious parents who attempted to bribe an examining doctor.

He felt curiously dirty. And, now that he had betrayed FitzMaugham and the Cause, now that it was done, he had little idea why he had done it, why he had jeopardized the Popeek program, his position—his life, even—for the sake of one potentially tubercular baby.

Well, the thing was done.

No. Not quite. Later, when things had quieted down, he would have to finish the job by transferring all the men in the clinic to distant places and by obliterating the computer's memories of this morning's activities.

The annunciator chimed again. "Your brother is on the wire, sir."

Walton trembled imperceptibly as he said, "Put him on." Somehow, Fred never called unless he could say or do something unpleasant. And Walton was very much afraid that his brother meant no good by this call. No good at all.

Three

ROY WALTON watched his brother's head and shoulders take form out of the swirl of colors on the screen. Fred Walton was more compact, built closer to the ground than his rangy brother; he was a squat five-seven, next to Roy's lean six-two. Fred had always threatened to "get even" with his older brother as soon as they were the same size, but to Fred's great dismay he had never managed to catch up with Roy in height.

Even on the screen, Fred's neck and shoulders gave an impression of tremendous solidity and force. Walton waited for his brother's image to take shape, and when the time lag was over he said, "Well, Fred? What goes?"

His brother's eyes flickered sleepily. "They tell me you were down here a little while ago, Roy. How come I didn't rate a visit?"

"I wasn't in your section. It was official business, anyway. I didn't have time."

Walton fixed his eyes sharply on the caduceus emblem gleaming on Fred's lapel, and refused to look anywhere else.

Fred said slowly, "You had time to tinker with our computer, though."

"Official business!"

"Really, Roy?" His brother's tone was venomous. "I happened to be using the computer shortly after you this morning. I was curious—unpardonably so, dear brother. I requested a transcript of your conversation with the machine."

Sparks seemed to flow from the screen. Walton sat back, feeling numb. He managed to pull his sagging mouth back into a stiff hard line and say, "That's a criminal offense, Fred. Any use I make of a Popeek computer outlet is confidential."

"Criminal offense? Maybe so . . . but that makes two of us, then. Eh, Roy?"

"How much do you know?"

"You wouldn't want me to recite it over a public communications system, would you? Your friend FitzMaugham might be listening to every word of this, and I have too much fraternal feeling for that. Ole Doc Walton doesn't want to get his bigwig big brother in trouble—oh, no!"

"Thanks for small blessings," Roy said acidly.

"You got me this job. You can take it away. Let's call it even for now, shall we?"

"Anything you like," Walton said. He was drenched in sweat, though the ingenious executive filter in the sending apparatus of the screen cloaked that fact and presented him as neat and fresh. "I have some work to do now." His voice was barely audible.

"I won't keep you any longer, then," Fred said.

The screen went dead.

Walton killed the contact at his end, got up, walked to the window. He nudged the opaquer control and the frosty white haze over the glass cleared away, revealing the fantastic beehive of the city outside.

Idiot! he thought. *Fool!*

He had risked everything to save one baby, one child probably doomed to an early death anyway. And FitzMaugham knew—the old man could see through Walton with ease—and Fred knew, too. His brother, and his father-substitute.

FitzMaugham might well choose to conceal Roy's defection this time, but would surely place less trust in him in the future. And as for Fred . . .

There was no telling what Fred might do. They had never been particularly close as brothers; they had lived with their parents (now almost totally forgotten) until Roy was nine and Fred seven. Their parents had gone down off Maracaibo in a jet crash; Roy and Fred had been sent to the public crèche.

After that it had been separate paths for the brothers. For Roy, an education in the law, a short spell as Senator FitzMaugham's private secretary, followed last month by his sudden elevation to assistant administrator of the newly-created Popeek Bureau. For Fred, medicine, unsuccessful private practice, finally a job in the Happysleep section of Popeek, thanks to Roy.

And now he has the upper hand for the first time, Walton thought. *I hope he's not thirsting for my scalp.*

He was being ground in a vise; he saw now the gulf between the toughness needed for a Popeek man and the very real streak of softness that was part of his character. Walton suddenly realized that he had never merited his office. His only honorable move would be to offer his resignation to FitzMaugham at once.

He thought back, thought of the Senator saying, *This is a job for a man with no heart. Popeek is the cruelest organization ever legislated by man. You think you can handle it, Roy?*

I think so, sir. I hope so.

He remembered going on to declare some fuzzy phrases about the need for equalization, the immediate necessity for dealing with Earth's population problem.

Temporary cruelty is the price of eternal happiness, FitzMaugham had said.

Walton remembered the day when the United Nations had finally agreed, had turned the Population Equalization Bureau loose on a stunned world. There had been the sharp flare of flash guns, the clatter of reporters feeding the story to the world, the momentary highmindedness, the sense of the nobility of Popeek. . . .

And then the six weeks of gathering hatred. No one liked Popeek. No one liked to put antiseptic on wounds, either, but it had to be done.

Walton shook his head sorrowfully. He had made a

serious mistake by saving Philip Prior. But resigning his post was no way to atone for it.

He opaqued the window again and returned to his desk. It was time to go through the mail.

The first letter on the stack was addressed to him by hand; he slit it open and scanned it.

> *Dear Mr Walton,*
>
> *Yesterday your men came and took away my mother to be kild. She didn't do nothing and lived a good life for seventy years and I want you to know I think you people are the biggest vermin since Hitler and Stalin and when youre old and sick I hope your own men come for you and stick you in the furnace where you belong. You stink and all of you stink.*
>
> *Signed, Disgusted*

Walton shrugged and opened the next letter, typed in a crisp voicewrite script on crinkly watermarked paper.

> *Sir:*
>
> *I see by the papers that the latest euthanasia figures are the highest yet, and that you have successfully rid the world of many of its weak sisters, those who are unable to stand the gaff, those who, in the words of the immortal Darwin "are not fit to survive." My heartiest congratulations, sir, upon the scope and ambition of your bold and courageous program. Your Bureau offers mankind its first real chance to enter that promised land, that*

Utopia, that has been our hope and prayer for so long.

I do sincerely hope, though, that your Bureau is devoting careful thought to the type of citizen that should be spared. It seems obvious that the myriad spawning Asiatics should be reduced tremendously, since their unchecked proliferation has caused such great hardship to humanity. The same might be said of the Europeans who refuse to obey the demands of sanity; and, coming closer to home, I pray you reduce the numbers of Jews, Catholics, Communists, anti-Herschelites, and other freethinking rabble, in order to make the new reborn world purer and cleaner and . . .

With a sickly cough Walton put the letter down. Most of them were just this sort: intelligent, rational, bigoted letters. There had been the educated Alabaman, disturbed that Popeek did not plan to eliminate all forms of second-class citizens; there had been the Michigan minister, anxious that no left-wing relativistic atheists escape the gas chamber.

And, of course, there was the other kind—the barely literate letters from bereaved parents or relatives, accusing Popeek of nameless crimes against humanity.

Well, it was only to be expected, Walton thought. He scribbled his initials on both the letters and dropped them into the chute that led to files, where they would be put on microfilm and scrupulously stored away. FitzMaugham insisted that every letter received be read and so filed.

Some day soon, Walton thought, population equalization would be unnecessary. Oh, sure, euthanasia would stick; it was a sane and, in the long run, merciful process. But this business of uprooting a few thousand Belgians and shipping them to the open spaces in Patagonia would cease.

Lang and his experimenters were struggling to transform Venus into a livable world. If it worked, the terraforming engineers could go on to convert Mars, the bigger moons of Jupiter and Saturn, and perhaps even distant Pluto, provided some form of heating could be developed.

There would be another transition then. Earth's multitudes would be shipped wholesale to the new worlds. Perhaps there would be riots; none but a few adventurers would go willingly. But some would go, and that would be a partial solution.

And then, the stars. The faster-than-light project was top secret, so top secret that in Popeek only FitzMaugham knew what was being done on it. But if it came through . . .

Walton shrugged and turned back to his work. Reports had to be read, filed, expedited.

The thought of Fred and what Fred knew bothered him. If only there were some way to relive this morning, to let the Prior baby go to the chamber as it deserved. . . .

Tension pounded in him. He slipped a hand into his desk, fumbled, found the green, diamond-shaped pellet he was searching for, and swallowed the benzolurethrin almost unthinkingly. The tranquilizer was only partly successful in relaxing him, but he was able to work steadily, without a break, until noon.

He was about to dial for lunch when the private screen he and FitzMaugham used between their offices glowed into life.

"Roy?"

The director's face looked impossibly tranquil.

"Sir?"

"I'm going to have a visitor at 1300. Ludwig. He wants to know how things are going."

Walton nodded. Ludwig was the head American delegate to the United Nations, a stubborn, dedicated man who had fought Popeek for years; then he had seen the light and had fought just as strenuously for its adoption. "Do you want me to prepare a report for him?" Walton asked.

"No, Roy. I want you to be here. I don't want to face him alone."

"Sir?"

"Some of the UN people feel I'm running Popeek as a one-man show," FitzMaugham explained. "Of course, that's not so, as that mountain of work on your desk testifies. But I want you there as evidence of the truth. I want him to see how much I have to rely on my assistants."

"I get it. Very good, Mr. FitzMaugham."

"And another thing," the director went on. "It'll help appearances if I show myself surrounded with loyal young lieutenants of impeccable character. Like you, Roy."

"Thank you, sir," Walton said weakly.

"Thank *you*. See you at 1300 sharp, then?"

"Of course, sir."

The screen went dead. Walton stared at it blankly. He wondered if this were some elaborate charade of the old man's; FitzMaugham was devious enough. That last remark, about loyal young lieutenants of impeccable character . . . it had seemed to be in good faith, but was it? Was FitzMaugham staging an intricate pretense before deposing his faithless protégé?

Maybe Fred had something to do with it, Walton thought. He decided to have another session with the computer after his conference with FitzMaugham and Ludwig. Perhaps it still wasn't too late to erase the damning data and cover his mistake.

Then it would be just his word against Fred's. He might yet be able to brazen through, he thought dully.

He ordered lunch with quivering fingers, and munched drearily on the tasteless synthetics for a while before dumping them down the disposal chute.

Four

AT PRECISELY 1255 Walton tidied his desk, rose and for the second time that day, left his office. He was apprehensive, but not unduly so; behind his immediate surface fears and tensions lay a calm certainty that FitzMaugham ultimately would stick by him.

And there was little to fear from Fred, he realized now. It was next to impossible for a mere lower-level medic to gain the ear of the director himself; in the normal course of events, if Fred attempted to contact FitzMaugham, he would automatically be referred to Roy.

No, the danger in Fred's knowledge was potential, not actual, and there might still be time to come to terms with him. It was almost with a jaunty step that Walton left his office, made his way through the busy outer office, and emerged in the outside corridor.

Fred was waiting there.

He was wearing his white medic's smock, stained yellow and red by reagents and coagulants. He was lounging against the curving plastine corridor wall, hands jammed deep into his pockets. His thick-featured, broad face wore an expression of elaborate casualness.

"Hello, Roy. Fancy finding *you* here!"

"How did you know I'd be coming this way?"

"I called your office. They told me you were on your way to the lift tubes. Why so jumpy, brother? Have a tough morning?"

"I've had worse," Walton said. He was tense, guarded. He pushed the stud beckoning the lift tube.

"Where you off to?" Fred asked.

"Confidential. Top-level powwow with Fitz, if you have to know."

Fred's eyes narrowed. "Strictly upper-echelon, aren't you? Do you have a minute to talk to a mere mortal?"

"Fred, don't make unnecessary trouble. You know—"

"*Can it.* I've only got a minute or two left of my lunch hour. I want to make myself perfectly plain with you. Are there any spy pickups in this corridor?"

Walton considered that. There were none that he knew of, and he knew of most. Still, FitzMaugham might have found it advisable to plant a few without advertising the fact. "I'm not sure," he said. "What's on your mind?"

Fred took a pad from his pocket and began to scrawl a note. Aloud he said, "I'll take my chances and tell you about it anyway. One of the men in the lab said another man told him you and FitzMaugham are both secretly Herschelites." His brow furrowed with the effort of saying one thing and writing another simultaneously. "Naturally, I won't give you any names yet, but I want you to know I'm investigating his background very carefully. He may just have been shooting his mouth off."

"Is that why you didn't want this to go into a spy pickup?" Walton asked.

"Exactly. I prefer to investigate unofficially for the time being." Fred finished the note, ripped the sheet from the pad and handed it to his brother.

Walton read it wordlessly. The handwriting was jagged and untidy, for it was no easy feat to carry on a conversation for the benefit of any concealed pickups while writing a message.

It said, *I know all about the Prior baby. I'll keep my mouth shut for now, so don't worry. But don't try anything foolish, because I've deposited an account of the whole thing where you can't find it.*

Walton crumpled the note and tucked it into his pocket. He said, "Thanks for the information, Fred. I'll keep it in mind."

"Okay, pal."

The lift tube arrived. Walton stepped inside and pressed *twenty-nine*.

In the moment it took for the tube to rise the one floor, he thought, *So Fred's playing a waiting game . . . He'll hold the information over my head until he can make good use of it.*

That was some relief, anyway. No matter what evidence Fred had already salted away, Walton still had a chance to blot out some of the computer's memory track and obscure the trail to that extent.

The lift tube opened; a gleaming sign listed the various activities of the twenty-ninth floor, and at the bottom of the list it said *D. F. FitzMaugham, Director*.

FitzMaugham's office was at the back of a maze of small cubicles housing Popeek functionaries of one sort or another. Walton had made some attempt to familiarize himself with the organizational stratification of Popeek, but his success thus far had been minimal. FitzMaugham had conceived the plan half a century ago, and had lovingly created and worked over the organization's structure through all the long years it took before the law was finally passed.

There were plenty of bugs in the system, but in general FitzMaugham's blueprint had been sound—sound enough for Popeek to begin functioning almost immediately after its UN approval. The manifold departments, the tight network of inter-reporting agencies, the fantastically detailed budget with its niggling appropriations for office supplies and its massive expenditures for, say, the terraforming project—most of these were fully understood only by FitzMaugham himself.

Walton glanced at his watch. He was three minutes late; the conversation with his brother had delayed him. But Ludwig of the UN was not known to be a scrupulously punctual man, and there was a high probability he hadn't arrived.

The secretary in the office guarding FitzMaugham's

looked up as Walton approached. "The director is in urgent conference, sir, and—oh, I'm sorry, Mr. Walton. Go right in; Mr. FitzMaugham is expecting you."

"Is Mr. Ludwig here yet?"

"Yes, sir. He arrived about ten minutes ago."

Curious, Walton thought. From what he knew of Ludwig he wasn't the man to arrive early for an appointment. Walton and FitzMaugham had had plenty of dealings with him in the days before Popeek was approved, and never once had Ludwig been on time.

Walton shrugged. If Ludwig could switch his stand so decisively from an emphatic anti-Popeek to an even more emphatic pro-Popeek, perhaps he could change in other respects as well.

Walton stepped within the field of the screener. His image, he knew, was being relayed inside where FitzMaugham could scrutinize him carefully before admitting him. The director was very touchy about admitting people to his office.

Five seconds passed; it usually took no more than that for FitzMaugham to admit him. But there was no sign from within, and Walton coughed discreetly.

Still no answer. He turned away and walked over to the desk where the secretary sat dictating into a voicewrite. He waited for her to finish her sentence, then touched her arm lightly.

"Yes, Mr. Walton?"

"The screen transmission seems to be out of order. Would you mind calling Mr. FitzMaugham on the annunciator and telling him I'm here?"

"Of course, sir."

Her fingers deftly flipped the switches. He waited for her to announce him, but she paused and looked back at Walton. "He doesn't acknowledge, Mr. Walton. He must be awfully busy."

"He *has* to acknowledge. Ring him again."

"I'm sorry, sir, but—"

"*Ring him again.*"

She rang, reluctantly, without any response. FitzMaugham preferred the sort of annunciator that had to be acknowledged; Walton allowed the girl to break in on his privacy without the formality of a return buzz.

"Still no answer, sir."

Walton was growing impatient. "Okay, devil take the acknowledgement. Break in on him and tell him I'm waiting out here. My presence is important inside."

"Sir, Mr. FitzMaugham absolutely forbids anyone to use the annunciator without his acknowledgement," the girl protested.

He felt his neck going red. "I'll take the responsibility."

"I'm sorry, sir—"

"All right. Get away from the machine and let *me* talk to him. If there are repercussions, tell him I forced you at gunpoint."

She backed away, horrified, and he slid in behind the desk. He made contact; there was no acknowledgement. He said, "Mr. FitzMaugham, this is Roy. I'm outside your office now. Should I come in, or not?"

Silence. He stared thoughtfully at the apparatus.

"I'm going in there," he said.

The door was of solid-paneled imitation wood, a couple of inches thick and probably filled with a good sturdy sheet of beryllium steel. FitzMaugham liked protection.

Walton contemplated the door for a moment. Stepping into the screener field, he said, "Mr. FitzMaugham? Can you hear me?" In the ensuing silence he went on, "This is Walton. I'm outside with a blaster, and unless I get any orders to the contrary, I'm going to break into your office."

Silence. This was very extraordinary indeed. He wondered if it were part of some trap of FitzMaugham's. Well, he'd find out soon enough. He adjusted the blaster aperture to short-range wide-beam, and turned it on. A soft even flow of heat bathed the door.

Quite a crowd of curious onlookers had gathered by now, at a respectful distance. Walton maintained the steady heat. The synthetic wood was sloughing away in dribbly blue masses as the radiation broke it down; the sheet of metal in the heart of the door was gleaming bright red.

The lock became visible now. Walton concentrated the flame there, and the door creaked and groaned.

He snapped the blaster off, pocketed it, and kicked the door soundly. It swung open.

He had a momentary glimpse of a blood-soaked white head slumped over a broad desk—and then someone hit him amidships.

It was a man about his own height, wearing a blue suit woven through with glittering gold threads; Walton's mind caught the details with odd clarity. The man's face was distorted with fear and shock, but Walton recognized it clearly enough. The ruddy cheeks, the broad nose and bushy eyebrows, belonged to Ludwig.

The UN man. The man who had just assassinated Director FitzMaugham.

He was battering his fists into Walton, struggling to get past him and through the wrecked door, to escape somewhere, anywhere. Walton grunted as a fist crashed into his stomach. He reeled backward, gagging and gasping, but managed to keep his hand on the other's coat. Desperately he pulled Ludwig to him. In the suddenness of the encounter he had no time to evaluate what had happened, no time to react to FitzMaugham's murder.

His one thought was that Ludwig had to be subdued.

His fist cracked into the other's mouth; sharp pain shot up through his hand at the impact of knuckles against teeth. Ludwig sagged. Walton realized that he was blocking the doorway; not only was he preventing Ludwig from escaping, he was also making it impossible for anyone outside to come to his own aid.

Blindly he clubbed his fist down on Ludwig's neck, spun him around, crashed another blow into the man's midsection. Suddenly Ludwig pulled away from him and ran back behind the director's desk.

Walton followed him . . . and stopped short as he saw the UN man pause, quiver tremulously, and topple to the floor. He sprawled grotesquely on the deep beige carpet, shook for a moment, then was still.

Walton gasped for breath. His clothes were torn, he was sticky with sweat and blood, his heart was pounding from unaccustomed exertion.

Ludwig's killed the director, he thought leadenly. *And now Ludwig's dead.*

He leaned against the doorpost. He was conscious of

figures moving past him, going into the room, examining FitzMaugham and the figure on the floor.

"Are you all right?" a crisp, familiar voice asked.

"Pretty winded," Walton admitted.

"Have some water."

Walton accepted the drink, gulped it, looked up at the man who had spoken. "Ludwig! How in hell's name—"

"A double," the UN man said. "Come over here and look at him."

Ludwig led him to the pseudo-Ludwig on the floor. It was an incredible resemblance. Two or three of the office workers had rolled the body over; the jaws were clenched stiffly, the face frozen in an agonized mask.

"He took poison," Ludwig said. "I don't imagine he expected to get out of here alive. But he did his work well. God, I wish I'd been on time for once in my life!"

Walton glanced numbly from the dead Ludwig on the floor to the live one standing opposite him. His shocked mind realized dimly what had happened. The assassin, masked to look like Ludwig, had arrived at 1300, and had been admitted to the director's office. He had killed the old man, and then had remained inside the office, either hoping to make an escape later in the day, or perhaps simply waiting for the poison to take effect.

"It was bound to happen," Ludwig said. "They've been gunning for the senator for years. And now that Popeek was passed . . ."

Walton looked involuntarily at the desk, mirror bright and uncluttered as always. Director FitzMaugham was sprawled forward, hands half-clenched, arms spread. His impressive mane of white hair was stained with his own blood. He had been clubbed—the simplest, crudest sort of murder.

Emotional reaction began. Walton wanted to break things, to cry, to let off steam somehow. But there were too many people present; the office, once sacrosanct, had miraculously become full of Popeek workers, policemen, secretaries, possibly some telefax reporters.

Walton recovered a shred of his authority. "All of you, *outside!*" he said loudly. He recognized Sellors, the building's security chief, and added, "Except you, Sellors. You can stay here."

The crowd melted away magically. Now there were just five in the office—Sellors, Ludwig, Walton, and the two corpses.

Ludwig said, "Do you have any idea who might be behind this, Mr. Walton?"

"I don't know," he said wearily. "There are thousands who'd have wanted to kill the director. Maybe it was a Herschelite plot. There'll be a full investigation."

"Mind stepping out of the way, sir?" Sellors asked. "I'd like to take some photos."

Walton and Ludwig moved to one side as the security man went to work. It was inevitable, Walton thought, that this would happen. FitzMaugham had been the living symbol of Popeek.

He walked to the battered door, reflecting that he would have it repaired at once. That thought led naturally to a new one, but before it was fully formed in his own mind, Ludwig voiced it.

"This is a terrible tragedy," the UN man said. "But one mitigating factor exists. I'm sure Mr. FitzMaugham's successor will be a fitting one. I'm confident you'll be able to carry on FitzMaugham's great work quite capably, Mr. Walton."

Five

THE NEW SIGN on the office door said:

ROY WALTON
Interim Director
Bureau of Population Equalization

He had argued against putting it up there, on the grounds that his appointment was strictly temporary, pending a meeting of the General Assembly to choose a new head for Popeek. But Ludwig had maintained it might be weeks or months before such a meeting could be held, and that there was no harm in identifying his office.

"Everything under control?" the UN man asked.

Walton eyed him unhappily. "I guess so. Now all I have to do is start figuring out how Mr. FitzMaugham's filing system worked, and I'll be all set."

"You mean you don't know?"

"Mr. FitzMaugham took very few people into his confidence," Walton said. "Popeek was his special brainchild. He had lived with it so long he thought its workings were self-evident to everyone. There'll be a period of adjustment."

"Of course," Ludwig said.

"This conference you were going to have with the director yesterday when he—ah, what was it about?" Walton asked.

The UN man shrugged. "It's irrelevant now, I suppose. I wanted to find out how Popeek's subsidiary research lines were coming along. But I guess you'll have to go through Mr. FitzMaugham's files before you know anything, eh?" Ludwig stared at him sharply.

Suddenly, Walton did not like the cheerful UN man.

"There'll be a certain period of adjustment," he repeated. "I'll let you know when I'm ready to answer questions about Popeek."

"Of course. I didn't mean to imply any criticism of you or of the late director or of Popeek, Mr. Walton."

"Naturally. I understand, Mr. Ludwig."

Ludwig took his leave at last, and Walton was alone in the late Mr. FitzMaugham's office for the first time since the assassination. He spread his hands on the highly polished desk and twisted his wrists outward in a tense gesture. His fingers made squeaking sounds as they rubbed the wooden surface.

It had been an uneasy afternoon yesterday, after the nightmare of the assassination and the subsequent security inquisition. Walton, wrung dry, had gone home early, leaving Popeek headless for two hours. The newsblares in the jetbus had been programmed with nothing but talk of the killing.

"A brutal hand today struck down the revered D. F. FitzMaugham, eighty-one, Director of Population Equalization. Security officials report definite prospects of solution of the shocking crime, and . . ."

The other riders in the bus had been vehemently outspoken.

"It's about time they let him have it," a fat woman in sleazy old clothes said. "That baby killer!"

"I knew they'd get him sooner or later," offered a thin, wispy-haired old man. "They *had* to."

"Rumor going around he was really a Herschelite . . ."

"Some new kid is taking over Popeek, they say. They'll get him too, mark my words."

Walton, huddling in his seat, pulled up his collar, and tried to shut his ears. It didn't work.

They'll get him too, mark my words.

He hadn't forgotten that prophecy by the time he reached his cubicle in upper Manhattan. The harsh words had drifted through his restless sleep all night.

Now, behind the safety of his office door, he thought of them again.

He couldn't hide. It hadn't worked for FitzMaugham, and it wouldn't for him.

Hiding wasn't the answer. Walton smiled grimly. If martyrdom were in store for him, let martyrdom come. The work of Popeek had to go forward. He decided he would conduct as much of his official business as possible by screen; but when personal contact was necessary, he would make no attempt to avoid it.

He glanced around FitzMaugham's office. The director had been a product of the last century, and he had seen nothing ugly in the furnishings of the Cullen Building. Unlike Walton, then, he had not had his office remodeled.

That would be one of the first tasks—to replace the clumsy battery of tungsten-filament incandescents with a wall of electroluminescents, to replace the creaking sash windows with some decent opaquers, to get rid of the accursed gingerbread trimming that offended the eye in every direction. The *thunkety-thunk* air-conditioner would have to go too; he'd have a molecusorter installed in a day or two.

The redecorating problems were the minor ones. It was the task of filling FitzMaugham's giant shoes, even on an interim basis, that staggered Walton.

He fumbled in the desk for a pad and stylus. This was going to call for an agenda. Hastily he wrote:

1. *Cancel F's appointments*
2. *Investigate setup in Files*
     a) Lang terraforming project
     b) faster-than-light
     c) budget-stretchable?
     d) locate spy pickups in building
3. *Meeting with section chiefs*
4. *Press conference with telefax services*
5. *See Ludwig . . . straighten things out*
6. *Redecorate office*

He thought for a moment, then erased a few of his numbers and changed. *Press conference* to 6. and *Redecorate office* to 4. He licked the stylus and wrote in at the very top of the paper:

> *0. Finish Prior affair.*

In a way, FitzMaugham's assassination had taken Walton off the hook on the Prior case. Whatever FitzMaugham suspected about Walton's activities yesterday morning no longer need trouble him. If the director had jotted down a memorandum on the subject, Walton would be able to find and destroy it when he went through FitzMaugham's files later. And if the dead man had merely kept the matter in his head, well, then it was safely at rest in the crematorium.

Walton groped in his jacket pocket and found the note his brother had slipped to him at lunchtime the day before. In the rush of events, Walton had not had a chance to destroy it.

Now, he read it once more, ripped it in half, ripped it again, and fed one quarter of the note into the disposal chute. He would get rid of the rest at fifteen-minute intervals, and he would defy anyone monitoring the disposal units to locate all four fragments.

Actually, he realized he was being overcautious. This was Director FitzMaugham's office and FitzMaugham's disposal chute. The director wouldn't have arranged to have his *own* chute monitored, would he?

Or would he? There was never any telling, with FitzMaugham. The old man had been terribly devious in every maneuver he made.

The room had the dry, crisp smell of the detecting devices that had been used—the close-to-the-ground, ugly metering-robots that had crawled all over the floor, sniffing up footprints and stray dandruff flakes for analysis, the chemical cleansers that had mopped the blood out of the rug. Walton cursed at the air-conditioner that was so inefficiently removing these smells from the air.

The annunciator chimed. Walton waited impatiently for a voice, then remembered that FitzMaugham had doggedly required an acknowledgement. He opened the channel and said. "This is Walton. In the future no acknowledgement will be necessary."

"Yes, sir. There's a reporter from *Citizen* here, and one from Globe Telefax."

"Tell them I'm not seeing anyone today. Here, I'll give them a statement. Tell them the gargantuan task of picking up the reins where the late, great Director FitzMaugham dropped them is one that will require my full energy for the next several days. I'll be happy to hold my first official press conference as soon as Popeek is once again moving on an even keel. Got that?"

"Yes, sir."

"Good. Make sure they print it. And—oh, listen. If anyone shows up today or tomorrow who had an appointment with Director FitzMaugham, tell him approximately the same thing. Not in those flowery words, of course, but give him the gist of it. I've got a lot of catching up to do before I can see people."

"Certainly, Director Walton."

He grinned at the sound of those words, *Director Wal-*

ton. Turning away from the annunciator, he took out his agenda and checked off number one, *Cancel FitzMaugham's appointments.*

Frowning, he realized he had better add a seventh item to the list: *Appoint new assistant administrator.* Someone would have to handle his old job.

But now, top priority went to the item ticketed zero on the list: *Finish Prior affair.* He'd never be in a better position to erase the evidence of yesterday's illegality than he was right now.

"Connect me with euthanasia files, please."

A moment later a dry voice said, "Files."

"Files, this is Acting Director Walton. I'd like a complete transcript of your computer's activities for yesterday morning between 0900 and 1200, with each separate activity itemized. How soon can I have it?"

"Within minutes, Director Walton."

"Good. Send it sealed, by closed circuit. There's some top-level stuff on that transcript. If the seal's not intact when it gets here, I'll shake up the whole department."

"Yes, sir. Anything else, sir?"

"No, that'll be—on second thought, yes. Send up a list of all doctors who were examining babies in the clinic yesterday morning."

He waited. While he waited, he went through the top layer of memoranda in FitzMaugham's desk.

There was a note on top which read, *Appointment with Lamarrre, 11 June—1215. Must be firm with him, and must handle with great delicacy. Perhaps time to let Walton know.*

Hmm, that was interesting, Walton thought. He had no idea who Lamarre might be, but FitzMaugham had drawn a spidery little star in the upper-right-hand corner of the memo sheet, indicating crash priority.

He flipped on the annunciator. "There's a Mr. Lamarre who had an appointment with Director FitzMaugham for 1215 today. If he calls, tell him I can't see him today but will honor the appointment tomorrow at the same time. If he shows up, tell him the same thing."

His watch said it was time to dispose of another fragment of Fred's message. He stuffed it into the disposal chute.

A moment later the green light flashed over the arrival bin; FitzMaugham had not been subject, as Walton had been in his previous office, to cascades of material arriving without warning.

Walton drew a sealed packet from the bin. He examined the seal and found it untampered, which was good; it meant the packet had come straight from the computer, and had not even been read by the technician in charge. With it was a typed list of five names—the doctors who had been in the lab the day before.

Breaking open the packet, Walton discovered seven closely-typed sheets with a series of itemized actions on them. He ran through them quickly, discarding sheets one, two, and three, which dealt with routine activities of the computer in the early hours of the previous day.

Item seventy-three was his request for Philip Prior's record card. He checked that one off.

Item seventy-four was his requisition for the key to the clinic's gene-sorting code.

Item seventy-five was his revision of Philip Prior's records, omitting all reference to his tubercular condition and to the euthanasia recommendation. Item seventy-six was the acknowledgement of this revision.

Item seventy-seven was his request for the boy's record card—this time, the amended one. The five items were dated and timed; the earliest was 1025, the latest 1037, all on June tenth.

Walton bracketed the five items thoughtfully, and scanned the rest of the page. Nothing of interest there, just more routine business. But item ninety-two, timed at 1102, was an intriguing one:

92: *Full transcript of morning's transactions issued at request of Dr. Frederic Walton, 932K104AZ.*

Fred hadn't been bluffing, then; he actually had possession of all the damning evidence. But when one dealt with a computer and with Donnerson micro-memory-tubes, the past was an extremely fluid entity.

"I want a direct line to the computer on floor twenty," he said.

After a brief lag a technician appeared on the screen. It was the same one he had spoken to earlier.

"There's been an error in the records," Walton said. "An error I wouldn't want to perpetuate. Will you set me up so I can feed a direct order into the machine?"

"Certainly, sir. Go ahead, sir."

"This is top secret. Vanish."

The technician vanished. Walton said, "Items seventy-three through seventy-seven on yesterday morning's record tape are to be deleted, and the information carried in those tubes is to be deleted as well. Furthermore, there is to be no record made of this transaction."

The voicewrite on floor twenty clattered briefly, and the order funneled into the computer. Walton waited a moment, tensely. Then he said, "All right, technician. Come back in where I can see you."

The technician appeared. Walton said, "I'm running a check now. Have the machine prepare another transcript of yesterday's activities between 0900 and 1200 and also one of today's doings for the last fifteen minutes."

"Right away, sir."

While he waited for the new transcripts to arrive, Walton studied the list of names on his desk. Five doctors— Gunther, Raymond, Archer, Hsi, Rein. He didn't know which one of them had examined the Prior baby, nor did he care to find out. All five would have to be transferred.

Meticulously, he took up his stylus and pad again, and plotted a destination for each:

Gunther . . . Zurich.

Raymond . . . Glasgow.

Archer . . . Tierra del Fuego.

Hsi . . . Leopoldville.

Rein . . . Bangkok.

He nodded. That was optimum dissemination; he would put through notice of the transfers later in the day, and by nightfall the men would be on their way to their new scenes of operation. Perhaps they would never understand why they had been uprooted and sent away from New York.

The new transcripts arrived. Impatiently Walton checked through them.

In the June tenth transcript, item seventy-one dealt

with smallpox statistics for North America 1822-68, and item seventy-two with the tally of antihistamine supply for requisitions for Clinic Three. There was no sign of any of Walton's requests. They had vanished from the record as completely as if they had never been.

Walton searched carefully through the June eleventh transcript for any mention of his deletion order. No, that hadn't been recorded either.

He smiled, his first honest smile since FitzMaugham's assassination. Now, with the computer records erased, the director dead, and the doctors on their way elsewhere, only Fred stood in the way of his chance of escaping punishment for the Prior business.

He decided he'd have to take his chances with Fred. Perhaps brotherly love would seal his lips after all.

Six

THE LATE Director FitzMaugham's files were spread over four floors of the building, but for Walton's purposes the only ones that mattered were those to which access was gained through the director's office alone.

A keyboard and screen were set into the wall to the left of the desk. Walton let his fingers rest lightly on the gleaming keys.

The main problem facing him, he thought, lay in not knowing where to begin. Despite his careful agenda, despite the necessary marshaling of his thoughts, he was still confused by the enormity of his job. The seven billion people of the world were in his hands. He could transfer fifty thousand

New Yorkers to the bleak northern provinces of underpopulated Canada with the same quick ease that he had shifted five unsuspecting doctors half an hour before.

After a few moments of uneasy thought he pecked out the short message, *Request complete data file on terraforming project.*

On the screen appeared the words, *Acknowledged and coded; prepare to receive.*

The arrival bin thrummed with activity. Walton hastily scooped out a double handful of typed sheets to make room for more. He grinned in anguish as the paper kept on coming. FitzMaugham's files on terraforming, no doubt, covered reams and reams.

Staggering, he carted it all over to his desk and began to skim through it. The data began thirty years earlier, in 2202, with a photostat of a letter from Dr. Herbert Lang to FitzMaugham, proposing a project whereby the inner planets of the solar system could be made habitable by human beings.

Appended to that was FitzMaugham's skeptical, slightly mocking reply; the old man had kept everything, it seemed, even letters which showed him in a bad light.

After that came more letters from Lang, urging FitzMaugham to plead terraforming's case before the United States Senate, and FitzMaugham's increasingly more enthusiastic answers. Finally, in 2212, a notation that the Senate had voted a million-dollar appropriation to Lang—a minuscule amount, in terms of the overall need, but it was enough to cover preliminary research. Lang had been grateful.

Walton skimmed through more-or-less familiar documents on the nature of the terraforming project. He could study those in detail later, if time permitted. What he wanted now was information on the current status of the project; FitzMaugham had been remarkably silent about it, though the public impression had been created that a team of engineers headed by Lang was already at work on Venus.

He shoved whole handfuls of letters to one side, looking for those of recent date.

Here was one dated 1 Feb 2232, FitzMaugham to Lang: it informed the scientist that passage of the Equalization Act was imminent, and that Lang stood to get a substantial appropriation from the UN in that event. A jubilant reply from Lang was attached.

Following that came another, 10 May 2232, FitzMaugham to Lang: official authorization of Lang as an executive member of Popeek, and appropriation of— Walton's eyes bugged—five billion dollars for terraforming research.

Note from Lang to FitzMaugham, 14 May: the terraforming crew was leaving for Venus immediately.

Note from FitzMaugham to Lang, 16 May: best wishes, and Lang was instructed to contact FitzMaugham without fail at weekly intervals.

Spacegram from Lang to FitzMaugham, 28 May; arrived at Venus safely, preparing operation as scheduled.

The file ended there. Walton rummaged through the huge heap, hoping to discover a later communiqué; by FitzMaugham's own request, Lang should have contacted Popeek about four days ago with his first report.

Possibly it had gone astray in delivery, Walton thought. He spent twenty minutes digging through the assorted material before remembering that he could get a replacement within seconds from the filing computer.

He typed out a requisition for any and all correspondence between Director FitzMaugham and Dr. Herbert Lang that was dated after 28 May 2232.

The machine acknowledged, and a moment later replied, *This material is not included in memory banks.*

Walton frowned, gathered up most of his superfluous terraforming data, and deposited it in a file drawer. The status of the project, then, was uncertain: the terraformers were on Venus and presumably at work, but were yet to be heard from.

The next Popeek project to tack down would be the faster-than-light spaceship drive. But after the mass of data Walton had just absorbed, he found himself hesitant to wade through another collection so soon.

He realized that he was hungry for the sight of another human being. He had spent the whole morning alone, speaking to anonymous underlings via screen or annunciator, and requisitioning material from an even more impersonal computer. He wanted noise, life, people around him.

He snapped on the annunciator. "I'm calling an immediate meeting of the Popeek section chiefs," he said. "In my office, in half an hour—at 1230 sharp. Tell them to drop whatever they're doing and come."

Just before they started to arrive, Walton felt a sudden

sick wave of tension sweep dizzyingly over him. He pulled open the top drawer of his new desk and reached for his tranquilizer tablets. He suffered a moment of shock and disorientation before he realized that this was FitzMaugham's desk, not his own, and that FitzMaugham forswore all forms of sedation.

Chuckling nervously, Walton drew out his wallet and extracted the extra benzolurethrin he carried for just such emergencies. He popped the lozenge into his mouth only a moment before the spare figure of Lee Percy, first of the section chiefs to arrive, appeared in the screener outside the door.

"Roy? It's me—Percy."

"I can see you. Come on in, Lee."

Percy was in charge of public relations for Popeek. He was a tall, angular man with thick corrugated features.

After him came Teddy Schaunhaft, clinic coordinator; Pauline Medhurst, personnel director; Olaf Eglin, director of field agents; and Sue Llewellyn, Popeek's comptroller.

These five had constituted the central council of Popeek. Walton, as assistant administrator, had served as their coordinator, as well as handling population transfer and serving as a funnel for red tape. Above them all had been FitzMaugham, brooding over his charges like an untroubled Wotan; FitzMaugham had reserved for himself, aside from the task of general supervision, the special duties attendant on handling the terraforming and faster-than-light wings of Popeek.

"I should have called you together much earlier than this," Walton said when they were settled. "The shock, though, and the general confusion—"

"We understand, Roy," said Sue Llewellyn sympathetically. She was a chubby little woman in her fifties, whose private life was reported to be incredibly at variance with her pleasantly domestic appearance. "It's been rough on all of us, but you were so close to Mr. FitzMaugham. . . ."

There was sympathetic clucking from various corners of the room. Walton said, "The period of mourning will have to be a brief one. What I'm suggesting is that business continue as usual, without a hitch." He glanced at Eglin, the director of field agents. "Olaf, is there a man in your section capable of handling your job?"

Eglin looked astonished for a moment, then mastered himself. "There must be five, at least. Walters, Lassen, Dominic—"

"Skip the catalogue," Walton told him. "Pick the man you think is best suited to replace you, and send his dossier up to me for approval."

"And where do *I* go?"

"You take over my slot as assistant administrator. As director of field agents, you're more familiar with the immediate problems of my old job than anyone else here."

Eglin preened himself smugly. Walton wondered if he had made an unwise choice; Eglin was competent enough, and would give forth one hundred percent effort at all times—but probably never the one hundred two percent a really great administrator could put out when necessary.

Still, the post had to be filled at once, and Eglin could pick up the reins faster than any of the others.

Walton looked around. "Otherwise, activities of Popeek will continue as under Mr. FitzMaugham, without a hitch. Any questions?"

Lee Percy raised an arm slowly. "Roy, I've got a problem I'd like to bring up here, as long as we're all together. There's a growing public sentiment that you and the late director were secretly Herschelites." He chuckled apologetically. "I know it sounds silly, but I just report what I hear."

"I'm familiar with the rumor," Walton said. "And I don't like it much, either. That's the sort of stuff riots are made of." The Herschelites were extremists who advocated wholesale sterilization of defectives, mandatory birth control, and half a dozen other stringent remedies for overpopulation.

"What steps are you taking to counteract it?" Walton asked.

"Well," said Percy, "we're preparing a memorial program for FitzMaugham which will intimate that he was murdered by the Hershelites, who hated him."

"Good. What's the slant?"

"That he was too easygoing, too humane. We build up the Herschelites as ultrareactionaries who intend to enforce their will on humanity if they get the chance, and imply FitzMaugham was fighting them tooth and nail. We close the show with some shots of you picking up the great man's mantle, etcetera, etcetera. And a short speech from you affirming the basically humanitarian aims of Popeek."

Walton smiled approvingly and said, "I like it. When do you want me to do the speech?"

"We won't need you," Percy told him. "We've got plenty of stock footage, and we can whip the speech out of some spare syllables you left around."

Walton frowned. Too many of the public speeches of the day were synthetic, created by skilled engineers who split words into their component phonemes and reassembled them in any shape they pleased. "Let me check through my speech before you put it over, at least."

"Will do. And we'll squash this Herschelite thing right off the bat."

Pauline Medhurst squirmed uneasily in her chair. Walton caught the hint and recognized her.

"Uh, Roy, I don't know if this is the time or the place, but I got that transfer order of yours, the five doctors . . ."

"You did? Good," Walton said hurriedly. "Have you notified them yet?"

"Yes. They seemed unhappy about it."

"Refer them to FitzMaugham's book. Tell them they're cogs in a mighty machine, working to save humanity. We can't let personal considerations interfere, Pauline."

"If you could only explain why—"

"Yeah," interjected Schaunhaft, the clinic coordinator suddenly. "You cleaned out my whole morning lab shift down there. I was wondering—"

Walton felt like a stag at bay. "Look," he said firmly, cutting through the hubbub, "*I* made the transfer. I had reasons for doing it. It's your job to get the five men out where they've been assigned, and to get five new men in here at once. You're not required to make explanations to them—nor I to you."

Sudden silence fell over the office. Walton hoped he had not been too forceful, and cast suspicion on his actions by his stiffness.

"Whew!" Sue Llewellyn said. "You really mean business!"

"I said we were going to run Popeek without a hitch,"

Walton replied. "Just because you know my first name, that doesn't mean I'm not going to be as strong a director as FitzMaugham was."

Until the UN picks my successor, his mind added. Out loud he said, "Unless you have any further questions, I'll ask you now to return to your respective sections."

He sat slumped at his desk after they were gone, trying to draw on some inner reserve of energy for the strength to go on.

One day at the job, and he was tired, terribly tired. And it would be six weeks or more before the United Nations convened to choose the next director of Popeek.

He didn't know who that man would be. He expected they would offer the job to him, provided he did competent work during the interim; but, wearily, he saw he would have to turn the offer down.

It was not only that his nerves couldn't handle the grinding daily tension of the job; he saw now what Fred might be up to, and it stung.

What if his brother were to hold off exposing him until the moment the UN proffered its appointment . . . and then took that moment to reveal that the head of Popeek, far from being an iron-minded Herschelite, had actually been guilty of an irregularity that transgressed against one of Popeek's own operations? He'd be finished. He'd be laughed out of public life for good—and probably prosecuted in the bargain—if Fred exposed him.

And Fred was perfectly capable of doing just that.

Walton saw himself spinning dizzily between conflicting alternatives. Keep the job and face his brother's exposé?

Or resign, and vanish into anonymity? Neither choice seemed too appealing.

Shrugging, he dragged himself out of his chair, determined to shroud his conflict behind the mask of work. He typed a request to Files, requisitioning data on the faster-than-light project.

Moments later, the torrent began—rising from somewhere in the depths of the giant computer, rumbling upward through the conveyor system, moving onward toward the twenty-ninth floor and the office of Interim Director Walton.

Seven

THE next morning there was a crowd gathered before the Cullen Building when Walton arrived.

There must have been at least a hundred people, fanning outward from a central focus. Walton stepped from the jet-bus and, with collar pulled up carefully to obscure as much of his face as possible, went to investigate.

A small red-faced man stood on a rickety chair against the side of the building. He was flanked by a pair of brass flagpoles, one bearing the American flag and the other the ensign of the United Nations. His voice was a biting rasp— probably, thought Walton, intensified, sharpened, and made more irritating by a harmonic modulator at his throat.

An irritating voice put its message across twice as fast as a pleasant one.

He was shouting, "This is the place! Up here, in this building, that's where they are! That's where Popeek wastes our money!"

From the slant of the man's words Walton instantly thought: *Herschelite!*

He repressed his anger and, for once, decided to stay and hear the extremist out. He had never really paid much attention to Herschelite propaganda—he had been exposed to little of it—and he realized that now, as head of Popeek, he owed it to himself to become familiar with the anti-Popeek arguments of both extremist factions—those who insisted Popeek was a tyranny, and the Herschelites, who thought it was too weak.

"This Popeek," the little man said, accenting the awkwardness of the word. "You know what it is? It's a stopgap. It's a silly, soft-minded, half-hearted attempt at solving our problems. It's a fake, a fraud, a phony!"

There was real passion behind the words. Walton distrusted small men with deep wells of passion; he no more enjoyed their company than he did that of a dynamo or an atomic pile. They were always threatening to explode.

The crowd was stirring restlessly. The Herschelite was getting to them, one way or another. Walton drew back nervously, not wanting to be recognized, and stationed himself at the fringe of the crowd.

"Some of you don't like Popeek for this reason or that reason. But let me tell you something, friends . . . you're wronger than they are! We've got to get tough with ourselves! We have to face the truth! Popeek is an unrealistic half-solution to man's problems. Until we limit birth, establish rigid controls over who's going to live and who isn't, we—"

It was straight Herschelite propaganda, undiluted. Walton wasn't surprised when someone in the audience interrupted, growling, "And who's going to set those controls? You?"

"You trusted yourselves to Popeek, didn't you? Why hesitate, then, to trust yourselves to Abel Herschel and his group of workers for the betterment and purification of mankind?"

Walton was almost limp with amazement. The Herschelite group was so much more drastic in its approach than Popeek that he wondered how they dared come out with those views in public. Animosity was high enough against Popeek; would the public accept a group more stringent yet?

The little man's voice rose high. "Onward with the Herschelites! Mankind must move forward! The Equalization people represent the forces of decay and sloth!"

Walton turned to the man next to him and murmured, "But Herschel's a fanatic. They'll kill all of us in the name of mankind."

The man looked puzzled; then, accepting the idea, he nodded. "Yeah, buddy. You know, you may have something there."

That was all the spark needed. Walton edged away surreptitiously and watched it spread through the crowd, while the little man's harangue grew more and more inflammatory.

Until a rock arced through the air from somewhere, whipped across the billowing UN flag, and cracked into the side of the building, That was the signal.

A hundred men and women converged on the little man on the battered chair. "*We have to face the truth!*" the harsh voice cried; then the flags were swept down, trampled on. Flagpoles fell, ringing metallically on the concrete; the chair toppled. The little man was lost beneath a tide of remorseless feet and arms.

A siren screamed.

"Cops!" Walton yelled from his vantage point some thirty feet away, and abruptly the crowd melted away in all directions, leaving Walton and the little man alone on the street. A security wagon drew up. Four men in gray uniforms sprang out.

"What's been going on here? Who's this man?" Then, seeing Walton, "Hey! Come over here!"

"Of course, officer." Walton turned his collar down and drew near. He spotted the glare of a ubiquitous video camera and faced it squarely. "I'm Director Walton of Popeek," he said loudly, into the camera. "I just arrived here a few minutes ago. I saw the whole thing."

"Tell us about it, Mr. Walton," the security man said.

"It was a Herschelite." Walton gestured at the broken body crumpled against the ground. "He was delivering an inflammatory speech aimed against Popeek, with special reference to the late Director FitzMaugham and myself. I was about to summon you and end the disturbance, when the listeners became aware that the man was a Herschelite. When they understood what he was advocating, they—well, you see the result."

"Thank you, sir. Terribly sorry we couldn't have prevented it. Must be very unpleasant, Mr. Walton."

"The man was asking for trouble," Walton said. "Popeek represents the minds and hearts of the world. Herschel and his people seek to overthrow this order. I can't condone violence of any sort, naturally, but"—he smiled into the camera—"Popeek is a sacred responsibility to me. Its enemies I must regard as blind and misguided people."

He turned and entered the building, feeling pleased with himself. That sequence would be shown globally on the next news screenings; every newsblare in the world would be reporting his words.

Lee Percy would be proud of him. Without benefit either of rehearsal or phonemic engineering, Walton had delivered a rousing speech and turned a grisly incident into a major propaganda instrument.

And more than that, Director FitzMaugham would have been proud of him.

But beneath the glow of pride, he was trembling. Yesterday he had saved a boy by a trifling alteration of his genetic record; today he had killed a man by sending a whispered accusation rustling through a mob.

Power. Popeek represented power, perhaps the greatest power in the world. That power would have to be channeled somehow, now that it had been unleashed.

The stack of papers relating to the superspeed space drive was still on his desk when he entered the office. He had had time yesterday to read through just some of the earliest; then, the pressure of routine had dragged him off to other duties.

Encouraged by FitzMaugham, the faster-than-light project had originated about a decade or so before. It stemmed from the fact that the ion-drive used for travel between planets had a top velocity, a limiting factor of about ninety thousand miles per second. At that rate it would take some eighteen years for a scouting party to visit the closest star and report back . . . not very efficient for a planet in a hurry to expand outward.

A group of scientists had set to work developing a subspace warp drive, one that would cut across the manifold of normal space and allow speeds above light velocity.

All the records were here: the preliminary trials, the budget allocations, the sketches and plans, the names of the researchers. Walton ploughed painstakingly through them, learning names, assimilating scientific data. It seemed that, while it was still in its early stages, FitzMaugham had nurtured the project along with money from his personal fortune.

For most of the morning Walton leafed through documents describing projected generators, types of hull material, specifications, speculations. It was nearly noon when he came across the neatly-typed note from Colonel Leslie McLeod, one of the military scientists in charge of the ultra-drive project. Walton read it through once, gasped, and read it again.

It was dated 14 June 2231, almost one year ago. It read:

My dear Mr. FitzMaugham:
I'm sure it will gladden you to learn that we have
at last achieved success in our endeavors. The X-72

*passed its last tests splendidly, and we are ready to
leave on the preliminary scouting flight at once.*

McLeod

It was followed by a note from FitzMaugham to
McLeod, dated 15 June:

Dr. McLeod:
   *All best wishes on your great adventure, I trust
you'll be departing, as usual, from the Nairobi base
within the next few days. Please let me hear from
you before departure.*

FitzM.

The file concluded with a final note from McLeod to the
director, dated 19 June 2231:

My dear Mr. FitzMaugham:
   *The X-72 will leave Nairobi in eleven hours,
bound outward, manned by a crew of sixteen, including myself. The men are all impatient for the
departure. I must offer my hearty thanks for the
help you have given us over the past years, without
which we would never have reached this step.*
   *Flight plans include visiting several of the nearer
stars, with the intention of returning either as soon
as we have discovered a habitable extra-solar
world, or one year after departure, whichever first
occurs.*
   Sincere good wishes, and may you have as much

success when you plead your case before the United Nations as we have had here—though you'll forgive me for hoping that our work might make any population equalization program on Earth totally superfluous!

McLeod

Walton stared at the three notes for a moment, so shocked he was unable to react. So a faster-than-light drive was not merely a hoped-for dream, but an actuality—with the first scouting mission a year absent already!

He felt a new burst of admiration for FitzMaugham. What a marvelous old scoundrel he had been!

Faster-than-light achieved, and the terraforming group on Venus, and neither fact released to the public . . . or even specifically given to FitzMaugham's own staff, his alleged confidants.

It had been shrewd of him, all right. He had made sure nothing could go wrong. If something happened to Lang and his crew on Venus—and it was quite possible, since word from them was a week overdue—it would be easy to say that the terraforming project was still in the planning stage. In the event of success, the excuse was that word of their progress had been withheld for "security reasons."

And the same would apply to the space drive; if McLeod and his men vanished into the nether regions of interstellar space and never returned, FitzMaugham would not have had to answer for the failure of a project which, as far as the public knew, was still in the planning stage. It was a double-edged sword with the director controlling both edges.

The annunciator chimed. "Dr. Lamarre is here for his appointment with you, Mr. Walton."

Walton was caught off guard. His mind raced furiously. *Lamarre? Who the dickens—oh, that left-over appointment of FitzMaugham's.*

"Tell Dr. Lamarre I'll be glad to see him in just a few minutes, please. I'll buzz you when I'm ready."

Hurriedly he gathered up the space-flight documents and jammed them in a file drawer near the data on terraforming. He surveyed his office; it looked neat, presentable. Glancing around, he made sure no stray documents were visible, documents which might reveal the truth about the space drive.

"Send in Dr. Lamarre," he said.

Dr. Lamarre was a short, thin, pale individual, with an uncertain wave in his sandy hair and a slight stoop of his shoulders. He carried a large, black leather portfolio which seemed on the point of exploding.

"Mr. Walton?"

"That's right. You're Dr. Lamarre?"

The small man handed him an engraved business card.

T. ELLIOT LAMARRE
Gerontologist

Walton fingered the card uneasily and returned it to its owner. "Gerontologist? One who studies ways of increasing the human life span?"

"Precisely."

Walton frowned. "I presume you've had some previous dealings with the late Director FitzMaugham?"

Lamarre gaped. "You mean he didn't *tell* you?"

"Director FitzMaugham shared very little information with his assistants, Dr. Lamarre. The suddenness of my elevation to this post gave me little time to explore his files. Would you mind filling me in on the background?"

"Of course." Lamarre crossed his legs and squinted myopically across the desk at Walton. "To be brief, Mr. FitzMaugham first heard of my work fourteen years ago. Since that time, he's supported my experiments with private grants of his own, public appropriations whenever possible, and lately with money supplied by Popeek. Naturally, because of the nature of my work I've shunned publicity. I completed my final tests last week, and was to have seen the director yesterday. But—"

"I know. I was busy going through Mr. FitzMaugham's files when you called yesterday. I didn't have time to see anyone." Walton wished he had checked on this man Lamarre earlier. Apparently it was a private project of FitzMaugham's and of some importance.

"May I ask what this 'work' of yours consists of?"

"Certainly. Mr. FitzMaugham expressed a hope that someday man's life span might be infinitely extended. I'm happy to report that I have developed a simple technique which will provide just that." The little man smiled in self-satisfaction. "In short," he said, "what I have developed, in everyday terms, is immortality, Mr. Walton."

Eight

WALTON WAS becoming hardened to astonishment; the further he excavated into the late director's affairs, the less susceptible he was to the visceral reaction of shock.

Still, this stunned him for a moment.

"Did you say you'd perfected this technique?" he asked slowly. "Or that it was still in the planning stage?"

Lamarre tapped the thick, glossy black portfolio. "In here. I've got it all." He seemed ready to burst with self-satisfaction.

Walton leaned back, spread his fingers against the surface of the desk, and wrinkled his forehead. "I've had this job since 1300 on the tenth, Mr. Lamarre. That's exactly two days ago, minus half an hour. And in that time I don't think

I've had less than ten major shocks and half a dozen minor ones."

"Sir?"

"What I'm getting at is this: just why did Director FitzMaugham sponsor this project of yours?"

Lamarre looked blank. "Because the director was a great humanitarian, of course. Because he felt that the human life span was short, far too short, and he wished his fellow men to enjoy long life. What other reason should there be?"

"I know FitzMaugham was a great man . . . I was his secretary for three years." (*Though he never said a word about you, Dr. Lamarre*, Walton thought.) "But to develop immortality at this stage of man's existence . . ." Walton shook his head. "Tell me about your work, Dr. Lamarre."

"It's difficult to sum up readily. I've fought degeneration of the body on the cellular level, and my tests show a successful outcome. Phagocyte stimulation combined with—the data's all here, Mr. Walton. I needn't run through it for you."

He began to hunt in the portfolio, fumbling for something. After a moment he extracted a folded quarto sheet, spread it out, and nudged it across the desk toward Walton.

The director glanced at the sheet; it was covered with chemical equations. "Spare me the technical details, Dr. Lamarre. Have you tested your treatment yet?"

"With the only test possible, the test of time. There are insects in my laboratories that have lived five years or more—veritable Methuselahs of their genera. Immortality is not something one can test in less than infinte time. But beneath the microscope, one can see the cells regenerating, one can see decay combated. . . ."

Walton took a deep breath. "Are you aware, Dr. Lamarre, that for the benefit of humanity I really should have you shot at once?"

"*What?*"

Walton nearly burst out laughing; the man looked outrageously funny with that look of shocked incomprehension on his face. "Do you understand what immortality would do to Earth?" he asked. "With no other planet of the solar system habitable by man, and none of the stars within reach? Within a generation we'd be living ten to the square inch. We'd—"

"Director FitzMaugham was aware of these things," Lamarre interrupted sharply. "He had no intention of administering my discovery wholesale to the populace. What's more, he was fully confident that a faster-than-light space drive would soon let us reach the planets, and that the terraforming engineers would succeed with their work on Venus."

"Those two factors are still unknowns in the equation," Walton said. "Neither has succeeded, as of now. And we can't possibly let word of your discovery get out until there are avenues to handle the overflow of population already on hand."

"So you propose—"

"To confiscate the notes you have with you, and to insist that you remain silent about this serum of yours until I give you permission to announce it."

"And if I refuse?"

Walton spread his hands. "Dr. Lamarre, I'm a reasonable man trying to do a very hard job. You're a scientist—and a sane one, I hope. I'd appreciate your cooperation. Bear with me a few weeks, and then perhaps the situation will change."

Awkward silence followed. Finally Lamarre said, "Very well. If you'll return my notes, I promise to keep silent until you give me permission to speak."

"That won't be enough. I'll need to keep the notes."

Lamarre sighed. "If you insist," he said.

When he was again alone, Walton stored the thick portfolio in a file drawer and stared at it quizzically.

FitzMaugham, he thought, *you were incredible!*

Lamarre's immortality serum, or whatever it was, was deadly. Whether it actually worked or not was irrelevant. If word ever escaped that an immortality drug existed, there would be rioting and death on a vast scale.

FitzMaugham had certainly seen that, and yet he had sublimely underwritten development of the serum, knowing that if terraforming and the ultradrive project should fail, Lamarre's project represented a major threat to civilization.

Well, Lamarre had knuckled under to Walton willingly enough. The problem now was to contact Lang on Venus and find out what was happening up there. . . .

"Mr. Walton," said the annunciator. "There's a coded message arrived for Director FitzMaugham."

"Where from?"

"From space, sir. They say they have news, but they

won't give it to anyone but Mr. FitzMaugham."

Walton cursed. "Where is this message being received?"

"Floor twenty-three, sir. Communications."

"Tell them I'll be right down," Walton snapped.

He caught a lift tube and arrived on the twenty-third floor moments later. No sooner had the tube door opened than he sprang out, dodging around a pair of startled technicians, and sprinted down the corridor toward Communications.

Here throbbed the network that held the branches of Popeek together. From here the screens were powered, the annunciators were linked, the phones connected.

Walton pushed open a door marked *Communications Central* and confronted four busy engineers who were crowded around a complex receiving mechanism.

"Where's that space message?" he demanded of the sallow young engineer who approached him.

"Still coming in, sir. They're repeating it over and over. We're triangulating their position now. Somewhere near the orbit of Pluto, Mr. Walton."

"Devil with that. Where's the message?"

Someone handed him a slip of paper. It said, *Calling Earth. Urgent call, top urgency, crash urgency. Will communicate only with D. F. FitzMaugham.*

"This all it is?" Walton asked. "No signature, no ship name?"

"That's right, Mr. Walton."

"Okay. Find them in a hurry and send them a return message. Tell them FitzMaugham's dead and I'm his successor. Mention me by name."

"Yes, sir."

He stamped impatiently around the lab while they set to work beaming the message into the void. Space communication was a field that dazzled and bewildered Walton, and he watched in awe as they swung into operation.

Time passed. "You know of any ships supposed to be in that sector?" he asked someone.

"No, sir. We weren't expecting any calls except from Lang on Venus—" The technician gasped, realizing he had made a slip, and turned pale.

"That's all right," Walton assured him. "I'm the director, remember? I know all about Lang."

"Of course, sir."

"Here's a reply, sir," another of the nameless, faceless technicians said. Walton scanned it.

It read, *Hello Walton. Request further identification before we report. McL.*

A little shudder of satisfaction shook Walton at the sight of the initialed *McL.* at the end of the message. That could mean only McLeod—and *that* could mean only one thing: the experimental starship had returned!

Walton realized depressedly that this probably implied that they hadn't found any Earth-type worlds among the stars. McLeod's note to FitzMaugham had said they would search for a year, and would return home at the end of that time if they had no success. And just about a year had elapsed.

He said, "Send this return message: McLeod, Nairobi, X-72. Congratulations! Walton."

The technician vanished again, leaving Walton alone. He gazed moodily at the complex maze of equipment all around him, listened to the steady *tick-tick* of the communication devices, strained his ears to pick up fragments of conversation from the men.

After what seemed like an hour, the technician returned. "There's a message coming through now, sir. We're decoding it as fast as we can."

"Make it snappy," Walton said. His watch read 1429. Only twenty minutes had passed since he had gone down there.

A grimy sheet of paper was thrust under his nose. He read it:

> *Hello Walton, this is McLeod. Happy to report that experimental ship X-72 is returning home with all hands in good shape, after a remarkable one-year cruise of the galaxy. I feel like Ulysses returning to Ithaca, except we didn't have such a hard time of it.*
>
> *I imagine you'll be interested in this: we found a perfectly lovely and livable world in the Procyon system. No intelligent life at all, and incredibly fine climate. Pity old FitzMaugham couldn't have lived to hear about it. Be seeing you soon. McLeod.*

Walton's hands were still shaking as he pressed the actuator that would let him back into his office. He would have to call another meeting of the section chiefs again, to discuss the best method of presenting this exciting news to the world.

For one thing, they would have to explain away

FitzMaugham's failure to reveal that the X-72 had been sent out over a year ago. That could be easily handled.

Then, there would have to be a careful build-up: descriptions of the new world, profiles of the heroes who had found it, etcetera. Someone was going to have to work out a plan for emigration . . . unless the resourceful Fitz-Maugham had already drawn up such a plan and stowed it in Files for just this anticipated day.

And then, perhaps Lamarre could be called back now, and allowed to release his discovery. Plans buzzed in Walton's mind: in the event that people proved reluctant to leave Earth and conquer an unknown world, no matter how tempting the climate, it might be feasible to dangle immortality before them—to restrict Lamarre's treatment to volunteer colonists, or something along that line. There was plenty of time to figure that out, Walton thought.

He stepped into his office and locked the door behind him. A glow of pleasure surrounded him; for once it seemed that things were heading in the right direction. He was happy, in a way, that FitzMaugham was no longer in charge. Now, with mankind on the threshold of—

Walton blinked. *Did I leave that file drawer open when I left the office?* he wondered. He was usually more cautious than that.

The file was definitely open now, as were the two cabinets adjoining it. Numbly he swung the cabinet doors wider, peered into the shadows, groped inside.

The drawers containing the documents pertaining to terraforming and to McLeod's space drive seemed intact. But the cabinet in which Walton had placed Lamarre's portfolio—that cabinet was totally empty!

Someone's been in here, he thought angrily. And then the anger changed to agony as hé remembered what had been in Lamarre's portfolio, and what would happen if that formula were loosed indiscriminately in the world.

Nine

THE ODD PART of it, Walton thought, was that there was absolutely nothing he could do.

He could call Sellors and give him a roasting for not guarding his office properly, but that wouldn't restore the missing portfolio.

He could send out a general alarm, and thereby let the world know that there was such a thing as Lamarre's formula. That would be catastrophic.

Walton slammed the cabinet shut and spun the lock. Then, heavily, he dropped into his chair and rested his head in his arms. All the jubilation of a few moments before had suddenly melted into dull apprehension.

Suspects? Just two—Lamarre, and Fred. Lamarre because he was obvious; Fred because he was likely to do anything to hurt his brother.

"Give me Sellors in security," Walton said quietly.

Sellors' bland face appeared on the screen. He blinked at the sight of Walton, causing Walton to wonder just how ghastly his own appearance was; even with the executive filter touching up the transmitted image, sprucing him up and falsifying him for the public benefit, he probably looked dreadful.

"Sellors, I want you to send out a general order for a Dr. Lamarre. You'll find his appearance recorded on the entrance tapes for today; he came to see me earlier. The first name is—ah—Elliot. T. Elliot Lamarre, gerontologist. I don't know where he lives."

"What should I do when I find him, sir?"

"Bring him here at once. And if you catch him at home, slap a seal on his door. He may be in possession of some very important secret documents."

"Yes, sir."

"And get hold of the doorsmith who repaired my office door; I want the lock calibration changed at once."

"Certainly, sir."

The screen faded. Walton turned back to his desk and busied himself in meaningless paper work, trying to keep himself from thinking.

A few moments later the screen brightened again. It was Fred.

Walton stared coldly at his brother's image. "Well?"

Fred chuckled. "Why so pale and wan, dear brother? Disappointed in love?"

"What do you want?"

"An audience with His Highness the Interim Director, if it please His Grace." Fred grinned unpleasantly. "A private audience, if you please, m'lord."

"Very well. Come on up here."

Fred shook his head. "Sorry, no go. There are too many tricky spy pickups in that office of yours. Let's meet elsewhere, shall we?"

"Where?"

"That club you belong to. The Bronze Room."

Walton sputtered. "But I can't leave the building now! There's no one who—"

"Now," Fred interrupted. "The Bronze Room. It's in the San Isidro, isn't it? Top of Neville Prospect?"

"All right," said Walton resignedly. "There's a doorsmith coming up here to do some work. Give me a minute to cancel the assignment and I'll meet you downstairs."

"You leave now," Fred said. "I'll arrive five minutes after you. And you won't need to cancel anything. *I* was the doorsmith."

Neville Prospect was the most fashionable avenue in all of New York City, a wide strip of ferroconcrete running up the West Side between Eleventh Avenue and the West Side Drive from Fortieth to Fiftieth Street. It was bordered on both sides by looming apartment buildings in which a man of wealth might have as many as four or five rooms to his suite; and at the very head of the Prospect, facing downtown, was the mighty San Isidro, a buttressed fortress of gleaming metal and stone whose mighty beryllium-steel supports swept out in a massive arc five hundred feet in either direction.

On the hundred fiftieth floor of the San Isidro was the exclusive Bronze Room, from whose quartz windows might be seen all the sprawling busyness of Manhattan and the close-packed confusion of New Jersey just across the river.

The jetcopter delivered Walton to the landing-stage of the Bronze Room; he tipped the man too much and stepped within. A door of dull bronze confronted him. He touched his key to the signet plate; the door pivoted noiselessly inward, admitting him.

The color scheme today was gray: gray light streamed from the luminescent walls, gray carpets lay underfoot, gray tables with gray dishes were visible in the murky distance. A gray-clad waiter, hardly more than four feet tall, sidled up to Walton.

"Good to see you again, sir," he murmured. "You have not been here of late."

"No," Walton said. "I've been busy."

"A terrible tragedy, the death of Mr. FitzMaugham. He was one of our most esteemed members. Will you have your usual room today, sir?"

Walton shook his head. "I'm entertaining a guest—my brother, Fred. We'll need a compartment for two. He'll identify himself when he arrives."

"Of course. Come with me, please."

The gnome led him through a gray haze to another bronze door, down a corridor lined with antique works of art, through an interior room decorated with glowing lumifacts of remarkable quality, past a broad quartz window so clean as to be dizzyingly invisible, and up to a narrow door with a bright red signet plate in its center.

"For you, sir."

Walton touched his key to the signet plate; the door crumpled like a fan. He stepped inside, gravely handed the gnome a bill, and closed the door.

The room was tastefully furnished, again in gray; the Bronze Room was always uniformly monochromatic, though the hue varied with the day and with the mood of the city. Walton had long speculated on what the club precincts would be like were the electronic magic disconnected.

Actually, he knew, none of the Bronze Room's appurtenances had any color except when the hand in the control room threw the switch. The club held many secrets. It was FitzMaugham who had brought about Walton's admission to the club, and Walton had been deeply grateful.

He was in a room just comfortably large enough for two, with a single bright window facing the Hudson, a small onyx table, a tiny screen tastefully set in the wall, and a bar. He dialed himself a filtered rum, his favorite drink. The dark, cloudy liquid came pouring instantly from the spigot.

The screen suddenly flashed a wave of green, breaking the ubiquitous grayness. The green gave way to the bald head and scowling face of Kroll, the Bronze Room's doorman.

"Sir, there is a man outside who claims to be your brother. He alleges he has an appointment with you here."

"That's right, Kroll; send him in. Fulks will bring him to my room."

"Just one moment, sir. First it is needful to verify."

Kroll's face vanished and Fred's appeared.

"Is this the man?" Kroll's voice asked.

"Yes," Walton said. "You can send my brother in."

Fred seemed a little dazed by the opulence. He sat gingerly on the edge of the foamweb couch, obviously attempting to appear blasé and painfully conscious of his failure to do so.

"This is quite a place," he said finally.

Walton smiled. "A little on the palatial side for my tastes. I don't come here often. The transition hurts too much when I go back outside."

"FitzMaugham got you in here, didn't he?"

Walton nodded.

"I thought so," Fred said. "Well, maybe someday soon I'll be a member too. Then we can meet here more often. We don't see enough of each other, you know."

"Dial yourself a drink," Walton said. "Then tell me what's on your mind—or were you just angling to get an invite up here?"

"It was more than that. But let me get a drink before we begin."

Fred dialed a Weesuer, heavy on the absinthe, and took a few sampling sips before wheeling around to face Walton. He said, "One of the minor talents I acquired in the course of my wanderings was doorsmithing. It's really not very difficult to learn, for a man who applies himself."

"You were the one who repaired my office door?"

Fred smirked. "I was. I wore a mask, of course, and my uniform was borrowed. Masks are very handy things. They make them most convincingly, nowadays. As, for instance, the one worn by the man who posed as Ludwig."

"What do you know about—"

"*Nothing.* And that's the flat truth, Roy. I didn't kill FitzMaugham, and I don't know who did." He drained his drink and dialed another. "No, the old man's death is as much of a mystery to me as it is to you. But I have to thank you for wrecking the door so completely when you blasted your way in. It gave me a chance to make some repairs when I most wanted to."

Walton held himself very carefully in check. He knew exactly what Fred was gong to say in the next few minutes, but he refused to let himself precipitate the conversation.

With studied care he rose, dialed another filtered rum for himself, and gently slid the initiator switch on the electroluminescent kaleidoscope embedded in the rear wall.

A pattern of lights sprang into being—yellow, pale rose, blue, soft green. They wove together, intertwined, sprang apart into a sharp hexagon, broke into a scatterpattern, melted, seemed to fall to the carpet in bright flakes.

"Shut that thing off!" Fred snapped suddenly. "Come on! Shut it! *Shut it!*"

Walton swung around. His brother was leaning forward intently, eyes clamped tight shut. "Is it off?" Fred asked. "Tell me!"

Shrugging, Walton canceled the signal and the lights faded. "You can open your eyes, now. It's off."

Cautiously Fred opened his eyes. "None of your fancy tricks, Roy!"

"Trick?" Walton asked innocently. "What trick? Simple

decoration, that's all—and quite lovely, too. Just like the kaleidowhirls you've seen on video."

Fred shook his head. "It's not the same thing. How do I know it's not some sort of hypnoscreen? How do I know what those lights can do?"

Walton realized his brother was unfamiliar with wall kaleidoscopes. "It's perfectly harmless," he said. "But if you don't want it on, we can do without it."

"Good. That's the way I like it."

Walton observed that Fred's cool confidence seemed somewhat shaken. His brother had made a tactical error in insisting on holding their interview here, where Walton had so much the upper hand.

"May I ask again why you wanted to see me?" Walton said.

"There are those people," Fred said slowly, "who oppose the entire principle of population equalization."

"I'm aware of that. Some of them are members of this very club."

"Exactly. Some of them are. The ones I mean are the gentry, those still lucky enough to cling to land and home. The squire with a hundred acres in the Matto Grosso; the wealthy landowner of Liberia; the gentleman who controls the rubber output of one of the lesser Indonesian islands. These people, Roy, are unhappy over equalization. They know that sooner or later you and your Bureau will find out about them and will equalize them . . . say, by installing a hundred Chinese on a private estate, or by using a private river for a nuclear turbine. You'll have to admit that their dislike of equalization is understandable."

"Everyone's dislike of equalization is understandable," Walton said. "I dislike it myself. You got your evidence of that two days ago. No one likes to give up special privileges."

"You see my point, then. There are perhaps a hundred of these men in close contact with each other—"

"*What!*"

"Ah, yes," Fred said. "A league. A conspiracy, it might almost be called. Very, very shady doings."

"Yes."

"I work for them," Fred said.

Walton let that soak in. "You're an employee of Popeek," he said. "Are you inferring that you're both an employee of Popeek and an employee of a group that seeks to undermine Popeek?"

Fred grinned proudly. "That's the position on the nose. It calls for remarkable compartmentalization of mind. I think I manage nicely."

Incredulously Walton said, "How long has this been going on?"

"Ever since I came to Popeek. This group is older than Popeek. They fought equalization all the way, and lost. Now they're working from the bottom up and trying to wreck things before you catch wise and confiscate their estates, as you're now legally entitled to do."

"And now that you've warned me they exist," Walton said, "you can be assured that that's the first thing I'll do. The second thing I'll do will be to have the security men track down their names and find out if there was an actual conspiracy. If there was, it's jail for them. And the third thing I'll do is discharge you from Popeek."

Fred shook his head. "You won't do any of those things, Roy. You can't."

"Why?"

"I know something about you that wouldn't look good if it came out in the open. Something that would get you bounced out of your high position in a flash."

"Not fast enough to stop me from setting the wheels going. My successor would continue the job of rooting out your league of landed gentry."

"I doubt that," Fred said calmly. "I doubt it very much—because *I'm* going to be your successor."

Ten

CROSSCURRENTS of fear ran through Walton. He said, "What are you talking about?"

Fred folded his arms complacently. "I don't think it comes as news to you that I broke into your office this morning while you were out. It was very simple: when I installed the lock, I built in a canceling circuit that would let me walk in whenever I pleased. And this morning I pleased. I was hoping to find something I could use as immediate leverage against you, but I hadn't expected anything as explosive as the portfolio in the left-hand cabinet."

"Where is it?"

Fred grinned sharply. "The contents of that portfolio are now in very safe keeping, Roy. Don't bluster and don't threaten, because it won't work. I took precautions."

"And—"

"And you know as well as I what would happen if that immortality serum got distributed to the good old man in the street," Fred said. "For one thing, there'd be a glorious panic. That would solve your population problem for a while, with millions killed in the rush. But after that—where would you equalize, with every man and woman on Earth living forever, and producing immortal children?"

"We don't know the long-range effects yet—"

"Don't temporize. You damned well know it'd be the biggest upheaval the world has ever seen." Fred paused. "My employers," he said, "are in possession of the Lamarre formulas now."

"And with great glee are busy making themselves immortals."

"No. They don't trust the stuff, and won't use it until it's been tried on two or three billion guinea pigs. Human ones."

"They're not planning to release the serum, are they?" Walton gasped.

"Not immediately," Fred said. "In exchange for certain concessions on your part, they're prepared to return Lamarre's portfolio to you without making use of it."

"Concessions? Such as what?"

"That you refrain from declaring their private lands open territory for equalization. That you resign your post as interim director. That you go before the General Assembly and recommend me as your successor."

"*You?*"

"Who else is best fitted to serve the interests I represent?"

Walton leaned back, his face showing a mirth he scarcely felt. "Very neat, Fred. But full of holes. First thing, what assurance have I that your wealthy friends won't keep a copy of the Lamarre formla and use it as a bludgeon in the future against anyone they don't agree with?"

"None," Fred admitted.

"Naturally. What's more, suppose I refuse to give in and your employers release the serum to all and sundry. Who gets hurt? Not me; I live in a one-room box myself. But they'll be filling the world with billions and billions of people. Their beloved estates will be overrun by the hungry multitudes, whether they like it or not. And no fence will keep out a million hungry people."

"This is a risk they recognize," Fred said.

Walton smiled triumphantly. "You mean they're bluffing! They know they don't dare release that serum, and they think they can get me out of the way and you, their puppet, into office by making menacing noises. All right. I'll call their bluff."

"You mean you refuse?"

"Yes," Walton said. "I have no intention of resigning my interim directorship, and when the Assembly convenes I'm going to ask for the job on a permanent basis. They'll give it to me."

"And my evidence against you? The Prior baby?"

"Hearsay. Propaganda. I'll laugh it right out of sight."

"Try laughing off the serum, Roy. It won't be so easy as all that."

"I'll manage," Walton said tightly. He crossed the room and jabbed down on the communicator stud. The screen lit;

the wizened face of the tiny servitor appeared.

"Sir?"

"Fulks, would you show this gentleman out of my chamber, please? He has no further wish to remain with me."

"Right away, Mr. Walton."

"Before you throw me out," Fred said, "let me tell you one more thing."

"Go ahead."

"You're acting stupidly—though that's nothing new for you, Roy. I'll give you a week's grace to make up your mind. Then the serum goes into production."

"My mind is made up," Walton said stiffly. The door telescoped and Fulks stood outside. He smiled obsequiously at Walton, bowed to Fred, and said to him, "Would you come with me, please?"

It was like one of those dreams, Walton thought, in which you were a butler bringing dishes to the table, and the tray becomes obstinately stuck to your fingertips and refuses to be separated; or in which the Cavendishes are dining in state and you come to the table nude; or in which you float downward perpetually with never a sign of bottom.

There never seemed to be any way out. Force opposed force and he seemed doomed always to be caught in the middle.

Angrily he snapped the kaleidoscope back on and let its everchanging swirl of color distract him. But in the depth of the deepest violet he kept seeing his brother's mocking face.

He summoned Fulks.

The gnome looked up at him expectantly. "Get me a

jetcopter," Walton ordered. "I'll be waiting on the west stage for it."

"Very good, sir."

Fulks never had any problems, Walton reflected sourly. The little man had found his niche in life; he spent his days in the plush comfort of the Bronze Room, seeing to the wants of the members. Never any choices to make, never any of the agonizing decisions that complicated life.

Decisions. Walton realized that one particular decision had been made for him, that of seeking the directorship permanently. He had not been planning to do that. Now he had no choice but to remain in office as long as he could.

He stepped out onto the landing stage and into the waiting jetcopter. "Cullen Building," he told the robopilot abstractedly.

He did not feel very cheerful.

The annunciator panel in Walton's office was bright as a Christmas tree; the signal bulbs were all alight, each representing someone anxious to speak to him. He flipped over the circuit-breaker, indicating he was back in his office, and received the first call.

It was from Lee Percy. Percy's thick features were wrinkled into a smile. "Just heard that speech you made outside the building this morning, Roy. It's getting a big blare on the newsscreens. Beautiful! Simply beautiful! Couldn't have been better if we'd concocted it ourselves."

"Glad you like it," Walton said. "It really was off the cuff."

"Even better, then. You're positively a genius. Say, I

wanted to tell you that we've got the FitzMaugham memorial all whipped up and ready to go. Full channel blast tonight over all media at 2000 sharp . . . a solid hour block. Nifty. Neat."

"Is my speech in the program?"

"Sure is, Roy. A slick one, too. Makes two speeches of yours blasted in a single day."

"Send me a transcript of my speech before it goes on the air," Walton said. "I want to read and approve that thing if it's supposed to be coming out of my mouth."

"It's a natural, Roy. You don't have to worry."

"*I want to read it beforehand!*" Walton snapped.

"Okay, okay. Don't chew my ears off. I'll ship it to you posthaste, man. Ease up. Pop a pill. You aren't loose, Roy."

"I can't afford to be," Walton said.

He broke contact and almost instantly the next call blossomed on the screen. Walton recognized the man as one of the technicians from Communications, floor twenty-three.

"Well?"

"We heard from McLeod again, sir. Message came in half an hour ago and we've been trying to reach you ever since."

"I wasn't in. Give me the message."

The technician unfolded a slip of paper. "It says, 'Arriving Nairobi tonight, will be in New York by morning. McLeod.' "

"Good. Send him confirmation and tell him I'll keep the entire morning free to see him."

"Yes, sir."

"Oh—anything from Venus?"

The technician shook his head emphatically. "Not a peep. We can't make contact with Dr. Lang at all."

Walton frowned. He wondered what was happening to the terraforming crew up there. "Keep trying, will you? Work a twenty-four-hour-a-day schedule. Draw extra pay. But get in touch with Lang, dammit!"

"Y-yes, sir. Anything else?"

"No. Get off the line."

As the contact snapped Walton smoothly broke connection again, leaving ten more would-be callers sputtering. A row of lights a foot long indicated their presence on the line. Walton ignored them and turned instead to his newsscreen.

The 1400 news was on. He fiddled with the controls and saw his own face take form on the screen. He was standing outside the Cullen Building, looking right out of the screen at himself, and in the background could be seen a huddled form under a coat. The dead Herschelite.

Walton of the screen was saying, " . . . The man was asking for trouble. Popeek represents the minds and hearts of the world. Herschel and his people seek to overthrow this order. I can't condone violence of any sort, naturally, but Popeek is a sacred responsibility to me. Its enemies I must regard as blind and misguided people."

He was smiling into the camera, but there was something behind the smile, something cold and steely, that astonished the watching Walton. *My God,* he thought. *Is that genuine? Have I really grown so hard?*

Apparently he had. He watched himself turn majestically and stride into the Cullen Building, stronghold of

Popeek. There was definitely a commanding air about him.

The commentator was saying, "With those heartfelt words, Director Walton goes to his desk in the Cullen Building to carry out his weighty task. To bring life out of death, joy out of sadness—this is the job facing Popeek, and this is the sort of man to whom it has been entrusted. Roy Walton, we salute you!"

The screen panned to a still of Director FitzMaugham. "Meanwhile," the commentator went on, "Walton's predecessor, the late D. F. FitzMaugham, went to his rest today. Police are still hoping to uncover the group responsible for his brutal slaying, and report a good probability of success. Tonight all channels will carry a memorial program for this great leader of humanity. D. F. FitzMaugham, hail and farewell!"

A little sickened, Walton snapped the set off. He had to admire Lee Percy; the propaganda man had done his job well. With a minor assist from Walton by way of a spontaneous speech, Percy had contrived to gain vast quantities of precious air time for Popeek. All to the good.

The annunciator was still blinking violently; it seemed about to explode with the weight of pent-up, frustrated calls. Walton nudged a red stud at the top and Security Chief Sellors entered the screen.

"Sellors, sir. We've been looking for this Lamarre. Can't find him anywhere."

"What?"

"We checked him to his home. He got there, all right. Then he disappeared. No sign of him anywhere in the city. What now, sir?"

Walton felt his fingers quivering. "Order a tracer sent out through all of Appalachia. No, cancel that—make it country-wide. Beam his description everywhere. Got any snaps?"

"Yes, sir."

"Get them on the air. Tell the country this man is vital to global security. Find him, Sellors."

"We'll give it a try."

"Better than that. You'll *find* him. If he doesn't turn up within eight hours, shift the tracer to world-wide. He might be anywhere—and he has to be found!"

Walton blanked the screen and avoided the next caller. He called his secretary and said, "Will you instruct everyone now calling me to refer their business downstairs to Assistant Administrator Eglin. If they won't do that, tell them to put it in writing and send it to me. I can't accept any more calls just now." Then he added, "Oh, put me through to Eglin myself before you let any of those calls reach him."

Eglin's face appeared on the private screen that linked the two offices. The small man looked dark-browed and harried. "This is a hell of a job, Roy," he sighed.

"So is mine," Walton said. "Look, I've got a ton of calls on the wire, and I'm transferring them all down to you. Throw as many as you can down to the subordinates. It's the only way to keep your sanity."

"Thanks. Thanks loads, Roy. All I need now is some more calls."

"Can't be helped. Who'd you pick for your replacement as director of field agents?" Walton asked.

"Lassen. I sent his dossier to you hours ago."

"Haven't read it yet. Is he on the job already?"

"Sure. He's been there since I moved up here," Eglin said. "What—"

"Never mind," said Walton. He hung up and called Lassen, the new director of field agents.

Lassen was a boyish-looking young man with stiff sandy hair and a sternly efficient manner. Walton said, "Lassen, I want you to do a job for me. Get one of your men to make up a list of the hundred biggest private estates still unequalized. I want the names of their owners, location of the estates, acreage, and things like that. Got it?"

"Right. When will you want it, Mr. Walton?"

"Immediately. But I don't want it to be a sloppy job. This is top important, double."

Lassen nodded. Walton grinned at him—the boy seemed to be in good control of himself—and clicked off.

He realized that he'd been engaged in half a dozen high-power conversations without a break, over a span of perhaps twenty minutes. His heart was pounding; his feet felt numb.

He popped a benzolurethrin into his mouth and kept on going. He would need to act fast, now that the wheels were turning. McLeod arriving the next day to report the results of the faster-than-light expedition, Lamarre missing, Fred at large and working for a conspiracy of landowners—Walton foresaw that he would be on a steady diet of tranquilizers for the next few days.

He opened the arrival bin and pulled out a handful of paper. One thick bundle was the dossier on Lassen; Walton initialed it and tossed it unread into the Files chute. He would have to rely on Eglin's judgment; Lassen seemed competent enough.

Underneath that, he found the script of the Fitz-Maugham memorial program to be shown that evening. Walton sat back and started to skim through it.

It was the usual sort of eulogy. He skipped rapidly past FitzMaugham's life and great works, on to the part where Interim Director Walton appeared on the screen to speak.

This part he read more carefully. He was very much interested in the words that Percy had placed in his mouth.

Eleven

THE SPEECH that night went over well . . . almost.

Walton watched the program in the privacy of his home, sprawled out on the foamweb sofa with a drink in one hand and the text of Percy's shooting-script in the other. The giant screen that occupied nearly half of his one unbroken wall glowed in lifelike colors.

FitzMaugham's career was traced with pomp and circumstance, done up in full glory: plenty of ringing trumpet flourishes, dozens of eye-appealing color groupings, much high-pitched, tense narrative. Percy had done his job skillfully. The show was punctuated by quotations from FitzMaugham's classic book, *Breathing Space and Sanity*. Key government figures drifted in and out of the narrative webwork, orating sonorously. That pious fraud, M. Seymour Lanson, President of the United States, delivered a flowery speech; the old figurehead was an artist at his one function, speechmaking. Walton watched, spellbound. Lee Percy was a genius in his field; there was no denying that.

Finally, toward the end of the hour, the narrator said, "The work of Popeek goes on, though its lofty-minded creator lies dead at an assassin's hand. Director FitzMaugham had chosen as his successor a young man schooled in the ideals of Popeek. Roy Walton, we know, will continue the noble task begun by D. F. FitzMaugham."

For the second time that day Walton watched his own face appear on a video screen. He glanced down at the script in his hand and back up at the screen. Percy's technicians had done a brilliant job. The Walton-image on the screen looked so real that the Walton on the couch almost believed he had actually delivered this speech—although he knew it had been cooked up out of some rearranged stills and a few brokendown phonemes with his voice characteristics.

It was a perfectly innocent speech. In humble tones he expressed his veneration for the late director, his hopes that he would be able to fill the void left by the death of FitzMaugham, his sense of Popeek as a sacred trust. Half-listening, Walton began to skim the script.

Startled, Walton looked down at the script. He didn't remember having encountered any such lines on his first reading, and he couldn't find them now. "This morning," the pseudo-Walton on the screen went on, "we received *contact from outer space!* From a faster-than-light ship sent out over a year ago to explore our neighboring stars.

"News of this voyage has been withheld until now for security reasons. But it is my great pleasure to tell you tonight that the stars have at last been reached by man. . . . A new world waits for us out there, lush, fertile, ready to be colonized by the brave pioneers of tomorrow!"

Walton stared aghast at the screen. His simulacrum had returned now to the script as prepared, but he barely listened.

He was thinking that Percy had let the cat out for sure. It was a totally unauthorized newsbreak. Numbly, Walton watched the program come to its end, and wondered what the repercussions would be once the public grasped all the implications.

He was awakened at 0600 by the chiming of his phone. Grumpily he climbed from bed, snapped on the receiver, switched the cutoff on the picture sender in order to hide his sleep-rumpled appearance, and said, "This is Walton. Yes?"

A picture formed on the screen: a heavily-tanned man in his late forties, stocky, hair close-cropped. "Sorry to roust you this way, old man. I'm McLeod."

Walton came fully awake in an instant. "McLeod? Where are you?"

"Out on Long Island. I just pulled into the airport half a moment ago. Traveled all night after dumping the ship at Nairobi."

"You made a good landing, I hope?"

"The best. The ship navigates like a bubble." McLeod frowned worriedly. "They brought me the early-morning telefax while I was having breakfast. I couldn't help reading all about the speech you made last night."

"Oh. I—"

"Quite a crasher of a speech," McLeod went on evenly. "But don't you think it was a little premature of you to release word of my flight? I mean—"

"It was quite premature," Walton said. "A member of my staff inserted that statement into my talk without my knowledge. He'll be disciplined for it."

A puzzled frown appeared on McLeod's face. "But *you* made that speech with your own lips! How can you blame it on a member of your staff?"

"The science that can send a ship to Procyon and back within a year," Walton said, "can also fake a speech. But I imagine we'll be able to cover up the pre-release without too much trouble."

"I'm not so sure of that," said McLeod. He shrugged apologetically. "You see, that planet's there, all right. But it happens to be the property of alien beings who live on the next world. And they're not so happy about having Earth come crashing into their system to colonize!"

Somehow Walton managed to hang onto his self-control, even with this staggering news crashing about him. "You've been in contact with these beings?" he asked.

McLeod nodded. "They have a translating gadget. We met them, yes."

Walton moistened his lips. "I think there's going to be trouble," he said. "I think I may be out of a job, too."

"What's that?"

"Just thinking out loud," Walton said. "Finish your breakfast and meet me at my office at 0900. We'll talk this thing out then."

Walton was in full command of himself by the time he

reached the Cullen Building.

He had read the morning telefax and heard the newsblares: they all screamed the sum and essence of Walton's
speech of the previous night, and a few of the braver telefax
outfits went as far as printing a resumé of the entire speech,
boiled down to Basic, of course, for benefit of that substantial
segment of the reading public that was most comfortable
while moving its lips. The one telefax outfit most outspo-
kenly opposed to Popeek, *Citizen*, took great delight in
giving the speech full play, and editorializing on a subsequent sheet against the "veil of security" hazing Popeek
operations.

Walton read the *Citizen* editorial twice, savoring its
painstaking simplicities of expression. Then he clipped it out
neatly and shot it down the chute to public relations, marked
Attention: Lee Percy.

"There's a Mr. McLeod waiting to see you," his secretary informed him. "He says he has an appointment."

"Send him in," Walton said. "And have Mr. Percy come
up here also."

While he waited for McLeod to arrive, Walton riffled
through the rest of the telefax sheets. Some of them praised
Popeek for having uncovered a new world; others damned it
for having hidden news of the faster-than-light drive so long.
Walton stacked them neatly in a heap at the edge of his desk.

In the bleak, dark hours of the morning, he had expected to be compelled to resign. Now, he realized, he could
immeasurably strengthen his own position if he could control the flow of events and channel them properly.

The square figure of McLeod appeared on the screen.
Walton admitted him.

"Sir. I'm McLeod."

"Of course. Won't you sit down?"

McLeod was tense, stiffly formal, very British in his reserve and general bearing. Walton gestured uneasily, trying to cut through the crackle of nervousness.

"We seem to have a mess on our hands," he said. "But there's no mess so messy we can't muddle through it, eh?"

"If we have to, sir. But I can't help feeling this could all have been avoided."

"No. You're wrong. McLeod. If it *could* have been avoided, it would have been avoided. The fact that some idiot in my public relations department gained access to my wire and found out you were returning is incontrovertible; it happened, despite precautions."

"Mr. Percy to see you," the annunciator said.

The angular figure of Lee Percy appeared on the screen. Walton told him to come in.

Percy looked frightened—terrified, Walton thought. He held a folded slip of paper loosely in one hand.

"Good morning, sir."

"Good morning, Lee." Walton observed that the friendly *Roy* had changed to the formal salutation, *sir*. "Did you get the clipping I sent you?"

"Yes, sir." Glumly.

"Lee, this is Leslie McLeod, chief of operations of our successful faster-than-light project. Colonel McLeod, I want you to meet Lee Percy. He's the man who masterminded our little newsbreak last night."

Percy flinched visibly. He stepped forward and laid his slip of paper on Walton's desk. "I m-made a m-mistake last night," he stammered. "I should never have released that break."

"Damned right you shouldn't have," Walton agreed, carefully keeping any hint of severity from his voice. "You have us in considerable hot water, Lee. That planet isn't ours for colonization, despite the enthusiasm with which I allegedly announced it last night. And you ought to be clever enough to realize it's impossible to withdraw and deny good news once you've broken it."

"The planet's not ours? But—?"

"According to Colonel McLeod," Walton said, "the planet is the property of intelligent alien beings who live on a neighboring world, and who no more care to have their system overrun by a pack of Earthmen than we would to have extrasolar aliens settle on Mars."

"Sir, that sheet of paper . . ." Percy said in a choked voice. "It's—it's—"

Walton unfolded it. It was Percy's resignation. He read the note carefully twice, smiled, and laid it down. Now was his time to be magnanimous.

"Denied," he said. "We need you on our team, Lee. I'm authorizing a ten percent pay-cut for one week, effective yesterday, but there'll be no other penalty."

"Thank you, sir."

He's crawling to me, Walton thought in amazement. He said, "Only don't pull that stunt again, or I'll not only fire you but blacklist you so hard you won't be able to find work between here and Procyon. Understand?"

"Yes, sir."

"Okay. Go back to your office and get to work. And no

more publicity on this faster-than-light thing until I authorize it. No—cancel that. Get out a quick release, a followup on last night. A smoke screen, I mean. Cook up so much cloudy verbiage about the conquest of space that no one bothers to remember anything of what I said. And play down the colonization angle!"

"I get it, sir." Percy grinned feebly.

"I doubt that," Walton snapped. "When you have the release prepared, shoot it up here for my okay. And heaven help you if you deviate from the text I see by as much as a single comma!"

Percy practically backed out of the office.

"Why did you do that?" McLeod asked, puzzled.

"You mean, why did I let him off so lightly?"

McLeod nodded. "In the military," he said, "we'd have a man shot for doing a thing like that."

"This isn't the military," Walton said. "And even though the man behaved like a congenital idiot yesterday, that's not enough evidence to push him into Happysleep. Besides, he knows his stuff. I can't afford to discharge him."

"Are public relations men that hard to come by?"

"No. But he's a good one—and the prospect of having him desert to the other side frightens me. He'll be forever grateful to me now. If I had fired him, he would've had half a dozen anti-Popeek articles in the *Citizen* before the week was out. And they'd ruin us."

McLeod smiled appreciatively. "You handle your job well, Mr. Walton."

"I have to," Walton said. "The director of Popeek is paid

to produce two or three miracles per hour. One gets used to it, after a while. Tell me about these aliens, Colonel McLeod."

McLeod swung a briefcase to Walton's desk and flipped the magneseal. He handed Walton a thick sheaf of glossy color photos.

"The first dozen or so are scenes of the planet," McLeod explained. "It's Procyon VIII—number eight out of sixteen, unless we missed a couple. We checked sixteen worlds in the system, anyway. Ten of 'em were methane giants; we didn't even bother to land. Two were ammonia supergiants, even less pleasant. Three small ones had no atmosphere at all worth speaking about, and were no more livable-looking than Mercury. And the remaining one was the one we call New Earth. Take a look, sir."

Walton looked. The photos showed rolling hills covered with close-packed shrubbery, flowing rivers, a lovely sunrise. Several of the shots were of indigenous life—a wizened little four-handed monkey, a six-legged doglike thing, a toothy bird.

"Life runs to six limbs there," Walton observed. "But how livable can this place be? Unless your photos are sour, that grass is *blue* . . . and the water's peculiar looking, too. What sort of tests did you run?"

"It's the light, sir. Procyon's a double star; that faint companion gets up in the sky and does tricky things to the camera. That grass may look blue, but it's a chlorophyll-based photosynthesizer all the same. And the water's nothing but H_2O, even with that purple tinge."

Walton nodded. "How about the atmosphere?"

"We were breathing it for a week, and no trouble. It's pretty rich in oxygen—twenty-four percent. Gives you a bouncy feeling—just right for pioneers, I'd say."

"You've prepared a full report on this place, haven't you?"

"Of course. It's right here." McLeod started to reach for his briefcase.

"Not just yet," Walton said. "I want to go through the rest of these snapshots." He turned over one after another rapidly until he came to a photo that showed a strange blocky figure, four-armed, bright green in color. Its neckless head was encased in a sort of breathing mask fashioned from some transparent plastic. Three cold, brooding eyes peered outward.

"What's this?" Walton asked.

"Oh, that." McLeod attempted a cheerful grin. "That's a Dirnan. They live on Procyon IX, one of the ammonia-giant planets. They're the aliens who don't want us there."

Twelve

WALTON STARED at the photograph of the alien. There was intelligence there . . . yes, intelligence and understanding, and perhaps even a sort of compassion.

He sighed. There were always qualifications, never unalloyed successes.

"Colonel McLeod, how long would it take your ship to return to the Procyon system?" he asked thoughtfully.

McLeod considered the question. "Hardly any time, sir. A few days, maybe. Why?".

"Just a wild idea. Tell me about your contact with these—ah—Dirnans."

"Well, sir, they landed after we'd spent more than a week surveying New Earth. There were six of them, and they had their translating widget with them. They told us who they were, and wanted to know who we were. We told them. They said they ran the Procyon system, and weren't of a mind to let any alien beings come barging in."

"Did they sound hostile?" Walton asked.

"Oh, no. Just businesslike. We were trespassing, and they asked us to get off. They were cold about it, but not angry."

"Fine," Walton said. "Look here, now. Do you think you could go back to their world as—well as an ambassador from Earth? Bring one of the Dirnans here for treaty talks, and such?"

"I suppose so," McLeod said hesitantly. "If it's necessary."

"It looks as if it may be. You had no luck in any of the other nearby systems?"

"No."

"Then Procyon VIII's our main hope. Tell your men we'll offer double pay for this cruise. And make it as fast as you know how."

"Hyperspace travel's practically instantaneous," McLeod said. "We spent most of our time cruising on standard ion drive from planet to planet. Maneuvering in the subspace manifold's a snap, though."

"Good. Snap it up, then. Back to Nairobi and clear out of there as soon as you're ready. Remember, it's urgent you bring one of the aliens here for treaty talks."

"I'll do my best," McLeod said.

Walton stared at the empty seat where McLeod had

been, and tried to picture a green Dirnan sitting there, goggling at him with its three eyes.

He was beginning to feel like a juggler. Popeek activity proceeded on so many fronts at once that it quite dazzled him. And every hour there were new challenges to meet, new decisions to make.

At the moment, there were too many eggs and not enough baskets. Walton realized he was making the same mistake FitzMaugham had, that of carrying too much of the Popeek workings inside his skull. If anything happened to him, the operation would be fatally paralyzed, and it would be some time before the gears were meshing again.

He resolved to keep a journal, to record each day a full and mercilessly honest account of each of the many maneuvers in which he was engaged. He would begin with his private conflict with Fred and the interests Fred represented, follow through with the Lamarre-immortality episode, and include a detailed report on the problems of the subsidiary projects, New Earth and Lang's terraforming group.

That gave him another idea. Reaching for his voicewrite, he dictated a concise confidential memorandum instructing Assistant Administrator Eglin to outfit an investigatory mission immediately; purpose, to go to Venus and make contact with Lang. The terraforming group was nearly two weeks overdue in its scheduled report. He could not ignore that any longer.

The everlasting annunciator chimed, and Walton switched on the screen. It was Sellors, and from the look of abject terror on the man's face, Walton knew that something sticky had just transpired.

"What is it, Sellors? Any luck in tracing Lamarre?"

"None, sir," the security chief said. "But there's been another development, Mr. Walton. A most serious one. *Most* serious."

Walton was ready to expect anything—a bulletin announcing the end of the universe, perhaps. "Well, tell me about it," he snapped impatiently.

Sellors seemed about ready to collapse with shame. He said hesitantly, "One of the communications technicians was making a routine check of the building's circuits, Mr. Walton. He found one trunk-line that didn't seem to belong where it was, so he checked up and found out that it had been newly installed."

"Well, what of it?"

"It was a spy pickup with its outlet in your office, sir," Sellors said, letting the words tumble out in one blur. "All the time you were talking this morning, someone was spying on you."

Walton grabbed the arms of his chair. "Are you telling me that your department was blind enough to let someone pipe a spy pickup right into this office?" he demanded. "Where did this outlet go? And is it cut off?"

"They cut it off as soon as they found it, sir. It went to a men's lavatory on the twenty-sixth floor."

"And how long was it in operation?"

"At least since last night, sir. Communications assures me that it couldn't possibly have been there before yesterday afternoon, since they ran a general check then and didn't see it."

Walton groaned. It was small comfort to know that he had had privacy up till last evening; if the wrong people had listened in on his conversation with McLeod, there would be serious trouble.

"All right, Sellors. This thing can't be your fault, but keep your eyes peeled in the future. And tell Communications that my office is to be checked for such things twice a day from now on, at 0900 and at 1300."

"Yes, sir." Sellors looked tremendously relieved.

"And start interrogating the Communications technicians. Find out who's responsible for that spy circuit, and hold him on security charges. And locate Lamarre!"

"I'll do my best, Mr. Walton."

While the screen was clearing, Walton jotted down a memorandum to himself: *investigate Sellors*. So far, as security chief, Sellors had allowed an assassin to reach FitzMaugham, allowed Prior to burst into Walton's old office, permitted Fred to masquerade as a doorsmith long enough to gain access to Walton's private files, and stood by blindly while Lee Percy tapped into Walton's private wire and some unidentified technician strung a spy pickup into the director's supposedly sacred office.

No security chief could have been as incompetent as all that. It had to be a planned campaign, directed from the outside.

He dialed Eglin.

"Olaf, you get my message about the Venus rescue mission okay?"

"Came through a few minutes ago. I'll have the specs drawn up by tonight."

"Devil with that," Walton said. "Drop everything and send that ship out *now*. I've got to know what Lang and his crew are up to, and I have to know right away. If we don't produce a livable Venus, or at least the possibility of one, in a couple of days, we'll be in for it on all sides."

"Why? What's up?"

"You'll see. Keep an eye on the telefax. I'll bet the next edition of *Citizen* is going to be interesting."

It was.

The glossy sheets of the 1200 *Citizen* extruded themselves from a million receivers in the New York area, but none of those million copies was as avidly pounced on as was Director Walton's. He had been hovering near the wall outlet for ten minutes, avidly awaiting the sheet's arrival.

And he was not disappointed.

The streamer headline ran:

THINGS FROM SPACE NIX BIG POPEEK PLAN

And under it in smaller type:

Greenskinned Uglies Put Feet In
Director Walton's Big Mouth

He smiled grimly and went on to the story itself. Written in the best approved *Citizen* journalese, it read:

Fellow human beings, we've been suckered again. The Citizen *found out for sure this morning that the big surprise Popeek's Interim Director Walton yanked out of his hat last night has a hole in it.*

It's sure dope that there's a good planet up there

in the sky for grabs. The way we hear it, its just like earth only prettier, with trees and flowers (remember them?). Our man says the air there is nice and clean. This world sounds okay.

But what Walton didn't know last night came home to roost today. Seems the folks on the next planet out there don't want any sloppy old Earthmen messing up their pasture—and so we ain't going to have any New Earth after all. Wishy-washy Walton is a cinch to throw in the towel now.

More dope in later editions. And check the edit page for extra info.

It was obvious, Walton thought, that the spy pickup which had been planted in his office had been a direct pipe line to the *Citizen* news desk. They had taken his conversation with McLeod and carefully ground it down into the chatty, informal, colloquial style that made *Citizen* the world's most heavily-subscribed telefax service.

He shuddered at what might have happened if they'd had their spy pickup installed a day earlier, and overheard Walton in the process of suppressing Lamarre's immortality serum. There would have been a lynch mob storming the Cullen Building ten minutes after the *Citizen* hit the waves with its exposé.

Not that he was much better off now. He no longer had the advantage of secrecy to cloak his actions, and public officials who were compelled to conduct business in the harsh light of public scrutiny generally didn't hold their offices for long.

He turned the sheet over and searched for the editorial column, merely to confirm his expectations.

It was captioned in bold black:

ARE WE PATSIES FOR GREENSKINS?

And went on to say:

> *Non-human beings have said "Whoa!" to our plans for opening up a new world in space. These aliens have put thumbs down on colonization of the New Earth discovered by Colonel Leslie McLeod.*
>
> *Aside from the question of why Popeek kept word of the McLeod expedition from the public so long, there is this to consider—will we take this lying down?*
>
> *We've got to find space for us to live. New Earth is a good place. The answer to the trouble is easy: we take New Earth. If the greenskins don't like it, bounce 'em!*
>
> *How about it? What do we do? Mr. Walton, we want to know. What goes?*

It was an open exhortation to interstellar warfare. Dispiritedly, Walton let the telefax sheets skitter to the floor, and made no move to pick them up.

War with the Dirnans? If *Citizen* had its way, there would be. The telefax sheet would remorselessly stir the people up until the cry for war was unanimous.

Well, thought Walton callously, *a good war would re-duce the population surplus. The idiots!*

He caught the afternoon newsblares. They were full of the *Citizen* break, and one commentator made a pointblank demand that Walton either advocate war with the Dirnans or resign.

Not long afterward, UN delegate Ludwig called.

"Some hot action over here today," he told Walton. "After that *Citizen* thing got out, a few of the Oriental delegates started howling for your scalp on sixteen different counts of bungling. What's going on, Walton?"

"Plenty of spy activity, for one thing. The main problem, though, is the nucleus of incompetent assistants surrounding me. I think I'm going to reduce the local population personally before the day is out. With a blunt instrument, preferably."

"Is there any truth in the *Citizen* story?"

"Hell, yes!" Walton exclaimed. "For once, it's gospel! An enterprising telefax man rigged a private pipeline into my office last night and no one caught it until it was too late. Sure, those aliens are holding out. They don't want us coming up there."

Ludwig chewed at his lip. "You have any plans?"

"Dozens of them. Want some, cheap?" He laughed, a brittle, unamused laugh.

"Seriously, Roy. You ought to go on the air again and smooth this thing over. The people are yelling for war with these Dirnans, and half of us over here at the UN aren't even sure the damned creatures exist. Couldn't you fake it up a little?"

"No," Walton said. "There's been enough faking. I'm going on the air with the truth for a change! Better have all your delegates over there listening in, because their ears are in for an opening."

As soon as he was rid of Ludwig he called Lee Percy.

"That program on the conquest of space is almost ready to go," the public relations man informed him.

"Kill it. Have you seen the noon *Citizen?*"

"No; been too busy on the new program. Anything big?"

Walton chuckled. "Fairly big. The *Citizen* just yanked the rug out from under everything. We'll probably be at war with Procyon IX by sundown. I want you to buy me air space on every medium for the 1900 spot tonight."

"Sure thing. What kind of speech you want us to cook up?"

"None at all," Walton said. "I'm going to speak off the cuff for a change. Just buy the time for me, and squeeze the budget for all it's worth."

Thirteen

THE BRIGHT LIGHT of the video cameras flooded the room. Percy had done a good job; there was a representative from every network, every telefax, every blare of any sort at all. The media had been corralled. Walton's words would echo round the world.

He was seated behind his desk—seated, because he could shape his words more forcefully that way, and also because he was terribly tired. He smiled into the battery of cameras.

"Good evening," he said. "I'm Roy Walton, speaking to you from the offices of the Bureau of Population Equalization. I've been director of Popeek for a little less than a week, now, and I'd like to make a report—a progress report, so to speak.

"We of Popeek regard ourselves as holding a mandate from you, the people. After all, it was the world-wide referendum last year that enabled the United Nations to put us into business. And I want to tell you how the work of Popeek is going.

"Our aim is to provide breathing space for human beings. The world is vastly overcrowded, with its seven billion people. Popeek's job is to ease that overcrowdedness, to equalize the population masses of the world so that the empty portions of the globe are filled up and the extremely overcrowded places thinned out a little. But this is only part of our job—the short-range, temporary part. We're planning for the future here. We know we can't keep shifting population from place to place on Earth; it won't work forever. Eventually every square inch is going to be covered, and then where do we go?

"You know the answer. We go *out*. We reach for the stars. At present we have spaceships that can take us to the planets, but the planets aren't suitable for human life. All right, we'll *make* them suitable! At this very moment a team of engineers is on Venus, in that hot, dry, formaldehyde atmosphere, struggling to turn Venus into a world fit for oxygen-breathing human beings. They'll do it, too—and when they're done with Venus they'll move on to Mars, to the Moon, perhaps to the big satellites of Jupiter and Saturn too. There'll be a day when the solar system will be habitable from Mercury to Pluto—we hope.

"But even that is short-range," Walton said pointedly.

"There'll be a day—it may be a hundred years from now, or a thousand, or ten thousand—when the entire solar system will be as crowded with humanity as Earth is today. We have to plan for that day, too. It's the *lack* of planning on the part of our ancestors that's made things so hard for us. We of Popeek don't want to repeat the tragic mistakes of the past.

"My predecessor, the late Director FitzMaugham, was aware of this problem. He succeeded in gathering a group of scientists and technicians who developed a super space drive, a faster-than-light ship that can travel to the stars virtually instantaneously, instead of taking years to make the trip as our present ships would.

"The ship was built and sent out on an exploratory mission. Director FitzMaugham chose to keep this fact a secret. He was afraid of arousing false hopes in case the expedition should be a failure.

"The expedition was *not* a failure! Colonel Leslie McLeod and his men discovered a planet similar to Earth in the system of the star Procyon. I have seen photographs of New Earth, as they have named it, and I can tell you that it is a lovely planet . . . and one that will be receptive to our pioneers."

Walton paused a moment before launching into the main subject of his talk.

"Unfortunately, there is a race of intelligent beings living on a neighboring planet of this world. Perhaps you have seen the misleading and inaccurate reports blared today to the effect that these people refuse to allow Earth to colonize in their system. Some of you have cried out for immediate war against these people, the Dirnans.

"I must confirm part of the story the telefax carried today: the Dirnans are definitely not anxious to have Earth set up a colony on a world adjoining theirs. We are strangers to them, and their reaction is understandable. After all, suppose a race of strange-looking creatures landed on Mars, and proceeded with wholesale colonization of our neighboring world? We'd be uneasy, to say the least.

"And so the Dirnans are uneasy. However, I've summoned a Dirnan ambassador—our first diplomatic contact with intelligent alien creatures!—and I hope he'll be on Earth shortly. I plan to convince him that we're peacful, neighborly people, and that it will be to our mutual benefit to allow Earth colonization in the Procyon system.

"I'm going to need your help. If, while our alien guest is here, he discovers that some misguided Earthmen are demanding war with Dirna, he's certainly not going to think of us as particularly desirable neighbors to welcome with open arms. I want to stress the importance of this. Sure, we can go to war with Dirna for possession of Procyon VIII. But why spread wholesale destruction on two worlds when we can probably achieve our goal peacefully?

"That's all I have to say tonight, people of the world. I hope you'll think about what I've told you. Popeek works twenty-four hours a day in your behalf, but we need your full cooperation if we're going to achieve our aims and bring humanity to its full maturity. Thank you."

The floodlights winked out suddenly, leaving Walton momentarily blinded. When he opened his eyes again he saw the cameramen moving their bulky apparatus out of the office quickly and efficiently. The regular programs had returned to the channels—the vapid dancing and joke-making, the terror shows, the kaleidowhirls.

Now that it was over, now that the tension was broken, Walton experienced a moment of bitter disillusionment. He had had high hopes for his speech, but had he really put it over? He wasn't sure.

He glanced up. Lee Percy stood over him.

"Roy, can I say something?" Percy said diffidently.

"Go ahead," Walton said.

"I don't know how many millions I forked over to put you on the media tonight, but I know one thing—we threw a hell of a lot of money away."

Walton sighed wearily. "Why do you say that?"

"That speech of yours," Percy said, "was the speech of an amateur. You ought to let pros handle the big spiels, Roy."

"I thought you liked the impromptu thing I did when they mobbed that Herschelite. How come no go tonight?"

Percy shook his head. "The speech you made outside the building was different. It had emotion; it had punch! But tonight you didn't come across at all."

"No?"

"I'd put money behind it." Acidly Percy said, "You can't win the public opinion by being reasonable. You gave a nice smooth speech. Bland . . . folksy. You laid everything on the line where they could see it."

"And that's wrong, is it?" Walton closed his eyes for a moment. "*Why?*"

"Because they won't listen! You gave them a sermon when you should have been punching at them! Sweet reason! You can't be *sweet* if you want to sell your product to seven billion morons!"

"Is that all they are?" Walton asked. "Just morons?"

Percy chuckled. "In the long run, yes. Give them their daily bread and their one room to live in, and they won't give a damn what happens to the world. FitzMaugham sold them Popeek the way you'd sell a car without turbines. He hoodwinked them into buying something they hadn't thought about or wanted."

"They *needed* Popeek, whether they wanted it or not. No one needs a car without turbines."

"Bad analogy, then," Percy said. "But it's true. They don't care a blast about Popeek, except where it affects them. If you'd told them that these aliens would kill them all if they didn't act nice, you'd have gotten across. But this sweetness and light business—oh, no, Roy. It just doesn't work."

"Is that all you have to tell me?" Walton asked.

"I guess so. I just wanted to show you where you had a big chance and muffed it. Where we could have helped you out if you'd let us. I don't want you to think I'm being rude or critical, Roy; I'm just trying to be helpful."

"Okay, Lee. Get out."

"Huh?"

"Go away. Go sell ice to the Eskimos. Leave me alone, yes?"

"If that's the way you want it. Hell, Roy, don't brood over it. We can still fix things up before that alien gets here. We can put the content of tonight's speech across so smoothly that they won't even know we're—"

"*Get out!*"

Percy skittered for the door. He paused and said, "You're all wrought up, Roy. You ought to take a pill or something for your nerves."

Well, he had his answer. An expert evaluation of the content and effect of his speech.

Dammit, he had *tried* to reach them. Percy said he hadn't and Percy probably was right, little as Walton cared to admit the fact to himself.

But was Percy's approach the only one? Did you have to lie to them, push them, treat them as seven billion morons?

Maybe. Right now billions of human beings—the same human beings Walton was expending so much energy to save—were staring at the kaleidowhirl programs on their videos. Their eyes were getting fixed, glassy. Their mouths were beginning to sag open, their cheeks to wobble, their lips to droop pendulously, as the hypnosis of the color patterns took effect.

This was humanity. They were busy forgetting all the things they had just been forced to listen to. All the big words, like *mandate* and *eventually* and *wholesale destruction.* Just so many harsh syllables to be wiped away by the soothing swirl of the colors.

And somewhere else, possibly, a poet named Prior was listening to his baby's coughing and trying to write a poem—a poem that Walton and a few others would read excitedly, while the billions would ignore it.

Walton saw that Percy was dead right: Roy Walton could never have sold Popeek to the world. But FitzMaugham, that cagy, devious genius, did it. By waving his hands before the public and saying abracadabra, he bamboozled them into approving Popeek before they knew what they were being sold.

It was a lousy trick, but FitzMaugham had realized that it had to be done. Someone had killed him for it, but it was too late by then.

And Walton saw that he had taken the wrong track by trying to be reasonable. Percy's callous description of humanity as "seven billion morons" was uncomfortably close to the truth. Walton would have to make his appeal to a more subliminal level.

Perhaps, he thought, at the level of the kaleidowhirls, those endless patterns of colored light that were the main form of diversion for the Great Unwashed.

"I'll get to them, Walton promised himself. *There can't be any dignity or nobility in human life with everyone crammed into one sardine can. So I'll treat them like the sardines they are, and hope I can turn them into the human beings they could be if they only had room.*

He rose, turned out the light, prepared to leave. He wondered if the late Director FitzMaugham had ever faced an internal crisis of this sort, or whether FitzMaugham had known these truths innately from the start.

Probably, the latter was the case. FitzMaugham had been a genius, a sort of superman. But FitzMaugham was dead, and the man who carried on his work was no genius. He was only a mere man.

The reports started filtering in the next morning. It went much as Percy had predicted.

Citizen was the most virulent. Under the sprawling headline, *WHO'S KIDDING WHO?* the telefax sheet wanted to know what the "mealy-mouthed" Popeek director was trying to tell the world on all media the night before. They weren't sure, since Walton, according to *Citizen*, had been talking in "hifalution prose picked on purpose to befuddle John Q. Public." But their general impression was that Walton had proposed some sort of sellout to the Dirnans.

The sellout idea prevailed in most of the cheap telefax sheets.

"Behind a cloud of words, Popeek czar Walton is selling the world downstream to the greenskins," said one paper. "His talk last night was strictly bunk. His holy-holy words and grim face were supposed to put over something, but we ain't fooled—and don't you be fooled either, friend!"

The video commentators were a little kinder, but not very. One called for a full investigation of the Earth-Dirna situation. Another wanted to know why Walton, an appointed official and not even a permanent one at that, had taken it upon himself to handle such high-power negotiations. The UN seemed a little worried about that, even though Ludwig had made a passionate speech insisting that negotiations with Dirna were part of Walton's allotted responsibilities.

That touched off a new ruckus. "How much power does Walton have?" *Citizen* demanded in a later edition. "Is he the boss of the world? And if he is, who the devil is he anyway?"

That struck Walton harder than all the other blows. He

had been gradually realizing that he did, in fact, control what amounted to dictatorial powers over the world. But he had not yet fully admitted it to himself, and it hurt to be accused of it publicly.

One thing was clear: his attempt at sincerity and clarity had been a total failure. The world was accustomed to subterfuge and verbal pyrotechnics, and when it didn't get the expected commodity, it grew suspicious. Sincerity had no market value. By going before the public and making a direct appeal, Walton had aroused the suspicion that he had something hidden up his sleeve.

When *Citizen's* third edition of the day openly screamed for war with Dirna, Walton realized the time had come to stop playing it clean. From now on, he would chart his course and head there at any cost.

He tore a sheet of paper from his memo pad and inscribed on it a brief motto: *The ends justify the means!*

With that as his guide, he was ready to get down to work.

Fourteen

MARTINEZ, security head for the entire Appalachia district, was a small, slight man with unruly hair and deep, piercing eyes. He stared levelly at Walton and said, "Sellors has been with security for twenty years. It's absurd to suggest that he's disloyal."

"He's made a great many mistakes," Walton remarked. "I'm simply suggesting that if he's not utterly incompetent he must be in someone else's pay."

"And you want us to break a man on your say-so, Director Walton?" Martinez shook his head fussily. "I'm afraid I can't see that. Of course, if you're willing to go through the usual channels, you could conceivably request a change of personnel in this district. But I don't see how else—"

"Sellors will have to go," Walton said. "Our operation has sprung too many leaks. We'll need a new man in here at once, and I want you to double-check him personally."

Martinez rose. The little man's nostrils flickered ominously. "I refuse. Security is external to whims and fancies. If I remove Sellors, it will undermine security self-confidence all throughout the country."

"All right," sighed Walton. "Sellors stays. I'll file a request to have him transferred, though."

"I'll pigeonhole it. I can vouch for Sellors' competence myself," Martinez snapped. "Popeek is in good hands, Mr. Walton. Please believe that."

Martinez left. Walton glowered at the retreating figure. He knew Martinez was honest—but the security head was a stubborn man, and rather than admit the existence of a flaw in the security structure he had erected, Martinez would let a weak man continue in a vital postion.

Well, that blind spot in Martinez' makeup would have to be compensated for, Walton thought. One way or another, he would have to get rid of Sellors and replace him with a security man he could trust.

He scribbled a hasty note and sent it down the chute to Lee Percy. As Walton anticipated, the public relations man phoned minutes later.

"Roy, what's this release you want me to get out? It's fantastic—Sellors a spy? How? He hasn't even been arrested. I just saw him in the building."

Walton smirked. "Since when do you have such a high respect for accuracy?" he asked. "Send out the release and we'll watch what happens."

The 1140 newsblares were the first to carry the news. Walton listened cheerlessly as they revealed that Security Chief Sellors had been arrested on charges of disloyalty. According to informed sources, said the blares, Sellors was now in custody and had agreed to reveal the nature of the secret conspiracy which had hired him.

At 1210 came a later report: Security Chief Sellors had temporarily been released from custody.

And at 1230 came a still later report: Security Chief Sellors had been assassinated by an unknown hand outside the Cullen Building.

Walton listened to the reports with cold detachment. He had foreseen the move: Sellors' panicky employers had silenced the man for good. *The ends justify the means,* Walton told himself. There was no reason to feel pity for Sellors; he had been a spy and death was the penalty. It made no real difference whether death came in a federal gas chamber or as the result of some carefully faked news releases.

Martinez called almost immediately after word of Sellors' murder reached the blares. The little man's face was deadly pale.

"I owe you an apology," he said. "I acted like an idiot this morning."

"Don't blame yourself," Walton said. "It was only natural that you'd trust Sellors; you'd known him so long. But you can't trust anyone these days, Martinez. Not even yourself."

"I will have to resign," the security man said.

"No. It wasn't your fault. Sellors was a spy and a bungler, and he paid the price. His own men struck him down when that rumor escaped that he was going to inform. Just send me a new man, as I asked—and make him a good one!"

Keeler, the new security attaché, was a crisp-looking man in his early thirties. He reported directly to Walton as soon as he reached the building.

"You're Sellors' replacement, eh? Glad to see you, Keeler." Walton studied him. He looked tough and hard and thoroughly incorruptible. "I've a couple of jobs I'd like you to start on right away. First, you know Sellors was looking for a man named Lamarre. Let me fill you in on that, and—"

"No need for that," Keeler said. "I was the man Sellors put on the Lamarre chase. There isn't a trace of him anywhere. We've got feelers out all over the planet now, and no luck."

"Hmm." Walton was mildly annoyed; he had been wishfully hoping Sellors had found Lamarre and had simply covered up the fact. But if Keeler had been the one who handled the search, there was no hope of that.

"All right," Walton said. "Keep on the hunt for Lamarre. At the moment I want you to give this building a thorough scouring. There's no telling how many spy pickups Sellors planted here. Top to bottom, and report back to me when the job is done."

Next on Walton's schedule was a call from communications. He received it and a technician told him, "There's been a call from the Venus ship. Do you want it, sir?"

"Of course!"

"It says, 'Arrived Venus June fifteen late, no sign of Lang outfit yet. We'll keep looking and will report daily.' It's signed, 'Spencer.'"

"Okay," Walton said. "Thanks. And if any further word

from them comes, let me have it right away."

The fate of the Lang expedition, Walton reflected, was not of immediate importance. But he would like to know what had happened to the group. He hoped Spencer and his rescue mission had something more concrete to report tomorrow.

The annunciator chimed. "Dr. Frederic Walton is on the line, sir. He says it's urgent."

"Okay," Walton said. He switched over and waited for his brother's face to appear on the screen. A nervous current of anticipation throbbed in him.

"Well, Fred?" he asked at length.

"You've been a busy little bee, haven't you?" Fred said. "I understand you have a new security chief to watch over you."

"I don't have time to make conversation now," Walton snapped.

"Nor do I. You fooled us badly, with that newsbreak on Sellors. You forced us into wiping out a useful contact prematurely."

"Not so useful," Walton said. "I was on to him. If you hadn't killed him, I would have had to handle the job myself. You saved me the trouble."

"My, my! Getting ruthless, aren't we!"

"When the occasion demands," Walton said.

"Fair enough. We'll play the same way." Fred's eyes narrowed. "You recall our conversation in the Bronze Room the other day, Roy?"

"Vividly."

"I've called to ask for your decision," Fred said. "One way or the other."

Walton was caught off guard. "But you said I had a week's grace!"

"The period has been halved," Fred said. "We now see it's necessary to accelerate things."

"Tell me what you want me to do. Then I'll give you my answer."

"It's simple enough. You're to resign in my favor. If it's not done by nightfall tomorrow, we'll find it necessary to release the Lamarre serum. Those are our terms, and don't try to bargain with me."

Walton was silent for a moment, contemplating his brother's cold face on the screen. Finally he said, "It takes time to get such things done. I can't just resign overnight."

"FitzMaugham did."

"Ah, yes—if you call that a resignation. But unless you want to inherit the same sort of chaos I did, you'd better give me a little time to prepare things."

Fred's eyes gleamed. "Does that mean you'll yield? You'll resign in my favor?"

"There's no guarantee the UN will accept you," Walton warned. "Even with my recommendation, I can't promise a one hundred percent chance of success."

"We'll have to risk it," said Fred. "The important step is getting you out of there. When can I have confirmation of all this?"

Walton eyed his brother shrewdly. "Come up to my office tomorrow at this time. I'll have everything set up for you by then, and I'll be able to show you how the Popeek machinery works. That's one advantage you'll have over me. FitzMaugham kept half the workings in his head."

Fred grinned savagely. "I'll see you then, Roy." Chuckling, he added, "I knew all that ruthlessness of yours was just skin deep. You never were tough, Roy."

Walton glanced at his watch after Fred had left the screen. The time was 1100. It had been a busy morning.

But some of the vaguenesses were beginning to look sharper. He knew, for instance, that Sellors had been in the pay of the same organization that backed Fred. Presumably, this meant that FitzMaugham had been assassinated by the landed gentry.

But for what reason? Surely, not simply for the sake of assassination. Had they cared to, they might have killed FitzMaugham whenever they pleased.

He saw now why the assassination had been timed as it had. By the time the conspirators had realized that Walton was sure to be the old man's successor, Fred had already joined their group. They had ready leverage on the prospective director. They knew they could shove him out of office almost as quickly as he got in, and supplant him with their puppet, Fred.

Well, they were in for a surprise. Fred was due to appear at Walton's office at 1100 on the morning of the seventeenth to take over command. Walton planned to be ready for them by then.

There was the matter of Lamarre. Walton wanted the little scientist and his formula badly. But by this time Fred had certainly made at least one copy of Lamarre's documents; the threat would remain, whether or not Popeek recovered the originals.

Walton had twenty-four hours to act. He called up Sue

Llewellyn, Popeek's comptroller.

"Sue, how's our budget looking?"

"What's on your mind, Roy?"

"Plenty. I want to know if I can make an expenditure of—say, a billion, between now and nightfall."

"A *billion?* You joking, Roy?"

"Hardly." Walton's tone was grim. "I hope I won't need it all. But there's a big purchase I want to make . . . an investment. Can you squeeze out the money? It doesn't matter where you squeeze it from, either, because if we don't get it by nightfall there probably won't be a Popeek by the day after tomorrow."

"What *are* you talking about, Roy?"

"Give me a yes or no answer. And if the answer's not the one I want to hear, I'm afraid you can start looking for a new job, Sue."

She uttered a little gasp. Then she said, "Okay, Roy. I'll play along with you, even if it bankrupts us. There's a billion at your disposal as of now, though Lord knows what I'll use for a payroll next week."

"You'll have it back," Walton promised. "With compound interest."

His next call was to a man he had once dealt with in his capacity of secretary to Senator FitzMaugham. He was Noel Hervey, a registered securities and exchange slyster.

Hervey was a small, worried-looking little man, but his unflickering eyes belied this ratty appearance. "What troubles, you, Roy?"

"I want you to make a stock purchase for me, pronto. Within an hour, say?"

Hervey shook his head instantly. "Sorry, Roy. I'm all tied up on a hefty monorail deal. Won't be free until Wednesday or Thursday, if by then."

Walton said, "What sort of money will you be making on this big deal of yours, Noel?"

"Confidential! You wouldn't invade a man's privacy on a delicate matter like—"

"Will it be worth five million dollars for you, Noel?"

"Five million—hey, is this a gag?"

"I'm awfully serious," Walton said. "I want you to swing a deal for me, right away. You've heard my price."

Hervey smiled warmly. "Well, start talking, friend. Consider me hired."

A few other matters remained to be tended to hurriedly. Walton spent some moments talking to a communications technician, then sent out an order for three or four technical books—*Basic Kaleidowhirl Theory* and related works. He sent a note to Lee Percy requesting him to stop by and see him in an hour, and told his annunciator that for no reason whatsoever was he to be disturbed for the next sixty minutes.

The hour passed rapidly; by its end, Walton's head was slightly dizzy from too much skimming, but his mind was thrumming with new possibilities, with communications potentials galore. Talk about reaching people! He had a natural!

He flipped on the annunciator. "Is Mr. Percy here yet?"

"No, sir. Should I send for him?"

"Yes. He's due here any minute to see me. Have there been any calls?"

"Quite a few. I've relayed them down to Mr. Eglin's office, as instructed."

"Good girl," Walton said.

"Oh, Mr. Percy's here. And there's a call for you from Communications."

Walton frowned. "Tell Percy to wait outside a minute or two. Give me the call."

The communications tech on the screen was grinning excitedly. He said, "Subspace message just came in for you, sir."

"From Venus?"

"No, sir. From Colonel McLeod."

"Let's have it," Walton said.

The technician read, " 'To Walton from McLeod, via subspace radio. Have made successful voyage to Procyon system, and am on way back with Dirnan ambassador on board. See you soon, and good luck—you'll need it.' "

"Good. That all?"

"That's all, sir."

"Okay. Keep me posted." He broke contact and turned to the annunciator. Excitement put a faint quiver in his voice. "You can send in Mr. Percy now," he said.

Fifteen

WALTON LOOKED up at the public relations man and said, "How much do you know about kaleidowhirls, Lee?"

"Not a hell of a lot. I never watch the things, myself. They're bad for the eyes."

Walton smiled. "That makes you a nonconformist, doesn't it? According to the figures I have here, the nightly kaleidowhirl programs are top-ranked on the rating charts."

"Maybe so," Percy said cautiously. "I still don't like to watch them. What goes, Roy?"

"I've suddenly become very interested in kaleidowhirls myself," Walton said. He leaned back and added casually, "I think they can be used as propaganda devices. My brother's reaction to one gave me the idea, couple days ago, at the

Bronze Room. For the past hour or so, I've been studying kaleidowhirls in terms of information theory. Did you know that it's possible to get messages across via kaleidowhirl?"

"Of course," Percy gasped. "But the Communications Commission would never let you get away with it!"

"By the time the Communications Commission found out what had been done," Walton said calmly, "we wouldn't be doing it any more. They won't be able to prove a thing." Sarcastically he added, "After spending a lifetime in public relations, you're not suddenly getting a rush of ethics, are you?"

"Well . . . let's have the details, then."

"Simple enough," Walton said. "We feed through a verbal message—something like *Horoay for Popeek* or *I Don't Want War With Dirna*. We flash it on the screen for, say, a microsecond, then cover it up with kaleidowhirl patterns. Wait two minutes, then flash it again. Plenty of noise, but the signal will get through if we flash it often enough."

"And it'll get through deep down," Percy said. "Subliminally. They won't even realize that they're being indoctrinated, but suddenly they'll have a new set of opinions about Popeek and Dirna!" He shuddered. "Roy, I hate to think what can happen if someone else gets to thinking about this and puts on his own kaleidowhirl shows."

"I've thought of that. After the Dirna crisis is over—after we've put over our point—I'm going to take steps to make sure no one can use this sort of weapon again. I'm going to frame someone into putting on a propaganda kaleidowhirl, and then catch him in the act. That ought to be sufficient to wise up the Communications Commission."

"In other words," Percy said, "you're willing to use this technique *now*. But since you don't want anyone else to use it, you're willing to give up future use of it yourself as soon as the Dirna trouble is over."

"Exactly." Walton shoved the stack of textbooks over to the PR man. "Read these through first. Get yourself familiar with the setup. Then buy a kaleidowhirl hour and get a bunch of our engineers in there to handle the special inserts. Okay?"

"It's nasty, but I like it. When do you want the program to begin?"

"Tomorrow. Tonight, if you can work it. And set up a poll of some kind to keep check on the program's effectiveness. I want two messages kaleidowhirled alternately: one supporting Popeek, one demanding a peaceful settlement with the aliens. Have your pulse takers feel out the populace on those two propositions, and report any fluctuation to me immediately."

"Got it."

"Oh, one more thing. I suspect you'll have some extra responsibilities as of tomorrow, Lee."

"Eh?"

"Your office will have one additional medium to deal with. Telefax. I'm buying *Citizen* and we're going to turn it into a pro-Popeek rag."

Percy's mouth dropped in astonishment; then he started to laugh. "You're a wonder, Roy. A genuine wonder."

Moments after Percy departed, Noel Hervey, the securities and exchange slyster, called.

"Well?" Walton asked.

Hervey looked preoccupied. "I've successfully spent a couple of hundred million of Popeek's money in the last half-hour, Roy. You now own the single biggest block of *Citizen* stock there is."

"How much is that?"

"One hundred fifty-two thousand shares. Approximately thirty-three percent."

"Thirty-three percent! What about the other eighteen percent?"

"Patience, lad, patience. I know my job. I snapped up all the small holdings there were, very quietly. It cost me a pretty penny to farm out the purchases, too."

"Why'd you do that?" Walton asked.

"Because this has to be handled very gingerly. You know the ownership setup of *Citizen*?"

"No."

"Well, it goes like this: Amalgamated Telefax owns a twenty-six percent chunk, and Horace Murlin owns twenty-five percent. Since Murlin also owns Amalgamated, he votes fifty-one percent of the stock, even though it isn't registered that way. The other forty-nine percent doesn't matter, Murlin figures. So I'm busy gathering up as much of it as I can for you—under half a dozen different brokerage names. I doubt that I can get it all, but I figure on rounding up at least forty-five percent. Then I'll approach Murlin with a Big Deal and sucker him into selling me six percent of his *Citizen* stock. He'll check around, find out that the remaining stock is splintered ninety-seven different ways, and he'll probably let go of a little of his, figuring he still has control."

"Suppose he doesn't?" Walton asked.

"Don't worry," Hervey said confidently. "He will. I've got a billion smackers to play with, don't I? I'll cook up a deal so juicy he can't resist it—and all he'll have to do to take a flyer will be to peel off a little of his *Citizen* stock. The second he does that, I transfer all the fragmented stock to you. With your controlling majority of fifty-one percent, you boot Murlin off the Board, and the telefax sheet is yours! Simple? Clear?"

"Perfectly," Walton said. "Okay. Keep in touch."

He broke contact and walked to the window. The street was packed with people scrambling in every direction, like so many ants moving at random over the ground. Many of them clutched telefax sheets—and the most popular one was the *Citizen*. Many of them would gape and goggle at kaleidowhirl programs, come evening.

Walton suddenly tightened his fist. In just that way, he thought, Popeek was tightening its hold on the public by capturing the mass media. If Hervey's confidence had any justification in truth, they would own the leading anti-Popeek telefax sheet by tomorrow. With subtle handling over the course of several days, they could swing the slant of *Citizen* around to a pro-Popeek stand, and do it so surreptitiously that it would seem as though the sheet had never had any other policy.

As for the kaleidowhirl subterfuge—that, Walton admitted, was hitting below the belt. But he had resolved that all would be fair during the current crisis. There would be time enough for morality after war had been averted.

At about 1430 that day, Walton took advantage of a lull

in activities to have a late lunch at the Bronze Room. He felt that he had to get away from the confining walls of his office for at least some part of the afternoon.

The Bronze Room had adopted cerise as its color scheme for the day. Walton selected a private room, lunched lightly on baked chlorella steak and filtered rum, and dialed a twelve-minute nap. When the alarm system in the foam-web couch stirred him to wakefulness, he stretched happily, some of the choking tension having been washed out of him.

Thoughtfully, he switched on the electroluminescent kaleidoscope and stared at it. It worked on the same principle as the kaleidowhirl programs beamed over the public video, except that the Bronze Room provided closed-channel beaming of its own kaleidoscopic patterns; tending more to soft greens and pale rose, they were on a higher esthetic plane, certainly, than the jagged, melodramatic purples and reds the video channels sent out for popular consumption.

But it was with a certain new apprehension that Walton now studied the kaleidoscopic pattern. Now that he knew what a dangerous weapon the flashing colors could be, how could he be certain that the Bronze Room proprietors were not flashing some scarcely seen subliminal command at him this very moment?

He turned the set off with a brusque gesture.

The ends justify the means. A nice homily, he thought, which allowed him to do almost anything. It brought to mind the rationale of Ivan Karamazov: without God, everything is permissible.

But both God and Dostoevski seem to be obsolete these

days, he reminded himself. God is now a lean young man with an office on the twenty-ninth floor of the Cullen Building—and as for Dostoevski, all he did was write books, and therefore could not have been of any great importance.

He felt a tremor of self-doubt. Maybe it had been unwise to let kaleidowhirl propaganda loose on the world; once unleashed, it might not be so easily caged again. He realized that as soon as the Popeek campaign was over, he would have to make sure some method was devised for pre-checking all public and closed-channel kaleidoscopic patterns.

The most damnable part of such propaganda techniques, he knew, was that you could put over almost any idea at all without arousing suspicion on the part of the viewer. He wouldn't know he'd been tampered with; you could tell him so, after the new idea had been planted, and by then he wouldn't believe you.

Walton dialed another filtered rum, and lifted it to his lips with a slightly shaky hand.

"Mr. Ludwig of the United Nations called while you were out, sir," Walton was told upon returning to his office. "He'd like you to call him back."

"Very well. Make the connection for me."

When Ludwig appeared, Walton said, "Sorry I missed your call. What's happening?"

"Special session of the Security Council just broke up. They passed a resolution unanimously and shipped it on to the Assembly. There's going to be an immediate hearing to determine the new permanent head of Popeek."

Walton clamped his lips together. After a moment he said, "How come?"

"The Dirnan crisis. They don't want a mere interim director handling things. They feel the man dealing with the aliens ought to have full UN blessing."

"Should I interpret that to mean I get the job automatically?"

"I couldn't swear to it," said Ludwig. "General consensus certainly favors you to continue. I'd advise that you show up at the hearing in person and present your program in detail; otherwise they may stick some smoothtalking politico in your place. The noise is slated to start at 1100, day after tomorrow. The eighteenth."

"I'll be there," Walton said. "Thanks for the tip."

He chewed the end of his stylus for a moment, then hastily scribbled down the appointment. As of now, he knew he couldn't worry too strongly about events taking place the day after tomorrow—not with Fred arriving for a showdown the next morning.

The next day began busily enough. Hervey was the first to call.

"The *Citizen*'s sewed up, Roy! I had dinner with Murlin last night and weaseled him out of four percent of *Citizen* stock in exchange and for a fancy tip on the new monorail project out Nevada way. He was grinning all over the place—but I'll bet he's grinning out of the other side of his mouth this morning."

"Is it all arranged?" Walton asked.

"In the bag. I was up by 0700 and consolidating my

holdings—*your* holdings, I mean. Forty-seven percent of the stock I had fragmented in a dozen different outfits; the other two percent outstanding belonged to rich widows who wouldn't sell. I lumped the forty-seven percent together in your name, then completed the transfer on Murlin's four percent and stuck that in there too. *Citizen* telefax is now the property of Popeek, Roy!"

"Fine work. How much did it cost?"

Then he said, "Four hundred eighty-three million and some change. Plus my usual five percent commission, which in this case comes to about two and a quarter million."

"But I offered you five million," Walton said. "That offer still goes."

"You want me to lose my license? I spend years placing bribes to get a slyster's license, and you want me to throw it away for an extra couple million? Uh-uh. I'll settle for two and a quarter, and damn good doing I call that for a day's work."

Walton grinned. "You win. And Sue Llewellyn will be glad to know it didn't cost the whole billion to grab *Citizen*. You'll be over with the papers, won't you?"

"About 1000," the slyster said. "I've gotta follow through for Murlin on his monorail deal first. The poor sucker! See you in an hour."

"Right."

Rapidly Walton scribbled memos. As soon as the papers were in his hands, he'd serve notice on Murlin that a stock-holders' meeting was to be held at once. After that, he'd depose Murlin, fire the present *Citizen* editors, and pack the telefax sheet with men loyal to Popeek.

Fred was due at 1100. Walton buzzed Keeler, the new security chief, and said, "Keeler, I have an appointment with someone at 1100. I want you to station three men outside my door and frisk him for weapons as he comes in."

"We'd do that anyway, sir. It's standard procedure now."

"Good. But I want you to be one of the three. And make sure the two who come with you are tight-mouthed. I don't want *any* newsbreaks on this."

"Right, sir."

"Okay. Be there about 1050 or so. About 1115, I'm going to press my door opener, and I want you and your men to break in, arrest my visitor, and spirit him off to the deepest dungeon security has. And leave him there. If Martinez wants to know what's going on, tell him I'll take responsibility."

Keeler looked vaguely puzzled, but merely nodded. "We frisk him first, then let him talk to you for fifteen minutes. Then we come in on signal and take him away. I've got it."

"This man's a dangerous anti-Popeek conspirator. Make sure he's drugged before he gets out of my office. I don't want him making noise."

The annunciator sounded. "Man from Communications has a message for you, Mr. Walton."

He switched over from Keeler to Communications and said, "Go ahead."

"From McLeod, Mr. Walton. We just got it. It says, 'Arriving Nairobi on the 18th, will be in your office with Dirnan following morning if he feels like making the trip.

Otherwise will you come to Nairobi?"

"Tell him yes, if necessary," Walton said.

He glanced at his watch. 0917. It looked like it was going to be hectic all day.

And Fred was due at 1100.

Sixteen

HERVEY SHOWED up at 1003, grinning broadly. He unfolded a thick wad of documents and thrust them at Walton.

"I hold in my hand the world's most potent telefax sheet," Hervey said. He flipped the documents casually onto Walton's desk and laughed. "They're all yours. Fifty-one percent, every bit of it voting stock. I told Murlin about it just before I left him this morning. He turned purple."

"What did he say?"

"What *could* he say? I asked him offhandedly if he knew where all the outstanding *Citizen* stock was, and he said yes, it was being held by a lot of small holders. And then I told him that somebody was buying out the small holders, and that I was selling my four percent. That's when he started to change colors. When I left he was busy making phone calls, but I don't think he'll like what he's going to find out."

Walton riffled through the papers. "It's all here, eh? Fine work. I'll put through your voucher in half an hour or so, unless you're in a hurry."

"Oh, don't rush," Hervey said. He ran a finger inside his collar. "Couple of security boys outside, y'know. They really gave me a going-over."

"I'm expecting an assassin at 1100," Walton said lightly. "They're on the lookout."

"Oh? A close friend?"

"A relative," Walton said.

Fred arrived promptly at 1100. By that time Walton had already set the machinery in operation for the taking-over of *Citizen.*

The first step had been to call Horace Murlin and confirm the fact that Popeek now owned the telefax sheet. Murlin's fleshy face was a curious shade of rose-purple; he sputtered at Walton for five minutes before admitting he was beaten.

With Murlin out of the way, Walton selected a new editorial staff for the paper from a list Percy supplied. He intended to keep the reporting crew of the old regime intact; *Citizen* had a fantastically efficient newsgathering team, and there was no point in breaking it up. It was the policy-making level Walton was interested in controlling.

The 1000 edition of *Citizen* was the last under the old editors. They had received word from Murlin about what had happened, and by 1030, when Walton sent his dismissal notices over, they were already cleaning out their desks.

That 1000 edition was a beauty, though. The lead headline read:

ARE WE CHUMPS FOR THE GREENSKINS?

And most of the issue was devoted to inflammatory pro-war anti-Popeek journalism. A full page of "letters from the readers"—actually transcribed phone calls, since few of *Citizen*'s readers were interested in writing letters—echoed the editorial stand. One "letter" in particular caught Walton's attention.

It was from a Mrs. P.F. of New York City Environ, which probably meant Jersey or lower Connecticut, and it was short and to the point:

To the Editor—
Hooray for you. Popeek is a damned crime and that Walton criminal ought to be put away and we ought to kill those greenskins up there before they kill us. We gotta have room to live.

Kill them before they kill us. Walton snickered. All the old hysterias, the old panic reactions, come boiling up again in times of stress.

He looked at his hand. It was perfectly steady, even though his wrist watch told him Fred would be here in just a few minutes. A week ago, a situation like this would have had him gobbling benzolurethrin as fast as he could unwrap the lozenges.

The ghostly presence of FitzMaugham seemed to hover

in the room. *The ends justify the means*, Walton told himself
grimly, as he waited for his brother to arrive.

Fred was dressed completely in black, from his stylish
neo-Victorian waistcoat and the bit of ribbon at his throat to
the mirror-bright leather pumps on his feet. The splendor of
his clothing was curiously at odds with the coarseness of his
features and the stockiness of his body.

He walked into Walton's office at the stroke of 1100 and
sighed deeply—the sigh of a man about to take permanent
possession. "Good morning, Roy. I'm on time, as always."

"And looking radiant, my dear brother." Walton gestured appreciatively at Fred's clothes. "It's been a long time
since I've seen you in anything but your lab smock."

"I gave notice at the lab yesterday, right after I spoke to
you. I'm no longer an employee of Popeek. And I felt I
should dress with the dignity suitable to my new rank." He
grinned buoyantly. "Well, ready to turn over the orb and
scepter, Roy?"

"Not exactly," Walton said.

"But—"

"But I promised you I'd resign in your favor today,
Fred. I don't think I ever used those words, but I certainly
implied it, didn't I?"

"Of course you did. You told me to come here at 1100
and you'd arrange the transfer."

Walton nodded. "Exactly so." He waited a long moment and then said quietly, "I lied, Fred."

He had chosen the words carefully, for maximum impact. He had not chosen wrongly.

For a brief instant Fred's face was very pale against the blackness of his garb. Total disbelief flickered across his eyes and mouth.

Walton had considered his brother's mental picture of him—the elder brother, virtuous, devoted to hard work, kind to animals, and just a little soft in the head. Also, extremely honest.

Fred hadn't expected Walton to be lying. And the calm admission stunned him.

"You're not planning to go through with it, then?" Fred asked in a dead voice.

"No."

"You realize what this means in terms of the serum, don't you? The moment I get out of here and transmit your refusal to my employers, they'll begin wholesale manufacture and distribution of the Lamarre serum. The publicity won't be good, Roy. Nor the result."

"You won't get out of here," Walton said.

Another shock wave rippled over Fred's face. "You can't be serious, Roy. My employers know where I am; they know what I'm here for. If they don't hear from me within twenty-four hours, they'll proceed with serum distribution. You can't hope to—"

"I'll risk it," Walton interrupted. "If nothing else, I'll have a twenty-four hour extension. You didn't really think I could hand Popeek over to you on a platter, Fred? Why, I don't even know how secure my *own* position is here. So I'm afraid I'll have to back down on my offer. You're under arrest, Fred!"

"*Arrest!*" Fred sprang from his seat and circled around

the desk toward Walton. For a moment the two brothers stared at each other, faces inches apart. Walton put one hand on his brother's shoulder and, gripping tightly, forced him around to the front of the desk.

"You had this all planned, didn't you?" Fred said bitterly. "Yesterday, when you talked to me, you knew this was what you were going to do. But you said you'd yield, and I believed you! I don't fool easy, but I thought I had you pegged because you were my brother. I *knew* you. You wouldn't do a sneaky thing like this."

"But I did," Walton said.

Suddenly, Fred jumped. He charged at Walton blindly, head down.

In the same motion, Walton signaled for Keeler and his men to break in, and met Fred's charge. He caught his brother in midstride with a swinging punch that sent his head cracking back sharply.

Fred's face twisted and writhed, more in astonishment than pain. He stepped back, rubbing his chin. "You've changed," he said. "This job's made you tough. A year ago you would never have done this to me."

Walton shrugged. "Look behind you, Fred. And this time you can trust me."

Fred turned warily. Keeler and two other gray-clad security men stood there.

"Drug him and take him away," Walton said. "Have him held in custody until I notify Martinez."

Fred's eyes widened. "You're a *dictator!*" he said hoarsely. "You just move people around like chessmen, Roy. Like chessmen."

"Drug him," Walton repeated.

Keeler stepped forward, a tiny hypodermic spray cupped in his hand. He activated it with a twitch of his thumb and touched it to Fred's forearm. A momentary hum droned in the office as the vibrating spray forced the drug into Fred's arm.

He slumped like an empty sack. "Pick him up," Keeler ordered. "Take him and let's get going."

The story broke in the 1300 edition of *Citizen*, and from the general tone of the piece Walton could see the fine hand of Lee Percy at work.

The headline was:

GUY TRIES TO KNOCK OFF POPEEK HEAD

After the usual string of subheads, all in the cheerful, breezy, barely literate *Citizen* style, came the body of the story:

> A guy tried to bump Popeek top number Roy Walton today. Security men got there in time to keep Walton from getting the same finisher as dead Popeek boss FitzMaugham got last week.
>
> Walton says he's all right; the assassin didn't even come close. He also told our man that he expects good news on the New Earth bit soon. We like the sound of those words. Popeek may be with the stream after all. Who knows?

The voice was that of *Citizen*, but the man behind the

voice was thinking a little differently. Had the previous editors of *Citizen* been handling the break, the prevailing tone would most likely have been too-bad-he-missed.

Walton called Percy after the edition came out. "Nice job you did on our first *Citizen*," he said approvingly. "It's just what I want: same illiterate style, but a slow swerving of editorial slant until it's completely pro-Popeek."

"Wait till you see tomorrow's paper. We're just getting the hang of it! And we'll have our first kaleidowhirl show at 2000 tonight. Cost a fortune to buy in, but we figured that's the best hour."

"What's the buried message?"

"As you said," Percy told him. "A pro-Popeek job and some pacifist stuff. We've got a team of pollsters out now, and they say the current's predominantly going the other way. We'll be able to tell if the kaleidowhirl stuff works out, all right."

"Keep up the good work," Walton said. "We'll get there yet. The alien isn't due to arrive for another day or so—McLeod gets into Nairobi tomorrow some time. I'm going to testify before the UN tomorrrow, too. I hope those UN boys are watching our pretty color patterns tonight."

Percy grinned. "Boy, you bet!"

Walton threw himself energetically into his work. It was taking shape, now. There were still some loose ends, of course, but he was beginning to feel that some end to the tangle of interlocking intrigues was in sight.

He checked with a public recreation director and discovered there would be a block forum on West 382nd Street at 1830 that night. He made a note to attend, and arranged to have a synthetic mask fashioned so he wouldn't have to reveal his own identity.

Twenty-four hours. In that time, Fred's employers would presumably be readying themselves to loose Lamarre's serum on the world; an extraterrestrial being would be landing on Earth—and, by then, Walton would have been called to render an account of his stewardship before the United Nations.

The annunciator chimed again. "Yes?" Walton said.

"Mr. O'Mealia of Mount Palomar Observatory, calling long distance to talk to you, sir."

"Put him on," Walton said puzzledly.

O'Mealia was a red-faced individual with deep-set, compelling eyes. He introduced himself as a member of the research staff at Mount Palomar. "Glad I could finally reach you," he said, in a staccato burst of words. "Been trying to call for an hour. Made some early-morning observations of Venus a little while ago, and I thought you'd be interested."

"Venus? What?"

"Cloud blanket looks awfully funny, Mr. Walton. Blazing away like sixty. Got the whole staff down here to discuss it, and the way it looks to us there's some sort of atomic chain-reaction going on in Venus' atmosphere. I think it's those terraforming men you Popeek folk have up there. I think they've blown the whole place up!"

Seventeen

WALTON STEPPED off the jetbus at Broadway and West 382nd Street, paused for a moment beneath a street lamp, and fingered his chin to see if his mask were on properly. It was.

Three youths stood leaning against a nearby building. "Could you tell me where the block meeting's being held?" Walton asked.

"Down the street and turn left. You a telefax man?"

"Just an interested citizen," Walton said. "Thanks for the directions."

It was easy to see where the block meeting was; Walton saw streams of determined-looking men and women entering a bulky old building just off 382nd Street. He joined them and found himself carried along into the auditorium.

Nervously he found a seat. The auditorium was an old one, predominantly dark brown and cavernous, with row after row of hard wooden folding chairs. Someone was adjusting a microphone on stage. A sharp metallic whine came over the public address system.

"Testing. Testing, one two three . . ."

"It's all right, Max!" someone yelled from the rear. Walton didn't turn around to look.

A low undercurrent of murmuring was audible. It was only 1815; the meeting was not due to start for another fifteen minutes, but the hall was nearly full, with more than a thousand of the local residents already on hand.

The fifteen minutes passed slowly. Walton listened carefully to the conversations around him; no one was discussing the Venus situation. Apparently his cloud of censorship had been effective. He had instructed Percy to keep all word of the disaster from the public until the 2100 newsblares. By that time, the people would have been exposed to the indoctrinating kaleidowhirl program at 2000, and their reaction would be accordingly more temperate—he hoped.

Also, releasing the news early would have further complicated the survey Walton was trying to make by attending this public meeting. The Index of Public Confusion increased factorially; one extra consideration for discussion and Walton's task would be hopelessly difficult.

At exactly 1830, a tall, middle-aged man stepped out on the stage. He seized the microphone as if it were a twig and said, "Hello, folks. Glad to see you're all here tonight. This is an important meeting for us all. In case some of you don't know me—and I do see some new faces out there—I'm Dave

Forman, president of the West 382nd Street Association. I also run a little law business on the side, just to help pay the rent." (Giggles.)

"As usual in these meetings," Forman went on, "we'll have a brief panel discussion, and then I'll throw the thing open to you folks for floor discussion. The panelists tonight are people you all know—Sadie Hargreave, Dominic Campobello, Rudi Steinfeld. Come on out here, folks."

The panelists appeared on the stage diffidently. Sadie Hargreave was a short, stout, fierce-looking little woman; Campobello was chunky, balding, Steinfeld tall and ascetic. Walton was astonished that there should be such camaraderie here. Was it all synthetic? It didn't seem that way.

He had always remained aloof, never mingling with his neighbors in the gigantic project where he lived, never suspecting the existence of community life on this scale. But, somehow, community life had sprung up in this most gargantuan of cities. Organizations within each project, within each block perhaps, had arisen, converting New York into an interlocking series of small towns. *I ought to investigate the grass roots more often,* Walton thought. *Caliph Haroun-al-Raschid having a night on the town.*

"Hello, folks," Sadie Hargreave said aggressively. "I'm glad I can talk to you tonight. Gosh, I want to speak out. I think it's crazy to let these thing-men from outer space push us around. I for one feel we ought to take strong action against that space world."

Cries of "Yeah! Yeah! Go to it, Sadie!" rose from the audience.

Skillfully she presented three inflammatory arguments

in favor of war with Dirna, backing up each with a referent of high emotional connotation. Walton watched her performance with growing admiration. The woman was a born public relations technician. It was too bad she was on the other side of the fence.

He saw the effect she had: people were nodding in agreement, grimacing vehemently, muttering to themselves. The mood of the meeting, he gathered, was overwhelmingly in favor of war if Dirna did not yield New Earth.

Dominic Campobello began his address by inviting all and sundry to his barber shop; this was greeted with laughter. Then he launched into a discourse on Popeek as an enemy of mankind. A few catcalls, Walton noted, but again chiefly approval. Campobello seemed sincere.

The third man, Rudi Steinfeld, was a local music teacher. He, too, spoke out against Popeek, though in a restrained, dryly intellectual manner. People began yawning. Steinfeld cut his speech short.

It was now 1900. In one hour Percy's kaleidowhirl program would be screened.

Walton stayed at the block meeting until 1930, listening to citizen after citizen rise and heap curses upon Popeek, Dirna, or Walton, depending on where his particular ire lay. At 1930 Walton rose and left the hall.

He phoned Percy. "I'm on West 382nd Street. Just attended a block meeting. I'd say the prevailing sentiment runs about ninety percent agin us. We don't have the people backing our program any more, Lee."

"We never did. But I think we'll nail 'em now. The kaleidowhirl's ready to go, and it's a honey. And I think

Citizen will sell 'em too! We're on our way, Roy."

"I hope so," Walton said.

He was unable to bring himself to watch Percy's program, even though he reached his room in time that night. He knew there could be no harm in watching—at least not for him—but the idea of voluntarily submitting his mind to external tampering was too repugnant to accept.

Instead he spent the hour dictating a report on the block meeting, for benefit of his pollster staff. When he was done with that, he turned to the 2100 edition of *Citizen*, which came clicking from the telefax slot right on schedule.

He had to look hard for the Venus story. Finally he found it tucked away at the bottom of the sheet.

ACCIDENT ON VENUS

A big blowup took place on the planet Venus earlier today. Sky-men who watched the popoff say it was caused by an atomic explosion in the planet's atmosphere.

Meanwhile, attempts are being made to reach the team of Earth engineers working on Venus. No word from them yet. They may be dead.

Walton chuckled. *They may be dead*, indeed! By now Lang and his team, and the rescue mission as well, lay dead under showers of radioactive formaldehyde, and Venus had been turned into a blazing hell ten times less livable than it had been before.

Percy had mishandled the news superbly. For one thing, he had carefully neglected to link Lang with Popeek in any way. That was good connotative thinking. It would be senseless to identify Popeek in the public mind with disasters or fiascos of any kind.

For another, the skimpy insignificance of the piece implied that it had been some natural phenomenon that sent Venus up in flames, not the fumbling attempts of the terraformers. Good handling there, too.

Walton felt cheerful. He slept soundly, knowing that the public consciousness was being properly shaped.

By 0900, when he arrived at his office, the pollsters had reported a ten percent swing in public opinion, in the direction of Popeek and Walton. At 1000, *Citizen* hit the slots with an extra announcing that prospects for peaceful occupation of New Earth looked excellent. The editorial praised Walton. The letters-to-the-editor column, carefully fabricated by Lee Percy, showed a definite upswing of opinion.

The trend continued, and it was contagious. By 1100, when Walton left the Cullen Building and caught a jetcopter for United Nations Headquarters, the pro-Popeek trend in public opinion was almost overwhelming.

The copter put down before the gleaming green-glass facade of UN Headquarters; Walton handed the man a bill and went inside, where a tense-faced Ludwig was waiting for him.

"They started early," Ludwig said. "It's been going on since 1000."

"How do things look?"

"I'm puzzled, Roy. Couple of die-hards are screaming for your scalp, but you're getting help from unexpected quarters. Old Mögens Snorresen of Denmark suddenly got up and said it was necessary for the safety of mankind that we give you a permanent appointment as director of Popeek."

"*Snorresen?* But hasn't he been the one who wanted me bounced?"

Ludwig nodded. "That's what I mean. The climate is changing, definitely changing. Ride the crest, Roy. The way things look now, you may end up being swept into office for life."

They entered the giant Assembly hall. At the dais, a black-faced man with bright teeth was speaking.

"Who's that?" Walton whispered.

"Malcolm Nbono, the delegate from Ghana. He regards you as a sort of saint for our times."

Walton slipped into a seat in the gallery and said, "Let's listen from here before we go down below. I want to catch my breath."

The young man from Ghana was saying ". . . Crisis points are common to humanity. Many years ago, when my people came from their colonial status and achieved independence, we learned that painstaking negotiations and peaceful approaches are infinitely more efficacious than frontal attack by violent means. In my eyes, Roy Walton is an outstanding exponent of this philosophy. I urge his election as director of the Bureau of Population Equalization."

A heavy-bearded, ponderous man to Nbono's right shouted "Bravo!" at that point, and added several thick Scandinavian expletives.

"That's good old Mögens. The Dane really is on your side this morning," Ludwig said.

"Must have been watching the kaleidowhirl last night," Walton murmured.

The delegate from Ghana concluded with a brief tremolo cadenza praising Walton. Walton's eyes were a little moist; he hadn't realized he was a saint. Nbono tacked on an abrupt coda and sat down.

"All right," Walton said. "Let's go down there."

They made a grand entrance. Ludwig took his seat behind the neon *United States* sign, and Walton slid into the unoccupied seat to Ludwig's right. A definite stir of interest was noticeable.

The secretary-general was presiding—beady-eyed Lars Magnusson of Sweden. "I see Mr. Walton of Popeek has arrived," he commented. "By a resolution passed unanimously yesterday, we have invited Mr. Walton this morning to address us briefly. Mr. Walton, would you care to speak now?"

"Thank you very much," Walton said. He rose.

The delegates were staring at him with great interest . . . and, somewhere behind them, obscured by the bright lights of the cameras, there were, he sensed, a vast multitude of onlookers peering at him from the galleries.

Onlookers who had seen Percy's kaleidowhirl last night, evidently. A thunderous wave of applause swept down on him. *This is too easy*, he thought. *That kaleidowhirl program seems to have hypnotized everybody.*

He moistened his lips.

"Mr. Secretary-General, members of the Assembly,

friends; I'm very grateful for this chance to come before you on my own behalf. It's my understanding that you are to choose a permanent successor to Mr. FitzMaugham today. I offer myself as a candidate for that post."

He had planned a long, impassioned, semantically loaded speech to sway them, but the happenings thus far this morning convinced him it was unnecessary. The kaleidowhirl had done the work for him.

"My qualifications for the post should be apparent to all. I worked with the late Director FitzMaugham during the formative days of Popeek. Upon his death I succeeded to his post and have efficiently maintained the operation of the Bureau during the eight days since his assassination.

"There are special circumstances which dictate my continuation in office. Perhaps you know of the failure of our terraforming experiments—the destruction of our outpost on Venus, and the permanent damage done to that planet. The failure of this project makes it imperative that we move outward to the stars to relieve our population crisis."

He took a deep breath. "In exactly four hours," he said, "a representative of an alien race will land on Earth to confer with the director of Popeek. I cannot stress too greatly the importance of maintaining a continuity of thought and action within our Bureau. Bluntly, it is essential that *I* be the one who deals with this alien. I ask for your support. Thank you."

He took his seat again. Ludwig was staring at him, aghast.

"Roy! What kind of a speech was that? You can't just *demand* the job! You've got to give reasons! You have to—"

"Hush," Walton said. "Don't worry about it. Were you

watching the kaleidowhirls last night?"

"Me? Of course not!"

Walton grinned. "*They* were," he said, gesturing at the other delegates. "I'm not worried."

Eighteen

WALTON LEFT the Assembly meeting about 1215, pleading urgent Popeek business. The voting began at 1300, and half an hour later the result was officially released.

The 1400 *Citizen* was the first to carry the report.

WALTON ELECTED POPEEK HEAD

The General Assembly of the United Nations gave Roy Walton a healthy vote of confidence today. By a 95-0 vote, three abstaining, he was picked to succeed the late D. F. FitzMaugham as

*Popeek czar. He has held the post on a temporary
basis for the past eight days.*

Walton rang up Percy. "Who wrote that *Citizen* piece
on me?" he asked.

"I did, chief. Why?"

"Nicely done, but not enough sock. Get all those
three-syllable words out of it by the next edition. Get back to
the old *Citizen* style of jazzy writing."

"We thought we'd brush it up a little now that you're
in," Percy said.

"No. That's dangerous. Keep to the old style, but re-
vamp the content. We're rolling along, now. What's new
from the pollsters?"

"Fifty percent swing to Popeek. You're the most popular man in the country, as of noon. Churches are offering up
prayers for you. There's a move afoot to make you President
of the United States in place of old Lanson."

"Let Lanson keep his job," Walton chuckled. "I'm not
looking for any figurehead jobs. I'm too young. When's the
next *Citizen* due?"

"At 1500. We're keeping up hourly editions until the
crisis is over."

Walton thought for a moment. "I think 1500's too early.
The Dirnan arrives in Nairobi at 1530 our time. I want a big
splash in the 1600 edition—but not a word before then!"

"I'm with you," Percy said, and signed off.

A moment later the annunciator said, "There's a
closed-circuit call for you from Batavia, sir."

"From where?"

"Batavia. Java."

"Let's have it, " Walton said.

A fleshy face filled the screen, the face of a man who had lived a soft life in a moist climate. A rumbling voice said, "You are Walton."

"I am Walton."

"I am Gaetano di Cassio. Pleased of making the acquaintance, Signor Director Walton. I own rubber plantation in the area here."

Walton's mind immediately clicked off the top name on the list of landed proprietors Lassen had prepared for him:

di Cassio, Gaetano. 57. Holdings estimated at better than a billion and a quarter. Born Genoa 2175, settled in Amsterdam 2199. Purchased large Java holding 2211.

"What can I do for you, Mr. di Cassio?"

The rubber magnate looked ill; his fleshy face was beaded with globules of sweat. "Your brother," he grunted heavily. "Your brother worked for me. I sent him to see you yesterday. He has not come back."

"Indeed?" Walton shrugged. "There's a famous phrase I could use at this point. I won't."

"Make no flippancies," di Cassio said heavily. "Where is he?"

Walton said, "In jail. Attempted coercion of a public official." He realized di Cassio was twice as nervous and tense as he was.

"You have jailed him," di Cassio repeated flatly. "Ah, I see. Jail." The audio pickup brought in the sound of stertorous breathing. "Will you not free him?" di Cassio asked.

"I will not."

"Did he not tell you what would happen if he would not

be granted his request?"

"He told me," Walton said. "Well?"

The fat man looked sick. Walton saw that the bluff was going to be unsuccessful; that the conspirators would not dare put Lamarre's drug into open production. It had been a weapon without weight, and Walton had not let himself be cowed by it.

"Well?" Walton repeated inflexibly.

"You trouble me sorely," said di Cassio. "You give my heart pain, Mr. Walton. Steps will have to be taken."

"The Lamarre immortality serum—"

The face on the screen turned a leaden gray. "The serum," di Cassio said, "is not entered into this talking."

"Oh, no? My brother Fred made a few remarks—"

"Serum *non esiste!*"

Walton smiled calmly. "A nonexistent serum," he said, "has, unfortunately, nonexistent leverage against me. You don't scare me, di Cassio. I've outbluffed you. Go take a walk around your plantation. While you still have it, that is."

"Steps will be taken," di Cassio said. But his malevolence was hollow. Walton laughed and broke contact.

He drew Lassen's list from his desk and inscribed a brief memo to Olaf Eglin on it. These were the hundred biggest estates in the world. Within a week, there would be equalized Japanese living on all of them.

He called Martinez of security. "I've ordered my brother Fred remanded to your care," he said.

"I know." The security man sounded peeved. "We can't hold a man indefinitely, not even on your say-so, Director Walton."

"The charge is conspiracy," Walton said. "Conspiracy

against the successful operation of Popeek. I'll have a list of the ringleaders on your desk in half an hour. I want them rounded up, given a thorough psyching, and jailed."

"There are times," Martinez said slowly, "when I suspect you exceed your powers, Director Walton. But send me the list and I'll have the arrests made."

The afternoon crawled. Walton proceeded with routine work on half a dozen fronts, held screened conferences with each of his section chiefs, read reports augmenting what he already knew of the Venus disaster, and gobbled a few benzolurethrin tranquilizers.

He called Keeler and learned that no sign of Lamarre had come to light yet. From Percy he discovered that *Citizen* had added two hundred thousand subscribers over-night. The 1500 edition had a lengthy editorial praising Walton, and some letters that Percy swore were genuine, doing the same.

At 1515 Olaf Eglin called to announce that the big estates were in the process of being dismembered. "You'll be able to hear the howls from here to Batavia when we get going," Eglin warned.

"We have to be tough," Walton told him firmly.

At 1517 he devoted a few minutes to a scientific paper that proposed terraforming Pluto by establishing synthetic hydrogen-fusion suns on the icy planet. Walton skimmed through the specifications, which involved passing a current of several million amperes through a tube containing a mixture of tritium and deuterium. The general idea, he gathered, was to create electromagnetic forces of near-solar intensity; a pulsed-reaction engine would supply a hundred megawatts of power continuously, at 10,000,000 degrees centigrade.

Has possibilities, Walton noted, and forwarded the plan on to Eglin. It sounded plausible enough, but Walton was personally skeptical of undertaking any more terraforming experiments after the Venus fiasco. There were, after all, limits to the public relations miracles Lee Percy could create.

At 1535 the annunciator chimed again. "Call from Nairobi, Africa, Mr. Walton."

"Okay."

McLeod appeared on the screen.

"We're here," he said. "Arrived safely half a microsecond ago, and all's well."

"How about the alien?"

"We have him in a specially constructed cabin. Breathes hydrogen and ammonia, you know. He's very anxious to see you. When can you come?"

Walton thought for a moment. "I guess there's no way of transporting him here, is there?"

"I wouldn't advise it. The Dirnans are very sensitive about traveling in such a low gravitational field. Makes their stomachs queasy, you know. Do you think you could come out here?"

"When's the earliest?"

"Oh—half an hour?" McLeod suggested.

"I'm on my way," said Walton.

The sprawling metropolis of Nairobi, capital of the Republic of Kenya, lay at the foot of the Kikuyu Hills, and magnificent Mount Kilimanjaro towered above it. Four million people inhabited Nairobi, finest of the many fine cities along Africa's eastern coast. Africa's Negro republics had built soundly and well after achieving their liberation from colonial status.

The city was calm as Walton's special jet decelerated for landing at the vast Nairobi airport. He had left at 1547 New York time; the transatlantic trip had taken two hours and some minutes, and there was an eight-hour time zone differential between Kenya and New York. It was now 0313 in Nairobi; the early-morning rain was falling right on schedule as the jet taxied to a halt.

McLeod was there to meet him. "The ship's in the hills, five miles out of town. There's a 'copter waiting for you here."

Moments after leaving the jetliner, Walton was shepherded aboard the 'copter. Rotors whirred; the 'copter rose perpendicularly until it hung just above the cloudseeders at 13,000 feet, then fired its jets and streaked toward the hills.

It was not raining when they landed; according to McLeod, the night rain was scheduled for 0200 in this sector, and the seeders had already been here and moved on to bring rain to the city proper. A groundcar waited for them at the airstrip in the hills. McLeod drove, handling the turboelectric job with skill.

"There's the ship," he said proudly, pointing.

Walton felt a sudden throat lump.

The ship stood on its tail in the midst of a wide, flat

swath of jet-blackened concrete. It was at least five hundred feet high, a towering pale needle shimmering brightly in the moonlight. Wideswept tailjets supported it like arching buttresses. Men moved busily about in the floodlighted area at its base.

McLeod drove up to the ship and around it. The flawless symmetry of the foreside was not duplicated behind; there, a spidery catwalk ran some eighty feet up the side of the ship to a gaping lock, and by its side a crude elevator shaft rose to the same hatch.

McLeod drew efficient salutes from the men as he left the car; Walton, only puzzled glares.

"We'd better take the elevator," McLeod said. "The men are working on the catwalk."

Silently they rode up into the ship. They stepped through the open airlock into a paneled lounge, then into narrow companionways. McLeod paused and pressed down a stud in an alcove along the way.

"I'm back," he announced. "Tell Thogran Klayrn that I've brought Walton. Find out whether he'll come out to talk to him."

"I thought he had to breathe special atmosphere," Walton said. "How can he come out?"

"They've got breathing masks. Usually they don't like to use them." McLeod listened at the earpiece for a moment, then nodded. To Walton he said, "The alien will see you in the lounge."

Walton had barely time to fortify himself with a slug of filtered rum when a crewman appeared at the entrance to the lounge and declared ostentatiously, "His Excellency, Thogran Klayrn of Dirna."

The alien entered.

Walton had seen the photographs, and so he was partially prepared. But only partially.

The photos had not given him any idea of size. The alien stood eight feet high, and gave an appearance of astonishing mass. It must have weighed four or five hundred pounds, but it stood on two thick legs barely three feet long. Somewhere near the middle of the column body, four sturdy arms jutted forth strangely. A neckless head topped the ponderous creature—a head covered entirely with the transparent breathing mask. One of the hands held a mechanical device of some sort; the translating machine, Walton surmised.

The alien's hide was bright-green, and leathery in texture. A faint pungent odor drifted through the room, as of an object long immersed in ammonia.

"I am Thogran Klayrn," a booming voice said. "Diplomasiarch of Dirna. I have been sent to talk with Roy Walton. Are you Roy Walton?"

"I am." Walton's voice sounded cold and dry to his own ears. He knew he was too tense, pressing too hard. "I'm very glad to meet you, Thogran Klayrn."

"Please sit. I do not. My body is not made that way."

Walton sat. It made him feel uncomfortable to have to crane his neck upward at the alien, but that could not be helped. "Did you have a pleasant trip?" Walton asked, temporizing desperately.

A half-grunt came from Thogran Klayrn. "Indeed it was so. But I do not indulge in little talk. A problem we have, and it must be discussed."

"Agreed." Whatever a diplomasiarch might be on Dirna, it was *not* a typical diplomat. Walton was relieved that it would not be necessary to spend hours in formalities before they reached the main problem.

"A ship sent out by your people," the alien said, "invaded our system some time ago. In command was your Colonel McLeod, whom I have come to know well. What was the purpose of this ship?"

"To explore the worlds of the universe and to discover a planet where we of Earth could settle. Our world is very overcrowded now."

"So I have been given to know. You have chosen Labura—or, in your terms, Procyon VIII—as your colony. Is this so?"

"Yes," Walton said. "It's a perfect world for our purposes. But Colonel McLeod has informed me that you object to our settling there."

"We do so object." The Dirnan's voice was cold. "You are a young and active race. We do not know what danger you may bring to us. To have you as our neighbors—"

"We could swear a treaty of eternal peace," Walton said.

"Words. Mere words."

"But don't you see that we can't even *land* on that planet of yours! It's too big, too heavy for us. What possible harm could we do?"

"There are races," said the Dirnan heavily, "which believe in violence as a sacred act. You have long-range missiles. How might we trust you?"

Walton squirmed; then sudden inspiration struck him. "There's a planet in this system that's as suitable for your people as Labura is for ours. I mean Jupiter. We could offer you colonial rights to Jupiter in exchange for the privilege of colonizing Labura!"

The alien was silent for a moment. Considering? There was no way of telling what emotions passed across that face. At length the alien said, "Not satisfactory. Our people have long since reached stability of population. We have no need of colonies. It has been many thousands of your years since we have ventured into space."

Walton felt chilled. *Many thousands of years!* He realized he was up against a formidable life form.

"We have learned to stabilize births and deaths," the Dirnan went on sonorously. "It is a fundamental law of the universe, and one that you Earthfolk must learn sooner or later. How you choose to do it is your own business. But we have no need of planets in your system, and we fear allowing you to enter ours. The matter is simple of statement, difficult of resolution. But we are open to suggestions from you."

Walton's mind blanked. Suggestions? What possible suggestion could he make?

He gasped. "We have something to offer," he said. "It might be of value to a race that has achieved population stability. We would give it to you in exchange for colonization rights."

"What is this commodity?" the Dirnan asked.

"Immortality," Walton said.

Nineteen

HE RETURNED to New York alone, later that night, too tired to sleep and too wide awake to relax. He felt like a poker player who had triumphantly topped four kings with four aces, and now was fumbling in his hand trying to locate some of those aces for his skeptical opponents.

The alien had accepted his offer. That was the one solid fact he was able to cling to, on the lonely night ride back from Nairobi. The rest was a quicksand of ifs and maybes.

If Lamarre could be found . . .

If the serum actually had any value . . .

If it was equally effective on Earthmen and Dirnans . . .

Walton tried to dismiss the alternatives. He had made a

desperately wild offer, and it had been accepted. New Earth was open for colonization, *if* . . .

The world outside the jet was a dark blur. He had left Nairobi at 0518 Nairobi time; jetting back across the eight intervening time zones, he would arrive in New York around midnight. Ultrarapid jet transit made such things possible; he would live twice through the early hours of June nineteenth.

New York had a fifteen minute rain scheduled at 0100 that night. Walton reached the housing project where he lived just as the rain was turned on. The night was otherwise a little muggy; he paused outside the main entrance, letting the drops fall on him. After a few minutes, feeling faintly foolish and very tired, he went inside, shook himself dry, and went to bed. He did not sleep.

Four caffeine tablets helped him get off to a running start in the morning. He arrived at the Cullen Building early, about 0835, and spent some time bringing his private journal up to date, explaining in detail the burden of his interview with the alien ambassador. Some day, Walton thought, a historian of the future would discover his journal and find that for a short period in 2232 a man named Roy Walton had acted as absolute dictator of humanity. The odd thing, Walton reflected, was that he had absolutely no power drive: he had been pitchforked into the role, and each of his successive extra-legal steps had been taken quite genuinely in the name of humanity.

Rationalization? Perhaps. But a necessary one.

At 0900 Walton took a deep breath and caller Keeler of security. The security man smiled oddly and said, "I was just about to call you, sir. We have some news, at last."

"News? What?"

"Lamarre. We found his body this morning, just about an hour ago: Murdered. It turned up in Marseilles, pretty badly decomposed, but we ran a full check and the retinal's absolutely Lamarre's."

"Oh," Walton said leadenly. His head swam. "Definitely Lamarre," he repeated. "Thanks, Keeler. Fine work. Fine."

"Something wrong, sir? You look—"

"I'm very tired," Walton said. "That's all. Tired. Thanks, Keeler."

"You called me about something, sir," Keeler reminded him gently.

"Oh, I was calling about Lamarre. I guess there's no point in—thanks, Keeler." He broke the contact.

For the first time Walton felt total despair, and, out of despair, came a sort of deathlike calmness. With Lamarre dead, his only hope of obtaining the serum was to free Fred and wangle the notes from him. But Fred's price for the notes would be Walton's job. Full circle, and a dead end.

Perhaps Fred could be induced to reveal the whereabouts of the notes. It wasn't likely, but it was possible. And if not? Walton shrugged. A man could do only so much. Terraforming had proved a failure, equalization was a stopgap of limited value, and the one extrasolar planet worth colonizing was held by aliens. Dead end.

I tried, Walton thought. *Now let someone else try.*

He shook his head, trying to clear the fog of negation that suddenly surrounded him. His thinking was all wrong; he had to keep trying, had to investigate every possible avenue before giving up.

His fingers hovered lightly over a benzolurethrin tablet, then drew back. Stiffly he rose from his chair and switched on the annunciator.

"I'm leaving the office for a while," he said hoarsely. "Send all calls to Mr. Eglin."

He had to see Fred.

Security Keep was a big, blocky building beyond the city limits proper, a windowless tower near Nyack, New York. Walton's private jetcopter dropped noiselessly to the landing stage on the wide parapet of the building. He contemplated its dull-bronze metallic exterior for a moment.

"Should I wait here?" the pilot asked.

"Yes," Walton said. With accession to the permanent dictatorship he rated a private ship and a live pilot. "I won't be here long."

He left the landing stage and stepped within an indicated screener field. There was a long pause. The air up here, Walton thought, is fresh and clean, not like city air.

A voice said, "What is your business here?"

"I'm Walton, director of Popeek. I have an appointment with Security Head Martinez."

"Wait a moment, Director Walton."

None of the obsequious *sirring* and *pleasing* Walton had grown accustomed to. In its way, the bluntness of address was as refreshing as the unpolluted air.

Walton's keen ears detected a gentle electronic whirr; he was being thoroughly scanned. After a moment the metal door before him rose silently into a hidden slot, and he found himself facing an inner door of burnished copper.

A screen was set in the inner door.

Martinez' face confronted him.

"Good morning, Director Walton. You're here for our interview?"

"Yes."

The inner door closed. This time, two chunky atomic cannons came barreling down to face him snout first. Walton flinched involuntarily, but a smiling Martinez stepped before them and greeted him. "Well, why are you here?"

"To see a prisoner of yours. My brother, Fred."

Martinez frowned and passed a delicate hand through his rumpled hair. "Seeing prisoners is positively forbidden, Mr. Walton. Seeing them in person, that is. I could arrange a closed-circuit video screening for you."

"Forbidden? But the man's here on my word alone. I—"

"Your powers, Mr. Walton, are still somewhat less than infinite. This is one rule we never have relaxed, and never will. The prisoners in the Keep are under constant security surveillance, and your presence in the cell block would undermine our entire system. Will video do?"

"I guess it'll have to," Walton said. He was not of a mind to argue now.

"Come with me, then," said Martinez.

The little man led him down a dim corridor into a side room, one entire wall of which was an unlit video screen. "You'll have total privacy in here," Martinez assured him. He did things to a dial set in the right-hand wall, and murmured a few words. The screen began to glow.

"You can call me when you're through," Martinez said. He seemed to glide out of the room, leaving Walton alone with Fred.

The huge screen was like a window directly into Fred's

cell. Walton met his brother's bitter gaze head on.

Fred looked demonic. His eyes were ringed by black shadows; his hair was uncombed, his heavy-featured face unwashed. He said, "Welcome to my palatial abode, dearest brother."

"Fred, don't make it hard for me. I came here to try to clarify things. I didn't *want* to stick you away here. I *had* to."

Fred smiled balefully. "You don't need to apologize. It was entirely my fault. I underestimated you; I didn't realize you had changed. I thought you were the same old soft-hearted dope I grew up with. You aren't."

"Possibly." Walton wished he had taken that benzolurethrin after all. Every nerve in his body seemed to be jumping. He said, "I found out today that Lamarre's dead."

"So?"

"So there's no possible way for Popeek to obtain the immortality serum except through you. Fred, I need that serum. I've promised it to the alien in exchange for colonization rights on Procyon VIII."

"A neat little package deal," Fred said harshly. "*Quid pro quo.* Well, I hate to spoil it, but I'm not going to tell where the *quo* lies hidden. You're not getting that serum out of me."

"I can have you mind-blasted," Walton said. "They'll pick your mind apart and strip it away layer by layer until they find what they want. There won't be much of *you* left by then, but we'll have the serum."

"No go. Not even you can swing that deal," Fred said. "You can't get a mind-pick permit on your lonesome: you need the President's okay. It takes at least a day to go through channels—half a day, if you pull rank. And by that time, Roy, I'll be out of here."

"What?"

"You heard me clear enough. *Out*. Seems you're holding me here on pretty tenuous grounds. Habeas corpus hasn't been suspended yet, Roy, and Popeek isn't big enough to do it. I've got a writ. I'll be sprung at 1500 today."

"I'll have you back in by 1530," Walton said angrily. "We're picking up di Cassio and that whole bunch. That'll be sufficient grounds to quash your habeas corpus."

"Ah! Maybe so," Fred said. "But I'll be out of here for half an hour. That's long enough to let the world know how you exercised an illegal special privilege and spared Philip Prior from Happysleep. Wiggle out of that one, then."

Walton began to sweat.

Fred had him neatly nailed this time.

Someone in security evidently had let him sneak his plea out of the Keep. Martinez? Well, it didn't matter. By 1500 Fred would be free, and the long-suppressed Prior incident would be smeared all over the telefax system. That would finish Walton; affairs were at too delicate an impasse for him to risk having to defend himself now. Fred might not be able to save himself, but he could certainly topple his brother.

There was no possible way to get a mind-pick request through before 1500; President Lanson himself would have to sign the authorization, and the old dodderer would take his time about it.

Mind-picking was out, but there was still one weapon left to the head of Popeek, if he cared to use it. Walton moistened his lips.

"It sounds very neat," he said. "I'll ask you one more

time; will you yield Lamarre's serum to me for use in my negotiations with the Dirnan?"

"Are you kidding? No!" Fred said positively. "Not to save your life or mine. I've got you exactly where I want you, Roy. Where I've wanted you all my life. And you can't wriggle out of it."

"I think you've underestimated me again," Walton said in a quiet voice. "And for the last time."

He stood up and opened the door of the room. A gray-clad security man hovered outside.

"Will you tell Mr. Martinez I'm ready to leave?" Walton said.

The jetcopter pilot was dozing when Walton reached the landing stage. Walton woke him and said, "Let's get back to the Cullen building, fast."

The trip took about ten minutes. Walton entered his office, signaling his return but indicating he wanted no calls just yet. Carefully, thoughtfully, he arranged the various strands of circumstance in his mind, building them into a symmetrical structure.

Di Cassio and the other conspirators would be rounded up by nightfall, certainly. But no time element operated there; Walton knew he could get mind-pick authorizations in a day or so, and go through one after another of them until the whereabouts of Lamarre's formula turned up. It was brutal, but necessary.

Fred was a different problem. Unless Walton prevented it, he'd be freed on his writ within hours—and when he revealed the Prior incident, it would smash Walton's whole fragile construct to flinders.

He couldn't fight habeas corpus. But the director of Popeek did have one weapon that legally superseded all others. Fred had gambled on his brother's softness, and Fred had lost.

Walton reached for his voicewrite and, in a calm, controlled voice, began to dictate an order for the immediate removal of Frederic Walton from Security Keep, and for his prompt transference to the Euthanasia Clinic on grounds of criminal insanity.

Twenty

EVEN AFTER that—for which he felt no guilt, only relief—
Walton felt oppressive foreboding hanging over him. Martinez phoned, late that day, to inform him that the hundred
landowners had been duly corralled and were being held in
the lower reaches of Security Keep.

"They're yelling and squalling," Martinez said, "and
they'll have plenty of high-power legal authority down here
soon enough. You'd better have a case against them."

"I'm obtaining an authorization to mind-blast the one
named di Cassio. He's the ringleader, I think." Walton
paused for a moment, then asked, "Did a Popeek 'copter
arrive to pick up Frederic Walton?"

"Yes," Martinez said. "At 1406. A lawyer showed up

here waving a writ, a little while later, but naturally we had no further jurisdiction." The security man's eyes were cold and accusing, but Walton did not flinch.

"1406?" he repeated. "All right, Martinez. Thanks for your cooperation."

He blanked the screen. He was moving coolly, crisply now. In order to get a mind-pick authorization, he would have to see President Lanson personally. Very well; he would see President Lanson.

The shrunken old man in the White House was openly deferential to the Popeek head. Walton stated his case quickly, bluntly. Lanson's watery, mild eyes blinked a few times at the many complexities of the situation. He rocked uneasily up and down.

Finally he said, "This mind-picking—it's absolutely necessary?"

"Absolutely. We must know where that serum is hidden."

Lanson sighed heavily. "I'll authorize it," he said. He looked beaten.

Washington to New York was a matter of some few minutes. The precious authorization in his hands, Walton spoke to di Cassio via the screener setup at Security Keep, informed him of what was going to be done with him. Then, despite the fat man's hysterical protests, he turned the authorization over to Martinez with instructions to proceed with the mind-pick.

It took fifty-eight minutes. Walton waited in a bare, austere office somewhere in the Keep while the mind-picking techniques peeled away the cortex of di Cassio's brain. By now Walton was past all ambivalence, all self-doubt. He thought of himself as a mere robot fulfilling a preset pattern of action.

At 1950 Martinez presented himself before Walton. The little security head looked bleak.

"It's done. Di Cassio's been reduced to blubber and bone. I wouldn't want to watch another mind-picking too soon."

"You may have to," Walton said. "If di Cassio wasn't the right one, I intend to go straight down the line on all hundred-odd of them. One of them dealt with Fred. One of them must know where the Lamarre papers are."

Martinez shook his head wearily. "No. There won't need to be any more mind-picking. We got it all out of di Cassio. The transcript ought to be along any moment."

As the security man spoke, an arrival bin in the office flashed and a packet arrived. Walton broke impatiently for the bin, but Martinez waved him away. "This is my domain, Mr. Walton. Please be patient."

With infuriating slowness, Martinez opened the packet, removed some closely-typed sheets, nodded over them. He handed them to Walton.

"Here. Read for yourself. Here's the record of the conversation between your brother and di Cassio. I think it's what you're looking for."

Walton accepted the sheets tensely and began to read:

Di Cassio: *You have a what?*
Fred Walton: *An immortality serum. Eternal life. You know. Some Popeek scientist invented it,*

and I stole his notebook from my brother's office. It's all here.

Di Cassio: *Buono! Excellent work. Excellent. Immortality, you say?*

Fred Walton: *Damned right. And it's the weapon we can use to pry Roy out of office. All I have to do is tell him he'd better get out of the way or we'll turn the serum loose on humanity, and he'll move. He's an idealist—stars in his eyes and all that. He won't dare resist.*

Di Cassio: *This is marvelous. You will, of course, send the serum formula to us for safe keeping?*

Fred Walton: *Like hell I will. I'm keeping those notes right where they belong—inside my head. I've destroyed the notebooks and had the scientist killed. The only one who knows the secret is yours truly. This is just to prevent double-crossing on your part, di Cassio. Not that I don't trust you, you understand.*

Di Cassio: *Fred, my boy—*

Fred Walton: *None of that stuff. You gave me a free hand. Don't try to interfere now.*

Walton let the transcript slip from his numb hands to the floor.

"My God," he said softly. "My God!"

Martinez' bright eyes flicked from Walton to the scattered papers on the floor. "What's the trouble? You've got Fred in your custody, haven't you?"

"Didn't you read the order I sent you?"

Martinez chuckled hollowly. "Well, yes—it was a Happysleep authorization. But I thought it was just a way of avoiding that writ . . . . I mean . . . your own *brother*, man."

"That was no dodge," Walton said. "That was a Happysleep order, and I meant it. Really. Unless there was a slipup, Fred went to the chamber four hours ago. And," said Walton, "he took the Lamarre formula along with him."

Alone in his office in the night-shadowed Cullen Building, Walton stared at his own distorted reflection mirrored in the opaqued windows. On his desk lay the slip of paper bearing the names of those who had gone to Happysleep in the 1500 gassing.

Frederic Walton was the fourth name on the list. For once, there had been no slip-ups.

Walton thought back over the events of the last nine days. One of his earliest realizations during that time had been that the head of Popeek held powers of life and death over humanity.

Godlike, he had assumed both responsibilities. He had granted life to Philip Prior; that had been the start of this chain of events, and the first of his many mistakes. Now, he had given death to Frederic Walton, an act in itself justifiable, but in consequence the most massive of his errors.

All his scheming had come to naught. Any help now would have to come from without.

Wearily, he snapped on the phone and asked for a connection to Nairobi. The interstellar swap would have to be canceled; Walton was unable to deliver the goods. Fred would have the final smirk yet.

Some minutes later, he got through to McLeod.

"I'm glad you called," McLeod said immediately. "I've been trying to reach you all day. The Dirnan's getting rather impatient; this low gravity is making him sick, and he wants to get going back to his home world."

"Let me talk to him. He'll be able to leave right away."

McLeod nodded and vanished from the screen. The alien visage of Thogran Klayrn appeared.

"I have been waiting for you," the Dirnan said. "You promised to call earlier today. You did not."

"I'm sorry about that," Walton told him. "I was trying to locate the papers to turn over to you."

"Ah, yes. Has it been done?"

"No," Walton said. "The serum doesn't exist any more. The man who invented it is dead, and so is the only other man who knew the formula."

There was a moment of startled silence. Then the Dirnan said, "You assured me delivery of the information."

"I know. But it can't be delivered." Walton was silent a long while, brooding. "The deal's off. There was a mixup and the man who had the data was—was inadvertently executed today."

"*Today*, you say?"

"Yes. It was an error on my part. A foolish blunder."

"That is irrelevant," the alien interrupted peevishly. "Is the man's body still intact?"

"Why, yes," Walton said, taken off guard. He wondered what plan the alien had. "It's in our morgue right now. But—"

The alien turned away from the screen, and Walton

heard him conferring with someone beyond the field of vision. Then the Dirnan returned.

"There are techniques for recovering information from newly dead persons," Thogran Klayrn said. "You have none of these on Earth?"

"Recovering information?" Walton stammered. "No, we don't."

"These techniques exist. Have you such a device as an electroencephalograph on Earth?"

"Of course."

"Then it is still possible to extract the data from this dead man's brain." The alien uttered a wistful wheeze. "See that the body comes to no harm. I will be at your city shortly."

For a moment Walton did not understand.

Then he thought, *Of course. It had to happen this way.*

He realized the rent in the fabric had been bound up, his mistakes undone, his conscience granted a reprieve. He felt absurdly grateful. That all his striving should have been ruined at the last moment would have been intolerable. Now, all was made whole.

"Thanks," he said with sudden fervor. "Thanks!"

14 May 2233 . . .

Roy Walton, director of the Bureau of Population Equalization, stood sweltering in the sun at Nairobi Spaceport, watching the smiling people file past him into the towering, golden-hulled ship.

A powerful-looking man holding a small child in his arms came up to him.

"Hello, Walton," he said in a majestic basso.

Walton turned, startled. "Prior!" he exclaimed, after a moment's fumbling.

"And this is my son, Philip," said Prior. "We'll both be going as colonists. My wife's already aboard, but I just wanted to thank you—"

Walton looked at the happy, red-cheeked boy. "There was a medical exam for all volunteer colonists. How did you get the boy through *this* time?"

"Legitimately," Prior said, grinning. "He's a perfectly healthy, normal boy. That potential TB condition was just that—potential. Philip got an A-one health clearance, so it's New Earth and the wide ranges for the Prior family!"

"I'm glad for you," Walton said absently. "I wish I could go."

"Why can't you?"

"Too much work here," Walton said. "If you turn out any poetry up there, I'd like to see it."

Prior shook his head. "I have a feeling I'll be too busy. Poetry's really just a substitute for living, I'm getting to think. I'll be too busy *living* up there to write anything."

"Maybe," said Walton. "I suppose you're right. But you'd better move along. That ship's due to blast pretty soon."

"Right. Thanks again for everything," Prior said, and he and the child moved on.

Walton watched them go. He thought back over the past year. *At least,* he thought, *I made one right guess. The boy deserved to live.*

The loading continued. One thousand colonists would go this first trip, and a thousand more the next day, and a thousand and a thousand more until a billion of Earth's multitudes were on the new world. There was a great deal of paperwork involved in transporting a billion people through space. Walton's desk groaned with a backlog of work.

He glanced up. No stars were visible, of course, in the midday sky, but he knew that New Earth was out there somewhere. And near it, Dirna.

Some day, he thought, *we'll have learned to control our growth. And that will be the day the Dirnans give us back our immortality formula.*

A warning siren sounded suddenly, and ship number one sprang up from Earth, hovered for a few instants on a red pillar of fire, and vanished. Director Walton looked blankly at the place where the ship had been, and, after a moment, turned away. Plenty of work waited for him back in New York.